THE HOMESTEADER

From a painting by W. M. Farrow.

"SOMETHING HAPPENED AND I WAS STRANGELY GLAD
AND CAME HERE BECAUSE I—I—JUST *HAD* TO SEE YOU,
JEAN."

THE HOMESTEADER

A Novel
BY
OSCAR MICHEAUX

Introduction to the Bison Book Edition
by Learthen Dorsey

Illustrated by W. M. Farrow

University of Nebraska Press
Lincoln and London

Introduction to the Bison Book Edition copyright © 1994 by the
University of Nebraska Press
Manufactured in the United States of America

First Bison Book printing: 1994
Most recent printing indicated by the last digit below:
10   9   8   7   6   5   4   3   2   1

Library of Congress Cataloging-in-Publication Data
Micheaux, Oscar, 1884–
The homesteader: a novel / by Oscar Micheaux; illustrated by W. M.
Farrow; introduction to the Bison book edition by Learthen Dorsey.
p.   cm.
ISBN 0-8032-8208-7
1. Frontier and pioneer life—South Dakota—Fiction.   2. Afro-
American pioneers—South Dakota—Fiction.   I. Dorsey,
Learthen.   II. Title.
PS3525.I1875H6   1994   C . 1
813'.52—DC20
94-6203
CIP

Reprinted from the original 1917 edition published by the Western
Book Supply Company, Sioux City, Iowa.

∞

BELOVED MOTHER
THIS
TO
YOU

CONTENTS

Introduction to the Bison Book Edition 1

EPOCH THE FIRST

CHAPTER   PAGE
I   Agnes 13
II   The Homesteader 21
III   At the Sod House 28
IV   She Could Never Be Anything to Him 37
V   When the Indians Shot the Town Up 43
VI   The Infidel, A Jew and A German 49
VII   The Day Before 56
VIII An Enterprising Young Man 61
IX   "Christine! Christine!" 75
X   "You Have Never Been This Way Before" . . . 80
XI   What Jean Baptiste Found in the Well 85
XII   Miss Stewart Receives a Caller 89
XIII The Coming of the Railroad 97
XIV   The Administrating Angel 107
XV   Oh, My Jean 115
XVI   "Bill" Prescott Proposes 123
XVII Harvest Time and What Came with It 131

EPOCH THE SECOND

I   Regarding the Intermarriage of Races 143
II   Which? 153
III   Memories — N. Justine McCarthy 159
IV   Orlean 174
V   A Proposal; A Proposition; A Certain Mrs. Pruitt
      — And a Letter 186
VI   The Prairie Fire 190
VII   Vanity 196
VIII Married 207
IX   Orlean Receives a Letter and Advice 212
X   Eugene Crook 221
XI   Reverend McCarthy Pays a Visit 227
XII   Reverend McCarthy Decides to Set Baptiste Right,
      But — 234
XIII The Wolf 240
XIV   The Contest 247

CONTENTS

CHAPTER   PAGE

XV   Compromised 252

XVI   The Evil Genius 259

XVII   The Coward 267

EPOCH THE THIRD

I   Chicago — The Boomerang 279

II   The Great Question 284

III   Glavis Makes A Promise 294

IV   The Gambler's Story 299

V   The Preacher's Evil Influence 305

VI   More of the Preacher's Work 311

VII   A Great Astronomer 317

VIII   N. Justine McCarthy Preaches a Sermon . . . 325

IX   What the People Were Saying 332

X   "Until Then" 339

XI   "It's the Wrong Number" 346

XII   Mrs. Pruitt Effects a Plan 354

XIII   Mrs. Merley 363

XIV   "Oh, Merciful God! Close Thou Mine Eyes!" . . 369

XV   "Love You — God, I Hate You!" 376

XVI   A Strange Dream 385

EPOCH THE FOURTH

I   The Drought 395

II   The Foreclosure 400

III   Irene Grey 407

IV   What Might Have Been 414

V   "Tell Me Why You Didn't Answer the Last Letter
I Wrote You" 421

VI   The Story 427

VII   Her Birthright "for a Mess of Pottage" . . . 436

VIII   Action 440

IX   Gossip 446

X   A Discovery — and a Surprise 456

XI   The Bishop's Inquisition 464

XII   The Bishop Acts 479

XIII   Where the Weak Must Be Strong 482

XIV   The Trial — the Lie — "As Guilty As Hell!" . . 488

XV   Grim Justice 495

XVI   A Friend 502

XVII   The Mystery 508

XVIII   "Vengeance is Mine. I Will Repay" 515

XIX   When the Truth Became Known 523

XX   As it Was in the Beginning 529

ILLUSTRATIONS

" Something happened and I was strangely glad and came here
because I — I just *had* to see you, Jean " . . . *Frontispiece*

FACING
PAGE

He was young, The Homesteader — just passed twenty-two —
and vigorous, strong, healthy and courageous 22

He raised on an elbow and looked into her face while she staggered forward in great surprise 35

" But, Jean, the cases are not parallel. What I did for you I
would have done for anybody. It was merely an act of
providence; but yours — oh, Jean, *can't you understand!* " . 138

" Miss Pitt was *so* anxious to meet you and I was, too, because
I think you and her would like each other. She's an awfully
good girl and willing to help a fellow " 159

" He's going to kill you out here to make him rich, and then
when you are dead and —" " Please don't, father ! " she almost screamed. She knew he was going to say: " in your
grave, he will marry another woman to enjoy what you have
died for," but she could not quite listen to that 245

He tried to throw off the uncanny feeling, but it seemed to
hang on like grim death. And as he stood enmeshed in its
sinister thraldom, he thought he saw her rise and point an
accusing finger at him 518

INTRODUCTION

By Learthen Dorsey

The Homesteader (1917) was Oscar Micheaux's third novel but its publication was the most singular event of his entire life. His first novel, *The Conquest* (1913), which was semi-autobiographical, describes the first twenty-nine years of his life after he left home to become a homesteader in South Dakota. It was successful enough to finance his first company, the Western Book and Supply Company in Sioux City (which became the Micheaux Book and Film Company in 1918).

The Homesteader is a reworking of *The Conquest*. The names of the original characters are changed. The white love interest is expanded, as is the political intrigue in the small towns of South Dakota. New characters with intriguing pasts are introduced, and Micheaux gives his own life much more melodrama and depth. His fictional name, Jean Baptiste, recalls the black Frenchman, Jean Baptiste Point du Sable, who established a trading post in 1779 that eventually became Chicago—as well as the biblical and saintly John the Baptist.[1]

Although *The Homesteader* does not include details of the Homestead Act or the political rivalries and competition for trade and rail connections which were much in evidence in *The Conquest,* the novel does provide a much more expansive treatment of South Dakota in the early twentieth century. Agnes Stewart, the daughter of a neighboring white farmer and the unnamed dream-girl in *The Conquest,* becomes a major character in this novel. She has a past, present, and a future. She saves Jean's life twice, once during a snowstorm in South Dakota, and they fall in love. The relationship between Jean and his neighbors is explored more fully here, and there is a subplot of murder and betrayal on the plains that involves the heroine. Micheaux also explores more fully how Jean obtains his first wife, Orlean McCarthy, who was his third and last choice. Because Agnes is white, Baptiste could not marry her, for such a love marriage would create a "chasm so deep socially that bridging was impossible." So Baptiste must search for black candidates. Orlean's character is similar to that of the Orlean of *The Conquest:* she is timid and weak-willed, but she harbors fury just below the surface. Her sister Ethel and father, the Reverend N. Justine McCarthy, are more treacherous here. Glavis, Ethel's husband, is the Claves of *The Conquest;* his character is unchanged.

The story lines of both novels are similar up to the point when Orlean is forced to return to Chicago, but in *The Homesteader* the subsequent meetings between Baptiste and Orlean's father are much more confrontational, particularly after his father-in-law breaks up the marriage by forcing Orlean to return to Chicago, where she sells the property that Baptiste had acquired for her. Baptiste brings suit against the Reverend, setting the stage for an ending that is tragic, melodramatic, and romantic.

Two young black filmmakers from Omaha—George P. Johnson and his brother Noble Johnson—thought *The Homesteader* was a novel waiting to be filmed. It had all of the ingredients of a successful movie script and western saga: it was inspirational, it was larger than life (and Jean Baptiste much more heroic than Oscar Devereaux in *The Conquest*), and it had a happy ending. George Johnson, the general booking agent of the Lincoln Film Company of Los Angeles (probably the second black film company established in the United States) began discussions with Micheaux about making a film from *The Homesteader* in 1918.[2]

The Lincoln Film Company, small and undercapitalized with a single studio in Los Angeles that Noble ran, made films that portrayed blacks in a positive light or made films that "filled the screen with strong black success images." The company concentrated on newsfilm of sports and western scenes or on plots portraying American individualism. Black film critics note that while the Johnson films contain the standard set pieces of the western genre and the character stereotypes of the period, they never present negative black images like comic buffoons, faithful servants, or singing and dancing half-wits.[3] So Micheaux's *Homesteader* would have been in good hands.

Still, filming *The Homesteader* was a tremendous gamble for the company, and consequently the Johnson brothers disagreed over the merits of doing it. Noble felt the story was much too advanced for the company and would not appeal to white movie audiences.[4] George met with Micheaux at Omaha in May and negotiation continued throughout the summer; they eventually signed a contract, whereby Micheaux would go to Los Angeles and supervise filming of *The Homesteader*. However, the contract was cancelled when Micheaux, once there, insisted upon directing the film himself.

To produce his own film, he sold stock in his company, now called the Micheaux Book and Film Company, to white farmers around Sioux City, Iowa, and also in South Dakota, Nebraska, and Oklahoma. Most of them he contacted on his returned trip from Los Angeles. He managed to raise $15,000. For one of the leading roles, he was able to secure

Evelyn Preer of the old Lafayette Players. She joined several bit players, described as light-skinned with nearly straight hair. Micheaux shot and cut the eight-reel film of *The Homesteader* in the old Selig studio in Chicago. After opening in New York in 1919, it grossed $5,000.[5] One film historian considered it a significant benchmark because, for the first time in an American film, a sexual relationship between a black man (Jean Baptiste, the homesteader in the novel) and a white woman (Agnes Stewart, Jean Baptiste's eventual wife) was not portrayed as the rape of a white woman.[6] Also, the relationship between Jean Baptiste and Agnes Stewart was appropriately vague and Victorian, and it does not appear to have been sexual until their marriage.

As Micheaux's film career took off, his company established branches in New York and Chicago.[7] From 1919 to 1943, Micheaux virtually abandoned the writing of fiction and literally taught himself the craft of filmmaking. He wrote scenarios, supervised filming, handled the bookkeeping.[8] To distribute and finance his films,* he would grant theater managers the first right to show them in return for money to finance more production. With that aim, Mi-

---

*Of the forty or some films produced by Oscar Micheaux, only ten have survived and are available for commercial release—the silent films, *Within Our Gates, Symbol of the Unconquered, Body and Soul,* and *Scar of Shame;* and the sound features, *The Girl from Chicago, God's Stepchildren, Lying Lips, Swing, Ten Minutes to Live,* and *Veiled Aristocrats.* In order of production, the films include—*The Homesteader* and *Within Our Gates* (1919); *The Brute* and *Symbol of the Unconquered* (1920); *Gunsaules Mystery* and *Deceit* (1921); *The Dungeon, The Virgin of the Seminole,* and *Son of Satan* (1922); *Jasper Landry's Will* (1923); *Body and Soul* (1924); *The Spider's Web* (1926); *The Millionaire* (1927); *When Men Betray* and *Easy Street* (1928); *Wages of Sin* (1929); *The Exile, Darktown Revue, Daughter of the Congo* (1931); *Veiled Aristocrats, Black Magic,* and *Ten Minutes to Live* (1932); *The Girl from Chicago, Ten Minutes to Kill* (1933); *Harlem after Midnight* (1934); *Lem Hawkin's Confession* (1935); *Swing, Temptation,* and *God's Stepchildren* (1938); *Lying Lips* (1939); *The Notorious Elinor Lee* (1940); *Underworld* (1947); and *The Betrayal* (1948).

cheaux also visited prospective theater managers accompanied by actors, who would perform scenes from the proposed film.[9]

The Micheaux Book and Film Company went bankrupt in 1928, and to continue production Oscar had to rely upon support from his second wife, Alice Russell, an actress whom he had married in 1929, and the backing of white financiers and theater owners.[10] In 1931 he produced the first all-black feature-length film, *The Exile,* another reworking of his experience on the South Dakota frontier.[11] Micheaux continued to produce the highly melodramatic films that were his trademark, but he met with increasing opposition from critics in the black community who felt that they reinforced the stereotyped and servile image of blacks found in those produced by the major Hollywood studios. If the white press criticized the quality of production and amateurish acting in Micheaux's films, the black press criticized his use of light-skinned black actors and his focus on interracial themes and "passing."[12]

Returning to writing fiction around 1943, Micheaux reworked the story *The Conquest,* this time as *The Wind from Nowhere* (1944). *The Case of Mrs. Wingate* (1945) combined the Nazi spy and detective genres with a black twist, and *The Story of Dorothy Stanfield* (1946) dealt with an insurance swindle. His last novel, *The Masquerade* (1947), a thinly disguised reworking of Charles W. Chesnutt's *The House behind the Cedars,* provides the tragic mulatto with a happier ending: instead of dying, she marries and escapes to the Midwest.[13]

Briefly, late in the forties, he returned to filmmaking. *The Betrayal,* produced in 1948, ran for three hours and flopped at the box office. Oscar Micheaux died at the age of sixty-seven in Charlotte, North Carolina, on March 26, 1951.[14]

The film of *The Homesteader* has not survived, but we still have the novel. It has pedagogic and historical value for the reader. As a period piece, the book provides a look at the black bourgeoisie in both a rural and urban context during the early twentieth century. It describes their interests and outlooks, their value systems and virtues, either as urban-ites in Chicago, as rural farmers in Illinois and Indiana, or as homesteaders on the Great Plains. Micheaux's descrip-tion of the Chicago South Side and its night life, replete with boarding houses and fine homes, creates the feel of a truly black urban community, and these descriptions are well worth waiting for and reading.

The novel also conveys a great deal about Micheaux, who speaks through his main protagonist, Jean Baptiste. Mi-cheaux was an ardent follower and supporter of Booker T. Washington, who was an outspoken educator and influen-tial assimilationist from 1893 to his death in 1915. Wash-ington advised African Americans to rely upon their own efforts, work hard to succeed, and to remain in the South instead of migrating to northern cities. In *The Homesteader,* Micheaux uses his protagonist to discuss why blacks have not achieved. This novel, like *The Conquest,* is used as a soap-box, but here Micheaux's polemics are much more inspi-rational than accusatory. For example, in one particular passage, he notes that Baptiste's deeds or successes are per-ceived as being a credit to the race, to "others who need the example." He goes on to write that in a moment of reflec-tions, Baptiste "paused and thought of his race. The indi-vidual here did not count so much, it was the cause. His race needed examples; they needed instances of successes to overcome the effects of ignorance and an animal vicious-ness that was prevalent among them" (p.109). In addition to needing examples, the race also needed to leave the cities and homestead on the plains, where there was room and opportunity for everything.

Finally, the reader will find *The Homesteader* an intriguing adventure. Micheaux taught himself to write, and his models may have been W. E. B. DuBois *(The Souls of Black Folks)* and Jack London *(Martin Eden)*.[15] And as a novice, he uses many literary devices to facilitate the flow of the novel. Some are more successful than others. In telling a far fuller story, he employs similar devices used to construct *The Conquest:* autobiography and polemics along with reflective dialogue or, if you will, monologues.

When the story begins, Jean Baptiste is given a full pedigree, which is remarkably similar to that of Micheaux. To give the other characters more depth, Micheaux provides them with a context or background. For example, Agnes Stewart comes from hard-working Scot-Irish stock. We learn very early in the novel that Agnes' father has an intriguing past, which foreshadows a happy ending. Augustus M. Barr, "an infidel"; Isaac Syfe, a Jew; and Peter Kaden—all of which we meet in South Dakota—are connected from the past, and their storyline is an interesting digression. In constructing these various story lines, Micheaux uses coincidence, flashbacks, trances, premonitions, and letters. Interposed with character development, storyline, and his plots, he also interjects polemics about the black community or inserts discussion about the state of society.[16] *The Homesteader* will hold your interest.

NOTES

1. Joseph A. Young, *Black Novelist as White Racist: The Myth of Black Inferiority in the Novels of Oscar Micheaux* (New York: Greenwood Press, 1989), pp. 74, 84.

2. Mark A. Reid, *Redefining Black Film* (Berkeley: University of California Press, 1993), p. 9.

3. Alfred D. Harrell, "Film's Early Black Auteurs," *Encore American & Worldwide New* (September 12, 1977), p. 36; Thomas Cripps, *Slow Fade to*

Black: the Negro in American Film, 1900–1942 (New York: Oxford University Press, 1993), pp. 75–76, 78–79, 173; Reid, *Redefining Black Film*, p. 9; and Donald Bogle, *Toms, Coons, Mulattoes, Mammies, & Bucks: an Interpretative History of Blacks in American Films* (New York: the Viking Press, 1973), p. 103.

4. Cripps, p. 82.

5. Cripps, p. 184; Chester J. Fontenot, Jr., "Oscar Micheaux, Black Novelist and Film Maker," in Virginia Faulkner with Frederick C. Luebke, *Vision and Refuge: Essays on the Literature of the Great Plains* (Lincoln: University of Nebraska Press, 1982), p. 118.

6. Fontenot, Jr., p. 118; Cripps, p. 184; Young, p. 66; and Reid, p. 12.

7. Fontenot, p. 118.

8. Fontenot, p. 122; J. Randall Woodland, "Oscar Micheaux," in *Dictionary of Literary Biography*, Vol. 50: *Afro-American Writers before the Harlem Renaissance* (Detroit: Gale Research, 1986), pp. 218–19.

9. Fontenot, p. 122.

10. Ibid.

11. Woodland, p. 222.

12. Ibid., pp. 222–23.

13. Fontenot, p. 123; Woodland, p. 224.

14. Ibid.

15. Young, pp. 20, 78.

16. Ibid., p. 75.

THE HOMESTEADER

EPOCH THE FIRST

LEADING CHARACTERS

AGNES, *Whose Eyes Were Baffling*

JEAN BAPTISTE, *The Homesteader*

JACK STEWART, *Agnes' Father*

AUGUSTUS M. BARR, *an Infidel*

ISAAC SYFE, *a Jew*

PETER KADEN, *The Victim*

N. JUSTINE McCARTHY, *a Preacher*

ORLEAN, *his Daughter, Without the Courage of Her Convictions*

ETHEL, *her Sister, Who Was Different*

GLAVIS, *Ethel's Husband*

EUGENE CROOK, *a Banker*

THE HOMESTEADER

CHAPTER I

AGNES

THEIR cognomen was Stewart, and three years had gone by since their return from Western Kansas where they had been on what they now chose to regard as a "Wild Goose Chase." The substance was, that as farmers they had failed to raise even one crop during the three years they spent there, so had in the end, therefore, returned broken and defeated to the rustic old district of Indiana where they had again taken up their residence on a rented farm.

Welcomed home like the "return of the prodigal," the age old gossip of "I told you so!" had been exchanged, and the episode was about forgotten.

But there was one in the family, the one with whom our story is largely concerned, who, although she had found little in Western Kansas to encourage her to stay there, had not, on the other hand, found much cheer back in old Indiana so long as they found no place to live but "Nubbin Ridge." Although but a girl, it so happened through circumstances over which she had no control, that whatever she thought or did, concerned largely the whole family's welfare or destiny.

Her father was a quaint old Scotchman, coming directly from Scotland to this country, a Highlander from the highest of the Highlands, and carried the accent still. But concerning her mother, she had never known her. Indeed, few had known her mother intimately; but it was generally understood that she had been the second wife of her father, and that she had died that Agnes might live. She was the only offspring by this marriage, although there were two boys by the first union. These lived at home with her and her father, but were, unfortunately, half-witted. Naturally Agnes was regarded as having been fortunate in being born of the second wife. But, what seemed rather singular, unlike her half brothers who were simple, she, on the other hand, appeared to be possessed with an unusual amount of wit; rare wit, extraordinary wit.

She was now twenty, and because she possessed such sweet ways, she was often referred to as beautiful, although, in truth she was not. Her face was somewhat square, and while there was a semblance of red roses in her cheeks when she smiled, her complexion was unusually white — almost pale. Her mouth, like her face, was also inclined to be square, while her lips were the reddest. She had a chin that was noticeable, due to the fact that it was so prominent, and her nose was straight almost to the point where it took a slight turn upwards. It was her hair, however, that was her greatest attraction. Unusually long, it was thick and heavy, of a flaxen tint, and was her pride. Her eyes, however, were a mystery — baffling. Sometimes when they were observed by others they were called blue, but upon second notice they might be taken for brown. Few really knew their exact color, and to most they were a puzzle. There was a flash about them at times that moved people, a peculiarity withal that even her father had never been able to understand. At such times he was singularly frightened, frightened with what he saw, and what he didn't see but felt. Always she then reminded him of her mother whom he had known only briefly before taking her as his wife. He had loved her, this wife, and had also feared her as he now feared this daughter when her eyes flashed.

Her mother had kept a secret from him — and the world! In trust she left some papers. What they contained he did not know, and would not until the day before she, Agnes, was to marry; and should she not marry by the time she reached thirty, the papers were to be given her then anyhow.

And so Jack Stewart had resigned himself to the situation; had given her the best education possible, which had not been much. She had gone through the grade schools, however, and barely succeeded in completing two years of the high school course. The love that he had been deprived of giving her mother because of her early death he had given to Agnes; she was his joy, his pride. She read to him because his eyes were not the best; she wrote his letters, consulted with him, assisted and conducted what business he had, and had avoided the society of young men.

So we have met, and know some little of the girl we are to follow. In the beginning of our story, we find her anything but contented. Living in quaint old " Nubbin Ridge," could not, to say the most, be called illustrious. It was a small district where the soil was very poor — as poor, perhaps, as Indiana afforded. So poor indeed, that it was capable of producing nothing but nubbins (corn) from which it derived its name. When a man went to rent a farm in " Nubbin Ridge " he was considered all in, down and out. . . . To continue life there was to grow poorer. It was a part of the state wherein no one had ever been known to grow rich, and Stewarts had proven no exception to the rule. But this story is to be concerned only briefly with " Nubbin Ridge," so we will come back to the one around whom it will in a measure center.

Her chief accomplishments since their disastrous conquest of Western Kansas had been the simple detail of keeping a diary. But at other times she had attempted musical composition and had even sent the same to publishers, one after another. Of course all she sent had duly come back, and she had by this time grown to expect the returned manuscripts as the inevitable. But since sending the same gave her a diversion, she had kept it up — and had today received a letter! A letter, that was all, and a short one at that; but even a letter in view of her previous experiences was highly appreciated. It stated briefly that her composition had been carefully examined — studied, but had, they very much regretted to inform her, been found unavailable for their needs. Although they had returned the same, they wished to say that she had shown some merit — "symptoms" she thought would have sounded better — and that they would always be patient and glad to examine anything she might be so kind as to submit!

She read the letter over many times. Not that she hoped that doing so would bring her anything, but because in her little life in "Nubbin Ridge" there was so little to break the usual monotonous routine. When she had read and studied it until she knew every letter by heart, she sighed, picked up her diary, and wrote therein:

There is little to record tonight. Today just passed was like yesterday, and yesterday was like the day before that, except it rained yesterday, and it didn't the day before. Papa and Bill and George have just completed picking corn — nubbins, the kind and only thing that grows in Nubbin Ridge. Verily does the name fit the production! We will perhaps have enough when it is sold to pay the rent, send to Sears & Roebuck for a few things, and that's all. George wants a gun and thinks he's worked hard enough this summer to earn one. He has found one in the catalogue that can be had for $4.85 and is all heart that papa will get it for him; along with four boxes of shells that will, all told, reach $6.00. Little enough, to say the least, for a summer's work! Bill has his mind set on a watch, but papa bought him a suit of clothes that cost $5.89 two months ago when we sold the hogs, so I don't think Bill will get in on anything this fall or winter. As for me, I would like to have a dress that I see can be had through a catalogue for a reasonable sum; but if it will crowd papa I will say nothing about it. He has the mortgage on the horses to pay, and by the time we get the few other necessities, it will not leave much, if anything.

LATER — Papa has been growing very restless of late. I don't wonder, either. Any one that had any energy, any spark of ambition, would grow restless or crazy in Nubbin Ridge! The very name smacks of poverty, ignorance and degeneration! But a real estate man from South Dakota has been in the neighborhood for a week, and has told some wonderful tales of opportunities out there. He has made it plain to papa that Western Kansas has been a failure to thousands of people for forty years; that South Dakota is different; that the rainfall is abundant; the climate is the best, and that every renter in Indiana should there proceed forthwith. I'm surprised that he should waste his time talking with papa who has no money, but he seems to be just as anxious for him to go as he is for others. Perhaps it's because he wishes a crowd. A crowd even though some are poor would, I imagine, appear more like business.

Bill and George are full for going, and papa has hinted to me as to whether I would like it. How should I know? It couldn't be worse than this place even if it was the jumping off place of all creation! I have about come to the place where I am willing to try anywhere once. There surely must be some place in this wide world where people have a chance to rise. Of course, with us — poor Bill and George, and papa's getting old, I don't suppose we will ever get hold of much anywhere. But the real estate man says we could all take homesteads; that in those parts—I cannot quite call the name, I'll study a while. . . . The Rosebud Country, is what he called it — there had been a great land opening, and there would be another in a few years. That we could go out now and rent on a place, raise big crops and get in good financial circumstances by the time the opening comes, go forth then and all take homesteads and grow rich! It sounds fishy — us growing rich; but since we have nothing we couldn't lose.

He says that people have grown wealthy in two years; that among the successful men — those who have made it quickly — is a colored man out there who came from — he couldn't say just where; but that if a colored man could make it, and get money together, surely any one else should. I will close this now because it is late, the light is low; besides I'm sleepy, and since that is surely one thing a person can do with success in " Nubbin Ridge," I will retire and have my share of it.

A MONTH LATER — It has happened! We are going West! The real estate man has gone back, and papa has been out there. He is carried away with the country. Says it is the greatest place on earth. I won't attempt to put down the wonders he has told of. Rich land to be rented for one-third of the crops — and we pay two-fifths in Nubbin Ridge where there is no soil, just a sprinkling of dust over the surface. Has rented a place already, and has made arrangements with the man that we owe to give him a year's time to pay the two hundred dollars. So we have enough to get out there and buy seed next spring! Everybody says we are going on another " Wild Goose Chase," but they would say that if we were going into the next county. It would seem better, however, if we would wait until spring, but Papa is getting ready to go right after Xmas. That settles it! I will make no more notes in this diary until we have reached the " promised land." In the meantime I am full of dreams, dreams, dreams! I had a strange dream last night; a real dream in which things happened! Always I have those day dreams, but last night I had a real dream. I dreamed that we went out to this country and that we rented and lived on a farm near the colored man the real estate man spoke of. I dreamed that he was an unusual man, a wonderful personality, and that we — he and I — became very close friends! That a strange murder occurred near where we went; a murder that no one could ever understand; but that in after years it was all made plain — and I was involved! Think of such a dream! Me being involved in anything; I, of " Nubbin Ridge!" I am sure that if I told out there the name of the place from where we came they would think we were crazy! But that was not all the dream — and it was all so plain! It frightens me when I think of it. I cannot realize how I could have had such a strange dream. I dreamed after we had been there a while that I fell in love — but it's the man I fell in love with which makes the dream so unusual, and — impossible! Yet there is a saying that nothing is impossible!

I will not record here or describe the one with whom I fell in love. Strangely I feel that I should wait. I cannot say why, but something seems to caution me; to tell me not to say more now.

There remains but one thing more. Yesterday I happened to glance at myself in the mirror. As if by magic I was drawn closer and studied myself, studied something in my features I had never seen before — at least not in that way. I observed then my hands. They, too, appeared unlike they had been before. It seems to have been the dream that prompted me to look — and the dream that revealed this about myself that I cannot understand. My eyes did not appear the same; they were as if — as if, they belonged to some other! My lips were red as usual; but there was about them something too I had not seen before: they appeared thicker, and as I studied them in the mirror more closely, I couldn't resist that singularity in my eyes. They became large and then small; they were blue, so blue, and then they were brown. It was when they appeared brown that I could not understand. I will close now for I wish to think. My brain is afire, I must think, think, think!

CHAPTER II

THE DAY was cold and dark and dreary. A storm raged over the prairie,— a storm of the kind that seem to come only over the northwest. Over the wide, unbroken country of our story, the wind screamed as if terribly angry. It raced across the level stretches, swept down into the draws, where draws were, tumbled against the hillsides, regained its equilibrium and tore madly down the other side, as if to destroy all in its path. A heavy snow had fallen all the morning, but about noon it had changed to fine grainy missiles that cut the face like cinders and made going against it very difficult. Notwithstanding, through it — directly against it at most times, The Homesteader struggled resolutely forward. He was shielded in a measure by the horses he was driving, whose bulks prevented the wind from striking him in the face, and on the body at all times. At other times — and especially when following a level stretch — he got close to the side of the front wagon with its large box loaded with coal, which towered above his head and shoulders.

Before him, but not always, the dim line of the trail, despite the heavy snow that had fallen that morning, was outlined. Perhaps it was because he had followed it — he and his horses — so often before in the two years since he had been West, that he was able to keep to its narrow way without difficulty today. And still, following it was not as difficult as following other trails, for it was an old, old trail. So old indeed was it, that nobody knew just how old it was, nor how far it reached. It was said that Custer had gone that way to meet his massacre; that Sitting Bull knew it best; but to The Homesteader, he hoped to be able to follow it only as long as the light of day pointed the way. When night came — but upon that he had not reckoned! To be caught upon it by darkness was certain death, and he didn't want to die.

He was young, The Homesteader — just passed twenty-two — and vigorous, strong, healthy and courageous. His height was over six feet and while he was slender he was not too much so. His shoulders were slightly round but not stooped. His great height gave him an advantage now. He followed his horses with long, rangy strides, turning his head frequently as if to give the blood a chance to circulate about and under the skin of his wide forehead. The fury of the storm appeared to grow worse, judging from the way the horses shook their bridled heads; or perhaps it was growing colder. Almost continually some of the horses were striking the ice from their nosepoints; while very often The Homesteader had to rest the lines he held while he forced the blood to his finger tips with long swings of his arms back and forth across his breast.

His claim lay many miles yet before him, and his continual gaze toward the west was to ascertain how long the light of day was likely to hold out. Behind, far to the rear, lay the little town of Bonesteel which he had left that morning, and now regretted having done so. But the storm had not been so bad then, and because the snow was falling he had conjectured it would be better to reach home before it became too deep or badly drifted. As it was now he was encountering all this and some more

"Damn!" he cried as they passed down a slope to where

From a painting by W. M. Farrow.

HE WAS YOUNG, THE HOMESTEADER—JUST PASSED TWENTY-TWO — AND VIGOROUS, STRONG, HEALTHY AND COURAGEOUS.

the land divided, and where the wind seemed to hit hardest. His course lay directly northwest, straight against the wind which he could only avoid by hanging the lines over the lever of the brake and fall in behind the trail wagon. But this, unfortunately, placed him too far away from the horses. He had walked all the way, for to walk was apparently the only way to keep from freezing. He soon reached the other side of the draw, and when he had come to the summit beyond, he groaned. Ahead of him just above the dark horizon the sun came suddenly from beneath the clouds. On either side of it, great, gasping sun-dogs struggled. They seemed to vie with the red sinking orbit; and as he continued his anxious gazing in that direction they seemed to have triumphed, for as the sun sank lower and lower, they appeared suddenly empowered with a mighty force for only a few minutes later the sun had fallen into the great abyss below and the night was on!

"We can make it yet, boys," he cried to his horses as if to cheer them. And as if they understood, they crashed forward with such vigor that he was thrown almost into a trot to keep up.

As to how long it went on thus, or as to how far they had gone, he was not able to reckon; but out of the now pitch darkness he became conscious of a peculiar longing. He had a vision of his sod house that stood on the claim, and he saw the small barn with its shed and the stalls for four. He saw the little house again with its one room, the little monkey stove with an oven on the chimney, and imagined himself putting a pan of baking powder bread therein. He saw his bed, a large, wide, dirty —'tis true — but a warm bed, nevertheless. He fancied himself creeping under the covers and sleeping the sound way he always did. He could not understand his prolific thoughts that followed.

He thought of his boyhood back in old Illinois; he took stock of the surroundings he had left there; he lived briefly through the discontentment that had ultimately inspired him to come West. And then he had again those dreams. Regardless of where his train of wandering thoughts began or of where they followed, always they were sure to end upon this given point, the girl. The girl of his dreams — for he had no real girl. There had never been a real girl for Jean Baptiste, for this was his name. In the years that had preceded his coming hither, it had been one relentless effort to get the few thousands together with which to start when he finally came West. At that he had been called lucky. He had no heritage, had Jean Baptiste. His father had given him only the French name that was his, for his father had been poor — but this instant belongs elsewhere. His heritage, then, had been his indefatigable will; his firm determination to make his way; his great desire to make good. But we follow Jean Baptiste and the girl.

Only a myth was she. She had come in a day dream when he came West, but strangely she had stayed. And, singularly as it may seem, he was confident she would come in person some day. He talked with her when he was lonely, and that was almost every day. He told her why he had come West, because he felt it was the place for young manhood. Here with the unbroken prairie all about him; with its virgin soil and undeveloped resources; and the fact that all the east, that part of the east that was Iowa and Illinois had once been as this now was, had once been as wild and undeveloped and had not then been worth any more — indeed, not so much. Here could a young man work out his own destiny. As Iowa and Illinois had been developed, so could this — so *would* this also be developed.

And as railways had formed a network of those states, so in time would they reach this territory as well. In fact it was inevitable what was to come, the prime essential, therefore, for his youth, was to begin with the beginning — and so he had done.

So he had come, had Jean Baptiste, and was living alone with a great hope; with a great hope for the future of this little empire out there in the hollow of God's hand; with a great love, too, for her, his dream girl. So in his prolific visions he talked on with her. He told her that it was a long way to the railroad now — thirty-two miles. He had that far to haul the coal he and others burned. There were yet no fences, and while there were section lines, they were rarely followed. It was nearer by trail. But he was patient, he was perseverant. Time would bring all else — and her. He had visions of her, she was not beautiful; she might not be vivacious, for that belonged to the city; but she was good. Always he understood everything that was hers, and he was confident she would understand him. Her name was sweet and easily pronounced. How he loved to call it!

He staggered at times now and didn't know why. He had wanted to be home and in his bed where he could sleep; but home as he now regarded it was too far. He couldn't make it, and didn't need to. Why should they blunder and pull so hard to get home when all about them was a place where they could rest. The prairie was all about; and he had slept on the ground before with only the soft grass beneath him. Why, then, must he continue on and on! The air was pleasant — warm and luxuriant, and he, Jean Baptiste, was very tired — oh, how tired he really was!

It was settled! He had gone far enough. He would

make his bed right where he was. He called to the horses. But somehow they didn't seem to hear. He called again then, he thought, louder, and still they failed to hear. He wondered at their stubbornness. They were good horses and had never disobeyed before. He called now again at the top of his voice, but they heeded him not; in the meantime forging onward, onward and onward! It occurred to him to drop the reins, but such had never been a custom. Within his tired, freezing and brain-fagged mind, there was a resolution that made him cling to them, but struggling to pull them down to a stop he continued.

And as he followed them now onward toward the sod house that stood on the claim, all realism seemed to desert him; he became a chilled mechanician; he seemed to have passed into the infinite where all was vague; where turmoil and peculiar strife only abided. . . . For Jean Baptiste did not understand that he was on the verge of freezing.

Stewarts were pleased with the country. They had arrived in early January. The weather had not been bad, although the wind blew much stronger here than it did in Indiana. However, they had not forgotten how it blew in Western Kansas and were therefore accustomed to it. The house upon the place they had rented was small, just four rooms, but it was well built and was warm. A village was not far. The people in it called it a town, but you see they were enthusiastic. To be more amply provided they could get what they needed at Gregory which was seven miles. Seven miles was not far to one who could ride horseback, and this Agnes had learned in Western Kansas.

" You had best not go to town today, my girl," cautioned Jack Stewart, her father, as she made ready to ride to

Gregory after ordering Bill to saddle Dolly, the gray mare that was their best.

"Tut, tut, papa," she chided. "This is a day to take the benefit of this wonderful air. The low altitude of Nubbin Ridge made me sallow; there was no blood in my cheeks. Here — ah, a nice horseback ride to Gregory will be the best yet for me!"

"I don't like the wind — and so much snow with it," he muttered, looking out with a frown upon his face.

"But the snow is not like it was," she argued, almost ready. "It's letting up."

"It's growing finer, which is evidence that it is growing colder."

"Better still," she cried, jumping about frolickingly, her lithe young body as agile as an athlete's. "Now, dada," she let out winsomely, "I shall dash up to Gregory, get all we need, and be back before the sun goes down!" And with that she kissed away further protest, swung open wide the door, stepped out and vaulted lightly into the saddle. A moment later she was gone, but not before her father cried:

"If you should be delayed, stay the night in town. Above all things, don't let the darkness catch you upon the prairie!"

CHAPTER III

SHE enjoyed the horseback ride to Gregory. Although she trembled at times from the sting of the intense cold, the exercise the riding gave her body kept the blood circulating freely, and she made the trip to the little town without event.

Once there, after thawing the cold out of her face and eyes, she proceeded to do her trading, filling the saddle-bags to their fullest.

"Which way do you live from town?" inquired the elderly man who waited upon her at the general store where she was doing her trading.

"Seven miles southeast," she replied.

"Indeed!" he cried as if surprised. "But you didn't come from there today — this afternoon? That would be directly against this storm!"

She nodded.

"Well, now, who would have thought you could have made it! 'Tis an awful day without," he cried as he regarded her in wonder.

"It *wasn't* warm, I admit," she agreed; "but I didn't seem to mind it so much!"

"You will not go back today — rather tonight?"

"Oh, yes."

"But it would be very risky. Look! It's grown dark already!" She looked out and observed that it had really

28

grown almost pitch dark during the few minutes she had lingered inside. She was for a moment at a loss for a reply, then, conscious that the wind would be to her back, she laughed lightly as she said:

" Oh, I shan't mind. It will take me less than forty minutes, and then it'll all be over," and she laughed low and easily again. The man frowned as he pursued:

" I don't like to see you start, a stranger in such a night as this. Since settlement following a trail is rather treacherous. One may leave town on one, but be on some other before they have gone two miles. And while the wind will be to your back, the uncertainty of direction, should you happen to look back or even around, is confusing. One loses sense of the way they are going. I'd suggest that you stick over until morning. It would be safer," he concluded, shaking his head dubiously.

" Oh, I am not afraid," she cried cheerfully. She was ready then, and with her usual dash, she crossed the short board walk, vaulted into the saddle, and a few minutes later the dull clatter of her horse's hoofs died in the distance.

With the wind to her back she rode easily. She enjoyed the exercise the riding gave her, and was thrilled instead of being frightened over what was before her. She followed quite easily the trail that had taken her into the village. In due time she passed a house that she had observed when going in that stood to one side of the trail, and then suddenly the mare came to an abrupt halt. She peered into the darkness before her. A barbwire fence was across the trail. She could not seem to recall it being there on her way in. Yet she argued with herself that she might have come around and not noticed it. For a moment she was in doubt as to which way to go to get around it. As she viewed it, it did not extend perhaps more than a quarter mile or a half at the most, after which she could come around to the other side and strike the trail again. She gave the ever faithful mare rein and they sailed down the fence line to where she estimated it must shortly end.

She did not know that this was the old U-Cross fence, and that because it stood on Indian land, it had not been taken up when the great ranch had been moved into the next county when giving up to the settler. In truth only a few steps to her right she had left the trail she had followed into town. The old trail had been cut off when The Homesteader in whose house she had seen the light, had laid out his claim, and it was this which caused the confusion. She did not know that one could go to town, or to the railroad today and returning on the morrow, find the route changed. Homesteaders were without scruples very often in such matters. The law of the state was that before a followed trail was cut off, it should be advertised for five weeks in advance to that effect; but not one in twenty of the settlers knew that such a law existed.

So Agnes Stewart had ridden fully two miles before she became apprehensive of the fact that she had lost her way. Now the most practical plan for her would been to have turned directly about and gone back to where she had started down the fence. But, charged with impatient youth, she sought what she felt to be the quickest way about. Now upon looking closely she could see that wires hung down in places and that a post here and there had sagged. She urged the mare over a place and then, once over, went in the direction she felt was home. The stiff, zero night air had somewhat dulled her, and she made the mistake of looking back, thereby confusing her direction to the point where after a few minutes she could not have sworn in what direction she was going, except that the wind was still at her back.

She peered into the darkness before her. She thought there would be lights of homesteaders about, and while there was, the storm made it impossible for her to see them. After a time she became alarmed, and recalled her father's warning, also the store-keeper's. But her natural determination was to go on, that she would get her bearings, presently. So, with a jerking of her body as if to stimulate circulation of the blood, she bent in the saddle and rode another mile or more. She had crossed draws, ascended hills, had stumbled over trails that always appeared to lead in the wrong direction, and at last gave up for lost at a summit where the wind and fine snow chilled her to the marrow. She was thoroughly frightened now. She thought to return to Gregory, but when she turned her eyes against the wind, she could catch no sight of anything. She was sure then that she could not make it back there had she wished to. Not knowing what to do she allowed the mare to trot ahead without any effort to direct her. She had not gone far before she realized that they were following a level stretch. And because she seemed to keep warm when the horse moved, she allowed the mare to continue. A half mile she estimated had been covered when out of the darkness some dark shape took outline. She peered ahead; the mare was ambling gently toward it, and she saw after a time that it was a quaint, oblong structure, a sod house apparently, many of which she had observed since coming West into the new country. She was relieved. At least she was not to freeze to death upon the prairie, a fact that she had begun to regard as a possibility a few minutes before. The mare fell into a walk and presently came up to a low, square house, built of sod, with its odd hip roof reposing darkly in the outline. She called, " Hello," and was patient. The wind bit into her, and she was conscious of the bitter cold, and that she was beginning to feel its severe effects. There was no response, and she called again, dismounting in the meantime. When she saw ho one she went around to where she observed a low door at which she knocked vigorously. From all appearances the place was occupied, but no one was at home. She tried the knob. It gave, and she pushed the door open cautiously. All was darkness within. Then, dropping the bridle reins she ventured inside. She could not understand why her feet made no sound upon the floor, but in truth there was no floor except the earth. She felt in her coat pocket and presently produced a match. When the flaring light illuminated the surroundings, she gazed about. It was, she quickly observed, a one room house. There was at her side a monkey stove with an oven on the pipe; while at her left stood a table with dishes piled thereupon. There was also a lantern on the table and this she adjusted and lighted before the blaze died. She swung this about, and saw there was a bed with dirty bed clothing, also a trunk, some boxes and what nots.

"A bachelor, I'd wager," she muttered, and then blushed when she considered her position. She looked about further, and upon seeing fuel, proceeded to build a fire. This done, she passed outside, found a path that extended northwest, and, leading the horse, soon came to a small barn. Here she saw two stalls with a manger filled with hay. She had to push the mare back to keep her from entering and making herself at home. She passed around the barn and entered the door of a small shed, for cattle obviously, but empty. Hay was in the manger, and, taking the bits from the mare's mouth, she tied the reins to the manger, unsaddled, and, leaving the shed after fastening the door, she carried the saddle with her to the house.

The little stove was roaring from the fire she had started, and she was surprised to find the room becoming warm. She placed the saddle in a convenient position and lifted her cap, whereupon her heavy hair fell over her shoulders. She caught it up and wound it into a braid quickly, guiltily. . . . She unbuttoned her coat then, and took a seat.

"There is no one here," she muttered to herself. "So since I don't know the way home, and there's no one here to tell me, guess I'll have to give it up until morning." She was thoughtful then. This *was* something of an adventure. Lost upon the prairie: a bachelor's homestead: there alone. Then suddenly she started. From the storm swept outside she thought she caught a sound, and thereupon became quickly alert, but the next moment her tension relaxed. It was only the wind at the corner of the house. The room had become warm, she was uncomfortable with the heavy coat about her. She was conscious, moreover, that her eyes were heavy, sleep was knocking at her door. She shook off the depression and fell again to thinking. She wondered who could live there and she continued in her random thinking until shortly, unconsciously, she fell into a doze.

She could not recall whether she had dozed an hour or a minute, but she was awakened suddenly and jumped to her feet; for, from the storm she had caught the sound of horses and wagons passing the house at only a short distance. She stood terrified. Her eyes were wide, her lips were apart as she listened to the grinding of the wagon wheels — and they went directly toward the barn. Then all was silent, and she placed her hand to her heart, to still the frightened beating there. She heard the horses shake in their harness, and came to herself. The man of the place had returned; she had taken charge of his house, he a bachelor and she a maid. She felt embarrassed. She got into her coat and buttoned it about her hurriedly; and then drawing the cap over her head, she waited, expectantly, although she was sure that time sufficient had expired, whoever drove the teams had not come toward the house. She could hear the horses, but she could not ascertain that they were being unhitched. She was undecided for a moment, then, catching up the lantern, she quickly went outside. Two wagons loaded heavily with coal greeted her. She passed to the front and found four horses, white with the frost from perspiration, standing hitched to the loads. She passed to their heads. No one was about, and she was puzzled. She passed around to the other side, and as she did so, stumbled over something. With the lantern raised, she peered down and then suddenly screamed when she discovered it was a man. Then, on second thought, fearing he had fallen from the wagon and become injured, she put her arm through the bail of the lantern, reached down, caught him by the shoulders and shook him. He was not injured, she was relieved to see; but *what was* the matter? In the next moment she gave a quick start. She realized in a twinkling then, that the man was freezing — perhaps already frozen!

With quick intuition she reached and caught him beneath the arms, and turning, dragged him to the house. She opened the door, and lifting his body, carried him in her arms across the room and laid him upon the bed. Then, realizing that the night was severely cold, she rushed out, closing the door behind her, and a half hour later had the horses unhitched, unharnessed and tied in their stalls. This done she returned hurriedly to the house to find the man still unconscious, but breathing heavily. She did not know at once what to do, but going to his feet, took off his shoes. This was rather difficult, and she feared that from the way they felt, his feet were frozen. She rubbed them vigor-

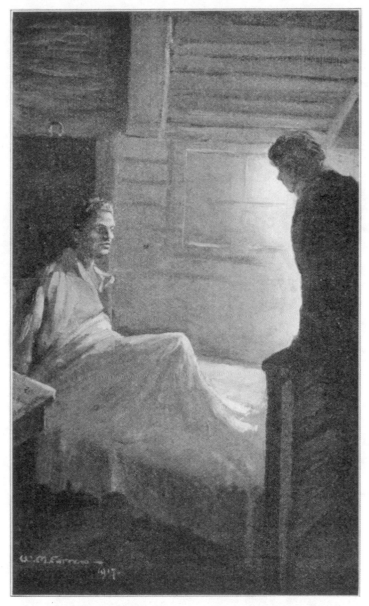

From a painting by W. M. Farrow.

HE RAISED ON AN ELBOW AND LOOKED INTO HER FACE
WHILE SHE STAGGERED IN GREAT SURPRISE.

ously, and was relieved after a time to feel the blood circulating and the same giving forth warmth. She sighed with relief and then pulling off the heavy gloves, she exercised the same proceeding with the hands, and was cheered to feel them give forth warmth after a time. She unbuttoned the coat at his throat, and rolling him over, managed to get it off of him. Next she unbuttoned the collar, drew off the cap, and for the first time saw his face. It was swollen and very dark, she thought. She brought the lantern closer and looked again. She gave a start then and opened her mouth in surprise. Then she fell to thinking. She went back to the chair beside the fire and reflected.

"It is all the same, of course," she said to herself. "But I was just surprised. It all seems rather singular," she mused, and tried to compose herself. The surprise she had just experienced, had, notwithstanding her effort at self possession, disconcerted her. She turned suddenly, for she had caught the sound of a noise from the bed. She got up quickly and went to him. He had turned from his side to his back. She stood over him with the lantern raised. To see him better she leaned over, holding the lantern so that her face was full in the light. She had unbuttoned her coat at the throat, and seeking more comfort, had also removed the cap she wore. She had, however, forgotten her hair which had been held about her head by the cap and it now fell in braids over her slender shoulders. On the instant the man's eyes opened. He raised on an elbow, looked into her face, smiled wanly, and murmured:

"It is you, Agnes. You have come and oh, I am glad, for I have waited for you so long." In the next breath he had fallen back upon the bed and was sleeping again, while she staggered in great surprise. *Who was this man* that he should call her name and say that *he* had waited?

But with Jean Baptiste, he snored in peace. His dream had come true; the one of his vision had come as he had hoped she would. But Jean Baptiste was not aware of the debt he owed her; that through strange providence in getting lost she had come into his sod house and saved his life. 'But what he was yet to know, and which is the great problem of our story, the girl, his dream girl, Agnes Stewart, happened to be white, while he, Jean Baptiste, The Homesteader, was a Negro.

CHAPTER IV

SHE COULD NEVER BE ANYTHING TO HIM

JEAN BAPTISTE slept soundly all the night through, snoring loudly at times, turning frequently, but never awakening. And while he slept, unconscious of how near he had come to freezing to death upon the prairie, but for the strange coincidence of Agnes Stewart's having gotten lost and finding him, she sat near, listening to the dull roar of the storm outside at times; at other times casting furtive, anxious and apprehensive glances toward the bed, half in fear. More because the position she realized herself to be in was awkward, not to say embarrassing.

Her eyes became heavy as the night wore on, and she arose and walked about over the dirt floor in an attempt to shake off the inertia. And in the meantime, the man she had saved slept on, apparently disturbed by nothing. Presently she approached him shyly, and, taking the coat he had worn and which lay near, she spread it carefully over him, then tiptoed away and regarded him curiously. Her life had never afforded character study in a broad sense; but for some reason, which she could not account for, she strangely trusted the sleeping man. And because she did, she was not in fear lest he awaken and take advantage of the compromising circumstances. But in her life she had met and known no colored people, and knew directly little about the Negro race beyond what she had read. Therefore to find herself lost on the wide plains, in a house alone with one, a bachelor Homesteader, with a terrific storm without, gave her a peculiar sensation.

When the hand of the little clock upon the table pointed to two o'clock a. m., she put coal on the fire, became seated in a crude rocking chair that proved notwithstanding, to be comfortable, and before she was aware of it, had fallen asleep. Worn out by the night's vigil, and the unusual circumstances in which she found herself, she slept soundly and all sense of flying time was lost upon her. The storm subsided with the approach of morn, and the sun was peeping out of a clear sky in the east when she awakened with a start. She jumped to her feet. Quickly her eyes sought the bed. It was empty. The man had arisen. She looked out through the little window. The blizzard had left the country gray and streaked. Buttoning her coat collar about her throat, she adjusted her cap by pulling it well down over her head, and ventured outside.

Never had she looked upon such a scene as met her eyes! Everywhere, as far as she could see, was a mantle of snow and ice. Here the snow had been swept into huge drifts or long ridges; while there it sparkled in the sun, one endless, unbroken sheet of white frost and ice. Here and there over the wide expanse a lonesome claim shack reposed as if lost; while to the northwest, she could see the little town to which she had gone the afternoon before, rising heroically out of the snow. Upon hearing a sound, she turned to find The Homesteader leading her horse, saddled and bridled from the barn. She turned her eyes away to hide the confusion with which she was suddenly overcome, and at the same time to try to find words with which to greet him.

" Good morning," she heard from his lips, and turned her face to see him touch the cap he wore.

"Good morning, sir," she returned, smiling with ease, notwithstanding her confusion of a moment before.

"I judge that you must have become lost, the why you happened along," said he pleasantly, courteously.

"I did," she acknowledged, marveled at finding herself so much at ease in his presence, and him conscious. In the same instance she took quick note of his speech and manner, and was strangely pleased.

"I see," she heard him mutter. She had cast her eyes away as if to think, but now turned again toward him to find him regarding her intently. She saw him give a quick start, and catch his breath as if in surprise, whereupon she turned her eyes away. But she did not understand the cause of his start; she did not understand that while he had recognized her as his dream girl, that only then had he realized that she was white, while he had naturally supposed his dream girl would be of his own blood, Ethiopian.

He lowered his eyes as this fact played in his mind, and as he hesitated, she again turned her eyes upon him and regarded him wonderingly. And in that moment the instance of the night before when he had awakened and looked up into her eyes for the first time when she stood over him, and had uttered the words she would never as long as she lived, forget, came back. "*It is you, Agnes. You have come and, oh, I am glad, for I have waited for you so long.*" "How did he know my name and come to say what he did?" was the question she now again, as she had been doing all the night through, asked herself. She prayed that she might find a way to ask him — how deeply her curiosity to know was aroused. And then, while she was so deeply engrossed, abruptly he raised his head, and his eyes fell searchingly again upon her. He saw and wondered at the curious intentness he saw there, and as he did so, he caught that something in her eyes; he saw what she had seen before leaving Indiana; and as she had been when she had seen it, he too, was strangely moved and could not understand. Apparently he forgot all else as the changing color of her eyes held him, and while so, unconsciously he advanced a step nearer her. She did not move away, but stood as if in a thraldom, with a feeling stealing over her that somewhere she had seen and known him once. . . . But where — *where, where!* She had *never* known an *Ethiopian,* she full well recalled; but she was positive that she had seen this man somewhere before. Then *where — where, where!*

As for the man, Jean Baptiste, he seemed to relax after a time, and looked away. He had seen her at last; she had been his dream girl; had come in a dream and as she stood before him she was all his wondrous vision had portrayed. Her face was flushed by the cold air, and red roses in full bloom were in her cheeks; while her beautiful hair, spread over her shoulders, and fanned by a light breeze, made her in his eyes a picture of enchantment. When he observed her again and saw that her eyes were blue and then again were brown, he was still mystified; but what was come over Jean Baptiste now was the fact, the Great fact: *The fact that between him and his dream girl was a chasm so deep socially that bridging was impossible.* Because she was white while he was black, according to *the custom of the country and its law,* she could never be anything to him. . . . .

Her back was to the rising sun, and neither had observed that it was mounting higher in the eastern skies. She suppressed the question that was on her lips to ask him, the eternal question, and in that instant he came out of his trance. He turned to her, and said:

" It was sure fortunate for me that you lost your way,"

and so saying his eyes went toward the place she had found him, and she understood. She could not repress a happy smile that overspread her face. He saw it and was pleased.

"It was rather providential; but I would forget it. To think that you might have frozen to death out there makes me shudder when I recall it."

"I cannot seem to understand what came over me — that I was in the act of freezing while I walked."

"It was a terrible night," she commented. "I, too, might have frozen, but for the good fortune of my horse finding your house."

"Isn't it strange," he muttered abstractedly.

"I hadn't the least idea where I was," said she, musingly.

"Such a coincidence."

"Indeed it was ——, but please, shall we forget it," and she shuddered slightly.

"Yes," he replied readily. "Where do you live?"

She pointed to where the smoke curled from the chimney of their home, a mile and a half away.

"The Watson place? I see. You are perhaps, then, newcomers here?"

"We are," and she smiled easily. He did also. He handed her the bridle reins then, and said:

"I trust you will pardon my forgetfulness. Indeed I was so absorbed in the fact that I had been saved, that I forgot to — to be courteous."

"Oh, no, sir!" she cried quickly. "You did not. You —" and then she broke off in her speech. It occurred to her that she was saying too much. But strangely she wanted to go on, strangely she wanted to know more of him: from where he had come; of his life, for already she could see that he was a gentleman; an unusual person — but he was speaking again.

" You have become chilled standing there — it is severely cold. Step back into the house and warm yourself before you start. I will hold your horse while you do so." And he reached for the bridle reins.

She looked up into his face, and again trusted him; again she experienced a peculiar gratitude, and turning she obeyed him. As she stood inside over the little monkey stove a moment later, she could see him, and appreciated how thoughtful he was.

She returned after a few minutes, stood beside the animal he had brought and was ready to go. Suddenly she vaulted into the saddle. She regarded him again intently, while he returned the same a bit abstractedly. She started to urge the mare forward, and then she drew her to a stop before she had gotten fully started. Impulsively she leaned forward and stretched her hand toward him. Mechanically he took it. She unconsciously gripped his, as she said:

" I'm glad it happened. . . . That I became lost and — and — you were saved." His dark face colored with gratitude, and he had an effort to keep from choking when he tried to reply. In the meantime, she bestowed upon him a happy smile, and the next moment her horse had found the trail and was dashing along it toward the place she lived.

And as she went homeward over the hill, the man in whose life she was later to play such a strange and intimate part, stood looking after her long and silently.

CHAPTER V

THE CLAIM of Jean Baptiste, containing 160 acres of land, adjoined the little town of Dallas on the north, and it was one of the surprises that Agnes Stewart had not wandered into it when she found the sod house and had later found Jean Baptiste in the snow.

The town had been started the winter before. A creek of considerable depth, and plenty of water ran to the south of it a half mile, and up this valley the promoters of the town contended that the railroad would build. It came up the same valley many miles below where at a way station it suddenly lifted out of it and sought the higher land to Bonesteel. Now the promoters, because the Railroad Company owned considerable land where the tracks left the valley to ascend to the highland, contended that it was the purpose of the railroad to split the trade country by coming up the valley, and that was why the town had been located where it was, on a piece of land that had once belonged to an Indian.

There were three other towns, platted by the government along a route that did not strike Dallas, and if the railroad should continue the route it was following where its tracks stopped west of Bonesteel, it was a foregone conclusion that it must hit the three government townsites.

This had ever been, and was, the great contention in the early days of the country of our story. But to get back to the characters in question, we must come back to the little town near the creek valley.

43

The winter preceding, when the town had been started, men had chosen to cast their lot with it, and by the time spring arrived, there was a half dozen or more business places represented. From Des Moines a man had come and started a lumber yard; while from elsewhere a man had cooperated with the promoters in establishing a bank. Two men, whose reputations were rather notorious, but who, nevertheless, were well fitted for what they chose, started a saloon. From a town that had no railroad in the state on the south, a man came with a great stock of merchandise. A weazened creature had been made postmaster; while a doctor, beliquored until he was uncertain, had come hither with a hope of redemption and had hung out his shingle. He was succeeding in the game of reform (?) as the best customer the saloon had. A tired man was conducting a business in a building that had been hauled many miles and was being used as a hotel. Many other lines of business were expected, but at this time the interest was largely in who the settlers were that had come, and those who were to come.

A beautiful quarter section of land joined the town on the east, and the man who had drawn it had already established his residence thereupon, so that he was known. On the south the land was the allotment of an Indian; while the same was true on the west. Naturally, when it was reported that a Negro held the place on the north, considerable curiosity prevailed to meet this lone Ethiopian.

But Jean Baptiste was a mixer, a jolly good fellow of the best type and by this time such was well known. As to where he had come from, we know; but his name had occasioned much comment because it was odd. To make it more illustrious, the settlers had added " Saint," so he was now commonly know as St. Jean Baptiste. The doctor, whose name was Slater, had improved even upon this. He called him "St. John the Baptist." But nobody took Doc very seriously. So full was he of red liquor most of the time, that he was regarded as a joke except in his profession. Here he was considered one of the best,— his redeeming feature.

The coal The Homesteader had hauled from Bonesteel was not all for himself, but for the lumber yard which sold it at fifteen dollars the ton, and the quality was soft, and not of the best grade at that.

He hauled it into town the morning following the episode of our story, and after unloading it and taking his check for the hauling, returned home, took care of his stock, and upon returning to town, forgot to relate anything concerning his experiences. . . . *Perhaps* he forgot. . . . Jean Baptiste could be depended upon to forget some things. . . . Especially the things that were best forgotten.

He walked across the quarter mile that lay between his claim and the town, and up to the saloon. Inside he encountered the usual crowd, Doc among them.

"Hello, there, St. John the Baptist," cried that one in beliquored delight. "Did you crawl through all that storm?"

"I'm here," laughed Baptiste. "How's Doc?"

"Finer'n a fiddle, both ends in the middle," and called for another drink. Just one. It is said that saloons would not be so bad if it was not for the treating nuisance. Well, Doc could be regarded here then, as practical, for he never bought others a drink.

"See you got your nose freezed, Baptiste," Doc laughed. Baptiste went toward the bar, took a look at himself, and laughed amusedly upon seeing the telltale darkness at the point of his nose, his cheeks and his forehead.

" T' hell, I didn't know that," he muttered.   The crowd laughed.

" Play you a game of Casino? " suggested Doc.

" You're on! " cried Baptiste.

After they had played awhile a Swede who lived across the creek entered, took a seat and drawing his chair near, watched the game.   Presently he spoke.   " The Indians are coming in today, so I guess there will be a shooting up the town."

The players paused and regarded each other apprehensively.   Others overheard the remark, and now exchanged significant glances.   This had been the one diversion of the long winter.   Indians who lived on the creek, coming into town, getting drunk, and then as a sally ride up and down the main street and shoot up the town.   The last time this had taken place, the bartender's wife had been frightened into hysterics.   And thereupon the bartender had sworn that the next time this was attempted, they would have to reckon with him.

The few people about became serious.   They knew the bartender was dangerous, and they feared the Indians, breeds, mostly, who made this act their pastime.   They were annoyed with such doings; but were inclined to lay the blame at the saloon door, for, although the law decreed that Indians should not be sold liquor they were always allowed to purchase all that they could possibly carry away with them inside and out.   So upon this announcement, those about prepared themselves for excitement.   The news quickly spread and to augment the excitement, a few minutes later the breeds in full regalia dashed into town.   They tied their horses at the front, and proceeded at once to the bar.

" Whiskey," they cried, shifting their spurred boots on the barroom floor.

"Sorry, boys, but I can't serve you," advised the bartender carelessly.

"What!" they cried.

"Can't serve you. It's agin' the law, yu' know."

"T' hell with the law!" exclaimed one.

"I didn't make it," muttered the bartender.

"You've been playing hell enforcing it," retorted another.

"Now, don't get rough, my worthy," cautioned the bartender.

"Give us what we called for, and none of this damn slush then," cried one, toying with the gun at his holster. The bartender observed this and got closer to the bar for a purpose. Those about, being of the peaceful kind, began shifting toward the door.

"We've been breakin' the law to serve you," said the bartender "and you've been breaking the law after we done it. Now the last time you were here you pulled off a 'stunt' that caused trouble. So I'll not serve you whiskey, and advise you that if you try shooting up the town again, there'll be trouble."

"Oh, is that so?" cried the bunch. "Well," sniffed one, who was more forward than the rest, "we'll just *show* you a trick or two. And, remember, when we've shot your little chicken coops full of holes, we are going to return and be served." With a hilarious laugh, they went outside, got into the saddles and had their fun. The population took refuge in the cellars in awed silence.

It was over in a few minutes and the breeds, true to their statement, returned to the saloon, and stood before the bar.

"Whiskey," they cried, and couldn't repress a grin. Ordinarily they were cowards, and their boldness had surprised even themselves.

" Whiskey? " said the bartender, nodding toward the speaker.

" That's my order! " the other cried uproarously. The bartender arranged several bottles in a row. This they did not understand at first. They did, however, a moment later.

" Very well," he cried of a sudden as his eyes narrowed, whereupon, with deliberation he caught the bottles one by one by the neck and as fast as he could let go, threw the same into the faces before him with all the force he could concentrate quickly. So quickly was it all done that those before him had not time to duck below the bar before many had been the recipients of the deluge. Within the minute there was a wild scramble for the door — all but three. For while the others disappeared over the hill toward the creek, Dr. Slater took thirty stitches or thereabouts in the faces of the recalcitrants.

CHAPTER VI

THE INFIDEL, A JEW AND A GERMAN

A MILE north from where stood the house of St. Jean Baptiste, there lived a quaint old man. He was a widower; at least this was the general opinion, especially when he so claimed to be. In a new country there may be found among those who settle much that is unusual, not to say quaint and oftentimes mysterious. And in the case of this man, by name illustrious, there was all this and some more.

Augustus M. Barr, he registered, and from England he hailed. How long since does not concern this story at this stage. Besides, he never told any one when, or why — well, he had been in America long enough to secure the claim he held and that was sufficient. But that Barr had been a man of some note back from where he came, there could be little doubt. Among the things to prove it, he was very much of a linguist, being well versed in English, French, Polish, German; the Scandinavian he thoroughly understood — and Latin, that was easy!

He had been a preacher and had pastored many years in a Baker street church, London. Then, it seems, he concluded after all that there was no God; there was no Satan nor Hell either — so he gave up the ministry and became an infidel. And so we have him. But there was something A. M. Barr had never told — but that was the mystery.

And while he will be concerned with our story, let us not forget that two miles and more west of the little town of Dallas, there lived another, a Jew. He was not a merchant, nor was he a trader; then, Jews who are not the one or the other are not the usual Jew, apparently. Well, Syfe wasn't, for that was his name, Isaac Syfe, and from far away Assyria he had come. He was dark of visage with dark hair, and piercing but lurking eyes with brows that ran together; while his nose was long and seemed to hang down at the point, reminding one of the ancient Judas. His mouth was small and close; and there was always a cigarette between the dark lips. He was of medium size, somewhere in the thirties, perhaps, lived alone, on a homestead that was his own, and so we have Isaac Syfe. But there is another still.

He lived about as far southwest of Dallas as Syfe lived to the west and, unlike Syfe, he was light, a blond, thick, short and stout. His neck was muscular and slightly bull like; while his features were distinctly Germanic: his face was rounded and healthy with cheeks soft and red, and they called him Kaden, Peter Kaden. He also held a claim, having purchased a relinquishment in the opening, lived alone as did Syfe and numerous other bachelors, and did his own cooking, washing and ironing.

Augustus M. Barr appeared very much impressed with Jean Baptiste. He was a judge of men, withal, and much impressed with Baptiste as a personality; but the fact that Baptiste had broken one hundred and thirty acres on his homestead and now had it ready for crop, the first year of settlement; and had wisely invested in another quarter upon which a girl had made proof, delighted Barr. He admired the younger man's viewpoint and optimism. So when Barr was in town, and the conversation happened around that way, he was ever pleased to speak his praise of Baptiste.

It was the day of the Indian episode when Barr, driving a team hitched to a spring wagon, came to town, hoping that the lumber yard had received the much needed coal.

"And how about the coal," cried Barr to the lumberman before he drew his team to a stop.

"Coal a plenty," replied the lumberman cheerfully.

"Good, good, good!" exclaimed Barr, his distinguished old face lighting up with great delight.

"Yep," let out the lumberman, coming toward the buggy. "I've weighed you, and round to the bin is the coal. St. Jean Baptiste arrived last night — that is, I think he got home last night, although he brought the coal this morning, two loads, four tons."

"Eighty hundred pounds of coal, you don't say! And it was Jean Baptiste who brought it! Now, say, wasn't that great! Not another man on this whole Reservation save he could have made it," he ended admiringly.

"Jean Baptiste is the man who can bring it if anybody," rejoined the other.

At this moment a large, stout man came driving up in a one horse rig.

"Any coal?" he called lazily from his seat.

"Plenty," cried Barr.

"Thank God," exclaimed the other, whose name was Stark, and who held the claim that cornered with the town on the northeast, and therefore joined with the Baptiste claim on the east.

"Thank Jean Baptiste," advised Barr. "He's the man that brought it."

"So?" said Stark thoughtfully. "When?"

"Yesterday."

"Yesterday?"

"That's what the lumberman said."

"Well, I'll be blowed!"

"You'll be warmed, I guess."

"Well, I should say!"

"That Baptiste is *some* fellow."

"Well, yes. Although I sometimes think he is a fool."

"Oh, not so rash!"

"Any man's a fool that would have left Bonesteel with loads yesterday."

"Then I suppose we should be thankful to the fool. A fool's errand will in this case mean many lazy men's comfort."

"And last summer you recall how it rained?"

"I sure do."

"Well, you know that fellow would go out and work in the rain."

"And has a hundred and thirty acres ready and into crop while I have but thirty."

"I have but ten, but —"

"You will be in the hole — at least behind at the end of this summer."

"But I'm advertised to prove up."

"And leave the country when you have done so."

"Well, of course. I have a house and lot and three acres back in Iowa."

"And Jean Baptiste has 320 acres. In a few years he will have a rich, wonderful farm that will be a factor in the local history and development of this country; it will also mean something for posterity."

"Well, I don't care."

"You drew your land and got it free excepting four dollars an acre to the government. Baptiste bought his and paid for the relinquishment. You were lucky, but it will be up to Jean Baptiste and his kind to make the country.

Had they been as you appear to be, we would perhaps all be in Jerusalem, or the jungle. Let's load the coal."

"Good lecture, that," muttered the lumberman when the two were at the bin. "Lot's o' truth in it, too. Old Stark needed it. He's too lazy to hitch up a team, so rides to town in that little buggy with one horse hitched to it."

"What are you talking about?" inquired another, coming up at this moment.

"Jean Baptiste."

"So?"

"Barr and Stark have just had a set-to about him."

"M-m?"

"Stark says a man that would come from Bonesteel a day like yesterday was a fool."

"Why will he partake of the fuel he brought to keep from freezing, then?"

"Well, Stark is too lazy to care. He's advertised to prove up, you know, and he always has something to say about working."

"Used to come to town after the mail during the rainy spell last summer, and upon seeing Baptiste at work in the field, cry ' Just look at that fool nigger, a workin' in the rain.'" Both laughed. A few minutes later the town was thrown into an uproar over the incident related in the last chapter.

Now it happened that day that Augustus M. Barr went to the postoffice and received a heavy envelope. He glanced through the contents with a serious face, and put the papers in his pocket. On the way to his claim, he took them out and went through them again, and returned them to his pocket. A few minutes later he reached into the pocket, drew out what he thought to be the papers, and silently tore them to threads, and flung the bundle of paper to the winds.

When Jean Baptiste left the town for his little sod house on the hill, he saw A. M. Barr just ahead of him. He followed the same route that Barr had taken, and when he reached the draw on the town site that lay between his place and the town, he espied some papers. He picked them up, continued on his way, and presently observed the torn ball of paper that Barr had cast away. He idly opened the package he held. He wondered at the contents and as he read them through he became curious. The papers had to do with something between Augustus M. Barr, Isaac Syfe, and Peter Kaden.

"Now that is singular," he said to himself. He continued to read through the papers, and as he did so, another fact became clear to him. Kaden was a sad character. And because he was so forlorn, never cultivated any friendship, lived alone and never visited, the people had begun to regard him as crazy. But now Jean Baptiste understood something that neither he, nor any of the people in the country had dreamed of. He read on. He recalled that the summer before a young lady, beautiful, refined but strange at times, had stayed at the Barr claim. Barr had introduced her as his niece. The people wondered at her seclusion. She had a fine claim. Barr had come to him once and spoken about selling it, stating that the girl had fallen heir to an estate in England and was compelled to return therewith. . . . Later he had succeeded in selling the place. She had disappeared; but he had never forgotten the expressions he had observed upon the face of Christine. . . . He had thought it singular at the time but had thought little of it since. He read further into the papers, and learned about some other person, a woman, but concerning her he could gather nothing definite. He could not understand about Christine either, except that she had fallen heir to nothing in England; was not there, but not more than three hundred miles from where he stood at that moment. But there was before him what he *did* understand, and which was that there was something between Augustus M. Barr, Isaac Syfe, and Peter Kaden, *and something was going to happen.*

CHAPTER VII

NEVER since the night at the sod house had Agnes Stewart been the same person. She could not seem to dismiss Jean Baptiste, and the instance of her providence in getting lost and thereby saving him, from her mind. His strange words and singular recognition of her was baffling. Being so very curious therefore, she had since learned that he was well known in the community and held in popular favor.

She knew little and understood less with regard to pre-destination; but she had, since meeting him, recalled that he was the one she had seen in her dream — and loved! She tried to laugh away such a freak; but do what she might, she grew more curious to see him again as the days passed; to talk with him, and learn at last what she was anxious to know — curious to know. *How did he come to utter her name and say that he had waited?*

And, coincident with this, she recalled anew what she had learned — which positively was little — regarding her mother. She had been told that she inherited that one's peculiarity; that her mother had possessed rare eyes, which in a measure explained her own. But she had not been told or knew why her mother had arranged the legacy as she had. Not until the day before she was to marry must she know. And then should she not have won a husband to herself by the time she had reached thirty, she was to have the same then, anyhow. Singular, but in a sense practical.

Well, it was so, and she could only sigh and be patient.

Most girls she had known back in " Nubbin Ridge " were usually married by the time they had reached her present age. But she was not quite like other girls, and did not even have a beau.

She wondered if the man she had saved had a sweetheart. And when she thought of this, she had a feeling that she would know in time. And as the days passed she began at last to believe that in some manner he would play a part in her own life. But Agnes Stewart was too innocent to know — at least appeared not to be aware of — *the custom of the country and its law,* and therefore could not appreciate the invisible and socially invincible barrier between them. 'Twas only the man Jean Baptiste she saw and reckoned according to what she understood. Therefore, because she could get nowhere in her wonderings, as a diversion she turned to the little diary and recorded therein:

JANUARY 20TH, 19 — I have not had the patience since arriving here to record any of the events that have transpired since we left Indiana. We have been here now nearly three weeks. Have not as yet had time to draw any conclusion with regard to the country, but this much I can cheerfully say — and which did not prevail back where we came from — there is spirit in the country, the spirit of the Pioneer.

The weather has been cold, cold every day since we arrived. Because we ran out of urgent provisions soon after coming here I ventured to go to Gregory, which is seven miles distant, for some more. I have been too much upset over what took place on that memorable trip to say much about it. Because I have never kept anything from him, I told papa how I started from the town, became lost, and stayed all night at a house and saved a man thereby. He has been so frightened over what happened that he will not let me go anywhere alone again — not even in the daytime. " Just think, my girl," he has said time and again, " supposing you had not stumbled into that house, you would surely have frozen to death on the plains! " I somehow feel that Dolly would have brought me home; but that is a matter for conjecture. But what I say to papa in return is: " Had I not gotten lost, that man that is known so well about the country must surely have suffered death! " This seems to pacify him, and he is pleased after all to know that my getting lost was so provident and opportune.

He has met the man, Jean Baptiste, (such an odd name,) and likes him very much — in fact, he is very much carried away with him. I have not seen him since the morning I left him at his sod house; but I cannot get out of my mind the events that passed while I was there. Always I can see him look up into my eyes with that strange recognition, and then as he turned, call " *Agnes, it is you. I'm glad you have come for I've waited for you so long.*" What that means I would give most half my life to know. I know that I shall never rest in peace until I have become well enough acquainted with him to ask him why and how he knew me. Then followed the morning when he talked to himself and did not know I heard. It is all so vivid in my mind.

Of late I have had an uncontrollable desire. I have wanted to know more of my mother. It seems that if I could have known her, I would understand myself better. I am positive now, that she must have been a rare person. That she was French and very high tempered, papa has told me; and also that she had lived in the West Indies before he met her, but that she was born in France. As to the legacy, he lays that to her peculiarity. She was always peculiar in a way, says he; and that at all times she was mysterious. She had been over almost all the world, and was wise in many things. He thinks I have inherited much of her wit, and that eventually it will express itself in some manner, which is all so strange. I hope, however, it will. To rise in some manner out of the simple, uneventful life I've lived would certainly be appreciated; but whatever it is I cannot conclude.

Should I ever rise in any way, I feel now it would be due in some manner to my meeting that strange colored man. I have wondered so often since meeting him, how it feels to be a Negro. Papa and I have discussed it often since. I understand there is a sort of prejudice against the race in this country; that in the South they are held down and badly treated; that in the North, even, they are not fairly treated. Papa and I were both agreed about it. We cannot understand why one should be disliked because his skin is dark; or because his ancestors were slaves. But withal I cannot understand how one could deal unfairly with them because of this. It is said that some of the race are very ignorant and vicious; that they very often commit the unspeakable crime. I suppose that is possible. If so, then they should be educated. Take this Jean Baptiste, for instance, an educated man, and what a gentleman! But papa, (he is very vindictive!) he says that only about half the colored people in this country are full blood; that in the days of slavery and since, even, the white man who is very often ready to abuse the black men, has been the cause of this mixture. . . . I should think their consciences would disturb them.

Oh, well, I am glad that I have grown up where prejudice against races is not a custom. My mother was French; my father Scotch all through, and because I know him and am so ingrained with his liberal traditions — even tho' he be poor,— I am at peace with all mankind.

We haven't all the money we need, and the fact worries me. Papa says he will hire Bill to some one if any one should need help. It might be that the colored man will hire him, maybe. They say he is going to hire a man. Papa intends to speak to him about it. The only thing that worries us is that we have to explain that weakness in Bill and George. George is impossible: too slow, talks too much, and would never earn his salt. But if one is patient with Bill until he catches on, he is an excellent worker, and faithful. I wish the colored man would give him the job. He owns the quarter that corners with us, which he expects to complete breaking out and putting into flax next summer, so we are told. If Bill could get that job it would be handy. Handy for Bill, for Mr. Baptiste, and for us.

We have not met many people as yet. Because it is so cold to get out, I haven't met any so to speak; but papa appears to be getting acquainted right along. We are going to town — to Gregory again Saturday. I am looking forward to it with pleasant anticipation. I sincerely trust it will be a beautiful day. In the meantime the clock has struck one, papa is turning over in bed and I can hear him. I'll hear his voice presently, so I will close this with hopes that Saturday will be a beautiful day and that I'll meet and become acquainted with some nice people.

CHAPTER VIII

WHEN JEAN BAPTISTE had found the papers belonging to Barr, and had come to understand that it had been Barr's intention to destroy the same, natural curiosity had prompted him to read into and examine what was in his possession.

But after having read them, and realizing fully to return the same then, would be to have Barr know, at least feel, that he was in possession of such a grave secret, would make their, up to this time agreeable, relationship rather awkward, he was at a loss as to what to do. So in the end he laid the papers away, and waited. If Barr should make inquiries for them, he would try to find some convenient way to return the same. But on after thought, he knew that Barr would hardly start an inquiry about the matter — even if he did come to realize he had lost instead of destroyed the papers.

A few days later he saw Peter Kaden in the village, and this time observed him more closely than had been his wont theretofore. Always sad, he so remained, and down in Baptiste's heart he was sorry for the wretch. It was after he had returned home and lingered at the fire that he heard a light knock at the door. He called " Come in." The door was opened and Augustus M. Barr stood in the doorway.

Baptiste was for a time slightly nervous. He was glad then that it was dark within the room, otherwise Barr must have seen him give a quick start.

"Ah-ha," began Barr, cheerfully, coming forward and taking the chair Baptiste placed at his disposal. "Quite comfortable in the little sod house on the claim."

"Quite comfortable," returned Baptiste evenly, his mind upon the papers so near. He didn't trust himself to comment. He waited for whatever was to happen.

"Suppose you are thinking about the big crop you will seed in the springtime," ventured Barr.

"Yes," admitted Baptiste, for in truth, the same had been on his mind before Barr put in his appearance. "Suppose you will put out quite a crop yourself in the spring," he ventured in return.

"Well, I don't know," said Barr thoughtfully. "I fear I'm getting a little old to farm — and this baching!" Baptiste thought about Christine who was not so far away instead of in England. . . . He marveled at the man's calm nerve. It did not seem possible that a man of this one's broad education could be so low as to resort to fallacies.

"No," he heard Barr again. "I don't think that I shall farm next summer. In fact I have about decided to make proof on my claim, and that is what I have called on you in regard to. I suppose I can count you as witness to the fact?" Baptiste was relieved. Barr still thought he had destroyed the papers. He was smiling when he replied:

"Indeed, I shall be glad to attest to the fact you refer to."

"Thanks," said Barr, and rose to go.

"No hurry."

"I must go into town on a matter of business," said Barr from the doorway. "Well," he paused briefly and then said, "I am applying for a date, and when that is settled I shall let you know."

"Very well. Good day."

" Good day, my friend," and he went over the hill.

Baptiste was thoughtful when he was gone. He looked after him and thought about the papers. He marveled again at the man's calmness. . . . Then suddenly he arose as a thought struck him, and going to his trunk, lifted from the top the last issue of the Dallas *Enterprise*. He glanced quickly through the columns and then his eyes rested on a legal notice. He smiled.

" Old Peter is going to make proof. . . . So is Barr. The eternal triangle begins to take shape. . . ." He got up and went to the door. Over the hill he saw Barr just entering the town. . . . " This is beginning to get interesting. . . . But I don't like the Kaden end of it. . . . I wish I could do something. . . . Something to help Kaden. . . ."

Saturday was a beautiful day. To Gregory from miles around went almost everybody. So along with the rest went Jean Baptiste. He fostered certain hopes,— had ulterior purposes in view. Firstly, it was a nice day, the town he knew would be filled; and secondly, he was subtly interested in Kaden. He had seen by the paper that he was advertised to make proof that day on his homestead. . . . Another thing, whenever he thought of Kaden, he could not keep Barr, and Syfe, and lastly, Christine, out of his mind. . . .

He found the little town filled almost to overflowing when he arrived. Teams were tied seemingly to every available post. The narrow board walks were crowded, the saloons were full, red liquor was doing its bit; while the general stores were alive with girls, women and children. A jovial day was ahead and old friendships were revived and new ones made. There is about a new country an air of hopefulness that is contagious. Here in this land had

come the best from everywhere: the best because they were
for the most part hopeful and courageous; that great army
of discontented persons that have been the forerunners of
the new world. Mingled in the crowd, Jean Baptiste regarded the unusual conglomeration of kinds. There were
Germans, from Germany, and there were Swedes from
Sweden, Danes from Denmark, Norwegians from Norway.
There were Poles, and Finns and Lithuanians and Russians;
there were French and a few English; but of his race he
was the only one.

As a whole the greater portion were from the northern
parts of the United States, and he was glad that they were.
With them there was no " Negro problem," and he was
glad there was not. The world was too busy to bother with
such: he was glad to know he could work unhampered. He
was looked at curiously by many. To the young, a man of
his skin was something rare, something new. He smiled
over it with equal amusement, and then in a store he walked
right into Agnes, the first time he had seen her since the
morning at the sod house. He was greatly surprised, and
rather flustrated,— and was glad again his skin was dark.
She could not see the blood that went to his face; while
with her, it showed most furiously.

As the meeting was unexpected, all she had thought and
felt in the weeks since, came suddenly to the surface in her
expression. In spite of her effort at self control, her blushing face evidenced her confusion upon seeing him again.
But with an effort, she managed to bow courteously, while
he was just as dignified. They would have passed and
gone their ways had it not been that in that instant another,
a lady, a neighbor and friend of Baptiste's, came upon them.
She had become acquainted with Agnes that day, and was

very fond of Baptiste. Although her name was Reynolds, she was a red blooded German, sociable, kind and obliging. She had not observed that they had exchanged greetings — did not know, obviously, that the two were acquainted; wherefore, her neighborly instincts became assertive.

Coming forward volubly, anxiously, she caught Baptiste by the hand and shook it vigorously. " Mr. Baptiste, Mr. Baptiste!" she cried, punctuating the hand shaking with her voice full of joy, her red, healthy face beaming with smiles. "How very glad I am to see you! You have not been to see us for an age, and I have asked Tom where you were. We feared you had gone off and done something serious," whereupon she winked mischievously. Baptiste understood and smiled.

" You are certainly looking well for an old bachelor," she commented, after releasing his hand and looking into his face seriously, albeit amusedly, mischievously. " We were at Dallas and got some of the coal you were brave enough to bring from Bonesteel that awful cold day. My, Jean, you certainly are possessed with great nerve! While that coal to everybody was a godsend, yet think of the risk you took! Why, supposing you had gotten lost in that terrific storm; lost as people have been in the West before! You must be careful," she admonished, kindly. " You are really too fine a young man to go out here and get frozen to death, indeed!" Baptiste started perceptibly. She regarded him questioningly. Unconsciously his eyes wandered toward Agnes who stood near, absorbed in all Mrs. Reynolds had been saying. His eyes met hers briefly, and the events of the night at the sod house passed through the minds of both. The next moment they looked away, and Mrs. Reynolds, not understanding, glanced toward Agnes.

She was by disposition versatile. But she caught her breath now with sudden equanimity, as she turned to Agnes and cried:

"Oh, Miss Stewart, you!" she smiled with her usual delight and going toward Agnes caught her arm affectionately, and then, with face still beaming, she turned to where Baptiste stood.

"I want you, Miss Stewart," she said with much ostentation, "to meet one of our neighbors and friends; one of the most enterprising young men of the country, Mr. Jean Baptiste. Mr. Baptiste, Miss Agnes Stewart." She did it gracefully, and for a time was overcome by her own vanity. In the meantime the lips of both those before her parted to say that they had met, and then slowly, understandingly, they saw that this would mean to explain. . . . Their faces lighted with the logic of meeting formally, and greetings were exchanged to fit the occasion.

For the first time he was permitted to see her, to regard her as the real Agnes. There was no embarrassment in her face but composure as she extended her small ungloved hand this time and permitted it to rest lightly in his palm. She smiled easily as she accepted his ardent gaze and showed a row of even white teeth momentarily before turning coquetishly away.

He regarded her intimately in one sweep of his eyes. She accepted this also with apparent composure. She was now fully normal in her composition. That about her which others had understood, and were inspired to call beautiful now seemed to strangely affect him.

Was it because he was hungry for woman's love; because since he had looked upon this land of promise and out of the visions she had come to him in those long silent days; because of his lonely young life there in the sod house she had communed with him; was it that he had imagined her sweet radiance that now caused him to feel that she was beautiful?

She had looked away only briefly, as if to give him time to think, to consider her, and then she turned her eyes upon him again. She regarded him frankly then, albeit admiringly. She wanted to hear him say something. She was not herself aware of how anxious she was to hear him speak; for him to say anything, would please her. And as she stood before him in her sweet innocence, all the goodness she possessed, the heart and desire always to be kind, to do for others as she had always, was revealed to him. His dream girl she was, and in reality she had not disappointed him.

If visionary he had loved her, he now saw her and what was hers. Her wondrous hair, rolled into a frivolous knot at the back of her head made her face appear the least slender when it was really square; the chestnut glint of it seemed to contrast coquettishly with her white skin; and the life, the healthy, cheerful life that now gave vigor to her blood brought faint red roses to her cheeks; roses that seemed to come and go. Her red lips seemed to tempt him, he was captivated. He forgot in this intimate survey that she was of one race while he, Jean Baptiste, was of another. . . . And that between their two races, the invisible barrier, the barrier which, while invisible was so absolute, so strong, so impossible of melting that it was best for the moment that he forget it.

While all he saw passed in a moment, he regarded her slenderness as she stood buttoned in the long coat, and wondered how she, so slight and fragile, had been able to lift his heavy frame upon the bed where he had found himself. And still before words had passed between them, he saw her again, and that singularity in the eyes had come back; they were blue and then they were brown, but withal they were so baffling. He did not seem to understand her when they were like this, yet when so he felt strangely a greater right, the right to look into and feast in what he saw, regardless of *the custom of the country and its law.* . . . And still while he was not aware of it, Jean Baptiste came to feel that there was something between them. Though infinite, in the life that was to come, he now came strangely to feel sure that he was to know her, to become more intimately acquainted with her, and with this consciousness he relaxed. The spell that had come from meeting her again, from being near her, from holding her hand in his though formally, the exchange of words passed and he gradually became his usual self; the self that had always been his in this land where others than those of the race to which he belonged were the sole inhabitants. He was relieved when he heard Mrs. Reynolds' voice:

" Miss Stewart and her folks have just moved out from Indiana, Jean, and are renting on the Watson place over east of you; the place that corners with the quarter you purchased last fall, you understand."

" Indeed! " Baptiste echoed with feigned ignorance, his eyebrows dilating.

" Yes," she went on with concern. " And you are neighbors."

" I'm glad — honored," Baptiste essayed.

" He is flattering," blushed Agnes, but she was pleased.

" And you'll find Mr. Baptiste the finest kind of neighbor, too," cried Mrs. Reynolds with equal delight.

" I'm a bad neighbor, Miss Stewart," he disdained. " Our friend here, Mrs. Reynolds, you see, is full of flattery."

" I don't believe so, Mr. Baptiste," she defended, glad

to be given an opportunity to speak. "We have just become acquainted, but papa has told me of her, and the family, and I'm sure we will be the best of friends, won't we?" she ended with her eyes upon Mrs. Reynolds.

"Bless you, yes! Who could keep from liking you?" whereupon she caught Agnes close and kissed her impulsively.

"Oh, say, now," cried Baptiste, and then stopped.

"You're not a woman," laughed Mrs. Reynolds, "but you understand," she added reprovingly. Suddenly her face lit up with a new thought, and the usual smiling gave way to seriousness, as she cried:

"By the way, Jean. We hear that you are going to hire a man this spring, and that reminds me that Miss Stewart's father has two boys — her brothers — whom he has not work enough nor horses enough to use, so he wishes to hire one out." She paused to observe Agnes, who had also become serious and was looking up at her.

At this point she turned to Baptiste, and with a slight hesitation, she said:

"Do you really wish to hire a man — Mr.— a — Mr. Baptiste?" Saying it had heightened her color, and the anxiety in her tone caused her to appear more serious. She had turned her eyes up to his and he was for the instant captivated again with the thought that she was beautiful. His answer, however, was calm.

"I must have a man," he acknowledged. "I have more work than I can do alone."

"Why, papa wishes to hire Bill —" It was natural to say Bill because it was Bill they always hired, although George was the older; but since we know why George was never offered, we return to her. "I should say William," she corrected awkwardly, and with an effort she cast it out of her mind and went on: "So if — if you think you could — a — use him, or would care to give him the job," she was annoyed with the fact that Bill was halfwitted, and it confused her, which explains the slight catches in her voice. But bravely she continued, "That is, if you have not already given some one else the job, you could speak to papa, and he would be pleased, I'm sure." She ended with evident relief; but the thought that had confused her, being still in her mind, her face was dark with a confusion that he did not understand.

Hoping to relieve the annoyance he could see, although not understanding the cause of it, he spoke up quickly.

"I have not hired a man, and have no other in sight; so your suggestion, Miss, regarding your brother meets with my favor. I will endeavor therefore, to see your father today if possible, if not, later, and discuss the matter pro and con."

He had made it so easy for her, and she was overly gracious as she attempted to have him understand in some manner that her brother was afflicted. So her effort this time was a bit braver, notwithstanding as anxious, however, as before.

"Oh, papa will be glad to have my brother work for you, and I wish you would — would please not hire any other until you have talked with him." She paused again as if to gather courage for the final drive.

"You will find my brother faithful, and honest, and a good worker; but — but —" it seemed that she could not avoid the break in her voice when she came to this all embarrassing point, "but sometimes — he — he makes mistakes. He is a little awkward, a little bunglesome in starting, but if you would — could exercise just a little patience for a few days — a day, I am sure he would please you."

It was out at last. She was sure he would understand. It had cost her such an effort to try to make it plain without just coming out and saying he was halfwitted. She was not aware that in concluding she had done so appealingly. He had observed it and his man's heart went out to her in her distress. He remembered then too, although he had on their first meeting forgotten that he had been told all about her brothers, and had also heard of her.

"You need have no fear there, Miss Stewart," he wilfully lied. "I am the most patient man in the world." He wondered then at himself, that he could lie so easily. His one great failing was his impatience, and he knew it. Because he did and felt that he tried to crush it, was his redeeming feature in this respect. But the words had lightened her burden, and there was heightening of her color, as she spoke now with unfeigned delight:

"Oh, that is indeed kind of you. I am so glad to hear you say so. Bill is a good hand — everybody likes him after he has worked a while. It is because he is a little awkward and forgetful in the beginning that worries my father and me. So I'm glad you know now and will not be impatient."

In truth while she did not know it, Jean was pleased with the prospect. He had not lived two years in the country, the new country, without having experienced the difficulty that comes with the usual hired man. The class of men, with the exception of a homesteader, who came to the country for work usually fell into the pastime of gambling and drinking which seemed to be contagious, and many were the griefs they gave those by whom they were employed. And Jean Baptiste, now that she had made it plain regarding her brother, had something to say himself.

"There is one little thing I should like to mention, Miss

Stewart," he said with apparent seriousness. She caught her breath with renewed anxiety as she returned his look. In the next instant she was relieved, however, as he said: "You understand that I am baching, a bachelor, and the fare of bachelors is, I trust you will appreciate, not always the best." He paused as he thought of how she must feel after having seen the way he kept his house, and hoped that she could overlook the condition in which she knew he kept it. But if he was embarrassed at the thought of it, it was not so with her. For her sympathy went out to him. She was conscious of how inconvenient it must be to bach, to live alone as he was doing, and to work so hard.

"It is not always to hired men's liking to forego the meals that only women can prepare, and for that reason it is sometimes difficult for us to keep men."

"Oh, you will not have to worry as to that, Mr. Baptiste," she assured him pleasantly. She caught her breath with something joyous apparently as she turned to him. "You see, we live almost directly between your two places, and my brother can stay home and save you that trouble and bother." She was glad that she could be of assistance to him in some way, though it be indirectly. With sudden impulse, she turned to Mrs. Reynolds who had not interrupted:

"It will be nice, now, won't it?"

"Just dandy," the other agreed readily. "I am so glad we all three met here," she went on. "In meeting we have fortunately been of some service to each other. You will find Mr. Baptiste a fine fellow to work for. We let our boys go over and help him out when he's pushed, and we know he appreciates it to the fullest." She halted, turned now mischievously to Baptiste and cried:

"We are always after Jean that he should marry. Why,

just think what a good husband he would make some nice
girl." She had found her topic, had Mrs. Reynolds. Of
all topics, she preferred to jolly the single with getting
married to anything else, so she went on with delight.

" He goes off down to Chicago every winter and we wait
to see the girl when he returns, but always he disappoints
us." She affected a frown a moment before resuming:
" It is certainly too bad that some good girl must do without
a home and the happiness that is due her, while he lives
there alone, having no comfort but what he gets when he
goes visiting." She affected to appear serious and to have
him feel it, while he could do nothing but grin awkwardly.

" Oh, Mrs. Reynolds, you're hard on a fellow. My!
Give him a chance. It takes two to make a bargain. I
can't marry myself." He caught the eyes of Agnes who
was enjoying his tender expression. Indeed the subject
appealed to him, and he had found it to his liking. She
blushed. She enjoyed the humor.

" I suspect Mrs. Reynolds speaks the truth," she said
with affected seriousness, but found it impossible to down
the color in her flaming cheeks nevertheless.

" Oh, but you two can jolly a fellow." He became serious now as he went on: ". But it isn't fair. There is no
girl back in Chicago; there is no girl anywhere for me."
He was successful in his affectation of self pity, and her
feelings went out to him in her words that followed:

" Now that is indeed, too bad, for him, Mrs. Reynolds,
isn't it? Perhaps he is telling the truth. The girls in
Chicago do not always understand the life out here, and
cannot make one feel very much encouraged." She wondered at her own words. But she went on nevertheless.
" Even back in Indiana they do not understand the West.
They are — seem to be, so narrow, they feel that they

are living in the only place of civilization on earth." Her logical statement took away the joke. They became serious. The store was filling and the crowd was pushing. So they parted.

A few minutes later as Baptiste passed down the street, he saw Peter Kaden coming from the commissioners' office. Across the way he observed Barr and Syfe stop and exchange a few words. The next moment they went their two ways while he stood looking after them.

CHAPTER IX

" CHRISTINE, CHRISTINE! "

ONE WEEK from the day Peter Kaden made proof at Gregory on the homestead he held, the court record showed that he had transferred the same to some unknown person. In the course of events it was not noticed by the masses. It was because Jean Baptiste was expecting something of the kind that he happened to observe the record of the transfer in the following week's issue of the paper. He couldn't get the incident out of his mind, and he found his eyes wandering time and again in the direction of the house of Augustus M. Barr in the days that followed.

From what he had gleaned from the papers, he was sure that something sinister was to occur in that new land soon. He tried in vain to formulate some plan of action — rather, some plan of prevention. But the plot, the intrigue, or whatever it may be called, was deep. It had taken root before either had ever seen the country they now called home. And because of its intricate nature, he could formulate no plan toward combatting the thing he felt positively in his veins was to take place.

Over the hill two miles and more the claim shack of Peter Kaden could not be seen. But he could always feel where it was and the events that went on therein. This healthy, but sad, forlorn German had aroused his sympathy, and always when he thought of him, strangely he thought of Christine.

The days passed slowly and things went on as usual.

He saw Barr occasionally and as often saw the dark Syfe. He read as was his wont, and then one evening when his few chores were done, he had a desire to walk. He drew on his overcoat, and, taking a bucket, he walked slowly down the slope that led up to his house, to the well a quarter mile distant. He could never after account for the strange feeling that came and went as he ambled toward the well. He reached it in due time, filled his bucket, and was in the act of returning when out of the night he caught the unmistakable sound of horses' hoofs. Some one on horseback was coming. He set the bucket down and bent his ears more keenly to hear the sound.

Yes, they were hoof beats, an unusual clatter. He gave a start. Only one horse in the neighborhood made such a noise with the hoofs when moving, for he had heard the same before, and that horse belonged to A. M. Barr, and was a pacer. Christine had use to ride him. And when he recalled it, he became curious. Christine was not there, he knew, unless she had come that day, which was not likely. . . . Then *who rode the horse?* He had never seen Barr on horseback. . . . They were coming from about where Barr's house stood, coming in his direction along the road. He estimated at that moment they must be about a quarter of a mile away. He listened intently. Onward they came, drawing closer all the while. He got an inspiration. Why should he be seen? He moved back from the road some distance. There was no moon and the night was dark, but the stars filled the night air with a dim ray. He lay upon the ground as the horseman drew nearer. Presently out of the shadow he caught the dim outline of the rider. He saw that a heavy ulster was worn, and the collar of the same was around the rider's neck, almost concealing the head; but he recognized the rider as A. M. Barr.

"Now where can he be going," he muttered to himself, standing erect as he listened to the hoof beats on the road below. He pondered briefly. "Why does he never ride in the daytime?" From down the road the sound of hoof beats continued. And then Baptiste was again inspired.

"Kaden!" he cried, and fell into deep thought.

At his left was a small creek, usually dry. This stream led in an angling direction down toward the larger stream south of the town. It led directly toward the claim of Peter Kaden, although the homestead lay beyond the creek. By following it, one could reach Kaden's house in about two-thirds the distance if going by trail.

A few minutes later Jean Baptiste was speedily following the route that led to the creek. He paused at intervals and upon listening could hear the hoof beats along the trail in the inevitable direction. He reached the creek in a short time, found his way across it, and once on the other side, he hurried through a school section to Kaden's cabin that was joined with this on the south. He crossed the school section quickly, and in the night air he could smell, and presently came to see, the smoke curling from the chimney. He approached the house cautiously. He was glad that poor Kaden didn't keep a dog. When he had drawn close enough to distinguish the objects before him, he saw Barr's horse tied out of the wind, on the south side of the little barn. He looked closer and observed another near. He reckoned that one to be Syfe's. "So the triangle is forming," he muttered.

He went up to the house noiselessly. He passed around its dark side to where he saw light emanating from the small window. He peered cautiously through it. Sitting on the side of the bed, Kaden's face met his gaze. He regarded it briefly before seeking out the others. Never, he felt, if he lived a hundred years would he ever forget the expression of agony that face wore! Upon its usual roundness, perceptible lines had formed; in the light of the dim lamp he caught the darkness about the eyes, the skin under almost sagging and swollen. He permitted his gaze to drift further, and to take in the proportions of the room.

On a stool near sat Syfe, the Jew. He wore his overcoat. Indeed, Baptiste could not recall having ever seen him without it about him; also he wore his thick, dark cap. His little mustache stood out over the small mouth, between the lips of which reposed the usual cigarette. He was drawing away easily at this, while his ears appeared to be attentive to what was going on. He was listening to Barr, who stood in the center of the room, talking in much excitement, making gestures; while he could see the agonized Kaden protesting. He could not catch all that was being said, but some of it. Barr, in particular, he observed, while speaking forcibly, was nevertheless controlled. It was Kaden whose voice reached his ears more often on the outside.

"I kept you from Australia. . . ." this from Barr. "They had you on shipboard. . . . Your carcass would be fit for the vultures now on that sand swept desert you were headed for. . . ."

"But I was innocent, I was innocent," protested Kaden. "I didn't go to Russia that trip. I didn't go to Russia, and to Jerusalem, I have never been!"

"But you hadn't proved it. You were done for. They had you, and all you could do or say wouldn't have kept you in England. It was I, me, do you understand. . . . You *do* understand that I kept you from going. I, me, who saved you. No law in this land could keep you here if they knew now where you were. . . ."

"But you forget Christine, my poor Christine! You have her, is that not enough? Oh, you are hard. You drive me most insane. Tell me about Christine. Give her back to me and all is yours."

A wind rose suddenly out of the west. A shed stood near, a shed covered over with hay and some poles that had been cut green, and the now dry leaves gave forth a moaning sound. He saw those inside start. With the noise, Baptiste knew he could hear no more, and might be apprehended. Stealthily he departed.

And all the way to the sod house that night he kept repeating what he had heard. *"Christine, Christine! You have her, is she not enough? Give her back and all is yours!"*

If he could only ascertain what was between Kaden and Christine — but it was all coming to something soon, and he knew that Augustus M. Barr was taking the advantage of some one; that Kaden was innocent but couldn't prove it; that Syfe was in some way darkly connected, and the eternal triangle held to its sinister purpose.

CHAPTER X

"YOU HAVE NEVER BEEN THIS WAY BEFORE"

WHEN AGNES STEWART found her father and they were ready to return home, she inquired: "Did he see you?"

"See who?"

"You? You don't understand. I mean the colored gentleman, Mr. Baptiste?"

"Why, no, my dear," her father replied wonderingly. "I saw him, but I had no word with him. I don't understand."

"Why, I met him. Mrs. Reynolds, who knows you — she and I became acquainted, and we met and had a long talk with Mr. Baptiste, and he is going to hire a man, so we discussed Bill. He said he would see you." Her father drew the team to a stop.

"I don't understand. I should see him, and I did, but he was talking with some fellows who live north of town. I think it was about horses. He went with them, so I suppose we may as well go on home and see him later."

"I'm so sorry," she said and showed it in her face. "I had hoped he would get to see you, and that it would all be settled and Bill would get the job."

"Don't be so out of hope," said he. "I have no doubt that we will get to see Mr. Baptiste, and talk it over."

"I am worried, because — you know, papa, when we have paid for the seed and feed, we will have very little left."

"Such a wonderful, such a thoughtful little girl I have," he said admiringly, stroking her hand fondly in the meantime. "I can't imagine how I could get along without my Aggie."

"See him and get Bill hired and I'll not worry any more."

"I'll do so, I'll do so tomorrow."

"You say you saw him going north of town?"

"Yes."

She was silent, while he was thoughtful. Presently he inquired of what passed when she met him.

She told him.

"I never spoke of having met him before."

"You didn't?"

"Why, no, papa. How could I? It would be hard to explain."

"Well, now, coming to think of it, it would, wouldn't it?"

"It *shouldn't,*" she said. She didn't relish the situation.

"Did he?"

"What?"

"Speak of it."

"Oh, no! He didn't . . ."

"I wonder has he ever."

"I don't think so."

"That is very thoughtful of him."

"It is. He is a real gentleman."

"So everybody says."

"And so pleasant to listen to."

"Indeed."

"Mrs. Reynolds is carried away with him. Says he's one of the most industrious and energetic young men of the country."

"Isn't that fine! But it seems rather odd, doesn't it? Him out here alone."

" It is indeed singular.   But he is just the kind of man a new country needs."

" If the country had a few hundred more like him we wouldn't know it in five years."

" In three years! " she said admiringly.

" How shall we explain in regards to Bill? . . ."

" I've explained."

" You have! "

" Oh, I didn't come out and say it in words, of course.   I didn't need to."

" Then how?   How did you make him understand? "

" It was easy.   It was easy because he is so quick witted. He seems to readily understand anything."

" I'll bet! "

" He spoke of the fact that being a bachelor it was awkward to keep hired men, and this fact seemed to worry him."

" But why didn't you explain that Bill could stay home? "

" I did."

" Oh! "

" And he was so relieved."

" I'm sure he was.   It is very inconvenient."

" It is.   And I feel rather sorry for him."

" Needs a wife."

She was silent.

" Wonder why he doesn't marry? "

" I don't know."

"Will make some girl a fine husband."

Silence.

" I guess he has a girl, though, and will likely marry soon."

" I don't think so."

" Why? "

" Well," she said slowly.   She blushed unseen and went

on: "Mrs. Reynolds joked him about it, and he denied it."

"But any man would do that. They like to be modest; to appear like they have no loves. It creates sympathy. Men are sentimental, too. They like sympathy."

"Yes, I suppose so," she said slowly, thoughtfully. "But I don't think he has a girl. In my mind he is a poor lonesome fellow. Just like he has no close friends. . . ."

He was silent now.

"I have thought about it since I met him."

"You have?"

"Why, yes. Certainly."

Her father laughed.

"Why are you laughing?" she asked, somewhat nettled.

"I was thinking."

"Thinking? Thinking of what?"

"Of Jean Baptiste."

"What do you mean?"

"Why, there is a good chance for you."

"Father!"

"Why not!"

"Father! How can you!"

He laughed. She acted as if angry. He looked at her mischievously. She did not grant him a smile.

"Tut, tut, Aggie! Can't you take a joke?"

"But you should not joke like that."

"Oh, come now. It pleased me to joke like that."

"Why should it please you?"

"Why, I have a sense of humor."

"A sense of humor?"

"Yes."

"But I don't see the joke?"

"Why, Aggie," he turned to her seriously. "Almost I don't think it is a joke."

" Father ! "

" Well, dear? You seem to be so interested in the man."

" Father, oh, father ! " and the next instant she was crying. He reached out and caught her fondly to him. "My girl, my girl, I didn't intend to upset you. Now be papa's little darling and don't cry any more ! "

" You have never been this way before," she sobbed. He caressed her more now.

" Well, dearest. You see. Well, your mother —"

" My mother ! " she sat quickly up.

" We are going to raise a great crop this year. I feel sure of it."

" But my mother ! "

" I think I know where I can get some good seed oats." They rode along in silence the rest of the way, consumed with their own thoughts. No words passed, but Agnes was thinking. She would never get out of her mind what her father had started to say. But he had stopped in time. . . . Her mind went back to the strange incidents in her life. She lived over again the day she had looked in the mirror and had seen that strange look, she connected it singularly with what her father had started to say. She was silent thereafter, but her soul was on fire.

CHAPTER XI

"WELL, my friend," said A. M. Barr, stopping before Baptiste's hut one day shortly after his visit to Kaden's, " I have my date and will make proof on the 22nd of March. I have listed you as one of my witnesses. Guess I may depend on you to be ready that day?"

"I shall remember it, Mr. Barr," answered Baptiste. "Have you rented your place yet?"

"No, I have not. Rather, not the buildings. My neighbor across the road, however, will put the thirty acres I have broken into crop, and break a few more."

"M-m."

"How much do you plan seeding this season?"

"All of both places anyhow."

"Ah, young man, I tell you, you are a worker! Such young men as you will be the making of this country. And you'll be rich in time."

"Oh, no," cried Baptiste disdainfully.

"If I were young and strong like you, I would be doing the same."

"You expect to go away when you have completed your proof. . . ."

"Well, I don't know," whereupon A. M. Barr cast a furtive glance in his direction. Baptiste pretended not to see it.

"What'll you do with your horses?" Another furtive glance.

" Well, I might advertise a sale," he said boldly. He cast a dark look in Baptiste's direction, which the other pretended not to see — but did see nevertheless. " Why, what could he know," was in Barr's mind. " Nothing," he answered his own question. A moment later he was the same Barr; the officious Englishman when he drove down the road a few minutes later, and none the wiser therefor.

March the twenty-second came and went, and Augustus offered proof on his homestead, and passed, Baptiste assisting him as witness.

Sunday was the next day, and when it came, all calm and beautiful, Baptiste realized that he did not have enough seed wheat to sow all his land that he wished put in wheat. A squaw man had raised a large crop to the southwest of him the year before, and this, he understood, was for sale. He decided to call on the squaw man, ascertain the fact, and if so, purchase a share of it for his purpose.

Accordingly, Sunday morning after he had breakfasted, and piled the dishes bachelor fashion (unwashed) he started out.

The route he took carried him directly by Peter Kaden's claim, and when he had gone that far, and found himself looking at the low, sod house that stood a few paces back from the road, he was curious. He paused unconsciously before the house and observed it idly a few moments.

He was struck with the quietness about, and at once became curiously apprehensive. No smoke emerged from the chimney. There was no evidence that any one was about. Impelled by his growing curiosity, he approached the house and knocked at the door. There was no response from within. He tried it again. Still no response. He tried the knob. It gave. He pushed the door open cautiously, and peered in. The house was empty but for the crude fur-

niture. He entered curiously and looked about. The bed
was spread over, there was no fire in the stove, the coldness
of the atmosphere within impressed him with a theory that
no fire had been in the stove that day or the night before.
The dishes were clean and piled on the table with a cloth
spread over them. He went outside, closing the door behind him and swept the surrounding country with his gaze
which revealed no Peter Kaden. He lowered his eyes in
thought as his lips muttered:

" Wonder where he is ?"

A path began at his feet. It led down to a draw some
two hundred yards away. He fell into it aimlessly and
followed its course for a short way. Presently, upon looking up, he saw a well at the side of the draw which obviously
was the terminus of the path.

Forthwith he made the well his objective. In that country
wells were not plentiful. The soil was of the richest and
blackest loam with a clay subsoil; but water except where
there was sand, was not easily found only in or near a
draw, or a flat. He reached the well, and, drawing aside
the bucket that reposed on the lid, he opened the well and
lowered the bucket to the water some thirty feet below.

The bright sun rays somewhat blinded him and for a
moment he could not see the water clearly. The bucket
struck, in due time, however, and he wondered why there
was no splash. He jerked it over, and when it struck again
there was the sound of water, but it appeared difficult to
sink it. He peered down into it again to ascertain what
the matter was. A wave of ripples caught his gaze, while
the bucket seemed to be resting on something. He gave
the rope another jerk and twist, and it came down bottom-
side up on the dark object.

" Hell," he muttered, " this well is dry!" He took another look. "No, it isn't dry. There is something in the well." Bending until his face was shaded by the shadow of the well, he searched below very closely with his eyes. He could distinguish that there was something; and that *the something* seemed to bobble. He withdrew the bucket, unfilled, and, allowing a few moments for the ripples to subside, he searched the darkness below again closely. He became conscious of a cold feeling stealing up his spine, then he caught and held his breath as slowly what was below took outline. It was not a dog, a coyote, a pig, or an animal of any kind. It was *something* else . . . and the *something* else had features that were familiar. At last realization was upon him, his fingers gripped the boards they held as he gradually straightened up.

"My God!" he cried at last, terror stricken.

For below him, with white face turned upward as if laughing, was the dead body of Peter Kaden.

CHAPTER XII

COINCIDENT with the finding of Peter Kaden's body in the well, certain things became public with regard to others. But to complete this part of it. After finding the body Jean Baptiste hurried into Dallas and gave the alarm. Excitement ran high for a time, and as it was Sunday, in a few hours the spot around the well was crowded. From over all the reservation the people came, and the consensus of opinion was that it was suicide. . . . Perhaps Jean Baptiste was the only one who had his doubts. If it *was* suicide, then he was positive it was a precipitated suicide.

Until the coroner arrived there was no disposition made of the remains, and when he did, the decision of suicide was sustained.

Since the man Baptiste had started to see was brought to the spot by the excitement, the business in hand was settled thereupon, and that evening, he went to call on the Stewarts with a view to hiring Bill.

He found Agnes alone, but was invited to enter. From her expression, he could see that he was expected, and while he waited for her father who had gone across the road, they fell into amiable conversation.

" Springtime is knocking at our door," he ventured.

" And I am glad to see it, and suppose you are also," she answered.

"Who isn't! It has been a very severe winter."

"I think so, too. Are the winters here as a rule as cold as this one has been?" How modest he thought she was. She was dressed neatly in a satin shirtwaist and tailored skirt; while from beneath the skirts her small feet incased in heavy shoes peeped like mice. Her neck rose out of her bodice and he thought her throat was so very round and white; while he noticed her prominent chin more today than he had before. He liked it. Nature had been his study, and he didn't like a retreating chin. It, to his mind, was an indication of weak will, with exceptions perhaps here and there. He reposed more confidence in the person, however, when the chin was like hers, so naturally he was interested. As she sat before him with folded hands, he also observed her heavy hair, done into braids and gathered about her head. It gave her an unostentatious expression; while her eyes were as he had found them before, baffling.

"Why, no, they are not," he said. "Of course I have not seen many — in fact this is the second; but I am advised that, as a rule, the winters are very mild for this latitude."

"I see. I hope they will always be so if we continue to live here," and she laughed pleasantly.

"How do you like it in our country?" he inquired now, pleased to be in conversation with her.

"Why, I like it very well," she replied amiably. "What I have seen of it, I think I would as soon live here as back in Indiana."

"I have been in Indiana myself."

"You have?" She was cheered with the fact. He nodded.

"Yes, all over. What part of Indiana do you come from?"

"Rensselaer," she replied, shifting with comfort, and

delighted that by his having been in Indiana, he was making their conversation easier.

"Oh, I see," she heard him.   "That is toward the northern part of the state."

"Yes," she replied in obvious delight.

"I have never been to that town, but I have been all around it."

"Well, well!"   She was at a loss in the moment how to proceed and then presently she said:

"You have traveled considerably, Mr. Baptiste, I understand."

He felt somewhat flattered to know that she had discussed him with others apparently.

"Well, yes, I have," he replied slowly.

"That must be fine.   I long so much to travel."

"You have not traveled far?"

"No.   From Indiana to Western Kansas where we were most starved out, and then back to Indiana and out here." He laughed, she also joined in and they felt nearer each other by it.

"And how do you like it, Mr. Baptiste?"

"Out here, you mean?"

"Yes, why, yes, of course," she added hastily.

"Why, I like it fine.   I'm thoroughly in love with the country."

"That's nice.   And you own such nice land, I don't wonder," she said thoughtfully.

"Oh, well," he replied, modestly, "I think I should like it anyhow."

"Of course; but when one has property — such nice land as you own, they have everything to like it for."

"I'm compelled to agree with you."

"I'm sorry we don't own any," she said regretfully.

"But of course in a way we are not entitled to. We didn't get in 'on the ground floor,' therefore we must be satisfied as renters."

He was silent but attentive.

"Papa never seems to have been very fortunate. It may be due to his quaint old fashioned manner, but he has never owned any land at all, poor fellow." She said the last more to herself than to him. He was interested and continued to listen.

"We went to Western Kansas with a little money and very good stock, and were dried out two years straight, and the third year when we had a good crop with a chance to get back at least a little of what we had lost, along came a big hail storm and pounded everything into the ground."

"Wasn't that too bad!" he cried sympathetically.

"It sure was! It is awfully discouraging to work as hard and to have sacrificed as much as we had, and then come out as we did. It just took all the ambition out of him."

"I shouldn't wonder," he commented tenderly.

"And then we went back to Indiana — broke, of course, and having no money and no stock; because we had to sell what we had left to get out of Western Kansas. So since 'beggars can't be choosers' we had to take what we could get. And that was a poor farm in a remote part of Indiana, in a little place that was so poor that the corn was all nubbins. They called it 'Nubbin Ridge.'"

He laughed, and she had to also when she thought of it.

"Well, we were able to live and pay a little on some more stock. Because my brothers didn't take much to run around with like other boys but stayed home and worked, we finally succeeded in getting just a little something together again and then a real estate man came along and told us about this place, so here we are." She bestowed a smile upon him and sighed. She had told more of themselves than she had intended, but it had been a pleasant diversion at that; moreover, she was delighted because he was such an attentive listener.

" So that is how you came here? " he essayed. " I have enjoyed listening to you. Your lives read like an interesting book."

" Oh, that isn't fair. You are joking with me! " Notwithstanding, she blushed furiously.

" No, no, indeed," he protested.

She believed him. Strangely she reposed such confidence in the man that she felt she could sit and talk with him forever.

" But it is certainly too bad that you have been so unfortunate. I am sure it will not always be so. You are perseverant, I see, and ' riches come to him who waits.' "

" An old saying, but I hope it will not wait too long. Papa is getting old, and — my brothers would be unable to manage with any effect alone. . . ." He understood her and the incident was overlooked.

" Your mother is dead? "

" Yes, my mother is dead, Mr. Baptiste."

" Oh."

" Died when I was a baby."

" Well, well. . . ."

" I never knew her."

" Well, I do say! " He paused briefly, while she was silent but thinking deeply. . . . Thinking of what her father had started to say and never finished.

" And I venture to say that you have just about raised yourself? "

She blushed.

" You must be a wonderful girl."

She blushed again and twisted her hands about. She tried to protest; but couldn't trust herself to say anything just then. How she liked to hear him talk!

"You have my best wishes, believe me," he was at a loss for the moment as to how to proceed.

"Oh, thank you." She didn't dare raise her eyes. He regarded her as she sat before him, blushing so beautifully, and wished they were of the same race. . . . Footsteps were heard at that moment, and both sat up expectantly. Quickly, then, she rose to her feet and went to the door and opened it in time to meet her father who was about to enter.

"Oh, it's you, father! I'm glad you've come. Mr. Baptiste is here to see you."

"Ah-ha, Mr. Baptiste, I am honored," cried Jack Stewart, her father, and he marched forward with outstretched hand and much ado; Scotch propriety.

"Glad to know you, Judge," Baptiste returned warmly, grasping the proffered hand.

"Be seated, be seated and make yourself comfortable; make yourself at home," he said, pushing forward the chair out of which Baptiste had risen. Agnes was smiling pleasantly. She could see that the two were going to become friends, for both were so frank in their demeanor.

"Now, Aggie, you must prepare supper for Mr. Baptiste and myself," he said, taking hold of her arm.

"Oh, no," disdained Baptiste. "Don't think of it!"

"Now, now, my worthy friend," admonished Stewart, and then stopped. "Why — you have met my daughter?"

"Yes, we have met," they spoke in the same breath, exchanging glances.

"Then, while you fix us something good to eat, we will discuss our business."

They found no difficulty in reaching a bargain in regard to Bill, the bargain being that Bill was to board home and sleep there also; and the consideration was to be one dollar per day, and by the time this was completed, Agnes called them to supper.

" This is an unexpected pleasure, even though it be an intrusion," said Baptiste as he was gently urged into a seat.

" Ah-ha, and I see you have a sense of humor," whereupon Jack Stewart's eyes glistened humorously behind the old style glasses he wore. Baptist colored unseen, while Agnes regarded him smilingly.

" We haven't much, but what is here you are welcome to," she said.

" It's a feast," said he.

" About as good as baching, anyhow," joined Stewart.

" Hush!"

" How do you like it?"

" Didn't I say hush?   That should be sufficient!"   Agnes took a seat and surveyed the table carefully to see that all was there. Her father was pious. He blessed the table, and when this was over, fell to eating with his knife.

" By the way," cried Baptiste near the end of the meal. " Did you hear the news?"

" What news," they asked in chorus.

" The man dead in the well."

" Is that so!" they exclaimed, shocked.

He then told them in detail all about the finding of the body, and the opinion that it was a suicide. They listened with the usual awe and curiosity. But Jean Baptiste did not voice his suspicions, or tell them anything he knew. At a later hour he took his leave.

And neither of the three realized then that the self-same

tragedy linked strangely an after event in their lives. But when Jean Baptiste went over the hill to his sod house that stood on the claim, Jack Stewart went outside and walked around for almost an hour. He was thinking. Thinking of something he knew and had never told.

CHAPTER XIII

THE COMING OF THE RAILROAD

I T IS NOT likely that the people in the neighborhood of Dallas would have ever known any more than they did regarding A. M. Barr, had it not been for two accounts. When proof had been offered by him on his homestead and a loan sought, to keep from invalidating the title to his land, he was compelled to admit that he was married; but, fortunately for him, it was not necessary to state when or how long he had been married, and this he obligingly did not state. But the surprise came when upon admittance, he then confessed to the promoters that he had married Christine. . . . Of course everybody was positive then that he had been married to Christine when he came to the country, and that he was married to her at the time she was holding the claim. Perjury was a penitentiary offense. He had sold her claim on pretense that she must go to England. Christine, as Baptiste had come to know by the papers he found, had not, of course, gone to England; but merely to Lincoln, Nebraska, where she was safe to keep silent about what she knew in regard to the subtle transactions of Augustus M. Barr.

The incident went the usual route of gossip, the people wondering how such a beautiful girl as Christine could be happy as the wife of an old, broken down infidel like Barr. But they never came into the truth, the whole truth; they never connected Barr with the dark Assyrian Jew, Isaac Syfe; nor were they aware that he had ever known the forlorn Peter Kaden. Only Jean Baptiste knew this, and that, although Barr called a sale and immediately left the country, there was something still to be completed. But Jean Baptiste didn't know then that it would all come back to him in such an unusual manner. However, the public learned a little more concerning the previous activities of this august contemporary before long. It came in the form of a sensational newspaper feature story. And was in brief to wit:

While pastor of the Baker Street church, London, Isaac M. Barr, and not Augustus, mind you, although there was no question about the two being one and the same became very much in the confidence of his flock. Of London's great middle class they were and possessed ambition, which Barr apparently appealed to. The result was that a great colony set sail for a land of promise, the land being Western Canada. The full details were not given; but it seems that Barr was the trustee and handled the money. On arrival, Barr suddenly disappeared and the good people from England never saw him again, which perhaps accounts in some measure for his becoming an infidel. . . . Who would not under such circumstances?

.

There is a feature regarding a new country—that is, a country that lays toward the western portion of the great central valley, that is always questioned, and is ever a source for knockers. But we should explain one thing that might be of benefit to those who would go west to settle and develop with hopes of success. And this is rainfall. In this country of our story, which lay near the line where central time is changed to mountain time, near the fifth principal meridian the altitude is about 2000 feet above the level of the sea, and the rainfall may be estimated accordingly. Rainfall is governed by altitude and is a feature beyond discussion. This is a very serious matter, and could multitudes of people going west to take homesteads, or settle, be impressed with the facts and know then what to expect, much grief could be avoided.

But unfortunately this is not so. Masses can be convinced — were convinced in the country of our story, and all the west beyond, in other parts, that rainfall was governed by cultivation. An erroneous idea! As has been stated, rainfall is governed by elevation: air pressures are such that when in contact with the heavy air due to the lower elevation, thunder showers and general rains fall more frequently on the whole and this can be certified by the record of any weather bureau, comparing the elevation to the amount of precipitation over a given period, say five or ten years. It is a fact, however, that in the most arid districts cloudbursts do occur, but they are always a detriment to the parts over which they may fall. And it is also true that in a given year or season, more rain may fall over a certain arid district than some well cultivated portion in a country where the fall of rain is beyond question.

Because of these contending features, many portions of the country have received a boom one season and failed to produce the next. When one year had proven exceedingly wet, the theory was that the whole climatic origin of the country had changed; drought had passed forever, and people and capital flowed in to sometimes go out, broken and shattered in spirits, hopes and finances later. Such instances hurt and hinder a country instead of helping it. If, in coming to the country of our story the masses of people could have understood that at an elevation of from two thousand to twenty-two hundred feet, the rainfall over a period of ten years would approximate an average of twenty-five inches annually, it is reasonable to suppose that they would expect dry years and wet years; some cold winters and some fair, open winters; some cloudbursts and some protracted droughts. But when the first years of settlement were accompanied by heavy rains, the boom that followed is almost beyond our pen to detail.

From over all the country people came hither; people with means, for it was the land of opportunity. The man who was in many cases wealthy in older portions of the country, had come there with next to and very often with nothing and had grown rich — not by any particular ability or concentrated effort on the part of himself; not by the making and saving, investing and profiting, but because in the early days the land was of such little value and brought so little when offered for sale that it had been a case of staying thereon; result, riches came in the advance later in the price according to demand.

Such was not the circumstances altogether in the land where Jean Baptiste had cast his lot in the hope for ultimate success. While opportunity was ripe, a few thousands had been expedient. For what could be had for a small amount here would have cost a far greater amount back east. But while land was selling and selling readily the country would and could not maintain its possible quota of development without railroad facilities. This question, therefore, was of the most urgent anxiety. When would the railroad be extended out of Bonesteel westward? At Bonesteel they said never. Others, somewhat more liberal said it *might* be extended in twenty years. They argued that since it had taken that many years after Bonesteel had been started before the company placed their tracks there, the same would in all probability hold with regards to the country and the towns west. So be it.

The promoters of the town of Dallas argued that it would

not be extended from Bonesteel at all; that when it was extended, it would come up the valley from the town some miles below Bonesteel, where the tracks lifted to the highlands. Meaning, of course that Dallas would be the only town in the newly opened portion of the country to get the railroad.

Jean Baptiste and Bill had seeded all the land that was under cultivation on Baptiste's property, and were well under way of breaking what was left unbroken, when Baptiste was offered a proposition that looked good to him. It was 200 acres joining his place near Stewart's, the property of an Indian, the allotee having recently expired. Under a ruling of the Department of the Interior, an Indian cannot dispose of an allotment under twenty-five years from the time he is alloted. This ruling is dissatisfactory to the Indian; for, notwithstanding all the rôles in which he is characterized in the movies and dramas as the great primitive hero, brave and courageous, the people of the West who are surrounded with red men, and know them, know that they wish to sell anything they might happen to possess as soon as selling is possible. Therefore, when one happens to expire, leaving his land to his heirs who can thereupon sell, dispose, give away or do what they may wish with the land, as long as it accords with the dictates of the Indian agent, the tract of land in question can be expected to pass into other hands forthwith.

The two hundred acres offered Jean Baptiste was convenient to his land, and was offered at twenty dollars per acre. Other lands about had sold as high as thirty dollars the acre. A thousand dollars down and a thousand dollars a year until paid was the bargain, and he accepted it, paying over the thousand, which was the last of the money he had brought from the East with him.

This was before something happened that turned the whole country into an orgy of excitement.

A few days after this one of the long rainy periods set in, and the little town was overrun with homesteaders, agreeing that the land that was broken was acting to their advantage: bringing all the good rains, and drought would never be again.

Then one day a man brought the news. The surveyors were in Bonesteel. It was verified by others, and really turned out to be true. The surveyors being in Bonesteel was an evident fact that the railroad would follow the highlands and would not come up the valley, and that settled Dallas as a town. It was doomed before a stake was set, and here passes out of our story, in so far as a railway in its present location was concerned. But whatever route a railroad took, it meant that the value to a homestead by the extension of the railroad would approximate to exceed ten dollars per acre. And Jean Baptiste now owned five hundred and twenty acres.

Since the work now in breaking the extra two hundred acres was before him, and was more than three miles from his homestead, he sought more convenience, by determining to approach the Stewarts with a request to board him.

It was a rainy day, when he called, only to find Jack Stewart out, while George and Bill were tinkering about the barn. They had not been informed of his purchase.

"Oh, it is you — Mr. Baptiste," cried Agnes upon opening the door in response to his knock. "Come right in."

"Where's the governor?" he inquired when seated.

"Search me," she laughed. "Papa's always out, rain or shine."

"Busy man."

"Yes. Busy but never gets anything by it, apparently."

She was full of humor, her eyes twinkled.   He was also.
It was a day to be grateful.   Rainfall, though it bring delay
in the work, such days always are appreciated in a new
country.   It made those there feel more confident.

"Lots of rain."

"Yes.   I suppose you are glad," she said interestedly.

"Well, I should be."

"We are, too.   It looks as if, should this keep up, we will
really raise a crop."

"Oh, it'll keep up," he said cheerfully, confidently.   "It
always rains in this country."

"How optimistic you are," she said, regarding him admiringly.

"Thanks."

She smiled then and bit her lip.

"How's your neighbors across the road?   I've never become acquainted with them."

"Their name is Prescott.   I don't know much about them;
but papa has met them."

"How many of them?"

"Three.   The man and wife and a son."

"A son?"

"M-m."

"How old is he — a young man?"

"M-m."

He smiled mischievously.

"Oh, it will be great," and she laughed amusedly.

"He farms with his parents?"

"I don't think so.   He has rented a few acres on the
place north of us.   Don't seem to be much force."

"You should wake him up."

"Humph!"

"My congratulations," irrelevantly.

"Please don't.   He's too ugly, too lazy; loves nothing but a stallion he owns, and is very uninteresting."

"Indeed!"   Suddenly he jumped up.   "I have forgotten that I came to see your dad."

"I can't say when papa will be home," she answered, going toward the door and looking out.

"I wanted to see him regarding a little business about boarding.   I wonder if he could board me?"

"He'll be home about noon, anyhow."

"That won't be so long, now," said he, regarding the clock.

"So you are tired of baching," she said with a little twinkle of the eyes.

"Oh, baching?   Before I started.   But that is not what has expedited my wishing to board.   I bought some more land.   Couple hundred acres of that dead Indian land over south."

"You did!"

"Why, yes."   He did not understand her exclamation.

"Oh, but you are such a wonderful man, and to be such a young man!"   She was not aware of the intimacy in her reference, and spoke thoughtfully, as if to herself more than to him.

He was flattered, and didn't know how to reply.

"You are certainly deserving of the high esteem in which you are held throughout the community," and still she was as if speaking to herself, and thoughtful.

He could not shut out at once the vanity she had aroused in him.   He wished to appear and to feel modest about it, however.   After all, he had most of the other land to pay for, which, nevertheless, gave him no worry.   His confidence was supreme.   He continued silent while she went on:

"It must be wonderful to be a young man and to be so courageous; to be so forceful and to be admired."

"Oh, you flatter me."

"No; I do not mean to. I am speaking frankly and what I feel. I admire the qualities you are possessed with. I read a great deal, and when I see a young man like you going ahead so in the world, I think he should be encouraged."

How very frankly, and considerately she had said it all. His vanity was gone. He saw her as the real Agnes. He saw in her, moreover, that which he had always longed for in his race. How much he would have given to have heard those words uttered by a girl of his blood on his trips back East. But, of course the West was foreign to them. They could not have understood as she did. But the kindness she had shown had its effect. He could at least admire her openly for what she was. He spoke now.

"I think you are very kind, Miss Stewart. I can't say when any one has spoken so sensibly to me as you have, and you will believe me when I say that such shall never be forgotten." He paused briefly before going on. "And it will always be my earnest wish that I shall prove worthy of such kind words." He stopped then, for in truth, he was too overcome with emotion, and could not trust himself to go on.

She stood with her back to him, and could he have seen her eyes he would also have observed tears of emotion. They were honest tears. She had spoken the truth. She admired the man in Jean Baptiste, and she had not thought of his color in speaking her conviction. But withal she felt strangely that her life was linked in some manner with this man's.

Her father's appearance at this moment served to break

the silent embarrassment between them, the embarrassment that had come out of what she had said.

They settled with regards to his boarding with them, and a few minutes later he took his leave. As he was passing out, their eyes met. Never had they appeared so deep; never before so soft. But in the same he saw again that which he had seen before and as yet could not understand.

CHAPTER XIV

NEVER before since Jean Baptiste had come West and staked his lot and future there, doing his part toward the building of that little empire out there in the hollow of God's hand, had he worked so hard as he did in the days that followed that summer. When the rains for a time ceased and the warm, porous soil had dried sufficiently to permit a return to the fields, from early morn until the sun had disappeared in the west late afternoons, did he labor. Observation with him seemed to be inherent. Ever since he had played as a boy back in old Illinois he had been deeply sensitive with regards to his race. To him, notwithstanding the fact that he realized that less than fifty years had passed since freedom, they appeared — even considering their adverse circumstances — to progress rather slowly. He had not as yet come fully to appreciate and understand why they remained always so poor; always the serf; always in the position to gain so little — but withal to suffer so much! Oh, the anguish it had so often given him!

His being in the West had come of an ulterior purpose. It has been stated that he was a keen observer. While so he had cultivated also the faculty of determination. By now it had became a sort of habit, a sort of second nature as it were. But there were certain things he could not seem to get away from. For instance: It seemed to him that the most difficult task he had ever encountered was to convince the average colored man that the Negro race could ever be anything. In after years he understood more fully why this was — but we deal with the present; those days when Jean Baptiste with a great ambition was struggling to " do his bit " in the development of the country of our story. He struggled with these problems at times until he became fatigued; not knowing that he could never understand until the time came for him to.

When he dined late one afternoon and found himself alone with Agnes, he spoke of being tired.

" You work too hard, Jean," she said, kindly.

" Perhaps so," he admitted. " And, still, the way I choose to see that is, that I'll not know the difference this time next year."

" That is quite possible," she agreed thoughtfully. " But your case is this, I think. You seem inspired by some high compulsion; some infinite purpose in the way you work, and in your mind this is so uppermost that you forget the limit of your physical self." She paused and gazed at the knife she held. Her mind appeared to deliberate, and he wondered at her deep logic. What a really mindful person she was, and still but a girl.

" I cannot help thinking of you and your effort here," she resumed, " and if I was asked, I would advise you to exercise more discretion in regard to yourself. To labor as you do, without regard to rain, sun, or time, is not practical. It would be very sad if, in conducting yourself as you do, something should happen to you before you had quite fulfilled that to which you are aspiring — not to accomplish altogether, but to demonstrate."

" You seem to have such a complete understanding of everything, Agnes," he said. " You appear to see so much deeper than the people I have met, to look so much beneath the surface and read what is there. I cannot always understand you." He paused while she continued in that thoughtful manner as if she had not heard what he said. "Now in your remark of a moment ago, you so defined a certain thing I would like to tell you. . . . But I shall not now. The instance is always so much in my mind that indeed, I lose sense of physical endurance; I lose sight of everything but the one object. It is not that I care so much for the fruits of my labor; but if I could actually succeed, it would mean so much to the credit of a multitude of others.— Others who need the example. . . ." He paused and thought of his race. The individual here did not count so much, it was the cause. His race needed examples; they needed instances of successes to overcome the effect of ignorance and an animal viciousness that was prevalent among them.

In this land, for instance, which had been advertised from one end of the country to the other; this land where four hundred thousand acres of virgin soil had been opened to the settler, he was about the only one of that race who had come hither, or paid the instance any attention. Such examples of neglected opportunity stood out clearly, and were recorded; and the record would give his race, claiming to be discriminated against, no credit. . . . Such examples of obliviousness to what was around them would be hard to explain away. So in his ambitious youth, Jean Baptiste's dream was to own one thousand acres of land. He was now twenty-three and possessed half that much. He conjectured that he could reach the amount by the time he was thirty — providing nothing serious happened to retard him. . . .

He had finished his meal and was ready to go back to that little place over the hill. The girl who had made proof on the homestead he had purchased, had lived fourteen months alone in a little sod house her father had built for her in which he now had his bed. She had come of a prosperous family in the East. She had come hither and put in the time, and the requirements, and had sold the land that he had bought at a good profit to herself. Such instances were common in that country, so common indeed, that little was thought of it. In his trips back East when Baptiste told of such opportunities, he was not taken seriously. The fact that the wealth of the great Central Valley was right at their door; that from the production there they purchased the food they ate; that sheep were raised whose wool was later manufactured into the very clothes they wore, had no meaning to them. And always he felt discouraged when he returned from a visit among them.

He had never seen Agnes so serious as she was that night. She arose and followed him to the door, and stood with him a moment before he left. Her eyes were tired and she appeared worried. He became possessed with an impulse to shake her hand. She seemed to sense his desire, and as he stepped out into the night, she extended it. He grasped and held it briefly. He whispered goodnight to her, and as he went through the yard and out into the road, she watched him from the open door until he was out of sight.

Jean Baptiste thought he had secured a bargain in a team he had purchased a week before, and, from all appearances he had. For, after working them a week, he found them model horses — apparently. As stated, he slept in the little sod house on the place near Stewart's, and also had a barn there in which he kept his horses while working. The morning following the conversation with Agnes, just related, he went out to curry and feed this team along with the other horses, and received a kick that was almost his ending. Right at the temple one spiked him, and he knew no more for hours.

" I wonder why Jean is so late," said Agnes, going to the

window and gazing up the road. He was a hardy eater and the fact that he was late for breakfast was unusual. They waited a while longer and then ate without him. Bill who had been to care for his horses at the place before breakfast, reported that he had seen Baptiste go into the barn. So he had arisen, that was sure; but why had he not come for his meal? The subject was dismissed by all except Agnes, who was strangely uneasy.

"Bill," said she, "see what is the matter with your boss when you go over, and tell him to come to breakfast."

Bill had no difficulty ascertaining, and returned quickly with the news.

"I knew it!" exclaimed Agnes, excitedly. "I just felt that something was the matter," whereupon she got into a light coat and followed her father and brothers to where he lay outside the barn door, bleeding freely from the temple.

They carried him into their house, and were cheered to see that the blood had ceased to flow. His head was bandaged while Bill went for Doc. Slater, who pronounced the wound serious but not fatal. He awakened later in the day and called for water. It was brought him forthwith by Agnes.

When he had drunk deeply and lay back weakly upon the pillow, he heard:

"How do you feel, Jean?" He looked around in the semi-darkness of the room, and upon seeing her, sighed before answering. When he did it was a groan. She came quickly to where he lay and bent over him.

"Jean," she repeated softly, tenderly. "How do you feel? Does your head pain you much?"

"Where am I?" he said, turning his face toward her. She put her hand lightly over his bandaged head.

"You're here, Jean. At Stewart's. You are hurt, do you understand?"

"Hurt?" he repeated abstractedly.

"Yes, hurt, Jean. You were kicked on the temple by one of your horses."

"Is that so?" and he suddenly sat up in the bed.

"Careful, careful," she cried, excitedly, pushing him gently back upon the pillow. He was silent as if in deep thought, while she waited eagerly. Presently she said in a low voice:

"Do you feel hurt badly, Jean?"

"I don't know." He raised his hand to his head as if trying to think more clearly. She caught his hands and held them as if trying to estimate his pulse, to see if he had any fever.

"How did you come to get kicked, Jean?" she asked, speaking in the same low tone.

"I don't know. When I opened the barn door I had a vision of one of the horses moving and I knew no more."

"You must be very careful and not start the bleeding again," she advised. "You bled considerably."

"And you say I am at your house. At where I board?"

"Yes, Jean."

He turned and stared at her, and for the first time seemed to be himself. He closed his eyes a moment as if to shut out something he did not wish to see.

"And you have me here and are caring for me?"

"We brought you here and are caring for you, Jean," she repeated.

"It is singular," said he.

"What is singular?"

"That you have twice happened to be where you can

serve me when I am injured or in danger." She was silent. She didn't know how to answer, or that there was to be any answer.

"Has a doctor been here?"

"Yes."

"What did he seem to think of it?"

"He said your wound was serious, but not fatal."

"Did he say I could get up soon?"

"He didn't say, Jean; but I don't think it would be wise." He groaned.

"Now you must be patient and not fret yourself into a fever," she said seriously.

"But I have so much work to do."

"That will have to wait. Your health is first," she said firmly.

"But the work should be done," he insisted.

"But you must consider your health before you can even think about the work."

He groaned again. She was thoughtful. She was considerate, and she could see that he would worry about his work and injure himself or risk fever.

"I'll speak to papa, and perhaps George can take your place for a few days, a week or until you can get out."

"You are so kind, Agnes," he said then. "You are always so thoughtful. I don't know how I can accept all you do for me."

"Please hush—don't mention it." She arose and presently returned with her father.

"Ah-ha," he always greeted. "So you've come to. Thought something would show up in that 'bargain.'"

"Please don't, father," admonished Agnes, frowningly.

"I'll look after everything while you are down, old man,"

said Stewart. "I'll start the horses you've been working this afternoon. Aggie has explained everything. I understand."

"I'm so thankful," he said, then closing his eyes, and a few minutes later had fallen asleep.

CHAPTER XV

OH, MY JEAN!

WHEN JACK STEWART left Indiana, and left owing the two hundred dollars which was secured by a chattel mortgage on his horses, he failed to do something he now had cause to regret. The man to whom he owed this money agreed to give him one year in which to pay it, but didn't renew the mortgage. He was a close friend of Jack's, and there had been no worry. But the man died; his affairs fell into the hands of an administrator, whose duties were to clean up, to realize on all due and past due matter. And because the note of Jack Stewart's was due and past due, the extension being simply a verbal one, the administrator wrote Jack demanding that he take up his note at once.

We know the circumstances of Jack Stewart; that be cause Jean Baptiste had hired his son Bill, and now was boarding with them, he was able to get along; but Jack Stewart had nothing with which to pay $200 notes. . . . So while Jean Baptiste was recovering from his illness, Jack Stewart had cause to be very much worried

Possessed, however, with a confidence, Jack took the matter up with the banker in the town where he received his mail. Now a common saying in a new country is: " I'm going to borrow five dollars and start a bank. . . ." Inferring that while there is, as a whole, an abundance of banks in a new country, they do not always have the wherewithal to loan. What they have is usually retained for the accommodation of their regular patrons, and they were unable to accommodate Jack, even had they wished to do so.

Now, he could have secured the money had he been a claimholder or a land owner. But Jack, being neither, found himself in a bad plight. He had Aggie write a long letter in which he tried to explain matters, and requested until fall to pay, as had been verbally agreed upon. But the class of people in the old East who regard the new West as a land of impossibilities, where drought burns all planted crops to crisp, where grasshoppers eat what is left, who still regard those who would stake their fortunes and chances in the West as fools, were not all dead.

The administrator happened to be one of this kind. He had no confidence in the country Jack wrote about, the crops he had planted; what he expected to reap, and no patience withal into the bargain. So he wrote Jack a brief letter, and also one to the bank in the town, sending the papers with it at the same time, with instructions to foreclose at a given time. And when Jack knew more of it, he was confronted with paying the note in thirty days or having his horse taken, and sold at auction.

Jean Baptiste recovered, went back to his work, and noticed that Jack Stewart and Agnes were much worried; but, of course, didn't understand the cause of it.

"Have you tried elsewhere, father?" said Agnes when they had gotten the notice giving them thirty days' grace.

"But I am not known, dear. There is not much money in a new country, and it is very difficult to get credit where there is nothing to lend."

"There must be some way to avoid this. Oh, that man, why couldn't he be reasonable!"

"It is always bad when one has to write. If I were

back in Indiana I could go and see this man and reason it out, but when a thousand miles is between us — it's bad!"

"If we could have only just three months."

"Two months," he exclaimed.

The days that followed were days of grave anxiety, of nervous anticipation for them. There was but one person they could turn to at such a time, and that was Jean Baptiste. Agnes thought of him, she started to speak with her father regarding him, but in the end did not bring herself to do so.

So the time went on, and the thirty days became twenty; and the twenty fell to ten; and the ten fell to five, and then Jean Baptiste could bear their worry no longer without speaking.

"You and your father have been very kind to me, Agnes, and I can see you are greatly worried about something. If I could help you in any way, I would be glad to do so."

She was so near to crying when she heard this that she had much difficulty keeping back the tears. But she managed to say:

"Why, it's nothing serious. Just a little matter, that's all," and she went into her room. He pondered. It was more than that. Of this he was sure. He left the house and came around to where Jack sat, and was moved by his expression. But Jack would say nothing. He could not understand. He tried to dismiss the subject from his mind, and so came Sunday, the day of days.

He was walking from his meal to his place to look over his crops, when from up the road he caught the sound of buggy-wheels. Two men, driving a single horse hitched to a light buggy were coming his way. When they caught sight of him, they hurried the animal forward slightly by touching him up with the whip, and beckoned to him to stop. Presently they drew up to where he stood and he recognized one as a homesteader, and having a claim near and the other as a professional dealer in horses. They exchanged greetings and some remarks about the weather and crops, and then the trader said:

"By the way, Jean, where does that old Scotchman live out this way? The old fellow who moved out here recently from Indiana?"

"That's the place there," and Baptiste pointed to the top of the house that could just be seen from where they stood.

"I see," said the other thoughtfully. "Wonder where that dappled gray mare he owns is grazing. I'd like to take a look at 'er."

"I think you will see her grazing in the pasture," said Baptiste curiously.

"How — what kind of animal is it?"

"Why, she's a hum-dinger," returned Baptiste more curiously. His curiosity aroused the other, who, looking at him said:

"Well, you see the old man is to be sold out — foreclosed, and I thought I'd take a look at his stuff and if I thought there was anything in it, I might save the old scout the humiliation by buying it."

"T' hell you say!" exclaimed Baptiste.

"Oh, yes. Hadn't you heard about it?"

"This is my first knowledge of it."

"Yes, the sheriff's coming to get the stuff Tuesday — that is, providing the old man don't come across with a couple of hundred before that time, and it is not likely he can, I don't think."

"Well, well!" Baptiste exclaimed, thinking of the worry

he had observed in the faces of Agnes and her father, and at last beginning to understand.

"Yes, it's rather bad, that. But this follows the old gent from where he comes, and he is not known here, so I guess I'll mosey along and take a look at the stuff — just a glance at it from the road, you understand. And if things look good, I'll drop by 'n see him later." Whereupon they went their way cheerfully, while Baptiste resumed his, thoughtfully.

He returned to his house by a roundabout way, and, later, hitching a team to a light buggy, he drove into the town where Jack traded and looked up the banker.

"Say, Brookings," he opened, "what kind of deal is the old Scotchman up against out there? You understand."

"Oh, yes!" exclaimed the cashier. "The old man out there on the Watson homestead! Well, it seems like the old fellow stands a good chance of being sold out." He then explained to Baptiste regarding the note and the circumstances.

"That don't look just right to me," muttered Baptiste when he had heard the circumstances.

"Well, now, it *isn't* right. But what can be done?"

"Can't you loan the old man the money?"

"I could; but I don't like letting credit to strangers and renters. If he could get a good man on his note I'd fix it out for him, since we've just received quite a sum for deposit."

"Well, if I should go it," said Baptiste suggestively. The other looked quickly up.

"Why, you! Gee, I'd take care of him for ten times the amount if you'd put your 'John Henry' on the note."

"Well, I'll be in town early in the morning," said Baptiste, turning to drive away.

"All right, Jean. Sure! I'll look for you."

The day was bright and lovely for driving, and Baptiste drove to his homestead, and from there to the Reynolds' where he had dinner and visited late. The next morning he went to the town, and when Jack Stewart, exhausted by the strain of worry under which he was laboring, came into town, having decided to try and sell the mare and one of the other horses, thereby leaving him only one with which to complete the cultivating of his corn and the reaping of his crops, he was called into the bank.

"Now if you'll just sign this, Mr. Stewart," said Brookings, "you can have until December first on that stuff."

"You mean the note!" the old man exclaimed, afraid to believe that he had heard aright.

"Yes, the note that is about to be foreclosed. You've been granted an extension." Jack Stewart was too overcome to attempt to comment. The realization that he was to be allowed to go on and not be sold out or be forced to dispose of his little stock at such a critical time, was too much for words. He caught up the pen, steadied his nerves, and wrote his name, not observing that the banker held a blotter over the lower line of the note. Jean Baptiste had cautioned him to do this. In view of the circumstances he had not wished Stewart or Agnes to know that he had gone cn the note.

Jack Stewart hurried home in a fever of excitement. He could not get there fast enough. He thought of Agnes, he did not wish her to have a minute more grief than what she had endured. He reached home and stumbled into the house, and to Agnes he said:

"Oh, girl, girl, girl! They have extended the note! The sheriff is not coming! We are saved, saved, saved!" He was too overcome with emotion and joy then to proceed.

He sank into a chair, while Agnes, carried away with excitement over the news, caressed him; said words of love and care until both had been exhausted by their own emotions. When they at last became calm, she turned to her father who now walked the floor in great joy.

"How did they come to extend the note, father?"

"Why — why, dear, that had never occurred to me! I became so excited when they told me that I had been granted an extension, I can only recall that I signed the note and almost ran out of the bank. The man had to call me back to give me my old note and mortgage. I don't know why they granted the extension." He stood holding his chin now and looking down at the floor as if trying to understand after all how it happened. Then his eyes opened suddenly wide. "Why, and, do you know, now, since I come to think of it, they did not take a new mortgage on the stock."

"I don't believe that the administrator had anything to do with it," she said after a time. "I know *that* man. He would sell his mother out into the streets. Now I wonder who has influenced the bank into giving us this time. . . ."

"Bless me, dear lord. But right now I am too tickled to try to think who. To be saved is enough all at once. Later, I shall try to figure out who has been my benefactor." And with this he left the house and went to walk with his joy in the fields where George was plowing corn, unconscious of the fact that the team he was driving was to have been seized on the morrow and sold for debt.

"Now I wonder *who* saved papa," Agnes said to herself, taking a seat by the window and gazing abstractedly out into the road. She employed her wits to estimate what had brought it about, and as she sat there, Jean Baptiste came driving down the road. He had not been there since break-

fast the morning before. He had taken his morning's meal
at the restaurant in the town. As he drove down the slope
that began above the house wherein she sat, his dark face
was lighted with a peaceful smile. He drove leisurely
along, concerned with the bright prospects of his four hundred acres of crop. He was so absorbed in his thoughts
that he passed on by without seeing Agnes at the window;
without even looking toward the house.

Upon seeing him Agnes had for the moment forgotten
what she was thinking about. But when he had passed
by, she was suddenly struck with an inspiration. She
jumped quickly to her feet: She raised her hands to her
breast and held them there as if to still a great excitement,
as she cried:

"Jean! Jean, Jean Baptiste! It was you, you, who did
it. It was you who saved my father, saved me; saved us
all! Oh, my Jean!"

She was overcome then with a great emotion. She sank
slowly upon a chair. And as she did so sobs broke from her
lips and she wept long and silently.

CHAPTER XVI

SUMMERTIME over the prairie country; summertime when the rainfall has been abundant, is a time of happiness to all settlers in a new land. And such a summer it was in the land of our story. God had been unusually kind to the settlers; he had blessed them with abundant moisture; with sunshine, not too warm and not too cold. The railroad was under course of construction and would be completed far enough west for the settlers from the most remote part — from the farthest corner of the reservation to journey with their grain or hogs, chickens or cattle to it and return to home the same day. And now the fields which had been seeded to winter wheat had turned to gold. Only a few thousand acres had been sowed over the county, and of this amount one hundred thirty acres grew on the homestead of Jean Baptiste. The season for its growth had been ideal, and the prospects for a bumper yield was the best. Ripe now, and ready to cut, the air was filled with its aroma.

He had brought a new self-binder from Gregory which now stood in the yard ready for action, its various colors green, red, blue and white, resplendent in the sunlight.

So now we see Jean Baptiste the cheerful, Jean Baptiste the hopeful, with hopes in a measure about realized; Jean Baptiste the Ethiopian in a country where he alone was black. He whistles at times, he sings, he is merry, cheery and gay.

But while Jean Baptiste was happy, cheerful and gay, there was in him what has been, what always will be that which makes us appreciate the courage that is in some men.

Bill Prescott, from the first day he had seen Agnes, had considered a match between her and himself a suggestive proposition. Bill Prescott might be referred to as a " feature." He was not so fortunate as to have been born handsome, and could not be called attractive. He had not, moreover, improved the situation by cultivation of wit, of art or pride. The West had meant no more to him than had the East, the South — or the West Indies, for that matter. Because Bill had no homestead, no deeded land, and had not tried to get any. His wealth consisted of a few horses, among which, an old, worn out, bought-on-credit-stallion, was his pride.

Of this stallion Bill talked. He told of his pedigree, tracing him back almost to the Ark. He was fond of tobacco, was Bill Prescott; he chewed, apparently, all the time. He had lost his front teeth; wore his thin hair long, and upon his small head a hat, oiled to the point where its age was a matter for conjecture. He had apparently appreciated that the wind blew outrageously over those parts at times, and, therefore, had hung a leather string to his hat which he pulled down over the back of his head to hold his hat in place. This succeeded in frumpling the long, thin hair and kept it in a dishevelled condition.

Now Bill had been a frequent caller at the Stewarts' home since they had come West. He did not always take the trouble to remove his hat when inside. That he was fond of Agnes was apparent, and smiled always upon seeing her, and at such times showed where his front teeth had been but where tobacco more frequently now was, with lazy delight.

He called this day wearing a clean, patched jumper over his cotton shirt. When once inside, sprawling his legs before him, and while Jack Stewart worked in the sun outside, repairing harness, he said to Agnes:

"Well, old girl, how'd you like to marry?" Agnes changed color a few times before she could decide whether to answer or not. In the meantime, patient and in no hurry, Bill grinned with pleasure at the ease with which he had started; showed tobacco where his teeth had been, and spat a pound of juice, with plenty of drippings trailing out the window by which she sat. It made considerable argument getting through the screen, but succeeded finally — most of it, the remainder, clung, hesitated, wavered, and finally giving up, dripped slowly to the ledge below.

"Dog-gone, myself," said Bill, getting up heavily from his chair, and going to the window and thumping it lightly, whereupon the hesitant amber, dashed in many directions about. Agnes had observed it all with calm disgust. Bill, however, not the least perturbed over his apparent breach of impropriety, became reseated, and resumed:

"Well?"

She turned her eyes slowly toward him, surveyed him coldly, and continued at her sewing.

Bill muttered something.

She regarded him again with cold disdain.

"Haw, haw!" he laughed loudly. "You don't pretend t' hear me, haw! haw! Then I guess you're stuck on that nigger you got a hangin' round here."

"Will you go!" she cried, as she quickly jumped to her feet and swung open the door. She controlled herself with considerable effort.

"Oh, ho! So that's the way you treat a white man — and honor a d—n nigger!" And with that he dashed out and passed to where the senior worked away over his harness. Jack Stewart saw and heard Bill approaching without looking up. He greeted:

" Ah-ha, William. And how are you today? "

Bill was struck with a sudden inspiration. In his way he really liked Agnes, and it was all settled in his mind to wed her. He realized now that he had rather bungled matters, and thereupon decided to exercise a little more discretion. So, choking down the anger that was in him, and swallowing a bit of tobacco juice at the same time, he said to Stewart.

" Good morning! Ah, by the way, Jack, I'd like to marry Agnes." So saying, he was pleased with himself again, and spat tobacco juice more easily in the next squirt. Jack continued working at his harness. For the moment he did not appear to comprehend, but presently he raised his eyes with the old style glasses before them, and surveyed Bill slowly.

" You want to do what? " he said, uncomprehendingly.

" To marry Agnes," Bill repeated calmly. He paused, looked away, sucked his soft mouth clean of amber and spat it tricklingly at Jack's feet, and looked up and at Jack with a wondrous smile.

Now Jack Stewart was possessed with certain virtues. He did not smoke, chew, drink, swear nor shave. He was rather put out, but with considerable effort at self control he managed to say:

" Well, if that's the way you feel about it, why don't you take it up with the girl? " Bill hesitated at this point, sucked his mouth clear again of tobacco juice, cleared his throat, spat the juice, and, after a hasty glance toward the house, decided not to mention that he had spoken with Agnes. He replied:

"Well, I thought it best to speak to you, and if it's all right with you, it ought to be all right with the gal."

Jack Stewart drew up, and then tried to relax. He did not think so much of Bill; but he did think the world of Agnes and wanted her respected by everybody. Moreover, he did not like to hear her "galled." He turned to William; he regarded him keenly, and then in a voice and words that were English, but accent that was very much Scotch, the which we will not attempt to characterize, he said:

"You're a joke. Just a great, big joke." He paused briefly, and then continued: "I'd like to be patient with you; but honestly, with you it wouldn't pay. You are not worth it. And in so far as my girl — any girl is concerned, I cannot imagine how you could even expect them to be interested." He paused and looked away, too full up to go ahead. In the meantime he heard Bill:

"Is that so!'"

"Is *it* so!" cried Stewart with a touch of vehemence. "Gad! See yourself. See how you go! Don't you observe what's around you close enough to see that girls want some sedateness; they admire in some measure cleverness, clothes, and — well, manhood!'"

"So I don't guess I have it?" retorted William, sneeringly.

"Oh, you bore me!" Jack returned disgustingly. He bent to his work in an attempt to forget it. And then he again heard from Bill:

"So that's the way yu' got it figgered out, eh!" He drew his mouth tight shut. He gave another soft suck that drew his skin close to his gums, and with his tongue, he cleared his mouth and spat tobacco, juice and all in a soft lump at Stewart's feet and said in unconcealed anger: "So that's the way you got me figgered out! And I want to say, now, that I don't think I want yer gal, anyhow. I'm a white man, I am. And what white man would want a gal that a nigger is allowed to hang aroun' and court!"

Jack Stewart was struck below the belt. He was fouled, and for a time everything went dark around him, he was so angry. He did not know that Jean Baptiste had saved him from losing his stock or being forced to sell them; he had never connected Baptiste and Agnes as being other than friends, and friends they had a right to be. But Jack Stewart *did* regard Jean Baptiste as a gentleman and gentlemen he respected. His knockout therefore was brief. He soon recovered. He could not speak, he could not even stammer; but with a sudden twitch of the tug his hands held, he came away around with it, and the heavy leather took Bill fairly in the mouth, in the middle of the mouth. And then Jack got his voice, and ready for another swing; but not before Bill found something, too. It was his feet.

"You stinkin', low down, pup!" cried Stewart, falling over from the force of the swing he had missed. "You trash of the sand hills! You tobacco chewin', ragga-muffin!" Getting his balance, and turning after William madly, he resumed: "You ornery, nasty, filthy, houn'! If I get my han's on you, I swear t' God I'll kill you."

But Bill Prescott now held the advantage. He was younger, and more fleet of foot; so therefore out ran Jack, who was left before he reached the gate, far to the rear, and Bill gained his side of the wide road with a safe lead. Jack finally came to a stop before getting off the premises with his blood boiling with such heat that he drew his hat off and beat himself with it. In the meantime, Agnes, who had witnessed the controversy from the gate, ventured out to where her father stood and taking him gently by the arm, she led him inside.

"My blood's up, my blood's up!" Jack kept crying and repeating. "That stinkin', triflin' peace a nothin', has been gittin' smart. Tryin' to low rate me; tryin' to low rate my girl. Insultin' Jean Baptiste! Dang him, dang him!"

"Father, father!" cried Agnes soothingly.

"Did you hear'm! Did you hear'm! Why, the low down, good for nothin', I'm a good mind to go cross the road and skin him alive!"

"Father, father!" begged Agnes.

"Did you hear what he said," insisted the infuriated senior.

"Yes, father," she confessed. "I heard him."

"You did! 'N that's worse!" Whereupon he tore loose and threw up his arms in an angered gesture.

"Now, papa," Agnes argued kindly. "I heard him, and what he said to you. He was in here and insul — spoke to me before he went out there. . . . I understand all about it. . . . So you must simply be calm — and forget it. That's all. . . ."

"I don't care so much for myself, but that he should speak about you and Baptiste! I just wish Baptiste could have heard him and just beat the gosh danged manure right out of him."

"Please be quiet, papa. Forget Bill Prescott and what he has tried to insinuate. . . . We understand *him* and what he *is,* and we understand Mr. Baptiste — and what *he is,* so let us just think of other things."

"Yes, Aggie, I suppose you're right. You always seem to be right. And I will try to forget it; but I'll say this much: If that ornery, lazy cuss ever crosses this road to my place again I'll thresh him within an inch of his life!"

"You've agreed to forget it, father. . . ."

" I agree again; but it's outrageous that he should say what he did about Jean Baptiste, now isn't it? "

" It is, father," she admitted with downcast eyes.

" Of course it is. Never was there more of a gentleman in the world than Jean Baptiste."

" Mr. Baptiste is a real gentleman," acknowledged Agnes again.

" There never was, and he knows it, the pup! "

Agnes was strangely silent, which Jack, in his excitement overlooked.

" And even if he should like my girl —"

" Father! "

" Well? "

" Oh, please hush! "

" I will, Aggie," he said slowly. He bent forward presently, folded her close, kissed her, and then placing his hat on his head, went back to his work. . . .

CHAPTER XVII

HARVEST TIME AND WHAT CAME WITH IT

HARVEST time, harvest time! When the harvest time is, all worries have passed. When the harvest time is, all doubts, droughts, fears and tears are no more. When the golden grain falls upon the canvas; when the meadow larks, the robins and all the birds of the land sing the song of harvest time, the farmer is happy, is gay, and confident.

And harvest time was on in the country of our story.

Jean Baptiste pulled his new binder before the barn, jumped from the seat, and before he started to unhitch, he gazed out over a stretch of land which two years before, had been a mass of unbroken prairie, but was now a world of shocked grain. Thousands upon thousands of shocks stood over the field like a great army in the distance. His crop was good — the best. And no crops are like the crop on new land. Never, since the beginning of time had that soil tasted tamed plant life. It had seemed to appreciate the change, and the countless shocks before him were evidence to the fact.

From where he stood when he had unhitched, he gazed across country toward the southeast where lay his other land. Only a part of which he could see. As it rose in the distance he could see the white topped oats; and just beyond he could see the deep purple of the flaxseed blossoms. He sighed contentedly, unharnessed his horses, let them drink, and turned them toward the pasture. He was not tired;

but he went to the side of the house which the sun did not strike, and sat him down.   At the furthest side of the field he observed Bill and George as they shocked away to finish. He was at peace again, as he always was, and thereupon fell into deep thought.

" My crop of wheat will yield not less than thirty bushels to the acre," he whispered to himself.   " And one hundred and thirty acres should then yield almost four thousand bushels.   I should receive at least eighty cents the bushel, and that would approximate about three thousand dollars, with seed left to sow the land again."   He paused in his meditation, and considered what even that alone would mean to him.   He could pay the entire amount on the land he had purchased, and perhaps a thousand or two more from the flax crop.   That would leave him owing but four hundred dollars on the land he had bought, and that amount he felt he would be able to squeeze out somewhere and have 520 acres clear!

He could not help being cheerful, perhaps somewhat vain over his prospects.   He was now just twenty-three and appreciated that most of his life was yet before him.   With, at the most, two or three more seasons like the present one, he could own the coveted thousand acres and the example would be completed.

That was the goal toward which he was working.   If he or any other man of the black race could acquire one thousand acres of such land it would stand out with more credit to the Negro race than all the protestations of a world of agitators in so far as the individual was concerned.

" It is things accomplished," he often said to himself. " It is what is actually accomplished that will get notice — and credit!   Damn excuses!   The best an excuse can secure is dismissal, and positively that is no asset."   He would then invariably think deeply into the conditions of his race, the race who protested loudly that they were being held down. Truly it was an intricate, delicate subject to try to solve with prolific thinkings. He compared them with the Jew — went away back to thousands of years before. Out of the past he could not solve it either. All had begun together. The Jew was hated, but was a merchant enjoying a large portion of the world commerce and success. The Negro was disliked because of his black skin — and sometimes seemingly for daring to be human.

At such times he would live over again the life that had been his before coming West. He thought of the multitudes in the employment of a great corporation who monopolized the sleeping car trade. Indeed this company after all was said, afforded great opportunities to the men. Not so much in what was collected in tips and in other devious ways, nor from the small salary, but from the great opportunity of observation that that particular form of travel afforded.

But so few made the proper effort to benefit themselves thereby. He continued to think along these lines until his thoughts came back to a point where in the past they were wont to come and stop. He could not in that moment understand why they had not been coming back to that selfsame point in recent months. . . . Since one cold day during the first month of that year. . . . He gave a start when he realized why, then sighed. It seemed too much for his thoughts just then. He regarded Bill and George at their task of trying to finish their work. Upon hearing a sound, he turned. Behind him stood Agnes.

" My, how you frightened me! " he cried.

She held in her hand a basket containing lunch for him and her brothers. This she had brought every day, but he had been so absorbed in his thoughts that he had quite forgotten that she was coming on this day as well. As she stood quietly before him, she seemed rather shorter than she really was, also more slender, and appeared withal more girlish than usual. Her eyes twinkled and her heavy hair drawn together at the back of her head, hung over her shoulders. Her sunkist skin was a bit tanned; her arms almost to the elbows were bare, brown and were very round. And as Jean Baptiste regarded her there in the bright golden sunlight she appeared to him like the Virgin Mary.

"You are tired," he cried, and pointed to a crude bench that reposed against the sod house, which he had just left in his prolific thinking of a moment before.

"Sit down, please, and rest yourself," he commanded. She obeyed him modestly, with a smile still upon her pleasant face.

"I judge that Bill and George will finish in a few minutes, so I'll wait, that we may all dine together. You'll be so kind as to wait until then, will you not?" he asked graciously, and bowed.

"Until then, my lord," she smiled, coquettishly.

"Thanks!" he laughed, good humoredly. Suddenly she cried:

"Oh, isn't it beautiful!" And swept her hands toward the field of shocked wheat. He had been looking away, but as she spoke he turned and smiled with satisfaction.

"It is."

"Just lovely," she cried, her eyes sparkling.

"And all safe, that's the best part about it," he said.

"Grand. I'm so glad you have saved it," she said with feeling.

"Thank you."

"You have earned it."

"I hope so. Still I thank you."

"It will bring you lots of money."

"I am hoping it will."

"Oh, it will."

"I was thinking of it before you came up."

"I knew it."

"You knew it!"

"I saw you from a distance."

"Oh. . . ."

"And I knew you were thinking."

"Oh, come now."

"Why shouldn't I? You're always thinking. The only time when you are not is when you are sleeping."

"You can say such wonderful things," he said, standing before her, the sun shining on his tanned features.

"Won't — ah — won't you be seated?" she invited. He colored unseen. She made room for him and he hesitatingly took a seat, at a conventional distance, on the bench beside her.

"Your other crops are fine, too," she said, sociably.

"I'm going over to look at them this afternoon."

"You should."

"Where is your father today?"

"Gone to town."

"Wish I'd known he was going; I'd had him bring out some twine for me. I think the oats will be ready to cut over on the other place right away, and I don't want to miss any time."

"No, indeed. A hail storm might come up." He glanced at her quickly. She was gazing across the field to where her halfwitted brothers worked, while he was thinking how thoughtful she was. Presently he heard her again.

"Why, if it is urgent — you are out, I — I could go to town and get the twine for you." She was looking at him now and he was confused. Her offer was so like her, so natural. Why was it that they understood each other so well?

"Oh, why, Agnes," he stammered, "that would be asking too much of you!"

"Why so? I shall be glad — glad to oblige you in any way. And it is not too much if one takes into consideration what you have done for — I'll be glad to go. . . ."

"Done for what?" he said, catching up where she had broken off, and eyeing her inquiringly.

She was confused and the same showed in her face. She blushed. She had not meant to say what she did. But he was regarding her curiously. He hadn't thought about the note. She turned then and regarded him out of tender eyes. She played with the bonnet she held in her lap. She looked away and then back up into his face, and her eyes were more tender still. In her expression there was almost an appeal.

"What did you mean by what you started to say, Agnes," he repeated, evenly, but kindly.

"I — I — mean what you did for papa. What — you — you did about that — that — note." It was out at last and she lowered her eyes and struggled to hold back the tears with great effort.

"Oh," he laughed lowly, relievedly. "That was nothing." And he laughed again as if to dismiss it.

"But it *was* something," she cried, protestingly. "It *was* something. It was *everything* to us." She ended with great emotion apparent in her shaking voice. He shifted. It was awkward, and he was a trifle confused.

"Please don't think of it, Agnes."

"But how can I keep from thinking of it when I know that had it not been your graciousness; your wonderful thoughtfulness, your great kindness, we would have been sold out — bankrupted, disgraced, oh, me!" She covered her face with her hands, but he could see the tears now raining down her face and dropping upon her lap.

"Oh, Agnes," he cried. "I wish you wouldn't do that! Please don't. It hurts me. Besides, how did you know it? I told Brookings that your father was not to know it. I did not want it known." He paused and his voice shook slightly. They had drawn closer and now she reached out and placed her small hand upon his arm.

"Brookings didn't tell. He didn't tell papa; but I knew." She was looking down at the earth.

"I don't understand," she heard him say wonderingly.

"But didn't you think, Jean, that *I* understood! I understood the very day — a few minutes after papa returned home, brought the old note and told me about the extension." She paused and looked thoughtfully away across the field. "I understood when you drove by a few minutes later. You had forgotten about it, I could see, and your mind was on other things; but the moment you came into my sight, and I looked out upon you from the window, I knew you had saved us."

Her hand still rested lightly upon his arm. She was not aware of it, but deeply concerned with what she was saying. Presently, when he did not speak, she went on. "I understood and knew that you had forgotten it — that you were too much of a man to let us know what you had done. I can't forget it! I have wanted to tell you how

I felt — I felt that I owed it to you to tell you, but I couldn't before."

"Please let's forget it, Agnes," she heard him whisper.

"I can keep from speaking of it, but forget it — never! It was so much like you, like the man that's in you!" and the tears fell again.

"Agnes, Agnes, if you don't hush, almost I will forget myself. . . ."

"I had to tell you, I *had* to!" she sobbed.

"But it is only a small return for what you did for me. Do you realize, Agnes, had it not been for you, I — I — would not be sitting here now? Oh, think of that and then you will see how little I have done — how very little I can ever do to repay!" His voice was brave, albeit emotional. He leaned toward her, and the passion was in his face. She grasped his arm tighter as she looked up again into his face out of her tear bedimmed eyes and cried brokenly:

"But Jean, the cases are not parallel. What I did for you I would have done for anybody. It was merely an act of providence; but yours — oh, Jean, *can't you understand!*" He was silent.

"Yours was the act of kindness," she went on again, "the act of a man; and you would have kept it secret; because you would never have had it known, because you would not have us feel under obligation to you. Oh, that is what makes me — oh, it makes me cry when I think of it." The tears flowed freely while her slender shoulders shook with emotion.

And when she had concluded, the man beside her had forgotten *the custom of the country, and its law* had passed beyond him. He was as a man toward the maid now. Beside him wept the one he had loved as a dream girl. Behind him was the house with the bed she had laid

From a painting by W. M. Farrow.

"BUT, JEAN, THE CASES ARE NOT PARALLEL. WHAT I
DID FOR YOU I WOULD HAVE DONE FOR ANY ONE; BUT
YOURS—OH, JEAN, *CAN'T YOU UNDERSTAND!*"

him upon when she saved his life.   And when he had awakened, before being conscious of where he was or what had
happened to him, he had looked into her eyes and had seen
therein his dream girl.   She was his by the right of God;
he forgot now that she was white while he was black.   He
only remembered that she was his, and he loved her.

His voice was husky when he answered:

"Agnes, oh, Agnes, I begged you not to.   I almost beseeched you, because — oh, don't you understand what is
in me, that I am as all men, weak?   To have seen you that
night — the night I can never forget, the night when you
stood over me and I came back to life and saw you.   You
didn't know then and understand that I had dreamed of
you these two years since I had come here: that out of
my vision I had seen you, had talked with you, oh, Agnes!"
She straightened perceptibly; she looked up at him with
that peculiarity in her eyes that even she had never come
to understand.   They became oblivious to all that was
about them, and had unconsciously drawn closer together
now and regarded each other as if in some enchanted
garden.   She sang to him then the music that was in her,
and the words were:

"Jean, oh, Jean Baptiste, you have spoken and now at
last *I* understand.   And do you know that before I left
back there from where I came, I *saw* you: I dreamed of
you and that I would know you, and then I came and so
strangely met and have known you now for the man you
are, oh, Jean!"

Gradually as the composure that had been theirs passed
momentarily into oblivion, and the harvest birds twittered
gayly about them, his man's arm went out, and into the
embrace her slender body found its way.   His lips found
hers, and all else was forgotten.

EPOCH THE SECOND

EPOCH THE SECOND

CHAPTER I

REGARDING THE INTERMARRIAGE OF RACES

IT WAS winter, and the white snow lay everywhere; icicles hung from the eaves. All work on the farms was completed. People were journeying to a town half way between Bonesteel and Gregory to take the train for their former homes; others to spend it with their relatives, and Jean Baptiste was taking it for Chicago and New York where he went as a rule at the end of each year.

He was going with an air of satisfaction apparently; for, in truth, he had everything to make him feel so — that is, *almost* everything. He had succeeded in the West. The country had experienced a most profitable season, and the crop he reaped and sold had made him in round numbers the sum of seven thousand five hundred dollars. He had paid for the two hundred acres of land he had bargained for; he had seeded more land in the autumn just passed to winter wheat which had gone into the winter in the best of shape; his health was the best. For what more could he have wished?

And yet no man was more worried than he when he stepped from the stage onto the platform of the station where he was to entrain for the East. . . . It is barely possible that any man could have been more sad. . . . To explain this we are compelled to go back a few months; back to the harvest time; to his homestead and where he sat with some one near, very near, and what followed.

" I couldn't help it — I loved you; love you — have loved you always! " he passionately told her.

For answer she had yielded again her lips, and all the love of her warm young heart went out to him.

" I don't understand you always, dear," he whispered. " Sometimes there is something about you that puzzles me. I think it's in your eyes; but I *do* understand that whatever it is it is something good — it couldn't be otherwise, could it? "

" No, Jean," she faltered.

" And did you wonder at my calling your name that night? "

" I have never understood that fully until now," she replied.

" You came in a vision, and it must have been divine, two years ago gone now," she heard him; " and ever since your face, dear, has been before me. I have loved it, and, of course, I knew that I would surely love you when you came."

Isn't it strange," she whispered.

" But beautiful."

" So beautiful."

" Was it providence, or was it God that brought you that night and saved me from the slow death that was coming over me, Agnes? "

" Please, Jean, don't! Don't speak again of that awful night! Surely it must have been some divine providence that brought me to this place; but I can never recall it without a tremor. To think that you would have died out there! Please, never tell me of it again, dear." She trembled and nestled closer to him, while her little heart

beat a tattoo against her ribs. They looked up then, as
across the field her halfwitted brothers were approaching.
It was only then that they seemed to realize what had transpired and upon realization they silently disembraced. What
had passed was the most natural thing in the world, true;
and to them it had come because it was in them to assert
themselves, but now before him rose the Custom of the
Country, and its law. So vital is this Custom; so much is
it a part of the body politic that certain states have went
on record against it. Not because any bad, or good, any
wealth or poverty was involved. It had been because of
sentiment, the sentiment of the stronger faction. . . .

So it ruled.

In the lives of the two in our story, no thought but to
live according to God's law, and the law of the land, had
ever entered their minds, but now they had while laboring
under the stress of the pent-up excitement and emotion
overruled and forgot the law two races are wont to
observe and had given vent and words to the feeling which
was in them. . . . They stood conventionally apart now,
each absorbed in the calm realization of their positions in
our great American society. They were obviously disturbed; but that which had drawn them to the position they
had occupied and declared, still remained, and that was
love.

So time had gone on as time will; never stopping for anything, never hesitating, never delaying. So the day went,
and the week and the month, and the month after that and
the month after that, until in time the holidays were near,
and Jean Baptiste was going away, away to forget that
which was more to him than all the world — the love of
Agnes Stewart.

He had considered it — he had considered it before he

caught the one he loved into his arms and said the truth that was in him. . . . But there was another side to it that will have much space in our story.

Down the line a few stations from where he now was, there lived an example. A man had come years ago into the country, there, a strong, powerfully built man. He was healthy, he was courageous and he was dark, because forsooth, the man was a Negro. And so it had been with time this man's heart went out to one near by, a white. Because of his race it was with him as with Jean Baptiste. Near him there had been none of his kind. So unto himself he had taken a white wife. He had loved her and she had loved him; and because it was so, she had given to him children. And when the children had come she died. And after she had died and some years had passed, he took unto himself another wife of the same blood, and to that union there had come other children.

So when years had passed, and these selfsame children had reached their majority, they too, took unto themselves wives, and the wives were of the Caucasian blood. But when this dark man had settled in the land below, which, at that time, had been a new country, he decided to claim himself as otherwise than he was. He said and said again, that he was of Mexican descent, mongrel, forsooth; but there was no *Custom Of The Country* with regard to the Mexican, mongrel though he be. But the people and the neighbors all knew that he lied and that he was Ethiopian, the which looked out through his eyes. But even to merely claim being something else was a sort of compromise.

So his family had grown to men and women, and they in turn brought more children into the world. And all claimed allegiance to a race other than the one to which they belonged.

Once lived a man who was acknowledged as great and much that goes with greatness was given unto him by the public. A Negro he was, but as a climax in his great life, he had married a wife of that race that is superior in life, wealth and achievements to his own, the Caucasian. So it had gone.

The first named, Jean Baptiste never felt he could be quite like. Even if he should disregard *The Custom Of The Country, and its law,* and marry Agnes, he did not feel he would ever attempt that. But to marry out of the race to which he belonged, especially into the race in which she belonged, would be the most unpopular thing he could do. He had set himself in this new land to succeed; he had worked and slaved to that end. He liked his people; he wanted to help them. Examples they needed, and such he was glad he had become; but if he married now the one he loved, the example was lost; he would be condemned, he would be despised by the race that was his. Moreover, last but not least, he would perhaps, by such a union bring into her life much unhappiness, and he loved her too well for that.

Jean Baptiste had decided. He loved Agnes, and had every reason to; but he forswore. He would change it. He would go back from where he had come. He would be a man as befitted him to be. He would find a girl; he would marry in his race. They had education; they were refined — well, he would marry one of them anyhow!

So Jean Baptiste was going. He would forget Agnes. He would court one in his own race. So to Chicago he now sped.

He had lived in the windy city before going West, and was very familiar with that section of the city on the south side that is the center of the Negro life of that great metropolis. Accordingly, he approached a station in the loop district, entered one of the yellow cars and took a seat. He looked below at the hurly-burly of life and action, and then his eyes took survey of the car. It was empty, all save himself and another, and that other was a girl, a girl of his race! The first he had seen since last he was in the city. How little did she know as she sat across the aisle from him, that she was the first of his race his eyes had looked upon for the past twelve months. He regarded her curiously. She was of that cross bred type that are so numerous, full bloods seemingly to have become rare about those parts. She was of a light brown complexion, almost a mulatto. She seemed about twenty-two years of age. Of the curious eyes upon her she seemed entirely unaware, finally leaving the train at a station that he was familiar with and disappeared.

At Thirty-first Street he left the train, fell in with the scattered crowd below and the dash of the city life was his again in a twinkling. He found his way to State Street, the great thoroughfare of his people. The novelty in viewing those of his clan now had left him, for they were all about. Even had he been blind he could have known he was among them, for was not there the usual noise; the old laugh, and all that went with it?

He hurried across and passed down Thirty-first to Dearborn Street, Darktown proper; but even when he had reached Federal, then called Armour, he had seen nothing but his race. He had friends — at least acquaintances, so to where they lived he walked briskly.

"And if it isn't Jean Baptiste, so 'elp me Jesus," cried the woman, as she opened the door in response to his knock, and without further ceremony encircled his neck with her arms, and kissed his lips once and twice. "You old dear!"

she exclaimed with him inside, holding him at arms' length and regarding him fondly. " How are you, anyhow? "

" Oh, fine," he replied, regarding her pleasantly.

" You are certainly looking good," she said, looking up into his face with fun in her eyes.   " Sit down, sit down and make yourself at home," she invited, drawing up a chair.

" Well, how's Chicago? " he inquired irrelevantly.

" Same old burg," she replied, drawing a chair up close.

" And how's hubby? "

" Fine! "

" And the rest of the family? "

" The same.   Pearl, too."

" Oh, Pearl. . . . How is Pearl? "

" Still single. . . ."

" Thought she was engaged to be married when I was here last year? "

" Oh, that fellow was no good! "

" What was the matter? "

" What's the matter with lots of these nigga' men 'round Chicago?   They can't keep a wife a posing on State Street."

" Humph! "

" It's the truth! "

" And how about the women?   They seem to be fond of passing along to be posed at. . . ."

" Oh, you're mean," she pouted. Then: " Are you married yet? "

" Oh, lordy! How could I get married? Not thirty minutes ago I saw the first colored girl I have seen in a year! "

" Oh, you're a liar! "

" It's the truth! "

" Is it so, Jean?   Have you really not seen a colored girl in a whole year? "

"I have never lied to you, have I?"

"Well, no. Of course you haven't; but I don't know what I would do under such circumstances. Not seeing nigga's for a year."

"But I've seen enough already to make up."

She laughed. "Lordy, me. Did you ever see so many 'shines' as there are on State Street!" She paused and her face became a little serious for a moment. "By the way, Jean, why don't you marry my sister?"

"You're shameful! Your sister wouldn't have me. I'm a farmer."

"Oh, yes she would. Pearl's getting tired of getting engaged to these Negroes around Chicago. She likes you, anyhow."

"Tut, tut," he laughed depreciatingly. "Pearl would run me ragged out there on that farm!" She laughed too.

"No, she wouldn't, really. Pearl is good looking and is tired of working."

"She's good looking, all right, and perhaps tired of working; but she wouldn't do out there on the farm."

"Oh, you won't do. I'll bet you are married already."

"Oh, Mrs. White!"

"But you're engaged?"

"Nope!"

"Jean. I'll bet you'll marry a white girl out there and have nothing more to do with nigga's."

"Now you're worse."

"And when you marry a white woman, I want to be the first one to shoot you — in the leg."

He laughed long and uproariously."

"You can laf all you want; but you ain't goin' through life lovin' nobody. You gotta girl somewhere; but do what you please so long as it don't come to that."

" Come to what? "

" Marrying a white woman."

" Wouldn't that be all right? "

She looked up at him with a glare. He smiled amusedly.
" Don't you laf here on a subject like that! Lord! I think
lots of you, but if I should hear that you had married a
white woman, man, I'd steal money enough to come there
and kill you dead! "

" Why would you want to do that? "

" *Why would I want to do that?* Humph! What you
want to ask me such a question for? The idea! "

" But you haven't answered my question? "

She glared at him again, all the humor gone out of her face.
Presently, biting at the thread in some sewing she was doing,
she said: " In the first place, white people and Negroes
have no business marrying each other. In the second place,
a nigga' only gets a po' white woman. And in the third
place, white people and nigga's don't mix well when it comes
to society. Now, supposin' you married a white woman
and brought her here to Chicago, who would you associate
with? We niggu's 's sho goin' to pass 'er up. And the
white folks — you better not look their way! "

He was silent.

" Ain't I done outlined it right? "

" You've revealed some very delicate points with regard
to the matter," he acknowledged.

" Of course I have, and you can't get away from it. But
that ain't all. Now, to be frank with yu'. I wouldn't ceh
so much about some triflin' no 'count nigga' marrying some
old white woman; but that ain't the kind no white woman
wants when she stoops so low as to marry a nigga'. Uh,
naw! Naw indeedy! She don't fool with nothin' like
that! She leaves that kind for some poor colored woman

to break her heart and get her head broken over. She marries somebody like you with plenty of money and sense with it, see!"

He laughed amusedly.

"No laffin' in it. You know I'm tellin' the truth. So take warning! Don't marry no white woman up there and come trottin' down here expectin' me to give you blessin'. Because if you do, and just as sure as my name is Ida White, I'm going to do something to you!"

"But a white woman might help a fellow to get up in the world," he argued.

"Yes, I'll admit that, too. But ouh burden is ouh burden, and we've got to bear it. And, besides, you c'n get a girl that'll help you when you really want a wife. That ain't no argument. Of course I'd like to see Pearl married. But you ain't going to fool with her, and I know it. Pearl thinks she would like it better if she could marry somebody from out of Chicago; but they'd all be the same after a month or so with her."

"Well," said he, "I'd better get over to the Keystone. You've interested me today. I've learned something regarding the amalgamation of races. . . ."

"I hope you have, if you had it in your mind. Anything else might be forgiven, but marrying a white woman — never!"

They parted then. She to her sewing, and Jean Baptiste to his thoughts. . . .

CHAPTER II

JEAN BAPTISTE returned to the West after two months' travel through the East, and the spring following, sowed a large crop of small grain and reaped a bountiful yield that fall. About this time the county just west of where he lived was opened to settlement, and a still larger crowd than had registered for the land in the county he lived came hither and sought a quarter section.

The opening passed to the day of the drawing, and when all the lucky numbers had secured their filings, contracts for the purchases of relinquishments began. By this time the lands had reached great values, and that which he had purchased a short time before for twenty dollars the acre, had by this time reached the value of fifty dollars the acre. And now he had an opportunity of increasing his possessions to the number coveted, one thousand acres.

He had paid a visit to his parents that winter, and found his sisters, who were mere children when he had left home, grown to womanhood, and old enough to take claims. So with them he had discussed the matter. Inspired by his great success, they were all heart and soul to follow his bidding; so thereupon it was agreed that he would try to secure three relinquishments on good quarters, and upon one or more of these they would make filings.

His grandmother, who had raised a family in the days of

slavery agreed and was anxious to file on one; one sister on another, and the third place,— was to be his bride's.

By doing this, he could have her use her homestead right, providing she filed on the claim before marrying him. So it was planned. But Jean Baptiste knew no girl that he could ask to become his wife, therefore this was yet to be. When he had given up his real love to be loyal to his race, he had determined on one thing: that marriage was a business, even if it was supposed to be inspired by love. But when Agnes was left out, he loved no one. Therefore it must be resolved into a business proposition — and the love to come after.

So, resigned to the fact, he set himself to choose a wife.

On his trip East the winter before he met two persons with whom he had since corresponded. One, the first, was a young man not long out of an agricultural college whose father was a great success as a potato grower. He and Jean became intimate friends. It now so happened that the one mentioned had a sister, and through him Jean Baptiste was introduced to her by mail.

Correspondence followed and by this time it had become very agreeable. She proved to be a very logical young woman, and Jean Baptiste was favorably impressed. She was, moreover, industrious, ambitious, and well educated. Her age was about the same as his, so on the surface he thought that they should make a very good match. So be it.

In the meantime, however, he had opened a correspondence with another whom he had met on his trip the winter before where she had been teaching in a coal mining town south of Chicago. The same had developed mutually, and he had found her agreeable and obviously eligible. Her father was a minister, a dispenser of the gospel, and while for reasons we will become acquainted with in due time, he had cultivated small acquaintance with preachers, he took only such slight consideration of the girl's father's profession that he had good cause to recall some time later.

About the time he was deeply engrossed in his correspondence with both the farmer's daughter and the young school teacher, he received a letter from a friend in Chicago introducing him to a lady friend of hers through mail. This one happened to be a maid on the Twentieth Century Limited, running between New York and Chicago. Well, Jean Baptiste was looking for a wife. Sentiment was in order, but it was with him, first of all, a business proposition. So be it. He would give her too a chance.

He was somewhat ashamed of himself when he addressed three letters when perhaps, he should have been addressing but one. It was not fair to either of the three, he guiltily felt; but, business was business with him.

From his friend's sister he received most delightful epistles, not altogether frivolous, with a great amount of common sense between the lines. But what was more to the point, her father was wealthy, and she must have some conception of what was required to accumulate and to hold. He rather liked her, it now seemed.

Now from the preacher's daughter he received also pleasing letters. Encouraging, but not to say unconventionally forward. He appreciated the fact that she was, a preacher's child, and naturally expected to conform to a certain custom.

But from New York he received the most encouragement. The position the maid held rather thrilled him. He loved the road — and she wrote such letters! It was plain to be seen here what the answer would be.

Which?

He borrowed ten thousand dollars, giving a mortgage

upon his land in security therefor. He purchased relinquishments upon three beautiful quarter sections of land in the county lying just to the west. The same, having to be homesteaded before title was acquired, had all ready been in part arranged for. His grandmother and sister were waiting to file on a place each — the third was for the bride-to-be. There remained a few weeks yet in which to make said selection; but, notwithstanding, all must be ready to make filing not later than the first day of October — and September at last arrived.

He became serious, then uneasy. Which? He wrote all three letters that would give either or all a right to hear the words from him, but did not say sufficient to any to give grounds for a possible breach of promise suit later.

He rather liked the girl whose father had made money. Yes, it so seemed — more than either of the other two. A match with her on the surface seemed more practical. But for some reason she did not reply within the time to the letter he had written her. Oh, if he could only have courted her; could have been in the position to have seen her of a warm night; to have said to her: "————." Poor Jean Baptiste your life might not have later come to what it did. . . .

He waited — but in vain. October was drawing dangerously near when at last he left for somewhere. Indeed he had not a complete idea where, but of one thing he had concluded, when he returned he would bring the bride-to-be.

At Omaha he made up his mind. The girl whose father had made money had had her chance and failed. He regretted it very much, but this was a business proposition, and he had two thousand dollars at stake that he would lose if he failed to get some one to file on that quarter section he had provided, on October first.

He was rather disturbed over the idea. He really would have preferred a little more sentiment — but time had become the expedient. "Of course," he argued, as he sped toward Chicago, "I'll be awfully good to the one I choose, so if it is a little out of the ordinary — why, I'll try to make up for it when she is mine."

With this consolation he arrived in Chicago, wishing that the girl who lived two hundred miles south of Omaha and whose father was well-to-do had replied to his letter. He really had chosen her out of the three. However, he resigned himself to the inevitable — one of the other two.

He left the train and boarded the South Side L. He got off again at Thirty-first Street, and found what he had always found before, State Street and Negroes. He was not interested in either this time. He had sent a telegram to New York from Omaha to the effect that he was headed for Chicago. It was to the maid, for she had drawn second choice. He planned to meet her at the number her dear friend — and the match maker, lived.

So it was to this number he now hurried.

"Oh, Mr. Baptiste," cried this little woman, whose name happened to be Rankin, and she was an old maid. She gave him her little hand, and was "delighted" to see him.

"And you've come! Miss Pitt will be so glad! She has talked of nobody but Mr. Baptiste this summer. Oh, I'm so glad you have come!" and she shook his hand again.

"I sent her a telegram that I was coming, and I trust she will let me know. . . ."

"She is due in tomorrow," cried their little friend, and her voice was like delicate music.

"I expect a telegram," he said evenly. "I am somewhat rushed."

"Indeed! But of course, you are a business man, Mr. Baptiste," chimed Miss Rankin with much admiration in her little voice. "How Miss Pitt will like you!"

Jean Baptiste smiled a smile of vanity. He was getting anxious to meet Miss Pitt himself — inasmuch as he expected to ask her to become his wife on the morrow.

"Ting-aling-aling!" went the bell on the street door, and little Miss Rankin rushed forth to open it.

"Special for Mr. Jean Baptiste," he heard and went to get it. After signing, he broke the seal a little nervously, and drawing the contents forth, read the enclosed message.

He sighed when it was over. Miss Pitt had been taken with a severe attack of neuralgia in New York, was indisposed and under the care of a physician, but would be in Chicago in six days. He studied the calendar on the wall. Six days would mean October second!

Too late, Miss Pitt, your chance is gone. And now we turn to the party of the third part who will follow us through our story.

From a painting by W. M. Farrow.

"MISS PITT WAS *SO* ANXIOUS TO MEET YOU AND I WAS, TOO, BECAUSE I THINK YOU AND HER WOULD LIKE EACH OTHER. SHE'S AN AWFULLY GOOD GIRL AND WILLING TO HELP A FELLOW."

CHAPTER III

"SHE will not be in tomorrow," said Baptiste, handing the letter to Miss Rankin.

"Oh, is that so!" cried Miss Rankin in a tone of deep disappointment, as she took the letter. "Now isn't that just too bad!"

"It is," agreed Baptiste. "I will not get to see her, since I shall have to return to the West not later than two or three days." He was extremely disappointed. He sat down with a sigh and rested his chin in his palm, looking before him thoughtfully.

"I'm sure sorry, so sorry," mused Miss Rankin abstractedly. "And you cannot possibly wait until next week?" she asked, anxiously.

He shook his head sadly.

"Impossible, absolutely impossible."

"It is certainly too bad. Miss Pitt was *so* anxious to meet you. And I was, too, because I think you and her would like each each other. She's an awfully good girl, and willing to help a fellow. Just the kind of a girl you need."

He shifted his position now and was absorbed in his thoughts. He had come back to his purpose. He was sorry for Miss Pitt; but he had also been sorry that Miss Grey had not answered his letter. . . . The association with neither, true, had developed into a love affair, so would not be hard to forget. He had agreed with himself that love was to come later. He had exercised discretion. Any one of the three was a desirable mate from a practical point of view. After marriage he was confident that they could conform sufficiently to each other's views to get along, perhaps be happy. Miss McCarthy was, in his opinion, the most intelligent of the three, as she had been to school and had graduated from college. He had confidence in education uplifting people; it made them more observing. It helped them morally. And with him this meant much. He was very critical when it came to morals. He had studied his race along this line, and he was very exacting; because, unfortunately as a whole their standard of morals were not so high as it should be. Of course he understood that the same began back in the time of slavery. They had not been brought up to a regard of morality in a higher sense and they were possessed with certain weaknesses. He was aware that in the days of slavery the Negro to begin with had had, as a rule only what he could steal, therefore stealing became a virtue. When accused as he naturally was sure to be, he had resorted to the subtle art of lying. So lying became an expedient. So it had gone. Then he came down to the point of physical morality.

The masters had so often the slave women, lustful by disposition, as concubine. He had, in so doing of course, mixed the races, Jean Baptiste knew until not more than one half of the entire race in America are without some trait of Caucasian blood. There had been no defense then, and for some time after. There was no law that exacted punishment for a master's cohabitation with slave women, so it had grown into a custom and was practiced in the South in a measure still.

So with freedom his race had not gotten away from these loose practices. They were given still to lustful, undependable habits, which he at times became very impatient with. His version was that a race could not rise higher than their morals. So in his business procedure of choosing a wife, one thing over all else was unalterable, she must be chaste and of high morals.

Orlean McCarthy, however she as yet appeared from a practical standpoint, could, he estimated rightly, boast of this virtue. No doubt she was equally as high in all other perquisites. But strangely he did not just wish to ask Miss McCarthy to become his wife. He could not understand it altogether. He was confident that no girl lived who perhaps was likely, as likely, to conform to his desires as she; but plan, do as he would, that lurking aversion still remained — infinitely worse, it grew to a fear.

He sighed perceptibly, and Miss Rankin, catching the same, was deeply sympathetic because she thought it was due to the disappointment he felt in realizing that he was not to see Miss Pitt on the morrow. She placed her arm gently about his shoulders, leaned her small head close to hio, and otrolrcd his hair with her other hand.

"Well," said he, after a time, and to himself, "I left the West to find a wife. I've lived out there alone long enough. I want a home, love and comfort and only a wife can bring that." He paused briefly in his mutterings. His face became firm. That will that had asserted itself and made him what he was today, became uppermost. He slowly let the sentiment out of him, which was at once mechanically replaced by a cold set purpose. He smiled then; not a sentimental smile, but one cold, hard, and singularly dry.

"Oh, by the way, Miss Rankin," he essayed, rising, apparently cheerful. "Do you happen to be acquainted with a family here by the name of McCarthy?"

"McCarthy?"

"Yes. I think the man's a preacher. A Rev. N. J. McCarthy, if I remember correctly." She looked up at him. Her face took on an expression of defined contempt as she grunted a reply.

"Humph!"

"Well . . ."

"Who doesn't know that old rascal!"

"Indeed!" he echoed, in affected surprise; but in the same instant he had a feeling that he was to hear just this. Still, he maintained his expression of surprise.

"The worst old rascal in the state of Illinois," she pursued with equal contempt.

"Oh, really!"

"Really — yes, *positively!*"

"I cannot understand?"

"Oh well," she emitted, vindictively. "You won't have to inquire far to get the record of N. J. McCarthy. Lordy, no! But now," she started with a heightening of color, "He's got a nice family. Two fine girls, Orlean and Ethel, and his wife is a good little soul, rather helpless and without the force a woman should have; but very nice. But that husband — forget him!"

"This is — er — rather unusual, don't you think?"

"Well, it is," she said. "One would naturally suppose that a man with such a family of moral girls as he has, would not be so — not because he is a preacher." She paused thoughtfully. "Because you know that does not count for a high morality always in our society. . . . But N. J. McCarthy has been like he is ever since I knew him. He's a rascal of the deep water if the Lord ever made one.

And such a hypocrite — there never lived! Added to it, he is the most pious old saint you ever saw! Looks just as innocent as the Christ — and treats his wife like a dog!"

"Oh, no!"

"No!" disdainfully. "Well, you'd better hush!" She paused again, and then as if having reconsidered she turned and said: "I'll not say any more about him. Indeed, I don't like to discuss the man even. He is the very embodiment of rascalism, deceit and hypocrisy. Now, I've said enough. Be a good boy, go out and buy me some cream." And smilingly she got his hat and ushered him outside.

"Well, now what do you think of that," he kept repeating to himself, as he went for the ice cream, "*what do you think of that?*" Suddenly he halted, and raised his hands to his head. He was thinking, thinking, thinking deeply, reflectively. His mind was going back, back, away back into his youth, his earliest youth — no! It was going — had gone back to his childhood!

"N. J. McCarthy, *N. J. McCarthy?* Where did *I know you!* Where, where, *where!*" His head was throbbing, his brain was struggling with something that happened a long time before. A saloon was just to his left, and into it he turned. He wanted to think; but he *didn't* want to think too fast. He took a glass of beer. It was late September, but rather warm, and when the cold beverage struck his throat, his mind went back into its yesterdays.

It had happened in the extremely southern portion of the state, in that part commonly referred to as "Egypt," where he then lived. He recalled the incident as it occurred about twenty years before, for he was just five years of age at the time. His mother's baby boy they called him, because he was the youngest of four boys in a large family of children. It was a day in the autumn. He was sure of this because his older brothers had been hunting; they had caught several rabbits and shot a few partridges. He had been allowed to follow for the first time, and had carried the game. . . . How distinctly it came back to him now.

He had picked the feathers from the quail, and had held the rabbits while his brothers skinned them. And, later, they had placed the game in cold water from their deep well, and had thereupon placed the pan holding the same upon the roof of the summer kitchen, and that night the frost had come. And when morning was again, the ice cold water had drawn the blood from the meat of the game, and the same was clear and white.

" Now, young man," his mother said to him the following morning, " you will get into clean cothes and stay clean, do you understand? "

" Yes, mama, I understand," he answered. " But, mama, why? " he inquired. Jean Baptiste had always asked such questions and for his doing so his mother had always rebuked him.

" You will ask the questions, my son," she said, raising his child body in her arms and kissing him fondly. " But I don't mind telling you." She stood him on the ground then, and pointed to him with her forefinger. " Because we are going to have company from town. Big people. The preachers. Lots of them, so little boys should be good, and clean, and be scarce when the preachers are around. They are big men with no time, or care, to waste with little boys! "

" M-um! " he had chimed.

" And, why, mama, do the preachers have no time for little boys? Were they not little boys once themselves? "

" Now, Jean! " she had admonished thereupon, " you are entirely too inquisitive for a little boy. There will be other company, also. Teachers, and Mrs. Winston, do you understand! So be good." With that she went about her dinner, cooking the rabbits and the quail that he had brought home the day before.

It had seemed an age before, in their spring wagon followed by the lumber wagon, the dignitaries of the occasion wheeled into the yard. He could not recall now how many preachers there were, except that there were many. He was in the way, he recalled, however, because, unlike his other brothers, he was not bashful. But the preachers did not seem to see him. They were all large and tall and stout, he could well remember. But the teachers took notice of him. One had caught him up fondly, kissed him and thereupon carried him into the house in her arms. She talked with him and he with her. And he could well recall that she listened intently to all he told her regarding his adventures of the day before in the big woods that was at their back. How beautiful and sweet he had thought she was. When she smiled she showed a golden tooth, something new to him, and he did not understand except that it was different from anything he had ever seen before.

After a long time, he thought, dinner was called, and, as was the custom, he was expected to wait. He had very often tried to reason with his mother that he could sit at the corner of the table in a high chair and eat out of a saucer. He had promised always to be good, just as good as he could be, and he would not talk. But his mother would not trust him, and it was understood that he should wait.

At the call of dinner he slid from the teacher's lap upon the floor and went outside. He peeped through the window from where he stood on a block. He saw them eat, and eat, and eat, He saw the quail the boys had shot disappear one after another into the mouths of the big preachers, and since he had counted and knew how many quail there were, he had watched with a growing fear. "Will they not leave one?" he cried.

At last, when he could endure it no longer, he ran into the house, walked into the dining room unseen, and stood looking on. Now, the teacher who had the golden tooth happened to turn and espy him and thereupon she cried:

"Oh, there is my little man, and I know he is hungry! Where did you go, sweet one? Come, now, quick to me," whereupon she held out loving arms into which he went and he had great difficulty in keeping back the tears. But he was hungry, and he had seen the last quail taken from the plate by a preacher who had previously taken two.

Upon her knee she had sat him, and he looked up into all the faces about. He then looked down into her plate and saw a half of quail. His anxious eyes found hers, and then went back to the plate and the half of quail thereon.

"That is for you, sweetness," she cried, and began to take from the table other good things, while he fell to eating, feeding his mouth with both hands for he was never before so hungry.

After a few moments he happened to lift his eyes from the plate. Just to the side of the beloved teacher, he observed a large, tall and stout preacher. He wore a jet black suit and around his throat a clerical vest fit closely; while around his neck he wore a white collar hind part before. The preacher's eyes had found Jean's and he gave a start. The eyes of the other were upon him, and they were angry eyes. He paused in his eats and gazed not understanding, into the eyes that were upon him. Then suddenly he recalled that he had observed that the preacher had been smiling upon the teacher. He had laughed and joked; and said many things that little Jean had not understood. As far as he could see, it appeared as if the teacher had not wished it; but the flirtation had been kept up.

At last, in his child mind he had understood. His crawling upon the teacher's lap had spoiled it all! The preacher was angry, therefore the expression in his eyes.

From across the table his mother stood observing him. She seemed not to know what to say or do, for it had always been so very hard to keep this one out of grown people's way. So she continued to stand hesitatingly.

"Didn't your mother say that you were to wait," growled the preacher, and his face was darker by the anger that was in it. This frightened Jean. He could find no answer in the moment to such words. His little eyes had then sought those of the teacher, who in reply drew him closely to her.

"Why, Reverend," she cried, amazed, "he's a little boy, a nice child, and hungry!" Whereupon she caressed him again. He was pacified then, and his eyes held some fire when he found the preacher's again. The others, too, had grown more evil. The preacher's lips parted. He leaned slightly forward as he said lowly, angrily:

"You're an impudent, ill mannered little boy, and you need a spanking!"

Then suddenly the child grew strangely angry. He couldn't understand. Perhaps it was because he had helped secure the quail, all of which the preachers were eating, and felt that in view of this he was entitled to a piece of one. He could not understand afterward how he had said it, but he extended his little face forward, close to the preacher's, as he poured:

"I ain't no impudent 'ittle boy, either! I went to hunt with my brothers yistidy and I carried all the game, and now you goin' eat it all and leave me none when I'm hungry. You're mean man and make me mad!"

As he spoke everything seemed to grow dark around him. He recalled that he was suddenly snatched from the teacher's lap, and carried to the summer kitchen which was all closed and dark inside. He recalled that switches were there, and that soon he felt them. As a rule he cried and begged before he was ever touched; but strangely then he never cried, and he never begged. He just kept his mouth shut tightly, and had borne all the pain inflicted by his mother, and she had punished him longer than she had ever done before. Perhaps it was because she felt she had to make him cry; felt that he *must* cry else he had not repented. After a time he felt terribly dazed, became sleepy, and gradually fell into a slumber while the blows continued to fall.

How long he slept he could not remember, but gradually he came out of it. There were no more blows then. Yet, his little body felt sore all over. When he looked up (for he was lying on his back in the summer kitchen), his mother sat near and was crying and wiping the tears with her apron, while over him bent the teacher, and she was crying also. And as the tears had fallen unchecked upon his face he had heard the teacher saying:

"It's a shame, an awful shame! The poor, poor little fellow! He was hungry and had helped to get the game. And to be punished so severely because he wanted to eat is a shame! Oh, Mrs. Baptiste, you must pray to your God for forgiveness!" And his mother had cried more than ever then.

Presently he heard a heavy footfall, and peeped upward to see his father standing over him. His father was fair of complexion, and unlike his mother, never said much and was not commonly emotional.   But when he was angry he was terrible, and he was angry now.   His blue eyes shone like fire.

" What is this, Belle," he cried in a terrible voice, " you've killed my boy about that d—n preacher ! "   His father stooped and looked closely into his face.   In fear he had opened his eyes.   " Jean ! " he heard his father breathe, " God, but it's a blessing you are alive, or there would be a dead preacher in that house."

" Oh, Fawn," his mother cried and fell on him, weeping. The teacher joined in to pacify him, and in that moment Jean was forgotten.   Stiffly he had slipped from the room, and had gone around near the kitchen step of the big house to a place where the dogs had their bed.   Here he kept a heavy green stick, a short club.   He passed before the door, and observed the preacher still sitting at the table, talking with Mrs. Winston.   He glared at him a moment and his little eyes narrowed to mere slits.   Then he thought of something else . . . It was Mose Allen, Mose Allen, a hermit who lived in the woods.   It was miles — in his mind — to where Mose lived, through heavy forests and timber ; but he was going there, he was going there to stay with old Mose and live in the woods.   He had done nothing wrong, yet had been severely punished.   Before this he had thought several times that when he became a man he would like to be a preacher, a big preacher, and be admired ; but, now — never !   He would go to old Mose Allen's, live in the woods — and hate preachers forever !

Later, deep into the forest he plodded.   Deep, deeper, until all about him he was surrounded with overgrowth, but resolutely he struggled onward.   He crossed a branch presently, and knew where he was.   The branch divided their land with Eppencamp's, the German.   From there the forest grew deeper, the trees larger, and the underbrush more tangled. But he was going to Mose Allen and remembered that that was the way. He grasped his green club tighter and felt like a hunter in the bear stories his big brothers had read to him. He crossed a raise between the branch and the creek where the water flowed deeply, and where they always went fishing. He paused upon reaching the creek, for there a footlog lay. For the first time he experienced a slight fear. He didn't like foot logs, and had never crossed one alone. He had always been carried across by his brothers; but his brothers were not near, and he was running away! So he took courage, and approached the treacherous bridge. He looked down at the whirling waters below with some awe; but finally with a grimace, he set his foot on the slick trunk of the fallen tree and started across. He recalled then that if one looked straight ahead and not down at the water, it was easy; but his mind was so much on the waters below. He kept his eyes elsewhere with great effort, and finally reached the middle. Now it seemed that he could not go one step further unless he saw what was below him. He hesitated, closed his eyes, and thought of the whipping he had received and the preacher he hated, opened them, and with calm determination born of anger, crossed safely to the other side.

He sighed long and deeply when he reached the other side. He looked back at the muddy waters whirling below, and with another sigh plunged into the forest again and on toward Mose Allen's.

He gained the other side of the forest in due time, and came into the clearing. A cornfield was between him and another forest, and almost to the other side of this Mose Allen lived. The sun was getting low, and the large oaks behind him cast great shadows that stretched before him and far out into the cornfield. He thought of ghosts and hurried on. He must reach Mose Allen's before night, that was sure.

It was a long way he thought when he reached the other side, and the forest before him appeared ominous. He was inclined to be frightened, but when he looked toward the west and home he saw that the sun had sunk and he plunged grimly again into the deep woodland before him.

Now the people of the neighborhood had made complaints, and it was common talk about the country, that chickens, and young pigs, and calves had been attacked and destroyed by something evil in the forests. At night this evil spirit had stolen out and ravaged the stock and the chickens.

Accordingly, those interested had planned a hunt for what was thought to be a catamount. It was not until he had gone deeply into the woods, and the darkness was everywhere about him, that he remembered the catamount. He stopped and tried to pick the briers out of his bleeding hands, and as he did so, he heard a terrible cry. He went cold with fear. He hardly dared breathe, and crouched in a hole he had found where only his shoulders and head were exposed. He awaited with abated breath for some minutes and was about to venture out when again the night air and darkness was rent by the terrible cry. He crouched deeper into the hole and trembled, for the noise was drawing nearer. On and on it came. He thought of a thousand things in one minute, and again he heard the cry. It was very near now, and he could hear the crunch of the animal's feet upon the dry leaves. And still on and on it came. Presently it was so close that he could see it. The body of the beast became dimly outlined before him and he could see the eyes plainly, as it swung its head back and forth, and its red eyes shone like coals of fire. Again the varmint rent the night air with its yell, as it espied its prey crouching in the hole.

By watching the eyes he observed the head sink lower and lower until it almost touched the earth. And thereupon he became suddenly calm and apprehensive. He held his breath and met it calmly, face to face. His club was drawn, his eyes were keen and intense. He waited. Suddenly the air was rent with another death rendering cry, and the beast sprung.

It had reckoned well, but so had he. He had, moreover, struck direct. The blow caught the beast on the point of its nose and muffled and spoiled its directed spring. He quickly came out of the hole and then, before the animal could get out of his reach, he struck it again with such force at the back of the head, that the beast was stunned. Again and again he struck until the head was like a bag of bones. When his strength was gone, and all was quiet, he became conscious of a drowsiness. He sank down and laid his head upon the body of the dead animal, and fell into a deep sleep.

And there they found him during the early hours of the morning and took him and the dead catamount home.

"Another beer, Cap'n?" he heard from the bartender. He quickly stood erect and gazed about in some confusion.

"Yes," he replied, throwing a coin upon the bar. He drank the beer quickly, went out, bought Miss Rankin the cream and after delivering it to her, went outside again and up State Street.

He was overcome with memories, was Jean Baptiste. He had a task to accomplish. He was going to Vernon Avenue where Miss McCarthy lived to ask her to become his wife.

And the preacher who had been the cause of his severe punishment twenty years before was her father, the Rev. N. J. McCarthy.

CHAPTER IV

ORLEAN

"OH, MAMA," cried Orlean E. McCarthy, coming hastily from the hallway into the room where her mother sat sewing, and handing her a note, "Mr. Baptiste is in the city and wishes to call at the earliest possible convenience."

"Indeed," replied her mother, affecting a serious expression, "this is rather sudden. Have you sent him word when he could?"

"Yes, mama, I wrote him a note and returned it by the boy that brought this one, that he could call at two o'clock." Her mother's gaze sought the clock automatically.

"And it is now past one," she replied. "You will have to get ready to receive him," she advised ceremoniously.

"All right, mama," said Orlean cheerfully, and suddenly bending forward, kissed her mother impulsively upon the cheek, and a moment later hurried upstairs.

"What is this I hear about somebody coming to call," inquired another, coming into the room at that moment. Mrs. McCarthy looked up on recognizing the voice of her younger daughter, Ethel, who now stood before her. She gave a perceptible start as she did so, and swallowed before she replied. In the meantime the other stood. regarding her rather severely, as was her nature.

She was very tall, was Ethel, and because she was so very thin she appeared really taller than she was. She did

174

not resemble her mother, who was a dumpy light brown skinned woman. She was part Indian, and possessed a heavy head of hair which, when let down, fell over her shoulders.

Ethel, on the other hand, was somewhat darker, had a thin face, with hair that was thick, but rather short and bushy. Her eyes were small and dark, out of which she never seemed to look straight at one. They appeared always to be lurking and without any expression, unless it was an expression of dislike. Forsooth, she was a known disagreeable person, ostentatious, pompous, and hard to get along with.

She was a bride of a few weeks and was then resting after a short honeymoon spent in Racine, Wisconsin, sixty miles north of Chicago.

"Why, Mr. Baptiste is coming. Coming to call on your sister. He has been corresponding with her for some time, you understand," her mother returned in her mild, trained manner.

"Oh!" echoed Ethel, apparently at a loss whether to be pleased, or displeased. She was as often one way as the other, so her mother was apprehensive of something more.

"I think you have met him, have you not?" her mother inquired.

"Yes, I've met him," admitted Ethel. "Last winter while teaching."

"And what do you think of him, my dear?"

"Well, he has some ways I don't like."

"What ways, please?" She had started to say "naturally" but thought better of it.

"Oh, he does not possess the dignity I like in a man. Struck me as much too commonplace."

"Oh," her mother grunted. She was acquainted with

Ethel's disposition, which was extremely vain. She loved pomp and ceremony, and admired very few people.

"What's he calling to see Orlean for?"

Her mother looked up in some surprise. She regarded her daughter keenly. "Why, my dear! Why do you ask such a question! Why do young men call to see any young ladies?" Both turned at this moment to see Orlean coming down the stairway, and attention was fastened upon her following.

"All 'dolled' up to meet your farmer," commented Ethel with a touch of envy in her voice. In truth she was envious. Her husband was just an ordinary fellow — that is, he was largely what she was making of him. It was said that she had found no other man who was willing to tolerate her evil temper and that, perhaps, was why she had married him. While with him, he had been anxious to marry her to satisfy his social ambition. Although an honest, hardworking fellow, he had come of very common stock. From the backwoods of Tennessee where his father had been a crude, untrained preacher, he had come to Chicago and had met and married her after a courtship of six years.

"You look very nice, my dear," said her mother, addressing Orlean. Between the two children there was a great difference. Although older, Orlean was by far the more timid by disposition. An obedient girl in every way, she had never been known to cross her parents, and had the happy faculty of making herself generally liked, while Ethel invited disfavor.

She was not so tall as Ethel, and while not as short as her mother, she was heavier than either. She was the image of her father who was dark, although not black. After her mother she had taken her hair, which, while not as fine, was nevertheless heavy, black and attractive. Her eyes were dark like her mother's, which were coal black. They were small and tender. Her expression was very frank; but she had inherited her mother's timidity and was subservient unto her father, and in a measure unto her younger sister, Ethel.

She was a year older than the man who was coming to see her, and had never had a beau.

"Do I look all right, mama?" she asked, turning so that she might be seen all around.

"Yes, my dear," the other replied. She always used the term "my dear." She had been trained to say that when she was a young wife, and had never gotten out of the habit.

"Now sit down, my daughter," she said judiciously, "and before the young man comes to call on you, tell me all about him."

"Yes, and leave out nothing," interposed Ethel.

"She is talking to your mother, Ethel. You will do her a favor by going to your room until it is over," advised their mother.

"Oh, well, if I'm not wanted, then I'll go," spit out Ethel wickedly, whereupon she turned and hastened up the stairs to her room and slammed the door behind her.

"Ethel has such a temper," her mother sighed deploringly. "She is so different from you, dear. You are like your mother, while she — well, she has her father's ways."

"Papa is not as mean as Ethel," defended Orlean, ever obedient to her mother, yet always upholding her father, it mattered not what the issue.

Her mother sighed again, shifted in her chair, and said no more on that subject. She knew the father better than Orlean, and would not argue. She had been trained not to. . . .

"Now where did you meet Mr. Baptiste, my dear?" she began.

"Where I taught last winter, mother," she replied obediently.

"And how did you come to meet him, daughter?"

"Why, he was calling on a girl friend of mine, and I happened along while he was there, and the girl introduced us."

"M-m. Was that the first time you had seen him?"

"No, I had met him on the street when he was on the way down there."

"I see. Did he speak to you on the street?"

"Oh, no, mother. He did not know me."

"But he might have spoken anyhow. . . ."

"But he was a gentleman, and he never spoke." She paused briefly, and then, her voice a trifle lower, said: "Of course he looked at me. But —"

"Well, any man would do that. We must grant that men are men. How were you impressed with him when you met him later at this friend's house?"

"Well, I don't know," returned Orlean hesitatingly. "He seemed to be a great talker, was very commonplace, dressed nicely but not showily. He knew quite a few people in Chicago that we know, and was born near the town in which I met him. He was just returning from New York, and — well, I rather admired him. He is far above the average colored man, I can say."

"M-m," her mother mused thoughtfully, and with an air of satisfaction. She couldn't think of anything more to say just then, and upon looking at the clock which showed ten minutes of two, she said: "Well, you had better go in the parlor, and after he has called, when convenient, call me and permit me to meet him. You will be careful, my dear, and understand that we have raised you to be a lady, and exercise your usual dignity."

" Yes, mama."

On the hour the street door bell was pulled with a jerk, and arising, Orlean went toward the door expectantly.

" Oh, how do you do," she cried, a moment later, her face lighted with a radiant smile as she extended her hand and allowed it to rest in that of Jean Baptiste's.

" Miss McCarthy," he cried, with her hand in one of his, and his hat in the other, he entered the door.

" May I take your hat? " asked Orlean, and taking it, placed it on the hall tree. In the meantime, his habitually observing eyes were upon her, and when she turned she found him regarding her closely.

" Come right into the parlor, please, Mr. Baptiste, and be seated." She hesitated between the davenport and the chairs; while he, without ado, chose the davenport and became seated, and the look he turned upon her commanded more than words that she, too, be seated. With a little hesitation, she finally sank on the davenport at a conventional distance, beside him.

" I was not certain, judging by your last letter, just when you would get here," she began timidly. He regarded her out of his searching eyes attentively. He was weighing her in the balance. He saw in those close glances what kind of a girl she was, apparently, for, after a respite, he relaxed audibly, but kept his eyes on her nevertheless.

" I was not certain myself," he said. " I am so rushed these days that I do not know always just what comes next. But I am glad that I am here at last — and to see you looking so well."

They exchanged the usual words about the weather, and other conventional notes, and then she called her mother.

"Mama, I wish you to meet Mr. Baptiste. Mr. Baptiste, this is my mother."

"Mr. Baptiste," said her mother, giving him her hand, "I am glad to know you."

"The same here, madam," he returned cheerfully. "Guess your health is good!"

"Very good, I'm glad to say."

They talked for a time, and all were cheered to find themselves so agreeable.

"I think I can slightly recall your people, Mr. Baptiste," her mother remarked, thoughtfully. "My husband, Dr. McCarthy," she said, giving him an honorary term, "pastored the church in the town near where you were born, many years ago."

"I do say," he echoed non-commitally.

"Do you recall it?" she asked.

He appeared to be thinking. . . . He hardly knew what to say, then, after some deliberation he brightened and said: "I think I do. I was very young then, but I think I do recall your husband. . . ."

"Your name — the name of your family has always remained in my mind," said she then, reflectively.

"Indeed. It is a rather peculiar name."

"It is so, I should say," she cried. "If it is quite fair, may I ask where or how your father came by such a name?"

"Oh, it is very simple. My father, of course, was born a slave like most — almost all Negroes previous to the war — and took the name from his master who I suppose was of French descent."

"Oh, that explains it. Of course that is natural. M-m; but it's a beautiful name, I must say."

He smiled.

" It is an illustrious name, also," she commented further.

" But the man who carries it in this instance, is much to the contrary notwithstanding," he laughed depreciatingly.

" It is a very beautiful day without, my dear," she said, addressing her daughter, " and perhaps Mr. Baptiste might like to walk out and see some of the town."

" I most assuredly would," he cried, glad of something for a change. He was restless, and estimated that if he felt the air, with her at his side, it might help him.

Orlean arose, went upstairs, and returned shortly wearing a large hat that set off her features. He rather liked her under it, and when they walked down the street together, he was conscious of an air of satisfaction.

" Where would you like to go? " she asked as they neared the intersection.

" For a car ride on the elevated," he replied promptly.

" Then we will go right down this street. This is Thirty-third, and there's an elevated station a few blocks from here."

They walked along leisurely, she listening attentively, while he talked freely of the West, his life there and what he was doing. When they reached the L. he assisted her upstairs to the station, and in so doing touched her arm for the first time. The contact gave him a slight sensation but he felt more easy when they had entered the car and taken a seat together. A moment later they were gazing out over the great city below as the cars sped through the air.

It was growing dark when they returned, and she invited him to dinner. He accepted and thereupon met Ethel and her husband.

Ethel was all pomp and ceremony, while her husband, with his cue from her, acted in the same manner, and they rather bored Jean Baptiste with their airs. He was glad

when the meal was over. He followed Orlean back to the
parlor, where they took a seat on the davenport again, and
drew closer to her this time. Soon she said: "Do you
play?"

"Lord, no!" he exclaimed; "but I shall be glad to listen
to you."

"I can't play much," she said modestly; "but I will
play what little I know." Thereupon she became seated
and played and sang, he thought, very well. After she
had played a few pieces, she turned and looked up at him,
and he caught the full expression of her eyes. He could
see that they were tender eyes; eyes behind which there was
not apparently the force of will that he desired; but Orlean
McCarthy was a fine girl. She was fine because she was
not wicked; because she was intelligent and had been carefully reared; she was fine because she had never cultivated
the society of undesirable or common people; but she was
not a fine girl because she had a great mind, or great
ability; or because she had done anything illustrious. And
this Jean Baptiste, a judge of human nature could readily
see; but he would marry her, he would be good to her; and
she would, he hoped, never have cause to regret having
married him. And thereupon he bent close to her, took
her chin in his hand and kissed her upon the lips. She
turned away when he had done this. In truth she was
not expecting such from him and knew not just how to
accept it. Her lips burned with a new sensation; she had
a peculiar feeling about the heart. She arose and went to
the piano and her fingers wandered idly over the keys as
she endeavored to still her beating heart.

Shortly she felt his hand upon her shoulder and she
turned to hear him say:

" Won't you come back into the parlor?   I — would like
to speak to you? "

She consented without hesitation, and arising followed
him timidly back to the seat they had occupied a few minutes
before. Again seated he drew closely but did not deign
to place his arm about her, looked toward the rear of the
house where the others were, and, seeing that the doors
were closed between them, sighed lightly and turned to her.

" Now, Miss McCarthy," he began, evenly. " I am going
to say something to you that I have never said to a woman
before." He paused while she waited with abated breath.

" I haven't known you long; but that is not the point.
What I should say is, that in view of our brief correspondence, it will perhaps appear rather bold of me to say
what I wish to. Yet, there comes a time in life when circumstances alter cases.

" Now, to be frank, I have always regarded matrimony as
a business proposition, and while sentiment is a very great
deal in a way, business considerations should be the first
expedient." She was all attention. She was peculiarly
thrilled. It was wonderful to listen to him, she thought,
and not for anything would she interrupt him. But *what*
did he mean; what was he *going* to say.

" Well, I, Miss McCarthy, need a wife. I want a wife;
but my life has not been lived where social intercourse with
girls of my race has been afforded, as you might understand." She nodded understandingly, sympathetically.
Her woman's nature was to sympathize, and what she did
was only natural with all women.

" It has not been my privilege to know any girl of my
race intimately; I am not, as I sit here beside you able to
conscientiously, or truly, go to one and say: ' I love you,

dear, and want you to be my wife,' in the conventional sense. Therefore, can I be forgiven if I say to you; if I ask you, Miss McCarthy," and so saying, he turned to her, his face serious, " to become my wife? "

He had paused, and her soul was afire. Was *this* a proposal or was it a play? For a time she was afraid to say anything. She wouldn't say no, and she was afraid to say yes, until — well, until she was positive that he had actually asked her to marry him. As it was, she hesitated. But it was so wonderful she thought. It was so beautiful to be so near such a wonderful young man, such a strong young man. The young men she had known had not been like this one. And, really, she wanted to marry. She was twenty-six, and since her sister had married, she had found life lonely. To be a man's wife and go and live alone with him must be wonderful. She was a reader, and he had sent her books. In all books and life and everything there was love. And love always had its climax in a place where one lived alone with a man. Oh, glorious! She was *ready to listen to anything he had to say.*

" Now, I do not profess love to you, Miss McCarthy, in trying to make this clear. I could not, and be truthful. And I have always tried to be truthful. Indeed, I could not feel very happy, I am sure, unless I was truthful. To pretend that which I am not is hypocrisy, and I despise a hypocrite. I am an owner of land in the West, and I believe you will agree with me, that it behooves any Negro to acquire all he can. We are such a race of paupers! We own so little, and have such little prestige. Thankfully, I am at present, on the high road to success, and, because of that, I want a wife, a dear, kind girl as a mate, the most natural thing in the world." She nodded unaware. What he was saying had not been said to her in that way; but the way he said it was so much to the point. She had not been trained to observe that which was practical; indeed, her father was regarded as a most impractical man; but she liked this man beside her now, and was anxious for him to go on. He did.

"I own 520 acres of very valuable land, and have consummated a deal for 480 more acres. This land is divided into tracts of 160 acres each, and must be homesteaded before the same is patented.

"Now, my grandmother, and also a sister are already in the West, and will homestead on two places. The other, I have arranged for you. The proceeding is simple. It will be necessary only for you to journey out West, file on this land as per my directions, after which we can be married any time after, and we can then live together on your claim. Do you understand?"

"I think so," she said a bit falteringly.

"Now, my dear, do not feel that I am a charter barterer; we can simply acquire a valuable tract of land by this process and be as we would under any other circumstances. Once you were out there all would be very plain to you, but at this distance, it is perhaps foreign to you, that I understand."

She looked up into his face trustingly. Right then she wanted him to kiss her. It was all so irregular; but he was a man and she a maid, and she had never had a love. . . . He seemed to understand, and passionately he caught her to him, and kissed her many, many times.

It was all over then, as far as she was concerned. She had not said yes or no with words, but her lips had been her consent, and she knew she would love him. It was the happiest hour in the simple life she had lived, and she was ready to become his forever.

CHAPTER V

A PROPOSAL; A PROPOSITION; A CERTAIN MRS. PRUITT —
AND A LETTER

"OH, MAMA, Mr. Baptiste has asked me to marry him," cried Orlean, rushing into the room and to the bed where her mother lay reading, after Jean Baptiste had left.

"Why, my child, this — this is rather sudden, is it not? Mr. Baptiste has known you only a few months and has been corresponding with you just a little while," her mother said with some excitement, suddenly sitting erect in the bed.

"Yes, mama, what you say is true, but he explained. He said — well, I can't quite explain, but he — he wants to marry me, mama, and you know — well, mama, you understand, don't you?"

"Yes, I understand. All girls want husbands, but it must be regular. So take off your clothes, dear, get into bed and tell me just what Mr. Baptiste did say."

The other did as instructed, and as best she could, tried to make plain what Jean had said to her regarding the land and all. She didn't make it very plain, and the matter rather worried her, but the fact that he had asked her to marry him, was uppermost in her mind, and she finally went to sleep happier than she had ever been in her life before.

"Now, when the young man calls today, you will have him take his business up with me," her mother instructed judiciously the following morning.

"He will explain it all, mama. He can do so very easily," she said, glad to be relieved of the difficult task. Yet she had her worries withal. Her mother was a very difficult person to explain anything to; besides, Orlean knew her mother was in constant fear of her father who was a Presiding Elder, traveling over the southern part of the state, and who came into the city only every few months. And if her mother was hard to make understand anything, her father was worse — and business, he knew next to nothing about although he was then five and fifty.

Jean Baptiste had accomplished a great many more difficult tasks than explaining to his prospective mother-in-law in regard to the land. When she seemed to have sensed what it all meant, he observed that she would give a peculiar little start, and he would have to try it all over again. In truth she understood better than she appeared to; but it was the girl's father whom she feared to anger — for in all her life she had never been able to please him.

But she found a way out along late that afternoon when a caller was announced.

The visitor was a woman possessed of rare wits, and of all the people that Mrs. McCarthy disliked, and of all who disliked Mrs. McCarthy, Mrs. Pruitt was the most pronounced. Yet, it was Mrs. Pruitt who settled the difficulty and saved the day for Orlean and Jean Baptiste. But as to why Mrs. Pruitt should dislike Mrs. McCarthy, and Mrs. McCarthy should dislike Mrs. Pruitt, there is a story that was known among all their friends and acquaintances.

When Miss Rankin had said what she did about Rev. N. J. McCarthy, she had not told all, nor had she referred to any woman in particular. She was not a scandal monger. But she knew as all Chicago knew, that in so far as the parties in question were concerned there was a friendship between Mrs. Pruitt and the Reverend that was rather subtle, and had been for years. And it was this which caused the two mentioned to dislike each other with an unspoken hatred.

But Mrs. McCarthy trusted Orlean's going eight hundred miles west to file on a homestead, and what might come of it, to Mrs. Pruitt rather than to herself. While she could — was aware of it — she did not dare venture anything to the contrary where it might come back to her husband's ears, she knew Mrs. Pruitt had more influence with her husband than had she. . . . Therefore when she invited Jean Baptiste to meet Mrs. Pruitt, who had met him years before, she breathed a sigh of relief.

It was over in a few hours. Mrs. Pruitt would accompany Orlean to the West and back, with Jean Baptiste paying expenses, and preparations were made thereto.

In two days they had reached Gregory where the great land excitement was on. From over all the country people had gathered, and the demand for the land had reached its greatest boom since Jean Baptiste had come to the country.

His sister and grandmother had arrived during his absence, and, after greeting them, he was handed a letter, which read:

My dear Mr. Baptiste:

Your most delightful letter was received by me today, and that you may see just how much I appreciate it, I am answering at *once* and hope you will receive the same real soon.

To begin with: the reason I have not answered sooner is quite obvious. I was away on a short visit, and only returned home today, to find that your *most* interesting letter had been here several days.   Think of it, and I would have given most *anything* to have had it sooner.

Well, in reference to what you intimated in your letter regarding the land up there, I am deeply interested.   Nothing strikes my fancy so much as homesteading — which I think you meant.   I would the best in the world like to hold down a claim, and am sure I would make a great homesteader.   But why write more! An hour with you will explain matters more fully than a hundred letters, so I will close with this : You hinted about coming down, and my invitation is to do so, and do so at *your earliest possible convenience.*   I am waiting with great anxiety your honored appearance.

In the meantime, trusting that you are healthy, hopeful and happy, please believe me to be,

Cordially, sincerely — and anxiously yours,

Irene Grey.

He regarded the letter a little wistfully, and the next moment tore it to bits, flung it to the winds, and went about his business.

CHAPTER VI

THE PRAIRIE FIRE

"MY MOTHER grabbed me, kissed and hugged me
time and again when I returned," Jean Baptiste
read in the letter he received from his wife-to-be
a few days after she had returned to the windy city, and he
was satisfied. "She had been so worried, you see, because
she had written father nothing about it, and this was the
first time in her married life that she has dared do anything
without a long consultation with him. But she is glad I
went now, and thinks you are a very sensible fellow therefor. Papa sent a telegram advising that he had been reap-
pointed Presiding Elder over the same district, and would
come into Chicago for a few days before entering into another year of the work.

"I am deluged with questions regarding the West, and
it gives me a great deal of pleasure to explain everything,
and of the wonderful work you are doing. Now, papa will
be home in a few days, and, knowing how hard he is to
explain anything to, I am preparing myself for quite a
task. I will close now. With love and kisses to you, believe me to be,

> "Your own,
> "ORLEAN."

Jean now went about his duties. His sister and grandmother were with him, and he had planned to put them on
their claims at once, so as to enable them to prove up as

soon as possible. Therefore to their places he hauled lumber, coal and provisions. Their claims lay some forty-five miles to the northwest beyond the railroad which now had its terminus at Dallas. And, referring to that, we have not found occasion to mention what had taken place in the country in the two years passed.

When the railroad had missed Dallas and struck Gregory and the other two government townsites, Dallas was apparently doomed, and in a few months most of the business men had gone, and the business buildings, etc., had been moved to Gregory. This town, because of the fact that it was only five miles from the next county line — the county that had been opened and which contained the land that Jean Baptiste had secured for his relatives and bride — was, for a time, expected to become the terminus. And to this end considerable activity had transpired with a view to getting the heavy trade that would naturally come with the opening and settlement of the county west, which had twice the area of the county in which Gregory lay.

Now, it was shortly after the railroad was under course of construction that one, the chief promoter of the townsite, called on the " town Dad's " of Gregory with a proposition. The proposition was, in short, to move Dallas to Gregory, and thereupon combine in making Gregory a real city.

Unfortunately for Gregory, her leaders were men who had grown up in a part of the country where the people did not know all they might have known. They consisted in a large measure of rustic mountebanks, who, because, and only because, Gregory happened to have been in the direct line of the railroad survey, and had thereby secured the road, took unto themselves the credit of it all. So, instead of entertaining the offer in a logical, business and appreciative manner, gave the promoter the big haw! haw! and turned their backs to him.

There was a spell of inactivity for a time on the part of the said promoter. But in the fall, when the ground had frozen hard, and the corn was being gathered, all that was left in the little town of Dallas, laying beside the claim of Jean Baptiste, was suddenly hauled five miles west of the town of Gregory. And still before the Gregory illogics had time even to think clearly, business was going on in what they then chose to call New Dallas — and the same lay directly on the line of the two counties, and where the railroad survey ended.

It is needless to detail the excitement which had followed this. " Lies, lies, liars! " were the epithets hurled from Gregory. " The railroad is in Gregory to stay; to stay for "— oh, they couldn't say how many years, perhaps a hundred; but all that noise to the west was a bluff, a simon pure bluff, and that ended it. That is, until they started the same noise over again. But it had not been a bluff. The tracks had been laid from Gregory to Dallas early in the spring that followed, and now Dallas was *the* town instead of Gregory, and the boom that had followed the building of the town, is a matter never to be forgotten in the history of the country.

Gregory's one good fortune was that she had secured the land office which necessitated that all filings should be entered there, and in this way got more of the boom that was occasioned by the land opening at the west than it had expected to when the railroad company had pushed its way west out of the town.

It was about this time while great excitement was on and thousands of people were in the town of Dallas that something occurred that came near literally wiping that town off the map. Jean Baptiste had loaded his wagons and was on the way from his land to the claims of his sister when the same came to pass.

The greatest danger in a new country comes after the grass has died in the fall and before the new grass starts in the spring. But in the fall when the grass is dry and crisp, and the surface below is warm and dry, is the time of prairie fires. No time could have been more opportune for such an episode than the time now was. The wind had been blowing for days and days, and had made the short grass very brittle, and the surface below as hot as in July. Jean Baptiste was within about a mile of where New Dallas now reposed vaingloriously on a hillside, her many new buildings rising proudly, defiantly, as if to taunt and annoy Gregory, against the skyline, when with the wind greeting him, he caught the smell of burning grass. He reached a hillside presently, and from there he could see for miles to the west beyond, and the sight that met his gaze staggered him.

" A prairie fire," he cried apprehensively, and urged his teams forward toward Dallas. One glance had been sufficient to *convince* him what it might possibly mean. A prairie fire with the wind behind it as this was, would bid no good for Dallas, and once there he could be of a little service, since he knew how to fight it.

When he arrived at the outskirts of the embryo city, he was met by a frightened herd of humanity. With bags and trunks and all they could carry; with eyes wide, and mouths gaped, in terror they were hurrying madly from the town to an apparent place of safety — a plowed field nearby. Miles to the west the fire and smoke rose in great, dark reddened clouds, and cast — even at that distance, dark shadows over the little city. As he drew into the town, he could see a line of figures working at fire breaks before the gloom. They were the promoters and the townspeople, and he imagined how they must feel with death possible — and destruction, positive, coming like an angry beast directly upon them.

Soon, Jean Baptiste, with wet horse blankets, was with them on the firing line. The speed at which the wind was driving the fire was ominous. Soon all the west was as if lost in the conflagration, for the sun, shining out of a clear sky an hour before was now shut out as if clouds were over all. The dull roar and crackle of the burning grass brought a feeling of awe over all before it. The heat became, after a time, intense; the air was surcharged with soot, and the little army worked madly at the firebreaks.

Rolling, tumbling, twisting, turning, but always coming onward, the hurricane presently struck the fire guards. In that moment it was seen that a mass of thistles, dried manure, and all refuse from the prairie was sweeping before it, as if to draw the fire onward. The fire plunged over the guards as though they had not been made, pushed back the little army and rushed madly into the town.

It was impossible now to do more. The conflagration was beyond control. Now in the town, an effort was therefore made to get the people out of their houses where some had even hidden when it appeared that all would be swept away in the terrible deluge of fire. One, two, three, four, five, six — ten houses went up like chaff, and the populace groaned, when, of a sudden, something happened. Like Napoleon's army at Waterloo there was a quick change. One of those rare freaks — but what some chose to claim in after years as the will of the Creator in sympathy with the hopeful builders, the wind gradually died down, whipped around, and in less than five minutes, was blowing from the east, almost directly against its route of a few minutes before. The fire halted, seemed to hesitate, and then like some cowardly thing, turned around and started back of the same ground it had raged over where it lingered briefly, sputtered, flickered, and then quickly died. And the town, badly frightened, hard worked, but thankful withal, was saved.

CHAPTER VII

VANITY

"MY FATHER is home, and, oh! but he did carry on when he was informed regarding my trip West to take the homestead," Orlean wrote her betrothed in her next letter. "He was so much upset over it that he went out of the house and walked in the street for a time to still his intense excitement. When he returned, however, he listened to my explanation, and, after a time, I was pleased to note that he was pacified. And still later he was pleased, and when a half day had passed he was tickled to death.

"Of course I was relieved then also, and now I am fully satisfied. I have not written you as soon as I should have on this account. I thought it would be best to wait until papa had heard the news and was settled on the matter, which he now is. He has written you and I think you should receive the letter about the same time you will this. He has never been anxious in his simple old heart for me to marry, but of course he understands that I must some day, and now that I am engaged to you, he appears to be greatly pleased.

"By the way, I have not received the ring yet, and am rather anxious. Of course I wish to be quite reasonable, but on the whole, a girl hardly feels she's engaged until she is wearing the ring, you know. Write me a real sweet letter, and make it long. In the meantime remember me as one who thinks a great deal of you,

"From your fond,
"ORLEAN."

Baptiste heard from his father-in-law-to-be in due time, and read the letter carefully, replying to the same forthwith.

We should record before going further that the incident which had happened between them in his youth had been almost as completely buried as it had been before the day of its recent resurrection. In his reply he stated that he would come into the city Xmas, which meant of course, that they would meet and come to understand each other better. He was glad that the formalities were in part through with, and would be glad when it was over. He did not appreciate so much ado where so little was represented, as it were. He had it from good authority without inquiry that the Reverend McCarthy had never possessed two hundred dollars at one time in his life, and the formalities he felt compelled to go through with far exceeded that amount already. And with this in mind he began gathering his corn crop which he had been delayed in doing on account of the stress of other more urgent duties.

He had been at work but a few days when snow began to fall. For days it fell from a northwesterly direction, and then turning, for a week came from an easterly direction. This kept up until the holidays arrived, therefore most of the corn crop over all the country was caught and remained in the field all the winter through. By the hardest work his sister and grandmother succeeded in reaching his place from their homesteads, and stayed there while he went into Chicago.

" Mr. Baptiste, please meet my father," said Orlean when he called, following his arrival in the city again. He looked up to find a tall, dark but handsome old man extending his hand. He regarded him, studied him carefully in a flash, and in doing so his mind went back twenty years; to a memorable day when he had been punished and had followed it by running away. He extended his hand and grasped the other's, and wondered if he also remembered. . . . They exchanged greetings, and if the other recalled him, he gave no evidence of the fact in his expression.

When he had sat beside the teacher, such a long time before, Baptiste recalled now, that at the back of the other's head there had been a white spot where the hair was changing color; but now this spot spread over all the head, and the hair was almost as white as snow. With his dark skin, this formed a contrast that gave the other a distinguished appearance which was noticeably striking. But his eyes did not meet with Baptiste's favor, though he was not inclined to take this seriously. But as he continued to glance at him at times during the evening he did not fail to see that the other seemed never to look straight and frankly into his eyes; and there was in his gaze and expression when he met Baptiste,— so Baptiste thought — a peculiar lurking, as if some hidden evil were looking out of the infinite depths of the other's soul. It annoyed Baptiste because every time he caught the other's gaze he recalled the incident of twenty years before, and wanted to forget it; declared he would forget it, and to that task he set himself, and apparently succeeded while in the city.

With Ethel and her husband, whose name was Glavis, he never got along at all. Ethel was pompous, and known to be disagreeable; while Glavis was narrow, and a victim of his wife's temper and disposition. So unless the talk was on society and " big " Negroes, which positively did not interest Jean Baptiste, who was practical to the superlative, there was no agreement.

So when Jean Baptiste returned West, he was conscious of a great relief.

The severe winter passed at last and with early spring everybody completed the gathering of the corn and immediately turned to seeding their crops. Work was plentiful everywhere, and to secure men to complete gathering his crop of corn, Baptiste had the greatest difficulty. Stewarts had failed to secure any land at all — either of the four in the drawing, and, being unable to purchase relinquishments on even one quarter at the large sum demanded therefor, had gone toward the western part of the state and taken free homesteads. As for Agnes, she had apparently passed out of his life.

He labored so hard in the cold, wet muddy fields in trying to get his corn out that he was taken ill, and was not able to work at all for days, and while so, he wrote his fiancée his troubles; and that since he was so indisposed, with a world of work and expense upon him she would do him a great favor if she would consent to come to him and be married.

Now the McCarthys had given Ethel a big wedding although her husband received only thirteen dollars a week for his work. Two hundred dollars, so it was reported, had been expended on the occasion. Such display did not appeal to the practical mind of Jean. He had lived his life too closely in accomplishing his purpose to become at this late day a victim of such simple vanity; the ultra simple vanity of aping the rich. Upon this point his mind was duly set. The McCarthys had started to buy a home the summer before which was quite expensive, and had entered into the contract with a payment of three hundred dollars. The Reverend had borrowed a hundred dollars on his life insurance and paid this in, while Glavis had paid another. Ethel had used what money she had saved teaching, to expend in the big wedding, so Orlean had paid the other hundred out of the money she had saved teaching school.

Now, if there was any big wedding for Orlean, then he, Jean Baptiste, knew that he would be expected to stand the expense. Therefore, Baptiste tried to make plain to Orlean in his letters the gravity of his position. She would be compelled to establish residence on her homestead early in May, and this was April, or forfeit her right and sacrifice all he had put into it.

But Orlean became unreasonable — Jean Baptiste reasoned. She set forth that she did not think it right for her to go away out there and marry him; that he should come to her. She seemed to have lost sense of all he had written her, regarding the crops, responsibilities, and other considerations. He wrote her to place it up to her mother and father, which she did, to reply in the same tenor. They had not agreed to it, either. He replied then heatedly, and hinted that her father was not a business man else he would have realized his circumstances, and, as man to man, appreciated the same.

The next letter he received had enclosed the receipt for the first payment of the purchase price of six dollars an acre, a charge the government had made on the land, amounting to some $210, in the first payment. She released him from his promise — but kept the ring.

" Now, don't that beat the devil! " he exclaimed angrily, when he read the letter. " As though this receipt is worth anything to me; or that it would suffice to get back the

$2,000 I paid the man for the relinquishment. The only thing that will suffice is, for her to go on the land, so I guess I'll have to settle this nuisance at once by going to Chicago and marrying her."

So he started for the Windy City.

At Omaha he sent a telegram to her to the effect that he was on the way, and would arrive in the city on the morrow.

He arrived. He called her up from the Northwestern station, and she called back that it was settled; she had given him her word. The engagement was off.

" Oh, foolish," he called jovially. . . . " It isn't," she called back angrily. . . . " Well," said he, " I'll call and see you. . . ." " No need," she said. . . . " But you'll see me," he called. . . . " Yes, I'll see you. I'll do you that honor. . . ."

Now when Jean Baptiste had called over the 'phone, Glavis had answered the call, and thereupon had started an argument that Orlean had concluded by taking the receiver from his hand. Of course she had jilted Jean Baptiste and had sent back the papers; moreover, she had declared she would not marry him — *under any circumstances.* But she would attend to that herself and did not need the assistance of her brother-in-law. . . .

Glavis was quite officious that morning — acting under his wife's orders. When the bell rang, although he should have been at his work an hour before he opened the door. Baptiste was there and Glavis started to say something he felt his wife would be pleased to know he said. But, being affected with a slight impediment of speech, his tongue became twisted and when he could straighten it out, Baptiste had passed him and was on his way to the rear of the house where Orlean stood pouting. Ethel stood near with her lips protruding, and Mrs. McCarthy, whom he had termed, "Little Mother Mary," stood nearby at a loss as to what to say.

"Indeed, but it looks more like you were waiting for a funeral than for me," as he burst in upon them. Pausing briefly, he observed the one who had declared everything against him, turned her face away and refused to greet him.

"What's the matter, hon'," he said gaily and laughed, at the same time gathering her into his arms.

"Will you look at that!" exclaimed Ethel, ready to start something. But Glavis, countered twice the morning so soon, concluded at last that it was his time to keep his place. So deciding, he cut his eyes toward Ethel, and said: "Now, Ethel, this is no affair of yours," and cautioned her still more with his eyes.

"No, Ethel," commanded Orlean, "This is *my* affair. I—" she did not finish, because at that moment Jean Baptiste had kissed her.

"It beats anything I ever witnessed," cried Ethel, almost bursting to get started.

"Then don't witness it," said Glavis, whereupon he caught her about the waist and urged her up the stairs and locked her in their room.

"You've been acting something awful like," chided Baptiste, with Orlean still in his arms. She did not answer just then. She could not. She decided at that moment, however, to take him into the parlor, and there tell him all she said she would. Yes, she would do that at once. So deciding, she caught him firmly by the arm, and commanded:

"Come, and I will get you told!"

He followed meekly. When they reached the parlor she was confronted with another proposition. Where would they sit? She glanced from the chairs to the davenport; but he settled it forthwith by settling upon the davenport. She hesitated, but before she had reached a decision, she found herself pulled down by his side — and dreadfully close. Well, she decided then, that this was better, after all, because, if she was close to him he could hear her better. She would not have to talk so loud. She did not like loud talking. It was too "niggerish," and she did not like that. But behold! He, as soon as she was seated, encircled her waist with his arm. Dreadful! Then, before she could tell him what she had made up all the night before to say to him, she felt his lips upon hers — and, my! they were so warm, and tender and soft. She was confused. Ethel and her father had said that the country where Jean lived was wild; that all the people in it were hard and coarse and rough — but Jean's kisses were warm, and soft and tender. She almost forgot what she had intended telling him. And just then he caught her to him, and that felt so — well, she did not know — could not say how it felt; but she was forgetting all she had planned to tell him. She heard his voice presently, and for a moment she caught sight of his eyes. They were real close to hers, and, oh, such eyes! She had not known he possessed such striking ones. How they moved her! She was as if hypnotized, she could not seem to break the spell, and in the meantime she was forgetting more of what she had made up her mind to say. He spoke then, and such a wonderful voice he seemed to have! How musical, how soft, how tender — but withal, how strong, how firm, how resolute and determined it was. She was held in a thraldom of strange delight.

"What has been the matter with my little girl?" And thereupon, as if they were not close enough, he gathered her into his arms. Oh, what a thrill it gave her! She had forgotten now, all she had had in mind to say and it would take an hour or so, perhaps a day, to think and remember it all over again. . . . "Hasn't she wanted to see me? Such beautiful days are these! Lovely, grand, glorious!" She looked out through the window. It *was* a beautiful day, indeed! And she had not observed it before.

"And hear the birds singing in the trees," she heard. And thereupon she listened a moment and heard the birds singing. She started. Now she had felt she was thoughtful. She really loved to listen to the twitter of birds — and it was springtime. It was life, and sunshine and happiness. She had not heard the birds before that morning, therefore it must have been because she had let anger rule instead of sunshine. And as if he had read her thoughts, she heard his voice again:

"And because you were angry — gave in to evil angriness and pouted instead of being cheerful, happy and gay, you have failed to observe how beautiful the sun shone, and that the birds were singing in the trees."

She felt — was sensitive of a feeling of genuine guilt.

"And away out west, where the sunshine kisses the earth, and the wheat, the corn, the flax, and the oats grow green in great fields, everybody there is about his duty; for, when the winter has been long, cold and dreary, the settlers must stay indoors lest they freeze. So with such days as these after the long, cold and dreary winters, everybody must be up and doing. For if the crops are to mature in the autumn time, they must be placed in the earth through seed in the springtime. But there is, unfortunately, one settler, called St. Jean Baptiste, by those who know him out there, who is not in his fields; his crops are not being sown; his fields — wide, wide fields, which represent many thousands of dollars, and long years of hard, hard work, are lying idle, growing to wild weeds!"

"But, Jean," she cried of a sudden. "It is not so?"

"Unfortunately it is so, my love!"

"Then — Jean — you must go — hurry, and sow your crops, also!" she echoed.

"For years and years has Jean Baptiste labored to get his fields as they are. For, in the beginning, they were wild, raw and unproductive, whereupon naught but coyotes, prairie dogs and wild Indians lived; where only a wild grass grew weakly and sickly from the surface and yielded only a prairie fire that in the autumn time burned all in its path; a land wherein no civilized one had resided since the beginning of time."

"Oh, Jean!"

"And he has longed for woman's love. For, according to the laws of the Christ, man should take unto himself a wife, else the world and all its people, its activity, its future will stop forthwith!"

"You are so wonderful!"

"Not wonderful, am I," quoth Baptiste. "Just a mite practical."

"But it is wonderful anyhow, all you say!"

"And yet my Orlean does not love me yet!"

"I didn't say that," she argued, thinking of what she had written him.

"Since therefore she has not said it, then methinks that she does not."

"I — I — oh, you — are awful!"

"And she will not go to live alone with me and share my life — and my love!"

"I — oh, I didn't say I wouldn't do all that." She was done for then. She had shot her last defense.

" Then you will? " he asked anxiously. " You will go back with me, and be mine, all mine and love me forever? "

She sought his lips and kissed him then, and he arose and caught her close to him and kissed her again and looked into her eyes, and she was then all his own.

CHAPTER VIII

"WHY — why — why, what does this mean!" exclaimed "Little Mother Mary" coming upon them at this minute. Notwithstanding the fact that she was surprised, it was obviously a glad surprise. She admired Jean Baptiste, and had been much upset over their little controversy. She understood the root of the trouble, and knew that it had been on account of what Baptiste had written and intimated in the letter regarding the Elder. Her husband did not admire real men, although of course, he was not aware of it. In truth, he admired no man, other than himself. And when others did not do likewise, he usually found excuses to disagree with them in some manner.

Jean Baptiste was not the type of man to make friends with her husband. He was too frank, too forward, too progressive in every way ever to become very intimate with N. Justine McCarthy. To begin with, Jean had never flattered his vanity as it was not his wont to give undue praise. And as yet he had no reason especially to admire the Reverend. That it had not been Orlean who had objected to coming West to marry him he was aware. Nor had it been her mother. It had been N. Justine who had a way of making his faults and shortcomings appear to be those of others — especially within his family, and in this instance his elder daughter bore the blame.

"What would you expect us to do, Little Mother," he said, turning a beaming face upon her.

" But — Orlean, I thought — I thought —"

" Oh, Mother," cried Jean Baptiste, " don't think. It will hurt you. Besides, it will not be necessary for you to think any more with regards to us now. We are as we were, and that is all. There is nothing wrong between us — never has been, nor between you and I now either, is there?" Whereupon he drew her down and upon the davenport and placed himself between her and her daughter.

" Now let's reason this thing out together," he began. " There is no need for quarreling. We'll leave that to idle, disagreeable people. The first thing in life is to know what you want — and then go get it. That's the way I do. When I proposed to Orlean I did so after due consideration. There has been some little disagreement with regards to my coming to get her, which was due to the fact that I have been so overrun with work until I really felt I had not the time to spare. However, here I am and ready to marry her. So let's get those who are concerned together and have it over with. What do you say to it?" he said, looking from one to the other. In the meantime, Ethel had crept down from upstairs to see what was going on, and saw the three on the davenport together, with Jean Baptiste in the middle. Whereupon, she turned and hurried back upstairs to where her husband was, with these words:

" Glavis, Glav—is," she cried all out of breath with exasperation. " I just wish you'd look! Just step down there and look!"

" Why, why — what is the matter, Ethel!" he cried, rising from his chair in some excitement.

" Why, that Jean Baptiste is sitting down there on the davenport with mama on one side of him and my sister on the other!"

" Oh, is that all!" he breathed with relief.

"Is that all!" she echoed in derision, her narrow little face screwed up.

"Well?"

"Will you 'well' me when that man just comes in here and takes the house and all that's in it!"

"Oh, Ethel." he argued. "Will you use some sense!"

"Will I use some sense! After what Orlean said? You remember well enough what she said, no longer than last night when she received that telegram. That she was through with that man; that she was not going to marry him, and had sent his old papers back to him to prove it!"

"Well, now, get all excited over the most natural thing in the world! Have you never seen a woman who never changed her mind — especially when there was a man in the case?"

"Of course I have," she shouted. "I am one who has never changed their mind!"

"I agree, and that is what's the matter with you," so saying, he made his get-away to avoid what would have followed.

"Now, you will have to deal with my husband in regard to this matter, Mr. Baptiste," admonished Mother Mary. She had given into him along with Orlean. It was useless to try to pit their weak wits against the commanding and domineering reason, the quick logic and searching intuition of Jean Baptiste. So they had quickly resigned to the inevitable, and left him to the rock of unreason, the Reverend N. J. McCarthy.

"All settled. I'll bounce right out and get him on the wire. Best words to send are: 'Please come to Chicago today. Important!' Will that be alright?"

"Jean Baptiste, you are a wonder!" cried Orlean, and, encircling his neck with her arms, kissed him impulsively.

In answer they received by special delivery a letter that night, stating that his honor, N. J., was on the way, and would arrive the following morning. Preparations were entered into at once therefore for a simple wedding, only Ethel holding aloft from the proceedings. It was while at the supper table that evening that Orlean took upon herself to try to set Baptiste right with what was before him in dealing with regards to her father.

"Now, my dear," she said lovingly, "if you would get along with papa, then praise him — you understand, flatter him a little. Make him think he's a king."

"Oh-ho!" he laughed, whereat she was embarrassed. "That's the 'bug,' eh!"

"Well," she hesitated, awkwardly, "he *is* rather vain."

Baptiste was thoughtful. Rev. McCarthy was vain. . . . He must be praised if one was to get along with him. . . . Make him think he was a king. His Majesty, Newton Justine, sounded very well as a title. All he needed now, then, was a crown. If necessary for peace in the family he would praise him, although it was not to his liking.

Jean Baptiste had little patience with people who must be praised. In his association he had chosen men, men who were too busy to look for or care for praise. But he failed to reckon then that he was facing another kind of person, one whom he was soon to learn.

His Majesty, Newton Justine, arrived on schedule the next morning, very serious of expression, and apparently tired into the bargain. Baptiste recalled when he saw him what he had been advised with regards to making him think he was a king. "Well," sighed Baptiste, "providing 'His Majesty' is not a despot, we may be able to get along for a day or two."

Later, when convenient, Baptiste attempted and was apparently successful in making the matter so plain that despite his reputed dislike for fair reasoning, the Elder was compelled to call his daughter and say:

"Now, Orlean, you have heard. Are you in love with this man?" The melting smile she bestowed him with was quite sufficient, so seeing, he continued:

"And do you wish to become his wife?" She looked down into her lap then, turned her hands in childish fashion, and replied in a very small voice:

"Yes."

"Then, that settles it," said the Elder, and thereafter made himself very amiable. By the morrow arrangements had been completed for a simple little home wedding, and at two o'clock, the ceremony was performed.

And when the bride and groom had been kissed according to custom, a storm without broke of a sudden, and the wind blew and the rain fell in torrents. So terrible became the storm that the piano, which some one played loudly, as if to shut out the roar of the storm outside, could hardly be heard. And in the meantime, so dark did it become that at two thirty the lights had to be turned on, the people could hardly distinguish each other in the rooms. Nor did the storm abate as the afternoon wore on, but continued in mad fury far into the night and the guests were compelled to leave in the downpour and wind.

And there were among those who departed, many who thought and did not speak. They were, for the most part, the new Negro, hence loathe to admit of superstitions — besides, they had great respect for the two who were about to start upon matrimony's uncertain journey. But regardless of what they might have said openly, it was a long time before they forgot.

"JEAN!" called Orlean three months later, as she came out of the house, the house where Stewarts had lived, and which Jean Baptiste had rented for the season so as to be near all his land in the older opened county. "I have something to tell you."

"What is it, dear?" he replied, drawing his horses to a stop, while she climbed on the step of the spring wagon he was riding in. He could see she was excited, and he was apprehensive.

She got up on the seat beside him, and placing her arms around him, began to cry. He petted her a moment and then, placing his hand under her chin, raised her head and said: "Well, now, my dear, what is the matter?" whereupon, he kissed her. Drawing his head down then, she whispered something in his ear.

"Oh!" he cried, his face suddenly aglow with an expression she had never seen in it before. The next instant he caught and drew her closely to him, and kissed her fondly. "I am so happy, dear; the happiest I have been since we married!"

"But, Jean!" she started and then hesitated. He appeared to understand.

"Now, my wife, you must not feel that way," he admonished. "That is the ultimate of young married life — children. Of course," he added, slowly, "couples are not always ready they feel, but such does not wait. We are not always ready to die, but old death comes when he gets ready and there's no use trying to argue a delay. So now, instead of looking distressed, just fancy what a great thing, a beautiful and heavenly thing after all it is, and be real nice." He kissed her again and assisted her from the buggy, and while he drove to his work she went into the house and picked up a letter.

It was from Ethel, and ran:

"*My dear sister:*

"I am writing you to say that I am very unhappy. You cannot imagine how disagreeable, how very inconvenient it is to be as I am. Never did I want a child — or children; but that silly man I'm married to is so crazy for a family that he has given me no peace.

"As a result I must sit around the house during these beautiful summer days and be satisfied to look out of the window and go nowhere. Oh, it is distressing, and I am so mad at times I can seem not to see! Can you sense it: Him so anxious for a family, when what he earns is hardly sufficient to keep us in comfort and maintain the payments on the home. I have tried to reason with him on the score, but it is no use at all. So while I sit around so angry I cannot see straight, he dances around gleefully, wondering whether it will be a girl or a boy!

"Now, I thought I would write you in time so that you could protect yourself. I am, therefore, sending you certain receipts which have been given me — but too late! They will not be again, though — trust me to attend to that! Don't wait too long, and use them as per direction. Do it and run no chance of getting to be as I am.

"I hope you are well and write me any time anything happens, and if these don't work, then tell me right quick and I will send you something that is sure. I depend on you taking care of yourself now, and don't let anybody put foolishness in your head.

"Hoping to hear from you soon, and that you are safe as yet, believe me to be, As ever your sister,

"ETHEL."

When she had completed the letter, she was thoughtful as her eyes wandered out to where her husband worked away in the field beyond. She tried to see a few months ahead. It was then midsummer, and Ethel and her father and all the girls were writing her already that they supposed they might as well not expect her until Xmas. But Jean had intimated already that he did not expect to go to Chicago Xmas. Still, that was several months away, and the dry weather of which he was complaining at the present, might be offset by rain soon. So she might get to see old Chicago Xmas after all. But she would be unable to go out if she did go to the city Xmas with what she knew now. She pondered, and while she did so, she read through certain receipts her sister had sent her. One was very simple, and she was tempted. It stated that the blossom of a certain weed was positive when made into a tea.

She was thoughtful a moment, and her eyes wandered again toward where her husband worked in the field. Finally they fell upon the creek that ran near the house, and she gave a start as she saw growing upon its banks, a peculiar weed with purple blossom. She wondered what kind of weeds they were. She made a mental note of the same and decided that when her husband came to luncheon she would ask him. She sighed then as she thought of the months to come, and what was to come with it. Presently, having nothing else urgent to do, she picked up paper, pen and ink and replied to Ethel's letter:

"*My dear sister:*
"Receipt of your recent letter is here acknowledged, and

in reply, will say that I have read the same carefully, and made a note of what you said.

"I hardly know how to reply to what you set forth in your letter, and I am not fully decided. But I might as well admit that I have just discovered that I also am to become a mother and, Jean, like Glavis, is tickled to death! I just told him this morning and he said it was the happiest moment he had experienced since we have been married.

"I am entirely at a loss what to do; but I will consult him regarding it. I don't think I ought to do as you advise — not let him know anything —because that would hardly be fair. He is just as good to me as he can be, and considers my every need. Sometimes I do not think he loves me as much as I would wish, but what can I do! He is my husband and gives me all his attention. I am, therefore, afraid that he will object to the measures you suggest. I am very much afraid he will, but I will ask him.

"He's a perfect dear, so jolly, so popular everywhere about, and, I repeat, so good to me that I hardly think my conscience would be clear if I did something in secret and something that he would not like.

"In the meantime, thanking you for your suggestions, and begging you not to act foolish, I am,
"Your affectionate sister,
"ORLEAN."

Jean Baptiste drove into the yard at noon singing cheerfully. He was met by his wife at the gate which she opened. The wind was blowing from the south, and the air was very hot. It had been blowing from that direction for days. He stopped singing while he unhitched the horses and gazed anxiously toward the northwest.

"What is it, dear?" she inquired, observing the old frown upon his face. He shook his head before replying, and tried to smile.

"This wind."

"The wind?"

"Yes. It's terribly hot. It's awfully drying. The oats are suffering, the wheat is hurt. I wish it would rain, and rain soon," whereat he shook his head again and his frown grew deeper.

He led the horses to the well to drink and while they were drinking she stood near, holding her hands and looking at the patch of strange weeds that were in blossom near. Presently she observed him, and, seeing that his mind was concerned with problems, she would satisfy her mind.

"Jean!" she called.

"Yes," he replied abstractedly.

"What kind of weeds are those?" and she pointed to the wild blossoms.

"Those!" he said, his mind struggling between what he was thinking about and the question. "Oh, those are evil weeds," he concluded, and turning, led his horses into the barn.

"Evil weeds!" she echoed. Slowly she turned and looked again. She was strangely frightened. Then taking courage, she went playfully to where they grew, and, gathering a bunch in a sort of bouquet, carried them into the house, laid them down, and began to place the meal upon the table.

"Why, Orlean," she heard, and turned to meet her husband. "What are you doing with these old things in here! My dear, you could find something better for the table than these things! Just outside the fence in the road roses are blooming everywhere, and the air is charged with their sweet fragrance." He paused briefly and held them to his nose. "And, besides, they stink. Booh!" he cried, holding them away. "They make me sick! Now, if you'll agree I'll throw these things away and run out into the road and get you a big bunch of roses. Will that be all right, dear?"

"Yes," she answered, and he did not understand why her eyes were downcast.

"Good!" he exclaimed, and she was glad to see that the frown upon his face was gone, if only for a while. "I'll bring you some nice flowers. You know," he paused in the doorway and turned to her, "I never liked this weed, anyhow. I have always connected them with all that's vile and evil." So saying, he turned and a few minutes later she heard his voice coming cheerfully from the road where he picked the various shades of roses.

"Now, my dear," said he pleasantly, "I have brought you a real bouquet," and he placed the vase containing the same in the center of the table, stood back and regarded the flowers admiringly.

"Why," he suddenly exclaimed, his eyes widening, "what is the matter?"

"Oh, nothing," she stammered more than spoke.

"Now there must be something?" While standing where he was he caught sight of Ethel's letter. Immediately she reached forth to snatch it from beneath his gaze. He made no effort to take it, but regarded her in the meantime wonderingly. The receipt concerning the weed lay in plain sight, and he could hardly help reading it. She caught it up then, while he still looked after her wonderingly. He raised his hand to his head and was thoughtful, before saying:

"Why were you so disturbed over me seeing the letter, Orlean? You have never been so before. Of course," he said, and hesitated, and then went on patiently, "I have no wish to pry into women's affairs or secrets, but I am curious to know why you acted as you did?"

She was an emotional girl. Never in her life had she violated the rules of her parents, and she had never thought of disobeying, or keeping secrets from her husband. When she was confronted with the situation, she broke down thereupon, and crying on his breast, told him all the letter contained, and what the receipt meant.

He listened patiently and when she was through he hesitated before speaking. After a moment he led her to the table, sat down, and fell to eating the luncheon.

"When we have dined," he paused after a few minutes to remark, "and you have washed the dishes, we will spare a few minutes for a talk, Orlean."

"Now," he resumed at the appointed time, "when we married, Orlean, it was my hope — and I feel sure 'twas yours, that we would live happily."

"Of course, Jean," she agreed tremulously.

"Then, dear, there are certain things we should come to an understanding thereto lest we find our lives at variance. To begin with, I wish your sister would not write you such letters as the one you received today. But, if she *must* and offer — yes, criminal advice, I trust *you* will not incline toward such seriously. You and I, as well as those who have gone before us; and as those who must perforce come after us, did not come into this world altogether by ours or others' providence. And if the world, and the people in the world are growing wicked, as yet, thank God, race suicide has not come to rule!" He was meditatively silent then for a time, gazing as if into space off across the sunkist fields.

"First," he resumed, "selfishness is a bad patient to nurse. Secondly, we must appreciate that ours — our lives have a duty to fulfill. Bringing children into the world and rearing them to clean and healthy man and womanhood is that duty — our greatest duty.   And now with regards to that receipt, or receipts.

"I will not seek to deny that such practices are not in some measure a custom.   Such very often are given thoughtlessly as to the infinite harm, ill health and unhappiness they might later bring.   But the fact that others cultivate and heed such is no reason, dear, do you feel, that we should?"

"No, Jean," she admitted without hesitation and very humbly.

"I feel more inspired to say this at this point in our new union, Orlean, because I cannot believe that it is your nature to be wicked; to wilfully practice and condone the wrong."

"Oh, Jean," she cried, moving toward him; laying her hands upon him, and seeking his eyes with her soul standing out in hers.   "You are so noble and so good," and in the next minute she was weeping silently upon his shoulder.

The dry weather continued over all the West, and for two weeks the wind remained in the south, and blew almost day and night.   Heretofore, it had been known to blow not more than a week at the most, before the heat would be broken by a rain.   And coincident with the heat and drought, the crops began to fire, plants of all kinds to wither, and every one in the country of our story became ominous.

But the Creator seemed to be with the struggling people of the new country, the drought was broken by rain before the crops were destroyed; the harvest was very good, and with the completion of the same, Orlean met her husband one evening with a letter, announcing that her father was coming to visit soon. And the next day they got another letter — no, a paper. It was a summons, and concerned Orlean.

CHAPTER X

EUGENE CROOK

TRIPP COUNTY, laying just to the west of the town of Dallas and where Jean Baptiste had purchased the relinquishments for his people was a large county and rich in soil. There had been little delay on the part of the railroad company in extending their line into it. But before this occurred — before even the county had been thrown open to the settlers, new promoters, conscious of the great success which had been achieved by the men who had promoted Dallas, purchased an allotment from an Indian, or a breed and started a town thereon almost directly in the center of the county in a valley of a creek known as the Dog Ear.

And it was about this time that a political ring was formed in the newer county for the avowed and subtle purpose of securing the county seat. Settlement on the whole had not as yet been possible, so the politics included the rabble. The cowboy, and the ex-cowboy; saloon men, bartenders — some freighters, squaw men and cattle thieves represented the voters. So it happened that before the bona-fide settlers had a chance in the way of political expression, they found the county organized, controlled and exploited by this ilk. But, as we have already stated, a town in the West — nor the East for that matter — is ever a town until a railway has found its way thither.

The difficulty began when the survey was run. Notwithstanding the fact that the county seat had been secured by the promoters of the town in the valley of the Dog Ear, the surveyors, from the route they took, did not seem to have had any orders to go via of Lamro, the county seat in question. On the contrary, they went smack through a section of land that had been secured in due time by the promoters who had made Dallas possible as a town.

Where the line of the survey stretched, less than two miles northwest of the county seat, they started a town, and were now bidding the townspeople and business men of the county seat to move their building over. A bitter fight was the answer — at the start. A railroad is everything almost to an aspiring town, and these people were capable of appreciating the fact. As a result, the little town in the valley a few months later, was no more. Another election was held and through the same the bona fide settlers asserted their rights and administered a severe rebuke by defeating the town in the valley and electing the new town which had been entitled Winner as the county seat.

Nevertheless, a few people remained in what was left of the valley town. Some were unable to move their buildings, others were indifferent, while others still remained there for purposes of their own.

Among those who remained, there was a banker, whose little bank reposed all alone with caves and broken sidewalks and all the leavings of the moved away town about. His name was Crook, Eugene Crook, and it was common knowledge that he was fond of his name and conducted his affairs so as to justify it. 'Gene Crook would rather, it was said, acquire something by beating some one in a deal than to secure it honestly. He possessed an auto, and had business to the northwest of the town some fifteen or eighteen miles, and had been seen in the neighborhood quite often.

Perhaps it was due in some measure to an unscrupulous character who had drawn a claim in those parts, and pretended to be homesteading there; but who in truth homesteaded more around the saloons of Winner and Crook's town than he did on the claim. His name was James J. Spaight.

James J. Spaight, and Eugene Crook were very close. 'Gene Crook had advanced Spaight considerable money towards his claim, and had him tied up in many ways, therefore, they were understood cohorts.

"They are never here," said Spaight, jumping from the auto and sweeping his hand about over a beautiful quarter section of land, one of the finest in the county.

"But I see a sod shack over in the draw," returned Crook. "They have apparently called themselves establishing a residence on the land."

"Yes; but let me tell you," said Spaight. "I can get you this piece of land — I can win it for you through contest. I know a thing or two, and I believe when we let the fellow know that we've got him dead to right, he'll weaken, and sell it to you for a song."

"Well," said Crook, thoughtfully, "we'll drive back to town and consult Duval about it."

On the way they drove by the homesteaders near and held subtle conversations with many, always in the end ascertaining how many times the people had been seen on the claim they had just left.

When they returned to the town in the valley, and retired into the private office of the little bank, Spaight went for Duval, a lawyer, who came forthwith. He was a tall, lean creature who attracted attention by his unusual height and leanness. He, also, was one of the "left overs." He was told of the beautiful homestead, and that the claimant had been seen only a few times there, and of the proposition to contest it.

"Who holds the place, did you say?" inquired Duval in his deep, droll voice, crossing his legs judiciously.

"Why, a nigger woman," said Spaight.

"A Negro woman?"

"Yes, what do you think of that?" pursued Spaight, his eyes widening. "I told Crook that if he worked a bluff good and right he could more than likely scare them out. A nigger in a white man's country!"

Crook smiled; Duval was thoughtful.

"What's her name — this Negress? Is she a single woman or married?"

"Why, she *was* single when she took it, of course. But she's got married since. I think the guy she married put up the money, and that's where we have them again."

"And the name?" inquired Duval again.

"Oh, yes, Baptiste. That's it. Jean Baptiste is her husband's name."

"Oh, hell!" cried Duval, and spat upon the floor.

"Why — what's the matter?" cried Crook and Spaight in chorus.

"I was struck with the joke."

"The joke?"

"Yes. The bluffing."

"But we don't understand?"

"Then you ought to. Jean Baptiste, huh! You'll bluff Jean Baptiste! Say, that's funny." Suddenly his face took on a cold hard expression. "Why, that's one of the shrewdest, one of the wisest, one of the most forcible men in this country. Have you never heard of Jean Baptiste? Oh, you fools! He's worth forty thousand dollars — made it himself and is not over twenty-five."

" Is that so?" they echoed, taken aback.

" Well, I should say so, and everybody in the county knows it."

" But they haven't lived on the place as they should!" protested Spaight, weakly.

" Something like yourself," laughed Duval. Spaight colored guiltily.

" But I can prove it," insisted Spaight.

" Well, in so far as that goes, I wouldn't doubt but they have not lived on the land. Baptiste owns a lot of land in the county east, and the chances are that he's been so busy that his wife has neglected to stay on the claim as she should have. Yes, that is quite likely."

" Then we can contest it?" cried Spaight.

" Of course. You can contest any place so far as that goes."

" Well, that's what we intend to do. And I have the goods on him and am sure we can win."

" They're all sure of that when they start," said Duval, sarcastically. " But I want to disillusion you. If you contest the place then do so with a realization of what we are up against. Don't go down there with any ' rough stuff ' or with a delusion that you are going to meet a weakling. Go down there with the calm, considerate understanding that you are going to vie with a man all through, and that man is Jean Baptiste. And while I'll take the case and do what I can, before we start, I'd advise that you keep away from that fellow as much as possible."

" Well, now, to be frank, Duval," said Crook, " What do you think of it anyhow?"

Duval regarded him closely a moment out of his small eyes. And then spoke slowly, easily, carefully. " Well, Crook, being frank with you, I don't think you can beat that fellow fairly. No one will beat Jean Baptiste in a fair fight. But of course," he added, "there are other ways. Yes, and when the time is right — if ever, you may try the *other* way."

CHAPTER XI

"WELL," said Baptiste to his wife, following the service of the summons. "We're up against a long, irksome and expensive contest case." Under his observation had come many of such. Only those who have homesteaded or have been closely related to such can in full appreciate the annoyance, the years of annoyance and uncertainty with which a contest case is fraught. Great fiction has been created from such; greater could be. Oh, the nerve racking, the bitterness and very often the sinister results that have grown out of one person trying to secure the place of another without the other's consent. Murder has been committed times untold as a sequel — but getting back to Jean Baptiste and his wife.

He was inclined to be more provoked than ordinarily, for the reason that by sending his wife — at least taking her to the homestead, he knew he could have avoided the contest. As a rule places are not contested altogether without a cause. He felt that it was — and it no doubt was — due to his effort to farm his own land and assist his folks in holding their claims as well. He had discovered before he married Orlean that she was likely to prove much unlike his sister, who possessed the strength of her convictions, for she was on the clinging vine order. Being extremely childish, this was further augmented by a stream of letters from Chicago, giving volumes of advice in re-

227

gards to something the advisors had not a very keen idea of themselves. He also was cautioned not to expose her. So she had, in truth only gone to her homestead when taken by him, returning when he did as well. The fact that he had arranged in regards to the renting of his land the next season would be no evidence to assist him before the bar that would hear his case.

The contest against his wife's homestead did not, of course alter his plans in any way. He would continue along the lines he had started. But there were other things that came to annoy him at the same time. Chiefly among these was his wife's father. Always there had to be some ado when it came to him. He had reared his daughter, as before intimated, to consider him of the world's greatest men — especially the Negro race's, and to avoid friction, Baptiste came gradually to see that he would almost have to be beholden unto this creature in whom he was positively not very deeply interested.

N. Justine McCarthy's accomplishments were of a nature which Baptiste would rather have avoided. The fact that he had been a Presiding Elder in one of the leading denominations of Negro churches out of which he managed to filch about a thousand a year, was in a measure foreign to his son-in-law. And the Reverend was not an informed or practical man.

The truth was that all the pretensions made to the Elder, flattering him into feeling he was a great man, Jean Baptiste came to regard as a deliberate fawning to flatter an extreme vanity. Far from being even practical, N. J. McCarthy was by disposition, environment and cultivation, narrow, impractical, hypocritical, envious and spiteful. As to how much he was so, not even did Jean Baptiste fully realize at the time, but came to learn later from experience.

He was expected in early October. The hearing of the contest was to convene a few days later, so as a greeting to his Majesty, he was to be given an opportunity to see Orlean on the stand and mercilessly grilled by non-sentimental lawyers. Baptiste was appreciative of what might result, and wished the visit could have been deferred for a while.

Another source of irritation continually, was Ethel's letters, and his wife's nervousness over the child that was to come. For the first time in her life she had been disobedient. Secretly she had, after many misgivings, fears and indecisions, brewed a tea from the weed as per Ethel's prescription — but in vain! Later, the guilt, the never-to-be-forgotten guilt; the unborn child that refused the poison, seemed to haunt her. And she could not tell her husband. But this was not all. Ethel's letters continued to come, filled with the same advice; the same suggestions; the same condemnation of motherhood — and she was compelled to keep it all a hopeless secret from the man she had sworn to love and obey.

One thing was agreed upon, they decided not to inform the Elder — at least, in so far as Orlean was concerned, she left it to Jean, and Jean, with as many troubles as he cared for and more, to deal with, was becoming perceptibly irritant. So with this state of affairs prevailing, the Reverend finally arrived for his long anticipated visit.

The letter advising the day he would arrive did not happen to reach them in time to meet him. Accordingly, neither was at the station to greet him, but, recalling that Baptiste had spoken of the Freedom and no narrow prejudices and customs to irk one, the Elder went forthwith to the leading hotel in Gregory where he was accorded considerable attention as a guest. This indeed satisfied his vanity, and he was taken much notice of by those about because of his distinguished appearance. A fact that he seldom ever lost sight of.

But Baptiste happened to be in town that night on horseback, and when the train had come and gone, he inquired carelessly of a fellow he met, and who had come in on the train, if he had seen a colored man aboard.

"Yes," said the other. "An elderly man, very distinguished looking."

"My father-in-law!" ejaculated Baptiste, and went forthwith to the hotel to find his erstwhile compatriot very much at ease among those filling the place.

"And it's a great way to greet me," exclaimed the Reverend, cheerfully, upon seeing him. Baptiste made haste to explain that he had not been aware of the day when he would arrive.

"Oh, that's all right, my son," said the other heartily. "And how is Orlean?"

"Fine! She'll be tickled to death to see you."

"And I her." The old gent was very cheerful. Such a trip was much to him. A life spent among the simple black people to whom he preached afforded little contrast compared with what was about him now. And, pompous by disposition, he was thrilled by the diversity. Baptiste decided thereupon to try to make his sojourn an agreeable one.

"Now, there is an old neighbor of mine in town with a buggy, and I'll see him and figure to have him take you out with him, as I am in on horseback."

"Very well," returned the Elder, and Baptiste went for the neighbor who happened to be a German with a very conspicuous voice. He found him at a saloon where the old scout was pretty well "pickled" from imbibing too freely in red liquor.

"Sure thing," he roared in his big voice when Baptiste stated his errand. "Bring him down here and I'll buy him a drink."

"But he's a preacher," cautioned Baptiste with a laugh.

"A preacher! Well, I'll be damned!" exclaimed the German, humorously. Whereupon he ordered drinks for the house, and two for himself. Baptiste grinned.

"I shall now depart," essayed the German, swaying not too steadily before the bar, and raising his glass, "to become sanctimonious and good," and drained his glass. The crowd roared.

"Where is he?" called the German loudly, as he drew his team to a stop before the hotel. Baptiste got out, went in and called to the Reverend. The other came forward quickly, carrying his bags and other accessories.

"Ah-ha!" roared the German from the buggy, sociably, "So there you are!"

"Why — Jean — the man is — drunk, is he not?" whispered the Elder.

"But he's alright — gets that way when he comes to town, but is perfectly safe withal." The Reverend stood for a moment, regarding the other dubiously.

"Come on, brother, and meet me!" called the German again in a voice sufficiently loud almost to awaken the dead.

"But, Jean," said the Reverend, lowly but apprehensively, "I don't know whether I want to ride with a drunken man or not."

Now it happened that the German's ears were very keen, and he overheard the Elder's remark, so without ceremony, and while the Reverend hesitated on the pavement, the German who did not like to be referred to as drunk, roared:

"Ah-ha! Naw, naw, naw! You don't have to ride with me! Naw, naw, naw!" And turning his horses about, he went back to the saloon where his voice rang forth a minute later in a raucous tune as he unloaded another schooner.

The Reverend beat a hasty retreat back into the hotel, while Baptiste called after him:

"I'll send Orlean for you in the morning," and went to look up his neighbor who had made himself so conspicuous.

"Well, now, if this doesn't beat all," cried the Reverend when he had kissed his daughter the following morning and they were spinning along the road on the way to the farm. "I would never have believed three months ago had some one said you could and would be driving these mules!"

"Oh, I have driven them fifty miles in a day — John!" she called suddenly to the off mule who was given to mischievous tricks.

"Well, well," commented the Reverend, "but it certainly beats all."

She was cheered and pleased to demonstrate what she had learned. They sailed along the country side in the autumn air, and talked of home, Ethel, her mother, Glavis and Jean. They came presently to Baptiste's homestead and viewed with great delight the admirable tract of land that stretched before them. She talked on cheerfully and told her father all that had passed, of how happy they were, but said nothing about her prospects of becoming a mother. When they had passed her husband's homestead and were nearing a corner where they must turn to reach

the house in which they were living, they passed an auto-
mobile carrying two men. They bowed lightly and the
men returned it.   When they had gotten out of hearing distance, one of the men whispered to the other:
" That's her! "
'Gene Crook thereupon turned and looked after the retreating figure of the girl in the buggy whose place he had
determined to secure through subtle methods.   But not even
'Gene Crook himself conceived of the unusual circumstances
that came to pass and brought him on a visit to these selfsame people, later.

CHAPTER XII

"NOW the first thing, daughter," said the Reverend, "when Jean comes and you have the time, is to go up and see your claim." Orlean swallowed, and started to tell him that it was contested; but on second thought, decided to leave the task to her husband, and said instead:

"I have a fine claim, papa. Jean says it is the best piece of land we have."

"Now isn't that fine!"

"It is," Orlean said, thinking of her husband.

"Your husband has a plenty, my dear, and we have been surprised that you have not been sending money to Chicago to have us buy something for you."

Orlean swallowed again and started to speak; to say that while her husband was a heavy land holder, the crops had not been the best the year before and were not as good this year as he had hoped for. Then she thought Jean could explain this better, also, instead she said:

"I — I haven't wanted for anything, papa."

"No, perhaps not. But you know papa always thinks of his baby; always buys her litle things and so on, you know." He paused, regarded her and the dress she wore. He recognized it as one that she had bought just before she had gotten married — forgetting that Jean Baptiste had paid for it — and said:

234

"And you have on the same dress you wore away from Chicago! Indeed, and that is a spring dress! Why do you not wear some of your summer dresses? Some you have bought since you have been married?"

"I haven't bought — my husband hasn't — I haven't needed any more clothes, really," she argued falteringly. He saw that she was keeping something back, and pursued:

"Why, dear, what do you mean! You don't mean to say that Jean hasn't bought you any dresses since he married you, and him owning so much land!"

"But I haven't needed any, papa — I have not asked him for any." He looked at her keenly. He saw that she was shielding the man she married, but with this he had no patience.

"Now, now, my dear. Jean ought not to treat my girl like that. He ought to buy you lots of things, and pretty things. I'm rather inclined to think he is miserly — have rather felt he was all the time." He paused briefly, posed in the way he did when preaching, and then went on. "Yes, you are sacrificing a great deal by coming away out here in a new country and living with him. Yes, yes, my dear. You see you are deprived of many conveniences; conveniences that you have been accustomed to." He looked around the little house; at its floor with only rugs, and its simple furniture. "Just compare this to the home you came out of. The good home. Yes, yes. I'm afraid that — that the rough life your husband has been living rather makes him forget the conventions my daughter has been accustomed to. Yes, I think so. I'm afraid I'll have to kind of — a — bring such to his attention that he might see his duty. Yes, my dear —"

"But, papa! I — I — think you had — better not. You see —" and she caught his arm and was thoughtful, looking downward in the meantime. She loved Jean Baptiste, but she was not a strong willed person by nature, training or disposition. She had inherited her mother's timidness. At heart she meant well to the man she married, but she had always been obedient to her father; had never sauced him and had never crossed him, which was his boast. Perhaps it was because of these things and that he knew it, that his nature asserted itself.

"I'm afraid you, like any newly married wife, are inclined to forget these things, rather accept your husband's excuse. Now your husband has a plenty, and can well afford to give to you. And, besides, you — he should not forget the sacrifices you are making for him. That is what he should see. Yes, yes. Now take Ethel," he suddenly turned to her. "Why, Glavis only makes thirteen dollars a week, and — why, Ethel makes him do just what she wants him to. Buys her a dress any time she wants it; a hat, a pair of shoes — and whatever she wishes. That's Ethel," he ended, forgetting to add that Glavis also bought and paid for the food Mrs. McCarthy ate, or that he, himself only brought — and never bought* things to eat only when he came into Chicago, three or five times a year — and sent a few things infrequently. But Orlean had taken a little courage. It was rather unusual, and she was surprised at herself. She was surprised that she dared even argue — just a little — with her father. He had always been accepted as infallible without question. To get along with him — have peace, her mother and she had always followed the rule of letting everything be his way, and be content with their own private opinion without expression as to conclusions. Moreover, whether he was right or wrong, abused or accused, the rule was to praise and flatter him notwithstanding. And at such times they could depend on him to do much for them. But she found her voice. Jean Baptiste was her husband, and she was not ungrateful. He gave her real love and husbandry, and it was perhaps her woman's nature to speak in defense of her mate. So she said:

"But Jean is not like Glavis, papa. They are two different men entirely."

"Well, yes, my dear," he said slowly, his dark face taking on a peculiar — and not very pleasant expression, " I'm afraid I will have to agree with you. Yes. They are different. Glavis is a fine boy, though. Don't own a thousand acres of land, but certainly takes care of home like a man. No, no. I never have to worry about anything. Just come home every few months to see that everything is all right — and find it so. Yes, that is Glavis. While Jean," and his mind went quickly back to an incident that had happened twenty-one years before, " is rather set in his ways. Yes, very much so, I fear. That is one of his failings. Some people would call it hard headed, but I should not quite call it that. No. Then, again," he paused a moment, looked at the floor and looked up. " He's crazy to get rich. You see, dear — of course you don't know that. Not old enough. That's where your father has the advantage over you — and Jean also. He's older. It's bad when a man is ambitious to get rich, for he is liable to work himself and his wife to death. Jean's liable to do that with you. Not like your old father, you know."

"Here he comes now," she cried excitedly, going quickly to the kitchen and making a fire and starting the meal. Her father looked after her. He looked out the window to where his son-in-law was unhitching his horses. He looked back to where his daughter was working nervously over the stove, and muttered to himself. "Has her trained to run like something frightened at his approach. That's the same spirit I tried to conquer twenty-one years ago and it is still in him. M-m. I'll have to look after that disposition." And with that he went outside to where his daughter's husband worked.

"Hello, Reverend," called Jean cheerfully. The "Reverend" darkened and glowered unseen. He did not like that term of address. Glavis called him "father." That was better. But he returned apparently as cheerful:

"Hello, my boy. So you are home to dinner?"

"Yes. Guess it's ready. She is very prompt about having my meals on time. Yes. Orlean is a good girl, and appreciates that I believe in always being on time," he rattled off.

"And how are the crops?"

"Not so good, not so good, I regret to say," said Jean moodily. "No; to be truthful, it is the poorest crop I have ever raised. Yes," he mused as if to himself. "And I need a good crop this year worse than I have ever needed one. Yes, I sure do.

"Indeed so. Got lots of expense. Borrowed ten thousand dollars to buy that land out there in Tripp County, and have none of it producing anything. And on top of that a guy comes along and slaps a contest on Orlean's place, and so I have that on my hands in addition to all the other burdens. So, believe me, it keeps me hopping."

"A contest on Orlean's place? What does that mean?"

"Does that mean! But of course you couldn't understand," whereat, Baptiste tried to explain to him what it meant.

"So you see you find us with our troubles." The Reverend made no reply to this.   Indeed, he had never been able to reply to Jean Baptiste.   In the first place, the man was ever too hurried; moreover, he understood so little regarding practical business matters until their relations had never been congenial.   When Jean had watered and fed his teams he came back to where the Elder stood and said:

"Well, Judge, we'll go in to dinner."   Now the Reverend was almost upset.   Such flat expressions!   Such a little regard for his caste.   Horrid!   He started to speak to him regarding his lack of manners, but that one had his face in the tub where the horses had drank, washing himself eagerly.   When he was through, he drew water from the well, and pouring it into a wash basin rinsed himself, and called for the towel.   No sooner had he done so than out of the house came Orlean with the goods.

"Wash up," cried Baptiste, pointing to the horse tub.

"Jean!" called his wife remonstratingly.   "You forget yourself.   Asking papa to wash where the horses have drank!   You must be more thoughtful!"

Baptiste laughed.   "Beg pardon, Colonel.   You see this open life has made me — er — rather informal.   But you'll get used to and like it with time.   Wash up and let's eat!"

"He's wild, just wild!" muttered the Reverend, as he followed them into the house.

CHAPTER XIII

THE WOLF

"NOW, ELDER," said Baptiste, getting up from the table without going through the usual formalities of resting a few minutes after the meal. "I've bought a building in town that I'm going to move onto Orlean's place. I'm preparing to jack it up and load it, so if you would like to come along, very well, we'll be glad to have you. But it's rather a rough, hard task, I'll admit."

"Now, now, son," started the Reverend, holding back his exasperation with difficulty. His son-in-law had never addressed him more than once by the same name. It was either Colonel, Judge, Reverend, Elder, or some other burlesque title in the sense used. He wanted to tell him that he should call him father, but before he had a chance to do so, that worthy had bounced out of the room and was heard from the barn. The Reverend looked after him with a glare.

"Dreadful!" he exclaimed when the other was out of hearing distance.

"What, papa?" inquired his daughter, regarding him questioningly. She had become accustomed to Jean's ways and did not understand her father's exclamation.

"Why, the man! Your husband!"

"Jean?"

"Such rough ways!"

"Oh," she exclaimed. "That's his way. He has always lived alone, you know. And is so ambitious. Is really compelled to hurry a little because he has so much to do."

"Well, I never saw the like. I'm afraid he and Ethel would never get along very well. No, he — is rather unusual."

"Oh, father. You must pay no attention to that! Jean is a fine fellow, a likeable man, and is loved by every one who knows him," she argued, trying to discourage her father's mood to complain. She had never been able to bring her father and husband very close. Perhaps it was because of their being so far apart in all that made them; but she was aware that Jean had never flattered her father, and that was very grave! No relation had ever risked that. Her father was accustomed to being flattered by everybody who was an intimate of the family, and Jean Baptiste had come into the family, married her, and apparently forgot to tell the Reverend that he was a great man. Moreover, from what she knew of her husband, he was not likely to do so. Her mother had tried to have Baptiste see it, she recalled, her little mother of whom Baptiste was very fond of. As has been stated it was generally known that her father was not very kind and patient, with her mother, and never had been.

It was, moreover, no secret that her father was unusually friendly with Mrs. Pruitt. But she was not supposed to let on that she was aware of such. If she was — and she certainly was — she did not mention the fact. Jean Baptiste knew of the Reverend's subtle practices, and in his mind condemned rather than admired him therefor. He knew that the Elder expected to be praised in spite of all these things. Now what would it all come to?

This thought was passing through Orlean's mind when she heard her father again:

"Now, he said something about a contest." She caught her breath quickly, swallowed, changed color, and then managed, hardly above a whisper, to say:

"Oh!"

"I don't understand. And he never takes the time to explain anything. Seems to take for granted that everybody should know, and tries to know it all himself, and it makes it very awkward," he said complainingly.

"It's all my fault, papa," Orlean admitted falteringly.

"Your fault!" the other exclaimed, not understanding.

"Yes," she breathed with eyes downcast.

"And what do you mean? How can it be your fault when you have sacrificed the nice home in Chicago for this wilderness?"

"But, papa," she faltered. "You have never been West before. You — you don't understand!"

"Don't understand!" cried the Reverend, anger and impatience evident. "What is there to understand about this wilderness?"

"Oh, papa," she cried, now beseechingly. "You —" she halted and swallowed what she had started to say. And what she had started to say was, that if he kept on like he had started, he would make it very difficult for her to be loyal to her husband and obedient to him as she had always been; as she was trying to be. Perhaps it was becoming difficult for her already. Subservience to her father, who insisted upon it, and obedience and loyalty to her husband who had a right and naturally expected it. It *was* difficult, and she was a weak willed person. Already her courage was failing her and she was beginning to sigh.

"It is very hard on my daughter, I fear," said the Elder, his face now full of emotion and self pity. "I worked all my life to raise my two darlings, and it grieves me to see one of them being ground down by a man."

"Oh, father, my husband is not cruel to me. He has never said an unkind word. He is just as good to me as a man can be — and I love him." This would have been sufficient to have satisfied and pacified any man, even one so unscrupulous. But it happens that in our story we have met one who is considerably different from the ordinary man. The substance of N. Justine McCarthy's vanity had never been fully estimated — not even by himself. Orlean did not recall then, that since she had been married she had not written her father and repeated what a great man he was. She had, on the other hand, written and told him what a great man her husband was. In her simplicity, she felt it was expected of her to tell that one or the other was great. But here she had encountered discouragement. Her husband apparently was considerably opposed to flattery. And she had difficulty to have him see that it was an evidence of faith on her part. But her husband had not seen it that way. He had disimissed it as a waste of time. and had gradually used his influence with her to other ends; to the road they were following; the road to ultimate success, which could only be achieved by grim, practical methods. And that was one of his words, practical. But her father was speaking again.

"Now I wish you would explain how you could be at fault for this contest upon your place, and why your husband accuses you of such?"

"But Jean does not accuse me of being at fault, father," she defended weakly. "I accuse myself. And if you will be just a little patient," she begged almost in tears, "I'll explain." He frowned in his usual way, while she sighed unheard, and then fell to the task before her.

"It is like this," she began with an effort at self control. "Jean has not wished to ask me to stay on my claim alone as his sister and grandmother have done, you see."

"Oh, so he has them living out there alone like cattle, helping him to get rich!"

"They do not live like cattle, father," she defended in the patient manner she had been trained to. "They have a horse and buggy that he has furnished them, and get all their needs at the stores which is charged to him. They have good neighbors, awfully nice white people — women, too, who live alone on their claims as his sister and grandmother are doing."

"But they are not like you, daughter. Those are all rough people. You cannot live like them. You have been accustomed to something."

She sighed unheard again and did not try to explain to his Majesty that most of the people — women included — were in a majority from the best homes in the East, as well as families; that many had wealth where she had none; and that Jean's sister had been graduated from high school and was very intelligent. It was difficult, and she knew it, to explain anything to her father; but she would endeavor to tell him of the contest.

"Well, father, since I was not on my place as I should have been, a man contested it, and now we must fight it out, Jean says, so that is it."

"M-m-m," sighed that one. "He's going to kill you out here to make him rich. And then when you are dead and —"

"Please, don't, father," she almost screamed. She knew he was going to say: "and in your grave, he will marry

From a painting by W. M. Farrow.

"HE'S GOING TO KILL YOU OUT HERE TO MAKE HIM RICH, AND THEN WHEN YOU ARE DEAD AND"—"PLEASE DON'T, FATHER!" SHE ALMOST SCREAMED. SHE KNEW HE WAS GOING TO SAY: "IN YOUR GRAVE, HE WILL MARRY AN-OTHER WOMAN TO ENJOY WHAT YOU HAVE DIED FOR," BUT SHE COULD NOT QUITE LISTEN TO THAT.

another woman and bring her in to enjoy what you have died for." But she could not quite listen to that. It was not fair. It was not fair to her and it was not fair to Jean. She was surprised at the way she felt. She forgot also, and for his benefit, that they had never been very happy at home when he was in Chicago. They had only pretended to be. It had been because of him being away all the time and their relation having been confined to letters that they had been contented. But Orlean had made herself believe for this occasion that when he came to visit, they were going to have a really pleasant time. And now so soon she was simply worn out. She had become more sensitive of her tasks in life than it had occurred to her she could ever be. For the first time she was getting the idea that, after all they were burdensome.

"Wouldn't you like to go to town, papa?" she cried, trying to be jolly. "Jean is ready now, and please come along and see the nice little house he has bought and is going to move on my claim." She was so cheerful, so anxious to have him enjoy his visit that his vanity for once took a back seat, and a few minutes later they were driving into Gregory.

As they drove along Baptiste told of what he was doing; discussing at length the West and what was being done toward its development. When they arrived in the town they approached the small but well made little building that he had purchased for $300, and went inside.

"Awfully small, my boy," said the Reverend, as they looked around.

"Of course," admitted Baptiste. "But it is not practical to invest in big houses in the beginning, you know. We must first build a good big barn, and that, I cannot even as yet afford."

"Places his horses before his wife, of course," muttered the Reverend, but obligingly unheard.

"And you say you intend to move it. Where? Not away down on that farm southeast?" he said, standing outside and looking up at the building.

"Oh, no," Baptiste returned shortly. "Onto Orlean's place, west of here."

"Oh. How far is that?"

"Not so far. About fifty miles."

"Good lord!" And the Reverend could say no more.

CHAPTER XIV

THE CONTEST

MOVING a building fifty miles across even a prairie is not an easy task, and before Jean Baptiste reached his wife's homestead with the building he had purchased, he had suffered much grief. And with the Reverend along, ever ready to keep their minds alive to the fact, it was made no easier. But because he was so chronic, he was left to grumble while his son-in-law labored almost to distraction into getting the building to the place before he would be compelled to turn back and face the contest which was scheduled for an early hearing. They succeeded in getting it within twenty miles of the claim when they were compelled to abandon the task for the time and return to Gregory to fight the contest.

This developed at times into a rather heated argument, and a prolonged one that tried the patience of all, dragging over a period of three days. It became obvious during the proceedings that the contestant and his cohorts desired as much as possible to keep away from Baptiste and on the other hand to concentrate their cross-fire upon his wife. But, expecting this, they found him on his guard, countering them at every angle, and, assisted by an able land attorney, he was successful in upsetting in a large way, their many subtle and well laid plans, causing them to fail in making the showing they had expected to.

To begin with their corroborating witness, James J. Spaight, developed before the close to more definitely corroborate for the defense. He had come to the trial with false testimony prepared, and had, under a fusillade of cross-examinations, broken down and impaired and weakened the prosectuion. In all such cases the one contesting is placed at a moral disadvantage, and the fact that Crook was a banker, fully able to have purchased relinquishment as others over all the county had done, was ever in the witness' mind, and did not help his case. Baptiste's wife proved much stronger after the first day. This was due largely to the fact that her father had been present on the first day, and had kept her so much alive to what she was sacrificing in struggling to assist her husband in his ambition to be rich, until she was perceptibly weak. The time limit on his ticket having about expired he had been compelled to return to Chicago the morning of the second day of the trial.

It was the consensus of opinion that she would retain her claim, though with so many cases to consider, it was obvious that it would take many months, and possibly a year to get a hearing — that is, before the officers of the local land offices could settle the case.

This done, Jean Baptiste returned and completed moving the house on the claim, fixed it up, dug a well, fenced in a small pasture and returned to gather his corn which amounted to about half a crop.

So time passed and the holidays approached and another phase in their relations took shape when the Reverend insisted that they come to Chicago to spend the holidays. It was very annoying. Orlean was expecting to become a mother in the early spring, and because they had never informed him of the fact, it brought considerable embarrassment to all.

It was difficult to explain to his Majesty that they would

not come into the city for the holidays. The Elder had insisted that he would send them tickets, and because Jean Baptiste had scoffed at the idea, trouble was brewing as a result. It was then he lost his patience.

"Can your father not understand, Orlean," he complained, with a deep frown, "that I cannot accept his charity? Because I have made up my mind not to go to Chicago, does not mean that I am not able to purchase our transportations there and back. It's the expense of the trip and what goes with it that has caused me to decide to dispense with it. But it's almost useless to try to reason anything with him, and I'll not waste the effort." Whereupon he would say no more.

He was having troubles of his own. He owed ten thousand dollars, and upon this, interest accrued every few months, and the rate was high. Besides, he had other pressing bills, and the grain he had raised was bringing very low prices. Therefore, he was in no mood to dally with a poverty poor preacher whose offer was more to show himself off and place Baptiste in a compromising position, than his desire for them to be home. He made no effort to appreciate the sentiments or to understand Jean Baptiste. And the fact that his daughter loved her husband and was willing to help him seemed to be lost sight of by N. Justine McCarthy. Being accustomed to having people flatter him as a rule, was so engraved in his shallow nature, that he was unable to see matters from a liberal point of view.

Their relations reached a climax when Orlean was with his sister on the claim a few days before the Yuletide. Baptiste received a letter addressed to her from the Elder. Thinking that, since she was on the claim, it might be something urgent, he opened it. It *was* urgent. It contained a money order covering the price of a ticket to Chicago with a trite note that he expected her soon, and that he, her husband, could come on later.

We shall not attempt to describe the anger that came over Jean Baptiste then. And, as is most likely the case when a man is angry, he does the thing he most likely would not do when his feelings are under control. With hands that trembled with anger, he turned the note over, wrote in a few words that he had defined his position with regards to coming to Chicago; that he would be obliged if the other would mind his own business; that he had married his wife and was trying to be a husband in every way to her; but that he was running his house, and was therefore returning the money therewith.

It served as a declaration of the war between the two that had been impending for months. We are too well acquainted with their regard for each other, so upon this we will not dwell; but upon receipt of Baptiste's letter, the Reverend sang his anger in a letter that fairly scorched the envelope in which it was enclosed. He threatened to turn the world over, and set it right again if the other did not do thus and so. To the threats, Baptiste made no reply. In a measure he was relieved; he had at last made his position clear to the other, and his wife, of course, was with him in the controversy. In view therefore, of the manner in which she had been trained, this made matters rather awkward. The yield of crops had not been one half the average, and it took almost all he had made to pay the interest, taxes and expenses. Baptiste was not cheerful; but Orlean was to become a mother, and he was a practical man. So together they passed a happy Xmas after all. In fact the only cloud upon their horizon of happiness was her father.

Evidently he voiced what he had done to near friends,

and they had not endorsed his action. Orlean was the wife of Jean Baptiste and if he expected her to stay with him, it was their affair, even if the Reverend had only intended to help. Attempting to force charity on others is not always sensible, so the Elder wrote later that it was " up to them," and if they had agreed to stay in the West Xmas, it was alright with him.

This was very considerate of him — apparently, after all the noise he had made, and Orlean was much relieved, and loved her father still. Her husband was also relieved, and forgot the matter for the time. But did the Reverend?

Well, that was not his nature. He never forgot things he should forget. Oh, no! He had not been a hypocrite forty years for nothing! In the meantime, the Xmas passed as it has for more than nineteen hundred years, winter set in, and the spring was approaching when the catastrophe occurred.

CHAPTER XV

COMPROMISED

"PLEASE don't go, Jean," she begged. "I don't want you to go. Stay with me."

"Now, Orlean," he said gently. "I have such a lot of work to do. I will go, tear down some of the old buildings on the homestead and be back before many days."

She cried for a time while he held her in his arms. Crying was nothing new with her. As the time for her delivery drew near, she was given to such spells. He was patient. After a few moments she dried her eys and said:

"Well, dear, you can go. But hurry back. I want you to be home then, you understand."

"Of course I want to be home then, wifey, and sure want it to be a boy."

"It *will* be a boy, Jean," she said with a strange confidence. "I believe it. I am sure it will."

"I shall love you always then, my wife. All our cares and burdens will vanish into the air, and we shall be as happy as the angels."

"Oh, Jean, you can make life seem so light."

"Life should be made to appear light, sweetheart," he said, caressing her. "Grandmother will be here with you and if you need for anything, draw a check and have the neighbors below bring it out. It is only three miles over the hill to Carter, you understand."

"By the way, dear," she said suddenly, going into the bedroom, and returning presently with a letter. "This is from mama. She writes that they have never told papa yet, and hopes that nothing serious will happen for then she would never — we would never be forgiven by him."

"Dear Little Mother Mary," he said fondly. "I hope nothing will happen, Orlean, for our sakes." And then he paused. He had started to say that he was not worried about her father's forgiveness. He had lost what little patience he had ever had with that one, and did not propose to be annoyed with his love, the love that he had to be continually making excuses and apologies to entertain. But before he had spoken he thought better of it, and decided to say nothing about it. His wife had been trained to regard her father as a king, and because he had succeeded in letting her see that after all he was just a Negro preacher with the most that went with Negro preachers in him, she had at last ceased to bore him with telling him how great her father was.

They were at her claim, and he was about to depart for his original homestead to clean up work preparatory to moving onto her claim permanently as he had intended to do. Already his wagons with horses hitched thereto stood near, and he was only lingering for a few parting words with her.

"I am kind of sorry we placed mother in this position," he heard her say as if talking more to herself than he.

"In what position, Orlean?"

"In keeping this a secret."

"From your father, you mean?" said he, frowning.

"Yes."

"Well, Orlean, I have tried to be a husband to you."

"And you have been, Jean."

"Then it is our business if I chose to keep such a secret."

" Yes, Jean," she said, lowering her eyes and thinking.

" But the one burden of our married life has been your father. I never anticipated that his love would be such a burden. Ever since we have been married we have had to waste our substance on fear over what he will think. He seems to lose sight of a husband's sentiment or right. I can fancy him in my position with regard to your mother before they had been married long. My God, if any father or mother would have ventured any suggestion as to how they should live or what they should do I can see him! "

His wife laughed.

" Have I spoken rightly? "

" Yes," she agreed and was momentarily amused.

" Yes. But he just makes our life a burden with his kind of love. Now take this matter for instance. Why should we be keeping this a secret from him — rather, why should I? It's just simply because I have too much other cares to be annoyed with a whole lot of to-do on his part. If he knew you were going to become a mother, he would just make our life unbearable with his insistences and love. Your mother knows it, and Ethel. Ethel who would have had you dispose of that innocent, knows it and keeps it from him, with fear all the while of what will come of it, should anything happen.

" Now, I'll say this much. I don't propose to make any excuses to him about anything I do or have you do hereafter. I'm going to be husband and master, and have nothing to do with what he does with regard to your mother. As long as I am good and kind to you, and don't neglect you, then I have a right, and positively will not be annoyed even by your father! "

" Please hush, Jean," she begged, her arms about him. But he was aroused. He had made himself forget as he should have forgotten the punishment he had been given twenty-two years before. But he did not like the man's conduct. Everywhere and with everybody back in Illinois who knew N. Justine McCarthy, he was regarded as an acknowledged rascal.

"Just look how he treats your mother!" She pulled at him and tried to still his voice; but speak he would. "If I was ever guilty of treating you as your father has treated your mother ever since he married her, I hope the Christ will sink my soul into the bottom-most pit of hell!"

"Jean, my God, please hush!"

"But I speak the truth and you know it. Would you like to look forward and feel that you had to go through all your life what your mother has endured?"

"Oh, no, no, no! But you must hush, Jean, in heaven's name, hush." He did then. The storm that had come over him had spent its force and he kissed her, turned then, went to where his teams stood, got into the front wagon, and looking back, drove upon his way.

"Poor Jean," murmured Orlean. "Father and he will never be friends and it makes it so hard for me." She continued to stand where he left her, looking after him until he had disappeared over the hills to the east.

Arriving at Gregory late that afternoon, Jean found a Lyceum concert, the number consisting of Negroes, one of whom, a girl, he had known some years before, for she had lived next door to where he then roomed.

He attended and afterward renewed their acquaintance. It so happened that a lumber company was going out of business in the next town east from Gregory, and some coal sheds there were for sale. Desiring something of the kind to use as a granary on his wife's claim, Baptiste journeyed hither the following day to look the same over.

Now it also happened that the same concerters were billed for the same town for an evening performance of that day. The day after being Sunday, and the company laying over until Monday, the days were passed together, with Baptiste scheduled to go out to his old place Sunday night.

It was a cheer to revive old acquaintances; to talk of Chicago and olden days with those who still lived there. It was a cheer to all, but Jean Baptiste had cause to regret it as we shall later see. In the meantime, he went to his old place as per schedule, returning to the little town the following morning, where he purchased a hundred foot shed and prepared to move it to his wife's claim forthwith.

A few miles only had been traversed before an intermittent thaw set in, the soft uncertain surface of the earth making it hazardous to pull a heavy load over. So when he reached his old place, he decided to leave it there, tear down his old granary and haul the lumber instead.

While in this act, his sister, who had been on a visit to Kansas, returned, and worried with regards to his wife, alone with his grandma out on the homestead, he hurried her therewith at once. The next day he was relieved to receive a letter from Orlean, advising that she was well, but to come home as soon as possible.

A week had passed and Saturday was upon him again before he was ready to make a start. Now there often comes in the springtime in the West, severe winds that may blow unchecked for days. And one came up just as Jean Baptiste had set out, and blew a terrific gale. It almost upset his wagons, and made driving very difficult. This was augmented further, because the wind was right in his face, and there was no way to avoid it. However, he finally reached a town about eleven miles west of Dallas, by the name of Colome that day. The next morning the wind had gone down and the day was beautiful, and he was cheered to think he could reach home that day, by getting started early. But bad luck was with Jean Baptiste that day, which was Sunday, and when he was going down a hill, the wagon struck a rocky place, bounced, and the right front wheel rolled out ahead of him. The axle had broken, and his load went down with a crash.

He went to a house he saw near, secured a wagon, and there met a man who had known his father, and had lived and run a newspaper in the same town near where he was born twenty-six years before. He wasted hours getting his load transferred to another wagon, and finally got started again. But not two miles had been covered before the coupling pole snapped, and his loads almost went down again. What trick of fate was playing him, he wondered, and swore viciously. Hours it took before the break was repaired, and he pulled into Winner, eighteen miles from home, late that night.

Early morning found him, however, resolutely on the way. He had covered about half the distance when he met a man who lived neighbor to him on his wife's claim, who told him he had tried to get him on the 'phone Saturday, at Gregory and again at Dallas; that his wife had given birth to a baby which had come into the world dead, on a Saturday.

He almost tumbled from the wagon when he heard this. "Dead!" he repeated. Finally he heard himself speaking, and in a voice that seemed to come from far away:

"Ah — well — did my wife have — attention?"

"Oh, yes," said the other. "Your sister, and two doctors. Yes, she had all the attention necessary. But I'm sorry for you, old man. It was sure a big, fine kid. She couldn't give it birth, so they had to kill it in order to save her life."

He started to resume his journey East, while Baptiste, now with unstrung nerves, started to resume his way West. But before his horses had gone many steps he suddenly drew them down to a halt, and, turning, heard the other call out: "I went to Carter and sent her father a telegram as per a request of hers. I suppose it was all right," and continued on his way.

"To him!" cried Baptiste inaudibly. "*To* him!" he repeated. "To him no doubt, that the baby — which he had not known was to be, had come and — dead!"

Mechanically he drove upon his way. He did not think, he did not speak. He said nothing for a long, long time; but down in his heart *Jean Baptiste knew that he was coming nearer to the parting of the ways.*

Back in old Illinois N. Justine McCarthy, upon receiving the telegram, he realized would in all probability depart at the earliest convenience for the West. And when he arrived, would learn still more than the message had told; would learn that he had been absent when his wife had given birth to the dead baby. Oh, his child, why could it not have lived. . . . Yes, she had had all the attention that was possible; but such would not be credited by N. Justine McCarthy. The fact that not every man had found it possible to be present at the bedside of their wives when children came, would not be considered by N. Justine McCarthy. *The fact that he himself had been absent when his own Orlean came into the world* would be no counter here. Jean Baptiste's absence at the critical time would serve as an excuse for the Reverend to vent his spite, and he would demand a toll. Jean Baptiste was compromised, and would have to make a sacrifice. . . .

CHAPTER XVI

THE EVIL GENIUS

"OH, JEAN," breathed Orlean, from the bed, "where have you been?"

He had come unto the house then, and the man in him was much downcast. He was, and had cause to feel discouraged, sorrowful and sad. So he explained to the one who lay upon the bed where he had been, and what had happened to him, and why he had been delayed.

She sighed when he was through and was sorry. For a long time he was on his knees at the bedside, and when an hour had passed, she reached and placed her arm about his neck, and was thankful that he was spared to her, and they would live on hopeful; but both felt their loss deeply.

"I sent papa a telegram," she said presently. Because he knew he made no answer. He knew the other would come, and he was resigned as to what would follow. She sighed again. Perhaps it was because she knew and also feared what was to follow. . . . She had not known her father her lifetime without knowing what must happen. But she loved her husband, and now in the weak state the delivery had left her she was struggling to withstand the subtle attack her father was sure to make.

Two days passed, and she was progressing toward health as well as could be expected. Since her marriage her health on the whole had improved wonderfully. The petty aches and pains of which she complained formerly had gradually disappeared, and the western air had brought health and vigor to her.

And then on the third day he arrived. Moreover, he brought Ethel with him. They rode over the hill that led to the claim in a hired rig, and Baptiste espied them as soon as they were in sight.

Our pen cannot describe what Jean Baptiste read in the eyes of N. J. McCarthy when he alighted from the buggy and went into the house. But suffice to say, that what had passed twenty-two years before had come back. There was to be war between them and as it had been then Baptiste was at a disadvantage, and must necessarily accept the inevitable.

Ethel was crying, and her tears meant more than words. She had never cried for love. It had always been something to the contrary. But we must turn to the one in bed — and helpless!

She saw her father when he stepped from the buggy, and understood what he carried behind his masklike face. He did not allow his eyes to rest on Jean Baptiste, and she noted this. She settled back upon the pillow, and tried to compose herself for the event that was to be. Her husband was compromised, and could not defend himself. . . . Therefore it fell upon her and from the sick bed to defend him.

He was inside the house now, and came toward her, and she was frightened when he was near and saw his face and what it held. Hatred within was there and she shuddered audibly. She closed her eyes to shut it out. Oh, the agony that came over her. She opened her eyes when his lips touched hers, and then began the struggle that was to be hers.

" Papa," she whispered, and in her voice there was a great appeal. " Don't blame Jean. Jean has burdens, he has responsibilities — he's all tied up! He's good to me, he loves me, he gives me all he has." But before she had finished, she knew that her appeal had fallen upon deaf ears. Her father had come — and he had brought a purpose to be fulfilled.

He caressed her; he said many foolish things, and she pretended to believe him; she made as if his coming had meant the saving of her life; but she knew behind all he pretended was the evil, the evil that was his nature, and the fear that filled her breast made her weaker; made her sick.

The doctor had said that she would be able to leave the bed in ten days, probably a week; but now with grim realization of what was before her she became weak, weaker, weakest. And all the time she saw that it was being charged to Jean Baptiste, and to his neglect.

We should perhaps try to make clear at this point in this story that Jean Baptiste could have settled matters in a very simple manner. . . . True, the manner in which he could have settled it, would be the manner in which wars could be avoided — by sacrificing principle. He could have gone to his Majesty and played a traitor to his nature by pretending to believe the Elder had been right and justified in everything; whereas, he, Jean Baptiste, had been as duly wrong. He could have acted in such a manner as to have his Majesty feel that he was a great man, that he had been honored by even knowing him, much less in being privileged to marry his daughter. This, in view of the fact that having been absent from her bedside at that crucial time, he was compromised, would have satisfied the Elder, and Baptiste would not have been compelled to forego all that later came to pass in their relations. *But Jean Baptiste had a principle, and was not a liar, nor a coward, nor a thief.* And, al-

though, he had been so unfortunte as not to have been by
the bedside of his wife during that hour, he could have senti-
mentally appeased his father-in-law, but Jean Baptiste had
not nor will he ever in the development of this story, sink
so low.   Of what was to come — and the most is — in this
story, Jean Baptiste at no time sacrificed his manhood for
any cause.

N. Justine McCarthy, and this is true of too many of
his race and to this cause may be attributed many of their
failures, was not a reader.   He never read anything but the
newspapers briefly and the Bible a little.   He was, therefore, not an informed man.   As a result he took little interest in, and appreciated less, what the world is thinking
and doing.   He had never understood because he had not
tried, what the people around where Jean Baptiste had come
were doing for posterity.   Yet he claimed very loudly to be
an apostle of the race — to be willing — and was — sacrificing his very soul for the cause of Ethiopia.   He took
great pride in telling and retelling how he had sacrificed for
his family — wife included.   As he was heard by others,
he had no faults; could do no wrong, and would surely
reach heaven in the end!

So while they lingered at the bedside of Orlean, he and
Ethel, as a pastime argued with each other, and involved
everybody but themselves with wrongs.   For instance, the
Reverend, affecting much piety, would in discussing his
wife, whom he ever did in terms regarding her faults, find
occasion to remark in a burst of self pity — and of self pity
he had an abundant supply:

" After all I have done for that woman; after all I have
sacrificed for her; after all the patience I have endured while
she has held me down — kept me from being what I would
have been and should, she is ever bursting out with:

' You're the meanest man in the world! You're the meanest man in the world!'" Whereupon he would affect a look of deep self pity and eternal mortification.

Unless we lengthen the story unnecessarily, we would not have the space to relate all he said in reference to his son-in-law in subtle ways during these days. But Jean Baptiste was too busy building a barn and other buildings to listen to these compliments the Elder was bestowing upon his wife with regard to him. "Yes, my dear," he said time and again, "If Jean was like your father, you would not be here now with your child lying dead in the grave. No, no. You would be in the best hospital in Chicago, with nurses and attendants all about you and your darling baby at your side," and, so saying, he would affect another sigh of self pity.

At first she had struggled to protest, but after a few days she gave up entirely and became resigned to the inevitable. She received an occasional diversion, however, when the Elder and Ethel entered into a controversy. Unlike Orlean, Ethel was not afraid of her father, especially when he had something to say about Glavis. The truth was, that while he so pretended, N. J. McCarthy had no more love for Glavis than he had for Baptiste; but he could tolerate Glavis because Glavis endeavored to satisfy his vanity. Baptiste, on the other hand, while he now accepted all his father-in-law chose to pour upon him in the way of rebuke for what he had done and should not have, and what he had not done and should have, he never told the Elder that he was a great man.

The first few days the Elder had held the usual prayer; but after some days he dispensed with this, and turned all his energy to rebuking Jean Baptiste, when he was out of sight.

"Now, don't you talk about Glavis," cried Ethel one day

when his Majesty had tired of abusing Baptiste and sought a diversion by remarking that Glavis had come from a stumpy farm in the woodlands of Tennessee. " No, you don't! Glavis is my husband and you can't abuse him to his back like you are doing Baptiste!"

" Just listen how she treats her father, Orlean," cried the Elder, overcome with self pity. Orlean then rebuked Ethel and chided her father. But the part which escaped her, was that Ethel defended her mate, while Orlean suffered to have hers rebuked at will. The greatest reason why Ethel and her father could not agree, as was well known, was that they were too much alike.

When Jean Baptiste had completed his barn, and his wife was out of danger, according to the doctor — but would never be according to the Elder — who insisted that the only cure would be for her to return to Chicago with them,— he was ready to go to work. His wife wanted to go to Chicago, for what the Reverend had done to her in the days he had sat by her and professed his great love, would have made her wish to go anywhere to appease him for even a day.

" Now, after the expense we have been to," said Baptiste, " I hardly know whether I can let you go to Chicago or not."

The Elder sighed, and said to her low enough for her husband's ears not to hear: " Just listen to that. After all I have done! Then I will have to pay your way to Chicago where I shall endeavor to save your life, your dear life which this man is trying to grind out of you to get rich."

" But I'll think it over," said Baptiste. " We have lots of work this summer, and will try to get caught up," and the next moment he was gone.

" Did you hear that, daughter? " said the Reverend, now

aloud, when the other's back was turned. "Oh, it's awful, the man you have married! Just crazy, crazy to get rich! And puts you after his work; after his horses; after his everything! And after all your poor old father has done for you," whereupon he let escape another sigh, and fell into tears of self pity.

Orlean stroked his head and swallowed what she would have offered in defense of the man she had married. It was useless to offer defense, he had broken this down long since.

"Yes, he is wanting to kill, to kill my poor daughter after all she has sacrificed," he sobbed, "and when you are dead and in your grave like your baby is out in this wild country," his voice was breaking now with sobs, "he will up and marry another woman to enjoy the fruits of your sacrifice!" He was lost in his own tears then, and could say no more.

"Now, dear," she suddenly heard her husband, and looked up to find that he had returned. He stooped and kissed her fondly, and then went on: "I am going up to my sister's homestead to start the men to work with the engine breaking the land and I must haul them the coal, which I will get at Colome. Now I will not be back for several days, but will make up my mind in the meantime as to whether I can let you go to Chicago or not."

"All right, dear," she said, raising from the bed and caressing him long and lingeringly. She could not understand how much she wanted him then, it seemed that she could hold him so forever. She kissed him again and again, and as he passed out of the room she looked after him long and lingeringly, and upon her face was a heavenly smile as he passed out of sight and disappeared over the hill. As he did so, the Elder got from his position at the other side of the

bed, went to the door, and also watched him out sight. As
he turned away, Baptiste's grandmother who had fed many
a preacher back there in old Illinois, the Reverend included,
started. She had seen his face, and what she had seen
therein had frightened her. When he went back into the
room and to the bed where Orlean lay, she dropped by the
table and buried her face in her old arms and sobbed, long
and silently. And a close observer could have heard these
shaken words:

"Poor Jean, poor Jean, poor Orlean, oh, poor Orlean!
You made all the fight you could but you were weak. You
were doomed before you started, for he knew you and knew
you were weak. But would to God that the world could end
today, for it will end tomorrow for you two. Poor Orlean,
poor Jean!"

CHAPTER XVII

THE COWARD

"HELLO, JEAN," cried a friend of his at Colome some days later, as he was leading his horses into the livery barn, after loading the coal he was hauling to the men who were breaking prairie on his sister's claim with a steam tractor. "Were those your folks I seen driving into town a while ago?"

"My folks?"

"Yeh. Three of them. A man and two women. One of the ladies appears to be sick."

"Oh," he echoed, and before he could or would have answered in his sudden surprise, the other passed on. It was some moments before he recovered from the shock the other's words had given him. He knew without stopping to think that the ones referred to were the Reverend, Ethel and his wife. He had written his wife a few days before that he would be home the following Sunday, and when he would be caught up in his hauling sufficiently and could spend a few days there.

"So he moves without my consent or bid," he breathed, and for a time he was listless from the feeling that overcame him. He attended to his horses, mechanically, had supper and went to verify what he had heard.

He had little difficulty in doing so, for the town was small, but that night, happened to be full of people, and the Reverend had found some difficulty in securing lodging. The day had not been a beautiful one by any means. It was in early April and the month had borrowed one of the dreary days of the previous month. Light snow had fallen, which, along toward evening had turned into a dismal sleet. A bad day to say the least, to be out, and a sick person of all things!

He went directly to the preacher when he saw him. He was aroused, and the insults he had suffered did not make him pleasant.

"Now, look here, Reverend McCarthy," he said and his tone revealed his feelings, "what kind of a 'stunt' are you pulling off with my wife?" And he blocked his way where they stood upon the sidewalk.

"Now, now, my son —"

"Oh, don't 'son' me," said the other impatiently. "You and I might as well come to an understanding right here to-night as any other time. We are not friends and you know it. We have never since we have known each other been in accord — not since we met — yes, twenty-two years ago. Oh, you remember it." The other started guiltily when Jean referred to his youth.

"You remember how my mother licked me for letting Miss Self help me upon her lap and fed me, thereby disturbing your illegitimate flirtation. . . ." The other's pious face darkened. But it was not his nature to meet and argue openly as men should and do. Always his counter was subtle. So while Jean Baptiste was in the mood to come to an understanding, to admit frankly to the other, that enemies they were, the Elder permitted a womanish smile to spread over his face and patted the other on the back, saying:

"Now, now, Jean. You are my daughter's husband, and it is no time or place to carry on like this. The girl lays sick over here and if you would be a husband you would go to her. Now let's dispense with such things as you refer to and go forth to the indisposed." He appeared more godly now than he had ever. Distrust was in the face of Baptiste. He knew the preacher was not sincere, but his wife, the girl he had married, lay ill. He suspicioned that the Elder had intended stealing her away without his knowledge; he knew, moreover, that all his affected tenderness was subtle; but he hushed the harsh words that were on his tongue to say and followed the other.

" Yes, my children," his pious face almost unable to veil the evil behind the mask, " here we are together," he said when he entered the room followed by Baptiste. Orlean was in bed and made no effort to greet her husband; while Ethel sat sulkily in a chair nearby and kept her mouth closed. Jean went to the bed and sat by his wife and regarded her meditatively. She did not seem to recognize him, and he made no effort to arouse her to express her thoughts which seemed to come and go. He was lost in thoughts, strange and sinister. Verily his life was in a turmoil. The life he had come into through his marriage had revived so many old and unpleasant memories that he had forgotten, until he was in a sort of daze. He had virtually run away from those parts wherein he had first seen the light of day, to escape the effect of dull indolence; the penurious evil that seemed to have gripped the populace, especially a great portion of his race. In the years Jean Baptiste had spent in the West, he had been able to follow, unhampered, his convictions. But now, the Reverend's presence seemed to have brought all this back.

In a conversation one day with that other he had occasion to mention the late James J. Hill, in his eulogy of the northwest and was surprised to find — and have the Reverend admit — that he had never even heard of him. Indeed, what the Elder knew about the big things in life would have filled a very small book. But when it came to the

virtues of the women in the churches over which he presided, he knew everything. And whenever they had become
agreeable in any way, it was sure to end with the Reverend
relating incidents regarding the social and moral conduct
of the women in the churches over which he presided.
Moreover, the Elder sought in his subtle manner, to dig into
the past life of members of Baptiste's family, of what any
had committed that could be used as a measure for gossip.
And this night, as they sat over Jean's wife whose sentiment
and convictions had been crushed, the Elder attempted to
dwell on the subject again.

" Yes, when your older sister taught in Murphysboro, and
got herself talked about because she drew a revolver on
Professor Alexander, that was certainly too bad."

" Looks as if she was able to take care of herself," suggested Baptiste, deciding to counter the old rascal at his own
game.

" But that's what I'm trying to show you, and you could
see it if you wasn't inclined to be so hard headed," argued
the Elder.

" We'll leave personalities out of it, if you please," said
Baptiste, coloring.

" Oh, but if your sister had had protection, such a de-
plorable incident would not have happened. Now, for instance," argued the Elder, " my girls have never had their
good names embarrassed with such incidents."

" Oh, they haven't," cried Baptiste, all patience gone.
" Then what about their half brother in East St. Louis, eh?
And the other one who died — was stabbed to death. Those
were yours, and you were never married to their mother ! "

The other's face became terrible. The expression upon
his face was dreadful to behold. He started to rise, but

Baptiste was not through. He was thoroughly aroused now, and all he had stood from this arch sinner had come back to him. Therefore, before the other could deny or do anything, said he:

"Oh, you needn't try to become so upset over it. Your morals are common knowledge to all the people of Illinois, and elsewhere. And let me tell you, you can — as you have — in your family, force those who know it and condemn it to keep quiet by making yourself so disagreeable that they will honey you up to get along with you. But it is not because they, or all those who know you, are not aware of it! That's your reputation, and some day you are going to suffer for it. You deliberately make people miserable to satisfy your infernal vanity; your desire to be looked upon and called great. Now right here you are bent upon crucifying your own daughter's happiness just because I haven't tickled your rotten vanity, and lied." He arose now, and pointed a threatening finger at the other.

"You are out to injure me, and you are taking advantage of your own child's position as my wife to do so. I'm going to let you go ahead. Orlean's a good girl, but she's weak like the mother that you have abused for thirty years! But remember this, N. J. McCarthy, and I've called you Reverend for the last time. The evil that you do unto others will some day be done unto you and will drag your ornery heart in its own blood. Mark my words!" And the next instant he was gone.

The other looked after him uneasily. The truth had come so forcibly, so impulsively, so abruptly, that it had for the time overcome his cunningness; but only for a moment after the other had disappeared was he so. He regained his usual composure soon enough, and he turned

to the sick woman for succor — to her whom he was dragging down to the gutter of misery for his own self
aggrandizement.

"Did you hear how he abused your father?" he cried,
the tears from his piggish eyes falling on her cheeks. She
reached and stroked his white hair, and mumbled weak
words.

"Oh, I never thought I would come to this — be brought
to this through the daughter that I have loved so much. Oh,
poor me, your poor old father," whereupon he wept bitterly.

"You see, you see," cried Ethel, who had risen and stood
over her, pointing her finger to Orlean as she lay upon the
bed. "This is what comes of marrying that man! I tried,
oh, I tried so hard to have you see that no good could come
of it, no good at all!" The other sighed. She was too
weak from mortification to reply in the affirmative, or the
negative.

"I tried, and I tried to have you desist, but you would!
When I had at last gotten you to quit him, and you swore
you had, no sooner did he come and place his arm about you
and whisper fool things in your ear, than did you but up
and consent to this. This, this, do you hear? This that
has brought your poor father to that!" and she stopped to
point to where that one lay stretched across the bed, sobbing.

The night was one long, miserable, quarrelsome night.
Ethel and the Elder wore themselves out abusing Baptiste,
and along toward morning all fell into a troubled sleep.

Baptiste met them the next morning as they came from
the rooms, and helped his wife across the street to a restaurant. When they had finished the meal, he said to her as
they came from the restaurant,

"Now, dear, I'll step into the bank here and get you
some money —"

" No, no, no, Jean," she said quickly, cutting him off before he completed what he had started to say.

" Well," and he started toward the bank again as if he had not understood her.

" No, no, no, Jean," she repeated, and caught his arm nervously. " No, don't ! "

" But you are going away, dear, and will surely need money ? " he insisted.

" Yes, but —Jean — Jean — I have money."

" You have money ? " repeated the other uncomprehendingly. " But how came you with money? That much money ? "

" I — I had — a — check cashed. That is — papa had one cashed for me."

" Oh, so that was it. M-m. *Your father* had it cashed for you ? " he understood then, and his suspicion that the Elder had intended taking her to Chicago without letting him know it was confirmed. They walked down the street toward the depot, and while she held nervously to his arm, his mind was concerned with his thoughts. It occurred to him that he should take his wife back to the claim right then. He felt that if she went to Chicago there would be trouble. He began slowly to appreciate that in dealing with Reverend McCarthy he was not dealing with a man; nor a near man. He was not dealing with a mere liar, or a thief, even — he was dealing with the lowest of all reptiles, a snake! Then why did not he, Jean Baptiste, act?

Perhaps if he had, we should never have had this story to tell. Jean Baptiste did not act. He decided to let her go. Beyond that he had no decision. It seemed that his mind would not work beyond the immediate present. Soon she heard him, as she clung to his arm, allowing her body to rest against his shoulder :

" How much for, Orlean? "

" Two — two — hundred dollars."

" Why — two hundred dollars! " he cried. " Why, Orlean, what has come over you? " She burst into tears then, and clung appealingly to him. And in that moment she was again his God-given mate.

" Besides," he went on, " I haven't such an amount in the bank, even." He looked up. A half a block in their lead walked Reverend McCarthy, carrying the luggage.

" Papa, p-a-pa! " called Orlean at the top of her voice. Pa-p-a," she called again and again until she fell into a fit of coughing. He halted, and was uneasy, Baptiste could see. They came up to him. Orlean was running despite her husband's effort to hold her back.

" Papa, papa! My God, give Jean back that money. Give it back, I say! Oh, I didn't want to do this, oh, I didn't want to! It was you who had me sign that check, you, you, you! " She was overcome then, and fell into a swoon in her husband's arms. He stood firmly, bravely, then like the Rock of Gibraltar. His face was very hard, it was very firm. His eyes spoke. It told the one before him the truth, the truth that was.

And as the other ran his hand to his inside vest pocket and drew forth the money, he kept saying in a low, cowardly voice:

" *It was her, it was her. She did it, she did it!* "

Baptiste took the money. He looked at it. He took fifty dollars from it and handed the amount to the other. He spoke then, in a voice that was singularly dry:

" I will not keep her from going. She can go; but you know I ought not let her."

They carried her to where the cars stood, and made her comfortable when once inside. She opened her eyes when

he was about to leave upon hearing the conductor's call.
She looked up into his eyes. He bent and kissed her. She
looked after him as he turned, and called: " Jean! "

" Yes, Orlean! "

" Goodby! "

He stood on the platform of the small western station
as the train pulled down the track. A few moments later
it disappeared from view, and she was gone.

EPOCH THE THIRD

EPOCH THE THIRD

CHAPTER I

CHICAGO — THE BOOMERANG

THE REVEREND McCARTHY had scored. He had succeeded in separating his daughter from the man she married. The fact that there was positively no misunderstanding between the two, was not seen or considered by him. Jean Baptiste had opposed him, and that was enough. He hated any member of his household, or any one related to the one of his household who dared disagree with him. Of course his "Majesty" did not see it that way. He saw himself as the most saintly man in the world and sympathized with himself accordingly. No man thought himself more unjustly abused than did N. Justine McCarthy.

But there were other things to complete. He had not wilfully participated in what had just passed — in fact, he had not meant to part the couple at all. He prided himself with having some judgment. He was merely undertaking that which in a way had grown common to him — the task of getting even.

Now he had estimated that he knew Jean Baptiste, although studying characters and their natural tendencies had not been a part of his theme in life. He felt albeit, that he had this one's tender spot clearly before him. To begin with: he put himself right with his own conscience by believing that Baptiste was a vain, selfish character, bent on one purpose — getting rich! He concluded — because he wished to — that Baptiste did not, and had never, loved Orlean. The fact that Orlean had not said anything to the contrary did not matter. He was her father, and therefore predicated and privileged to think and act for her. That was why he had always been of so much service, such fatherly help. He was protecting his daughter from the cruelty of men. But how he had planned it all!

"Now that hard-headed rascal," meaning of course his son-in-law, "is not going to lay down. Oh, no! My poor girl has that claim. He does not want her, but he does want the claim. To hold the claim, he must have her, and have her back on the claim. He's all war now; but when he realizes that to lose her is to lose the claim into the bargain — oh, well, I'll just set right down at home here and wait. Yes, I'll wait. He'll be coming along. And when he appears here, then I'll bend his ornery will into the right way of seeing things." So thereupon he took up his vigil, waiting for Jean Baptiste to put in his appearance.

But for some reason the other had not hastened to Chicago as soon as the Elder had anticipated he would. Three weeks had been consumed in the trip West, so he was somewhat behind in his church work. While it was true that ministers in some of the towns in his itinerary collected from the members at the quarterly conference and sent the money to him; on the other hand if he expected to get what was due him in any great measure, it was highly necessary that he be there in person. Accordingly, the time he spent in Chicago, waiting for the coming of his son-in-law that he might have the satisfaction of bending the other to his will began to grow long and irksome.

Moreover, if he sat at home, he was obliged to meet and greet the many visitors who called to see his sick daughter. More largely of course for the purpose of securing information for gossip, but compelling him therefore to make or offer some explanation. And here arose another phase of the case that was not pleasant. Following Jean Baptiste's marriage to Orlean, and after the Reverend had paid them his first visit, he had said a great deal in praise of his " rich " son-in-law. That he was so extremely vain, was why he had done this. It had tickled his vanity to have the people see his daughter marry so well, since it was well known about Chicago that Jean Baptiste was very successful. When the Elder had boasted to the people he met of the " rich " man his daughter had married, he wrote telling the young couple of it. To be referred to as " rich " he conjectured, should have flattered any man's vanity — it would have his — and he estimated that he was doing Baptiste a great favor when he let him know that he, the Elder, was advertising him as rich.

But the same had brought no response from that one. He had been too busy to take any interest in being praised. And even after the Elder had made his first visit, and returned and told of the wonders his daughter had married into, he still hoped this would soften Baptiste's disposition into praising and fawning upon him. It was not until Baptiste had returned the money he had sent his daughter for railway fare the Xmas before that the Reverend had thrown down the gauntlet and declared war. So the very thing he had played up a few months before, came back now to annoy him. Because he had never lived as he should have it was proving a boomerang. He had made a practice of pretending not to hear what was being said about him by others. But he could not seal his ears to the fact that the people were asking themselves and everybody else what had happened to his daughter, or between his daughter and the " rich " son-in-law. This was very uncomfortable, it was very annoying.

It was reported that he was compelled to go out West and
get her, and it was exasperating to explain all without
making it seem that what he had said a few months before
was boast, pure and simple.

"Yeh. All you could hear a few months ago, was the
'rich' man Orlean had married. Yeh. Mr. Mc. would
make it his business to get around so you had to ask
'im about them. Then he'd swell up lak a big frog and tell
all about it. Then of a sudden he jumps up and goes out
there and brings her back. Ump! Now I wonder what *is*
the mattah."

During these times, those of the household had little
peace. With impatience over Baptiste's not showing up so
he could read him the riot act, and his work being neglected;
with having to listen to no end of gossip that his meddling
had brought about, he became the most obstinate problem
imaginable about the house. All the love he had pretended
for Orlean while on the claim, was now changed to severe
chastisement. He no longer fondled and wasted hours
over her. She had no longer the convenient check book.
The fact that she had to have a little medicine, and that she
also had to have other necessities; that she had to eat — and
the most of this he was forced to provide, made him so
irritable, that those near prayed for the day when he would
leave. But if Jean Baptiste would only come so that he
could say to him what he had planned to say. Just to have
the opportunity to bend that stubborn will — that would be
sufficient to repay him for all he was now actually sacrificing.

As for "Little Mother Mary" these were the darkest
days of her never happy married life. Of all the men she
had met or known, she had truly admired and loved Jean
Baptiste more than any other. In truth it was her disposi-

tion to be frank, kind and truthful. She dearly loved her son-in-law for his manly frank and kind disposition. She trusted him, and, knowing that Orlean was of her disposition, weak and subservient to the will of those near, she had been relieved to feel that she had married the kind of man that would be patient and love a person with such a disposition.

She had been sincere in her praise of him to her many friends. She had told of him to everybody she knew or met. So much so indeed, that the Reverend on his last trip West in his daily rebuke, then had said: "And Mary has just sickened me with telling everybody she meets about Jean." Ethel had joined with him in this. The truth was that when her mother had sung her praise to the people regarding Jean Baptiste, there was nothing left to say about Glavis, but more especially about the Elder.

What the Reverend was forced to endure at this time, he promptly of course charged to the indiscretions of Jean Baptiste. If he had not done this, or if he had done that, the Elder would not have been forced to endure such annoyance. If he would only show up with his practical ideas in Chicago! Every morning when the door bell rang, he listened eagerly for the voice of his son-in-law. He watched the mail, and in assorting the letters, looked anxiously for the Western postmark. But a week passed, and no letter and no Jean Baptiste. Then at the end of two weeks, the same prevailed. And at the end of three weeks, he knew he would have to go to work or reckon with the bishop.

So on Tuesday of the following week, the Elder left for his work, and that same afternoon, Jean Baptiste arrived in Chicago.

CHAPTER II

THE DAYS that followed after the Elder had taken his wife away, were unhappy days for Jean Baptiste. In his life there were certain things he had held sacred. Chief among these was the marriage vow. While a strong willed, obviously firm sort of person, he was by nature sentimental. He had among his sentiments been an enemy of divorces. Nothing to him was so distasteful as the theory of divorce. He had always conjectured that if a man did not drink, or gamble, or beat his wife there could be no great cause for divorce; whereas, with the woman, if she was not guilty of infidelity a man could find no just cause, on the whole, to ask for a divorce. But whatever the cause be — even a just cause — he disliked the divorcing habit. He persisted in believing that if two people whose lives were linked together would get right down to a careful understanding and an appreciation of each other's sentiments, or points of view, they could find it possible to live together and be happy.

Fancy therefore, how this man must have felt when he arrived at the little house upon the wife's claim and found his grandmother alone. They had taken his wife and all her belongings. He lived in a sort of quandary in the days that followed. His very existence became mechanical. And one day while in this unhappy state, he chanced to find a little sun bonnet that they had evidently overlooked. She had bought it the summer before, and it was too small. But he recalled now that he had thought that it made her look very sweet. How much the bonnet meant to him now! He placed it carefully away, and when he was alone in the house in after days with only her memory as a companion he would get and bring it forth, gaze at it long and tenderly. It seemed to bring back the summer before when he had been hopeful and happy and gay. It brought him more clearly to realize and appreciate what marriage really meant and the sacred vow. And during these hours he would imagine he could see her again; that she was near and from under the little bonnet that was too small he communed with her and he would thereupon hold a mythical conversation, with her as the listener.

Was it all because Jean Baptiste loved his wife? What is there between love and duty? It had never been as much a question with Jean Baptiste as to how much he loved her as it was a question of duty. She was his wife by the decree of God and the law of the land. Whatever he had been, or might have been to others, therefore had gone completely out of his mind when he had taken her to him as wife. And now that she was away, to his mind first came the question, *why was she away?*

Yes, that was the great question. *Why was she away?* Oh, the agony this question gave the man of our story.

Not one serious quarrel had they ever had. Not once had he spoken harshly to her, nor had she been cross with him. Not once had the thought entered his mind that they would part; they they could part; that they would ever wish to part. In the beginning, true, there had been some little difficulties before they had become adjusted to each other's ways. But that had taken only a few months, after which they had gradually become devoted to each other. And so their lives had become. Out there in the "hollow of God's hand," their lives had become assimilated, they had looked forward to the future when there would be the little ones, enlarging their lives and duties.

And yet, why was his wife in Chicago without even a letter from her to him; or one from him to her? Why, why, *why?*

N. Justine McCarthy!

Oh, the hatred that began to grow — spread and take roots in the breast of this man of the prairie toward the man who had wilfully and deliberately wronged him, wrecked that which was most sacred to him. The days came and went, but that evil, twisting, warping hatred remained; it grew, it continued to grow until his very existence became a burden and a misery. No days were happy days to him. From the moment he awakened in the morning until he was lost in slumbers in the evening, Jean Baptiste knew no peace. While that perpetrator of his unhappiness waited impatiently in Chicago with plans to grind and humiliate him further, this man began to formulate plans also. With all the bitter hatred in his soul against the cause of his unhappiness, his plans were not the plans of "getting even," but merely to see his wife where no subtle influences could hamper her or warp her convictions and reason. He knew that to write to her would be but to prove useless. The letters would be examined and criticized by those around her. He knew that sending her money would be only regarded as an evidence of weakening on his part, and if he was to deal, weakness must have no place. So as to how he might see his wife, and give her an opportunity to appreciate duty, became his daily determination.

The great steam tractor, breaking prairie on his sister's homestead was diligently at its task, and while it turned over from twenty to thirty acres of wild sod each day, it also ate coal like a locomotive. So to it he was kept busy hauling coal over the thirty-five miles from Colome. On the land he was having broken (for he had teams breaking prairie in addition to the tractor) he had arranged to sow flaxseed. For two years preceding this date, crops had been perceptibly shorter, due to drought. Therefore seeds of all kind had attained a much higher price than previously. Flaxseed that he had raised and sold thousands of bushels of in years gone by for one dollar a bushel he was now compelled to pay the sum of $3.00 a bushel therefor.

So with a steam tractor hired at an average cost of $60 a day; with extra men in addition to be boarded; and with hauling the coal for the tractor himself such a distance and other expenses, Jean Baptiste, unlike his august-father-in-law, had little time or patience to sit around consuming his time and substance perpetrating a game of spite.

But he was positive that he would needs lose his mental balance unless he journey to Chicago and see his wife. Alone she would have time, he conjectured to think, to see and to realize just what she was doing. Why should they be separated? Positively there was nothing and never had been anything amiss between them, was what passed daily through his mind. Well, he decided that he would go to her as soon as he had arranged matters so he could. He was peeved when he recalled that the spring before he had been forced to make a trip to that same city that could as well have been avoided. But when anything had to be done, Jean Baptiste usually went after it and was through. In business where he was pitted against men, this was not difficult, and instead of disliking to face such music, he rather relished the zest it gave him. But when a man is dealing with a snake — for nothing else can a man who would sacrifice his own blood to vanity be likened to, it must be admitted that the task

worried Jean Baptiste. If N. Justine McCarthy had been a
reader, an observer, and a judge of mankind as well as a
student of human nature and its vicissitudes he could have
realized that murder was not short for such actions as he
was perpetrating. But here again Jean Baptiste was too
busy. He had no time to waste in jail — for even if killing the man who had done him such an injury be justified
he realized that justice in such cases works slowly. But
it would be vain and untruthful to say that with the bitterness in his heart, Jean Baptiste did not reach a point in his
mind where he could have slain in cold blood the man with
whom he was dealing.

At last came the time when he could be spared from his
farm, and to Chicago he journeyed. Positively this was one
trip to that city that gave him no joy. He estimated before
reaching there, that he should best not call up the house, but
bide his time and try to meet his wife elsewhere. But when
he arrived in the city, and not being a coward, he dismissed
this idea and went directly to the house in Vernon Avenue.

He was met at the door by " Little Mother Mary," who did
not greet him as she might have, but for certain reasons.
The most she could do even to live in the same atmosphere
with her husband was to pretend to act in accordance with
his sentiments. Baptiste followed her back to the rear room
where she took a seat and he sat down beside her. She had
uttered no word of greeting, but he came directly to the
point. " Where is Orlean? "

" She's out."

" Out where? "

" She just walked out into the street."

" How is she? "

" Better than when she came home," meaningly.

" When she was *brought* home," he corrected.

" Well? "

" But I am not here to argue whereof.   I am here to see her."

" But she's out."

" However, she'll return, I hope.   If not, then, where might I find her? "

" She'll return presently."

He was silent for a time while she regarded him nervously, listening in the meantime as if expecting some one.   She was afraid.   Her husband had left the city only that morning; but behind him he had left an escutcheon who could — and was, as capable of making matters as disagreeable.   It was Ethel, and Mrs. McCarthy was aware that that one was upstairs.   The household had been conducted according to the desires and dictates of the Elder.   Wherefore she was uneasy.   Baptiste observed her now, and made mental note as to the cause of the expression of uneasiness upon her face.

" What's the matter? " he asked.

She did not reply, but sighed.

" What's the matter, Mother Mary? " he asked kindly. Her love and admiration asserted itself momentarily in the look with which she replied to him.   How in that moment she wanted to tell him all, and to be to him as she had always wanted to be.   But only a moment was she so, then that look of hunted fear overspread her face again, and she turned uneasily toward the stairs.

" Won't you tell me what the matter is, mother? " she heard him again.   For answer the quick glance over her shoulder was sufficient.   It was as if to say. " Hush! Enemies are near! "   He then estimated that the Elder had gone to the southern part of the state, but Ethel must be near, and it was Ethel whom the mother feared.   He understood then, that the Reverend had a cunning way of having

Ethel do his bidding. Because she was possessed of his evil disposition, he could trust her to carry out anything on this order — that is, providing she disliked the person in question, and that was usually the case, for, like him, there were few people whom she really liked.

"What have you been doing to my child?" he heard from Mother Mary, presently. He studied her face again and saw that she was trying to reckon with him herself, although he knew that it mattered little what she thought or did on the whole.

"Has she told you what I have been doing to her?" he said. She shifted uncomfortably, looked around a little, listened for a sound that she expected to hear sooner or later, and then replied, and in doing so, he saw that she was again subservient to the old training.

"My husband told me," she countered.

"Oh," he echoed.

"You have not acted with discretion," she said again, and he understood her. Acting with "discretion" would been never to have given the Reverend an excuse for making that trip. . . .

"I have been good to your daughter; a husband to the best of my ability."

"But you — you — should not have blundered." Again he was reminded of what it meant to displease or give her husband any excuse.

"I did not agree in this room a year ago to be regardful of the opinion of others," he defended. "I agreed to the word of the law and of God. I have tried to fulfill that word. I did not intend to be absent when the child came." She shifted again uneasily, and her mind went back to the day Orlean was born and that her husband, too, had been away. . . .

" If I can see Orlean that will be sufficient," he said.

" She went to walk."

" Mother? "

She regarded him again, and then turned her eyes away for she could not stand to look long into his. The truth there would upset her and she knew it.

" Why must this be so? " She shifted uneasily again. Oh, if she could only be brave. If she could only dare — but she was not brave, Orlean was not brave. They had lived their lives too long subservient to the will of others to attempt bravery now. She rested her eyes on some sewing she pretended to do and waited. It could only be for a little while. Ethel must learn sooner or later of his presence, and then —! There would be a scene or he must go.

" It's a shame," said the other.

" You should have been careful," she returned meaningly. But in her mind was still the dream. If she could be brave. . . .

" Mother! " called some one sharply. Jean recognized the voice, the command. The other's face went pale for a moment, while her eyes closed. He understood. The worst had come. In the minutes they had been sitting there, she had almost dared hope that Orlean would return, and that in some way — perhaps it would have to come from heaven — they could fly. But chances now were gone. His cohort had appeared. " Who is it out there? " she asked, and came toward where they sat. She saw him then, and regarded him coldly. Through her mind shot the fact that her father had waited three weeks for him, and had just left that morning. Her disappointment was keen. For a moment she was frightened. In truth she held a fearsome admiration for the man, and then she stiffened. She had come back to herself;

to the fact that she had a reputation for being disagreeable. She turned to him, and said:

" What are you doing here? "

He answered her not. Her mother was trembling.

" Get out of this house! " she commanded, getting control of herself.

Baptiste was in a quandary. He recalled how he had seen her make her husband jump as if trying to get out of his skin when she was in her evil spasms.

" Did you hear! " she almost screamed.

" I am waiting for my wife," he replied then calmly.

" She is my sister! " she screamed again.

" I suppose I am aware of that."

" Then you cannot have her! "

" She is mine already."

" You're a liar! " she yelled, crying now, and her evil little face screwed up horribly in her anger. Mrs. Mc-Carthy was trembling as if a chill had come over her. Ethel suddenly flew to the 'phone. She got a number, and he heard her scream:

" Glavis! Glav—is. . . That man is here! . . . Glav—is! . . . That man is here! . . ." He could understand no more, then, but saw that she was frantic. He finally heard Mother Mary.

" You're wanted at the 'phone," she said, tremblingly. He got up and went to it. Ethel was dancing about the room like a demon.

" Hello! " he called.

" Hello! " came back. " Ah — ha — who — who — who is th-is? " the other sputtered, all excitement.

" Baptiste," replied the other, wondering at his excitement.

" Wh—at a—re yo—u do-i-ng a—t m-y h-o-u-s-e? "

"Oh, say," called back Baptiste. "There's nobody dead out here. Now calm yourself and say what you want to. I'm listening."

"We—ll," said the other, a little better controlled. "I ask what you are doing at my house?"

"Your house!" echoed Baptiste, uncomprehendingly. "Why, I do not understand you."

"I want to know what you are doing at my house after what you said about me!"

"At your house after what I said about you!" Baptiste repeated.

"Yes. You said I was 'nothing but a thirteen dollars a week jockey,' and all that." Baptiste was thoughtful. He had never said anything about Glavis — and then he understood. Some more of the Elder's work.

"Now, Glavis, I do not understand what you mean when you say what I said about you; but as for my being here, that is distinctly no wish of mine. But you know my wife is here, and it is her I am here to see. No other."

"But I want to see you downtown — you come down here!"

Baptiste was thoughtful. He knew that he could exert no influence over Orlean when she did return with Ethel acting as she was, so he might as well be downtown for the present as elsewhere. So he answered:

"Well, alright."

Ethel slammed and locked the door behind him, and he walked over to Cottage Grove Avenue and boarded a car.

CHAPTER III

GLAVIS MAKES A PROMISE

GLAVIS tried to appear very serious when Baptiste called at where he worked an hour later, but it was beyond him to be so. It was said that he was in the habit of trying to appear like the Reverend, but since the pretended seriousness of that one had never affected Jean Baptiste, Glavis' affectation had still less effect.

"Well, Glavis," he began pointedly. "I'm here as per your suggestion, and since it is quite plain what the matter is, we may as well come directly to the point."

"Well, yes, Baptiste, I guess I may as well agree with you," replied Glavis.

"Then, to begin with. That remark you made over the 'phone regarding what I had said about you, let me say is a falsehood pure and simple. What I said or would say to your back I will say to your face."

"Well, Baptiste," he replied quickly, and his expression confirmed the words that followed, "I believe you."

"I have no occasion to lie. It is very plain that our father-in-law and I are not in accord, and while it may be nothing to you perhaps, I do not hesitate to say that there is nothing wrong between Orlean and me — and never has been. It is all between her father and me, and he is using her as the means."

"Well, that is rather direct," suggested Glavis.

"Evidently so; but it's the truth and you know it. It is simply a case which you are supposed not to see all sides of."

" Now, Baptiste," defended Glavis, " I am no party to your wife's being here in Chicago."

" And I agree with you," returned Baptiste. " It is not your nature to make trouble between people, Glavis. I'll do you that honor. People are inclined to follow their natural bent, and yours, I repeat, is not to cause others misery. Therefore, you can rest assured that I do not mean to involve you in any of my troubles."

" That is sure manly in you, Baptiste," Glavis said heartily.

" But it is a fact, I venture, that you have been advised that I spoke ill of you — at least, I spoke disparagingly of you while your folks were in the West. Am I speaking correctly ? "

" I'll have to admit that you are," and he scowled a little.

" Do you believe these statements ? "

The other scowled again, but didn't have the courage to say that he did — or, perhaps to lie. He knew why he had been told what he had. To unite with the Reverend in his getting even with Baptiste, Glavis had been told that Baptiste had " run him down."

" Well, Glavis, the fact that my wife is at your home — under your roof — I, her husband, am therefore placed at a disadvantage thereby. You cannot help being indirectly implicated in whatever may happen."

" Now, now, Baptiste," the other cried quickly. " I do not want to have anything to do with you and Orlean's troubles. I —"

" It is *not* Orlean and my troubles, Glavis. It is her father's and my troubles."

Glavis shifted uncomfortably. Presently he said hesitatingly:

" The old man just left town this morning. Wished you and he could have had your outs together."

"Yes, it is too bad we did not. As I see it, I have no business with him. In him I am not interested, and never have been. Because I have held aloof from becoming so is the cause of the trouble. I was told before I married Orlean, and by her herself, that I should praise her father; that I should make him think that he was a king, if I would get along with him. Indeed, I did not, I confess, at the time consider it to be as grave as that, that I *had* this to do in order to live with Orlean."

It was positively uncomfortable to Glavis. He could find no words to disagree with the other because he knew that he spoke the truth. He knew that he had catered to the Reverend's vanity to be allowed to pay court to Ethel before he was married to her; he knew that he had done so since; and he knew — and did not always like it — that he was still doing so, and boarding the Reverend's wife into the bargain, and Orlean now was added thereto. He did not relish the task. He earned only a small salary that was insufficient for his own and his wife's needs. Up to a certain point his wife defied her father; but since she was so like him in disposition, and had been instrumental in assisting to separate Orlean and her husband, she had not the courage to rebel and compel — at least insist — that the Reverend take care of his wife and the daughter he had parted from her husband.

So it was all thrown onto Glavis. He made a few dollars extra each week by various means, and this helped him a little In truth, he wished that Orlean was with her husband, and knowing very well that there was where she wanted to be, he was inclined for the moment to try to help Baptiste. Besides, he rather admired the man. Few people could be oblivious to the personality of Baptiste and be honest with themselves. Even the Elder had always found it expedient to be disagreeable in order to dispel the effect of his son-in-law's frank personality.

"The way we are lined up, Glavis, you must appreciate that you cannot keep out of it. You are aware that I have no wish to hang around your abode; but I didn't come all the way from the West to fail to see Orlean. You know full well that Ethel would never let her meet me elsewhere, that her father has left orders to that effect. Now, what am I to do? If I call, your wife will make it so disagreeable that nothing can be accomplished."

"Dammit!" exclaimed Glavis suddenly. "It *isn't* all my fault or the old man's or my wife's! It's Orlean's!"

"Well," agreed Baptiste, thoughtfully, "on the whole, that is so."

"Of course it is! If Orlean was a woman she would be right out there with you now where she belongs!"

"And I agree with you again, Glavis. But Orlean *isn't* a woman, and that is what I have been trying to make her. She has never been a woman — wasn't reared so to be. By nature she is like her mother, and she has grown up according to her training."

"She cannot be two things at the same time," Glavis argued, "and that is a daughter to her father and a wife to you!"

"No, that is where the difficulty lay," said Baptiste. "But her father's influence over her is great, you will admit. She has been taught to agree with him, and that — I can never, nor will I try to do."

"It certainly beats hell!"

"It's the most awkward situation I have ever been placed in. But here's the idea: I took that girl for better or for worse. Now, what am I to do? Throw up my hands and quit, or try to see Orlean and get her around to reason?

It isn't Orlean. It's her father. So I have concluded to make some sort of a fight. Life and marriage are too serious just to let matters go like this."

"Yes, it is," agreed Glavis. "It certainly worries me. And it annoys me because it is so unnecessary." He was thoughtful and then suddenly he said:

"I'm sorry you let the old man — er — ah — get you mixed up like this." He appeared as if he wished to say more. To say that: "For when you let him get into it, the devil would be to pay! Keep him out of your affairs if you would live in peace."

"Well," said Baptiste, rising, "your time here belongs to the company you are working for, and not to me or my troubles. So I'm going to 'beat' it now out to Thirty-first Street."

"Well," returned Glavis, "believe me, Baptiste, I'm sorry for you, and for Orlean. It's rotten." It was remarkable how he saw what was causing it; but how he cleverly kept from directly accusing his father-in-law. "And I'll meet you at Thirty-first Street after supper. At the Keystone, remember." With that he grasped the other's hand warmly, and as Jean Baptiste went down the stairway from where Glavis worked, he knew that he had a friend who at least wanted to help right a most flagrant wrong. The only question was, would E. M. Glavis have the courage to go through with it?

Well, Glavis might have the courage — but *Ethel was his wife. And Jean Baptiste realized that of all things in the world, a woman's influence is the most subtle.*

CHAPTER IV

THE GAMBLER'S STORY

THE KEYSTONE was the oldest and most élite hostelry for Negroes in Chicago and the West for many years. It is located near Thirty-first and State Street, in the heart of the black belt of the southside of the city. It was built previous to the World's Fair and still maintains its prestige as the most popoular hangout for Negroes of the more ostentatious set. And it was here that Jean Baptiste went, following his departure with Glavis.

When Chicago was a "wide open" town, gambling had been carried on upstairs as a business. Porters, waiters, barbers and politicians who held the best jobs had always found their way eventually to the Keystone. Likewise did the Negroes in business and the professions and workers in all the trades, as well as mail carriers, mail clerks, and the men of the army and actors. In short the Keystone was the meeting place for men in nearly all the walks of life.

Always the freest city in the world for the black man, Chicago has the most Negroes in the mail service and the civil service; more Negroes carry clubs as policemen; more can be found in all the departments of the municipal courts, county commissioners, aldermen, corporation counsels, game warden assistants, and so on down. Indeed, a Negro feels freer and more hopeful in Chicago than anywhere else in the United States.

So it was such a crowd that Jean Baptiste encountered at the Keystone that day. There were two real estate men who had once run on the road with him and who had since succeeded in business; also there was another who was a county commissioner; and still another one, an army officer. So, upon seeing him they did all cry:

"Baptiste! Well, well, of all things! And how do you happen to be down here in the spring?"

"Oh, a little business," he returned, and joined with the crowd, bought a drink for them all, and was apparently jolly.

Among the number was a gambler by the name of Speed. He shook the visitor's hand heartily, and when the visit with the others was over, he went to a table and, sitting down, beckoned for Baptiste. When the other responded, he begged him to be seated, and then said:

"Now, I know what you are down here about — heard about it the day he brought her home." Baptiste regarded him wonderingly. "Yes, I understand," he said, making himself comfortable as if to tell a long story. "You are wondering how *I* come to understand about your father-in-law, and if you are not in a hurry, I'll tell you a little story."

"Well," said the other, "let's have a drink before you start."

"I don't care," and he beckoned to the bartender.

"Small bottle, a Schlitz," he said, and turned to Baptiste.

"Make it two," said the other, and turned to hear the story the other had to tell.

"It happened fifteen years ago," began Speed when their beer had been served. "I was a preacher then.— Hold on," he broke off at the expression on Baptiste's face.

"Yes, of course you can hardly believe it; but I was then a preacher. I was the pastor of the church in a little town, and I won't tell the name of the town; but it's all the same,

I was a preacher and pastor of this church. I had not been long ordained, and was ambitious to succeed as a minister. The charge had not been long created, and was, of course, not much of a place for money. But it so happened that a quarry was opened about the time I was sent there and it brought some hundred and fifty Negro families to live in the town, and in almost a twinkling, my charge became from among the poorest, to one of the best from a financial point of view. The men worked steadily and were paid well, and their families found quite a bit of work to do among the wealthy whites of the town.

" There were two young ladies living a few doors from where I preached, girls who made their own living, honestly, nice, clean girls, and I was much impressed with them. I sought, and finally succeeded in getting them interested in the church, and later began keeping company with one. Now here is where your folks come in. The Reverend Mc-Carthy — old Mac, I called him, was filling the same line he now is, Presiding Elder, and this church was in his itinerary. I was therefore under his recommendation. He had been visiting the church regularly, holding his quarterly conference every three months, and getting his little bit. It was shortly after I had started going with this young lady that McCarthy got awful nice and treated me so good until I became suspicious. Then one day it came out.

" ' By the way, Speed,' he said. ' Who're those girls living near the church?' I knew who he was referring to because I had seen him trying to smile on them the day before which had been a Sunday. But I pretends I don't know what or who he's talking about.

" ' Who?' I inquired as innocent as a lamb.

" ' Oh, those two girls living near the church,' and he called their names.

"'Why, they are two young ladies who came here not long ago,' I said, and waited.

"'Is *that* all?' he asked then, and I looked at him. He grinned, and said:

"'Aw, come on, Speed! Be a good fellow. Now, *are those girls* straight?' and he specified the one I had begun going with.

"'Why,' said I, 'Reverend McCarthy, I am surprised at you to ask such a question, or to offer such an insinuation. Besides,' I went on, 'Why?'

"'Aw, now, Speed,' he laughed easily, his big fat round face shaking. 'Be a *good* sport and put me onto these girls. Now, I'll tell you what I want you to do,' he said, drawing his chair close to mine. 'I'll make it my business to get back over here next Sunday night, and I want you to "*fix*" it for me with that one, and —' he winked in a way I did not at the time understand — but I did later —'I'll make it *right* with you. You understand,' he said, rising, '*I'll make it right with you.*'

"I was never so put out in my life. Here was this man, a minister of the Gospel, and a Presiding Elder, who had just deliberately delegated me to make a *previous* engagement for him without regard to morals — and with the girl I loved. I don't think he knew I was paying her court, but the moral was the same.

"I was outdone! But true to his words, the next Sunday night he was back!

"'Well, Speed,' he said when the services were over. 'What's the rip? Everything O. K.?' He was very anxious, and I'll never forget his face. But, I was afraid of the old rascal, still I hadn't lost my manhood at that. So I says:

"'Now, Reverend, you place me in a very awkward predicament. To begin with, I have the highest respect for those young ladies. And, again, even if I did not, I could not be expected to cohort as you suggested.'

" ' Aw, Speed,' he cut in. ' You're no good. Pshaw! I just know the older of those two girls is not straight — am positive of it. And you could ' fix things if you would,' and I detected a touch of angry disappointment in his tone.

" Well, to get out of it, I told the old rascal what I thought of his suggestion and left him. I never saw him again until near conference, and then not to speak with him. I was confident that I had satisfied the people, and that I would be sent back without any argument.

" So imagine when I went to conference and when the charges were being read off and I heard the Secretary call ' Reverend Speed to Mitchfield! ' instead of the town from which I had gone.

" I was just sick, man; so sick until I almost dropped dead on the floor! Oh, the agony it gave me! I finally got outside some way, and stood leaning against the church. How long I stood thus, I never knew; but the church let out by and by, while I still stood there — and let me explain. Mitchfield was a charge that contained exactly a dozen members—the Reverend McCarthy came out and I looked up straight into his eyes. . . . I knew then why I had been sent to Mitchfield instead of back to the charge I had been at.

" Well, I went to Mitchfield, and by working around town by the day, in connection with the charge, I managed to make it. Some months later, I married the girl I have spoken of, and we began to keep house in Mitchfield.

" It was pretty hard, and sometimes I don't wonder at what later happened. But to make a long story short, I was compelled to get work in a near-by town to make a living for me and my wife, and was gone all the week until Saturday night. At the end of six months, Reverend Mc-Carthy had taken my wife, and she had left me and was living in St. Louis!"

Baptiste was regarding him strangely.

"Have you heard the the rest of it?" the other paused to ask. "Well, Reverend McCarthy became the father of her two sons. One was killed some years ago, the other lives in St. Louis."

"But what — what became of their mother?" Baptiste inquired curiously.

"Her? What becomes of women who are deceived? If you visited St. Louis and the *district,* you might find her. She was there the last I heard of her."

"And you?"

"Me?" the other repeated in a strangely hollow voice. "You know what *I* am. A gambler, and with an old score to settle with that man if I ever get the chance."

CHAPTER V

THE PREACHER'S EVIL INFLUENCE

WITH all Ethel's excited ways, she was not to be reckoned a fool when she had in mind to accomplish some purpose. She understood full well, that it would be up to her at this time to keep Orlean from returning West with her husband, unless she recalled her father. This she did not wish to resort to, until she had exhausted all her force without avail. She appreciated the fact that Jean Baptiste could and would influence her husband as well as her mother, while as to Orlean, she would only need a half a chance to fall away from her influence and go back to her husband.

So with this in mind, Ethel, who had inherited from her father, much evil and the faculty of making people miserable began, as soon as Baptiste had left the house, to formulate plans to counter any effort on his part to see Orlean.

Her first move, therefore, was to recall Orlean who was visiting near, a fact which her mother had feared to tell Baptiste. She convinced her forthwith that she was sick, in danger, and sent her to bed, not telling her that Baptiste was even in town. She followed this by sending her mother to the kitchen, and keeping her there.

" Now what I must do — succeed in doing," she muttered to herself, " is to keep Orlean from seeing or meeting him in private and even in public for as much as an hour." She realized that keeping a man and wife apart was a grave task, and that she could not trust to the sympathy of any friends.

But one person could she trust to be an ally in the task she was trying to accomplish, and that was her father. She rather feared her husband at this time, for, while she held him under her control at most all times, he was by disposition inclined to be kind and good. And, although he was jealous of Baptiste in a measure, this did not reach proportions where he was likely to be a very ready accomplice with the plan in hand. Indeed, if it was left to him, Orlean would sleep in her husband's arms that very night!

" I wish papa had stayed just another day," she grumbled as she walked the floor and tried to formulate some effective plan of action. " To think that he left only this morning and that man came this afternoon!" She was provoked at such a coincidence. She did not like to think too deeply, or to scheme too long, for it hurt her. So she was compelled to take a chair for a time and rest her mind. She was not positive how long Baptiste would stay, and she would have difficulty in keeping her sister in bed for any length of time. But she decided to keep her in the house if she had to sit on guard at the front door.

And it was while she was yet undecided upon her plan of action, that Glavis came home. Once in a great while, when she wanted a change, a diversion, she would have his supper waiting. Other times it was left to her mother. He loved her in spite of all her evil, and was always pleased when she had his supper ready. So when she heard his footsteps outside, she was suddenly struck with an inspiration. She rushed toward the rear, and began hurriedly to set the table. Her mother had the meal ready, so she affected to be very cheerful when Glavis came into the room, and even kissed him fondly. He was so surprised, that the instance made him temporarily forget what was on his mind, which was just what she wished him to do.

"Where is Orlean?" he inquired after a time, whereupon his wife's face darkened.

"Oh, she's sick, and in bed," replied Ethel guardedly.

Glavis grunted. He was thinking. For a time he forgot all that was around him; his wife, the supper, his
work, all but Jean Baptiste and the wife that was being
harbored under the roof that he kept up. He suddenly got
up. He walked quickly out of the room and hurried upstairs while his wife's back was turned, and knocked at the
door of the room wherein Orlean was supposed to lay
sick.

"Come in," called the other.

"Oh, it's you, Glavis," she cried, dropping back into bed
when he entered the door.

"A—ah — Orlean," he said in his stammering sort of
way. "A — ah — how are you?"

"Why, I feel well, Glavis," she replied wonderingly. She
had never felt just right mentally since before she left the
West. And when she allowed herself to think, she found
that it hurt her. She had always been obedient — her
father had told her that time and again, and gave her great
credit for being so. "Think of it, my dear," he had so
often said, "in all your life you have never 'sassed' your
father, or contraried him," whereupon he would look
greatly relieved. So her father had laid down the rule she
was following — trying to follow. Her husband must certainly have been in grave error — not that she had observed
it, or that she had been badly treated by him, for she had
not. However, whenever she tried to see and understand
what it all meant, it hurt her. She was again the victim of
those nervous little spells that had harassed her before she
married, but which had strangely left her during that time.
But to do her father's will — for he never bid — always his

was an influence that seemed to need no words — she was trying. So she looked up at Glavis, and observed something unusual in his face.

"What is the matter, Glavis?" she inquired, sitting up in bed again. Glavis shifted about uneasily before replying.

"Ah — why — Orlean, it's Baptiste, your husband."

"Jean!" she cried, forgetting everything but her husband — forgetting that she had allowed herself to be parted from him. "What — what is the matter with him, Glavis? With Jean? Has something happened? Oh, I'm always so afraid something will happen to Jean!"

"No, no," exclaimed Glavis, pushing her gently back upon the pillow. "Nothing has happened. Ah — er — ah —"

"Oh, I'm so relieved," she sighed, as she fell over in the bed.

"He's here — in the city," she heard then from Glavis.

"He is!" she cried, sitting suddenly erect again. For a moment she hesitated, and then, raising her hand to her forehead as if in great pain, she groaned perceptibly. The next moment she had again sunk back upon the pillow, and her breath came hard. Perspiration stood upon her brow, and he saw it.

"Orlean, oh, Orlean," he cried then upon impulse. "Great God, this is a shame, a shame before God!" he lamented with great emotion.

Suddenly he rushed to the door and then halted as he heard his wife calling him from below. He turned to where Orlean lay in the bed, sick now for true.

"Aren't you coming down to supper, Orlean?" he called.

"No, Glavis. I am not hungry."

"But you should eat something, Orlean."

"No, Glavis," she repeated in a tired voice, a voice in which he detected a sigh. "I couldn't eat anything — now."

He looked at her a moment with great tenderness, let escape
a sigh, and then as if resigned to the inevitable, he turned
and passed down the stairway to where his wife waited
below.

She regarded him keenly, and during the meal, she kept
casting furtive glances in his direction. " I wonder what
he's been saying to Orlean? " she kept muttering to herself. She concluded then, that she would have to watch
him closely. He had never been in accord with her and
her father's plan, and they had borne false witness to influence him against Baptiste. But he had seen Baptiste she
knew, and was also aware of the fact that Glavis liked both
her sister and brother-in-law, and it was going to be a
task to keep him from following his natural inclination.

She thought about her father again, and wished that he
was in Chicago.

She had never been delegated to handle such a task alone,
and she disliked the immense responsibility that was now
upon her, and no one to stand with her in the conflict.

" Well, Ethel," Glavis said, arising from the table when
the meal was over, " I'm going to walk out for a while."

She started up quickly. Her lips parted to say that he
was going to meet Baptiste and conspire with him against
her father, but she realized that this would not be expedient.
He might revolt. She rather feared this at times, notwithstanding her influence over him, therefore she decided to exercise a little diplomacy. Accordingly she sank back into
the chair, and replied:

" Very well, dear."

He regarded her keenly, but she appeared to be inno-
cently completing her meal. He sighed to think that she
did not make herself disagreeable, the anticipation of which
had made him fear and dread the task that was before him.

But now he was compelled to feel a little grateful because she was apparently very prudent in the matter.

He hurried quickly to the hall tree, slipped into a light overcoat, and left the house. As he walked down the street, he was in deep thought.

CHAPTER VI

JEAN BAPTISTE was thoughtful for a long time after the other had left him. He had heard before he married Orlean that the Reverend was the father of two illegitimate children, but from Speed's story he had met the whole of it. Not only was he the father of two illegitimate children, but he had taken another man's wife to become so — and all this while he was one of the most influential men in the church!

This fact, however, did not cause Baptiste any wonderment. It was something he had become accustomed to. It seemed that the church contained so many of the same kind — from reports,— until it was a common expectation that a preacher was permitted to do the very worst things — things that nobody else would have the conscience to do. He arose presently and going to the bar, ordered another bottle of beer. He looked around the large room while he drank at the usual class who frequented the place. He knew that here and there among them were crooks, thieves, "con" men, gunmen, and gamblers. Many of these men had perhaps even committed murder — and that for money. Yet there was not one he was positive, that would deliberately separate a man and his wife for spite. And that was the crime this preacher father-in-law of his had committed.

Always in the mind of this man of the prairie this played. It followed him everywhere; it slept with him, arose with him, and retired with him. And all through long sleepless nights it flitted about in his dreams like an eternal spectre, it gave him no peace. Gradually it had brought him to a feeling that the only justifiable action would be to follow the beast to his lair and kill him upon sight. Often this occurred to him, and at such times he allowed his mind to recall murder cases of various phases, and wondered if such a feeling as he was experiencing, was the kind men had before committing murder. Then if so, what a relief it must be to the mind to kill. He had a vision of this arch hypocrite writhing at his feet, with death in his sinful eyes, and his tongue protruding from his mouth.

He drank the beer and then ordered liquor. Somehow he wanted to still that mania that was growing within him. He had struggled for happiness in the world, for success and contentment, and he did not wish his mind to dwell on the subject of murder. But he was glad that this man had left the city. A man might be able to accept a great deal of rebuke, and endure much; but sometimes the sight of one who has wronged him might cause him for a moment to forget all his good intentions and manly resolutions. Yes, he was glad that Reverend McCarthy had left the city, and he shuddered a little when he recalled with a grimace that he had traveled these many miles to see and reckon with his wife.

" Well, you are here," he heard then, and turned to greet Glavis.

" Oh, hello, Glavis," he returned with a tired expression about his eyes from the effect of the strain under which he had been laboring. " Have a drink."

" An old-time cocktail," Glavis said to the bartender. He then turned to Baptiste.

" Well, how's everything over home?" said Baptiste, coming directly to the point.

" Your wife's sick," said Glavis a little awkwardly.

" And I, her husband, cannot call and see her. I'm compelled to hear it from others and say nothing." He paused and the expression on his face was unpleasant to behold. Glavis saw it and looked away. He could not make any answer, and then he heard the other again.

" This is certainly the limit. I married that girl in good faith, and I'll bet that she has not told you or anybody else that. I mistreated her. But here we are, compelled to be apart, and by whom?" His face was still unpleasant, and Glavis only mumbled.

" That damn preacher!"

" Oh, Baptiste," cried Glavis, frowningly.

" Yes, I know — I understand your situation, Glavis. But you must appreciate what it is to be thrown into a mess like this. To have your home and happiness sacrificed to somebody's vanity. I'm compelled to stand for all this for the simple crime of not lauding the old man. All because I didn't tickle his vanity and become the hypocrite he is, for should I have said what he wanted me to say, then I would have surely lied. And I hate a liar!"

" But come, Baptiste," argued Glavis, " we want to figure out some way that you and your wife can get together without all this. Now let's have another drink and sit down."

" Well, alright," said the other disconsolately, " I feel as if it would do me good to get drunk tonight and kill somebody, —no, no, Glavis," he added quickly, " I'm not going to kill anybody. So you needn't think I am planning anything like that. I'm too busy to go to jail."

" Now, I'm willing to help you in any way I can, Baptiste," began Glavis, " as long as I can keep my wife out of it. I've got the darndest woman you ever saw. But she's my wife, and you know a man must try to live with the one he's married to, and that's why I am willing to help you."

They discussed plans at some length, and finally decided to settle matters on the morrow.

But when the morrow came, Ethel blocked all the plans. She refused to be sent away across town and let Baptiste come into the house and see his wife. She knew what that would mean, so she stood intrenched like the rock of Gibraltar. Other plans were resorted to, but with the same result. The days passed and Baptiste became obsessed with worry. He knew he should be back in the West and to his work; he began to lose patience with his wife for being so weak. If he could only see her he was certain that they would come to some agreement. Sunday came and went, and still he saw her not. Ethel took confidence; she smiled at the success with which she had blocked all efforts of communication. Baptiste wrote his wife notes, but these she intercepted and learned his plans. She convinced her sister that she was sick and should be under the care of a physician. This reached Baptiste, and he secured one, a brilliant young man who was making a reputation. He had known him while the other was attending the Northwestern Medical College, and admired him; but this too was blocked. For when he knocked at the door with the doctor at his side, they were forbade admittance. Thereupon Baptiste was embarrassed and greatly humiliated at the same time.

Ethel had a good laugh over it when they had left and cried: " He had his nerve, anyhow. Walking up here with a nigger doctor, the idea! I wish papa had been home, he'd have fixed him proper! Papa has never had one of those in his house, indeed not. No nigger doctor has ever attended any of us, and never will as long as papa has anything to do with it!"

Glavis finally succeeded in getting a hearing. By pleading and begging, he finally secured Ethel's consent to allow him to bring Baptiste to the house and sit near his wife for just thirty minutes — but no more. He did not apprise Baptiste of this fact nor of the time limit, but caught him by the arm and led him to the house as though he were a privileged character. He took notice of the clock when he entered, because he knew that Ethel, who was upstairs had done so. And he was very careful during the time to keep his eyes upon the clock. He knew that Ethel would appear at the expiration of thirty minutes and start her disagreeableness, so at the end of that time he quietly led Baptiste away after he had been allowed only to look at his wife, who was like a Sphinx from the careful dressing down she had had before and preparatory to his coming.

So, having carried out what he considered a bit of diplomacy, Glavis was relieved. Baptiste could expect no more of him, and so it ended.

Ethel wrote her father a cheerful letter and stated that that "hardheaded rascal" had been there from the West; but that Orlean had declined to see him but once, and had refused to go back at all, whereupon her father smiled satisfactorily.

Jean Baptiste returned to the West, defeated and downcast. He had for the first time in his life, failed in an undertaking. He had never known such before, he could not understand. But he was defeated, that was sure. Perhaps it was because he was not trained to engage in that particular kind of combat. He had been accustomed to dealing with men in the open, and was not prepared to counter the cunning and finesse of his newly acquired adversaries.

Over him it cast a gloom; it cast great, dark shadows, and

in the days that followed the real Jean Baptiste died and another came to live in his place. And that one was a hollow-cheeked, unhappy, nervous, apprehensive creature. He regarded life and all that went with it dubiously; he looked into the elements above him, and said that the world had reached a time whence it would change. The air would change, the earth would become hot, and rain would not fall and that drought would cover all the land, and the settlers would suffer. And so feeling, it did so become, and in the following chapter our story will deal with the elements, and with how the world did change, and how drought came, and what followed.

CHAPTER VII

A GREAT ASTRONOMER

NOT LONG AGO a man died who had made astronomy a specific study for sixty years. He knew the planets, Mars and Jupiter, and Saturn and all the others. He knew the constellations and the zodiac — in fact he was familiar with the solar system and all the workings of the universe. This man had predicted with considerable accuracy what seasons would be wet, and what seasons would be dry. He also foretold the seasons of warmth and those of cold. And he had said that about every twenty years, the world over would be gripped with drought. This drought would begin in the far north, and would cover the extreme northern portion of the country the first year. The second year it would reach further south, and extend over the great central valleys and be most severe near the northern tier of states. Following, it would go a bit further south the next year, and so on until it would finally disappear altogether.

So according to this man's prediction, the country of our story would experience a severe drought soon, preceded by a slight one as a forerunner. For two years the crops would be inferior but the following year would see it normal again.

So be it.

It had been dry the year before, and had been just a little bit so the year before that. We know by the shortage of crops Jean Baptiste had raised that such had been so. So, with hundreds of acres, and the sun shining hot, and the wind blowing from the south, it was no surprise when he became now, an altogether different person. (For you see the life — that life that makes men strong and fearless and cheerful had gone from the body of Jean Baptiste.) Then he began to grow uneasy. It is, perhaps, somewhat difficult to portray a drought and its subsequent disasters. We beg of you, however, that you go back to the early years in the peaceful, hopeful, vigorous country of our story: In the years that had been before when everything had pointed to success. Rainfall had been abundant; frost had waited until October before it showed his white coat upon the window sill. Land values had climbed and climbed, and had gone so high until only the moneyed could even reckon to own land. And Jean Baptiste controlled a thousand acres.

Over all the country, the pounding of steam and gasoline tractors filled the air with an incessant drumming; the black streaks everywhere told the story of conquest. The prairie was giving place to the inevitable settler, and hope was high in the hearts of all. So the wind had blown hot many days before the settlers became apprehensive of anything really serious.

Never since they had come to this country had they experienced such intense heat; such regular heat; such continued heat. A week passed and the heat continued. It blew a gale, and then a blast; but always it was hot, hot, hot!

Two weeks passed, and still it blew. Before this it had at least subsided at night, although it did begin afresh in the morning. But now it blew all night and all day, and each day it became hotter, the soil became dryer, and presently the crops began to fire.

" Oh, for a rain! " every settler cried. " For a rain, a rain, a rain! " But no rain came.

So every day there was the continual firing of the crops.

The corn had been too small in the beginning to require much moisture, and the dry weather had enabled the farmer to kill the weeds, so it stood the gaft quite well, for a time, and grew like gourd vines in the meantime. It was the wheat, the oats, the rye and the barley that were first to suffer. These were at their most critical stage, the time when tiny little heads must dare seek the light. And as they did so, the cruel heat met and burned them until thereupon they cried and died from grief. And still the drought continued.

No showers fell. The crops needed water. After the third week of such intense heat, the people groaned and said " '93 " had returned with all its attendant disaster. And still the wind kept blowing. The air grew hot, hotter; almost to stifling with the odor of the burning plants. The aroma mixed with the intense heat was suffocating. The grass upon the prairie gave up, turned its tiny blades to the sun and died to the roots, while all the grain of the land, slowly became shorter. It struggled, it bent, and at last turned what had pointed upward, downward, and also died of thirst.

And then the people awakened to the emergency. They began to take note of the fact that many had gone into debt so deeply until there were many who could never get out unless they sold their land! This had been so with poor managers, speculators, and others before. When they found that they were unable to make it, there had always remained the alternative of selling out. And this had been so easy, because the people at large wanted the land. So instead, heretofore, of retiring in defeat, the weakest had retired in apparent victory. " For my homestead, I received $8,000," or maybe it had been $10,000. So it had been. Great prices to all who wanted to sell. Only a small portion of them, however, had wanted to sell up to date.

But when the crops were surely a failure for the most part, hundreds and thousands and even more quarters were offered for sale. Then came the shock — the jolt that brought the people to a stern realization of what was before them. The buyers! There were no buyers! No, the buyers now when many wished to sell, stayed in Iowa, and Illinois and wherever they lived, and refused to come hither!

So, for the first time the people in the new country were face to face with a real problem. And this continued to be augmented by the intense heat. Hotter it had grown, and at last came a day when all the small grain was beyond redemption, only the corn and the flaxseed were yet a possibility. So to Jean Baptiste we now return.

He had written to his wife, and she had replied to his letter. He read them where he lived, on the homestead she had left, and longed simply for her to return. He lived with his mind in a dull quandary. It was useless to try to find consolation hating the cause of his troubles, so him, he tried much to forget. It would all come right some day, he still hoped, and worried between times over his debts. He had borrowed more money to develop his land; was behind in the interest, now, and also the taxes, and his wife wrote for money.

This was what Glavis had advised him to do — Send her money and all would be right. Yes, that was what Ethel and her mother and her father had all thought right. Send her money. But the day of plenty of money for Jean Baptiste was slipping. The burning, dried crop that lay in the field, would bring no money. But this he dared not write. If he wrote and told the woman he had married —

for a wife she surely was no more — that would be to tell the family. And that Prince of Evil, the Reverend, would say with his wonted braggadocio: " Um-m. Didn't I tell you right!, That is a wild country out there for wild people, only." So Baptiste kept what was ruining the crops to himself.

He sent her five dollars, and this brought the most pleasant letter he had yet received. It also brought one from Glavis, who followed the same with another, which was more to the point. It was this he wrote:

" CHICAGO, ILL., June, 30th, 191—

" Dear friend Baptiste:

" I have your recent letter, and it gives me a great pleasure to reply to it. You would have had my last letter sooner; but I left it to Ethel to mail, and this she did not do, so that explains the delay.

" Now we are getting along very well in Chicago, and hope the same prevails in the West. By the papers I read where considerable dry weather is prevailing over a part of the West, but hope it hasn't truck your part of the country. Appreciating, however, your disposition to come directly to a point, I will now turn to a subject that I am sure will be of greater interest to you than anything else, and which is Orlean, your wife.

" It gives me a pleasure to state that she appears more relieved of recent than she has since returning home. But I will not hesitate to tell you why. It is because of you, and you only. Always she talks of you — to me — and it pleases me to talk with her concerning you, for it is with you her mind is at all times. I fear that you cannot appreciate her now as you were once inclined to do; but really think you would be justified, fully so, if you did.

" Now, for instance, when you sent the money not long ago, it gave her great delight. That you haven't forgotten that she is your wife and have some regards, in spite of all, meant to her very much. She took it and bought her a pair of shoes, with a part; the other she spent to have pictures made so that she might send you one. And I speak truly that to send you one was the sole object in her having them made.

"The poor girl has suffered much — agonies. It is not her disposition to be as she has somehow been compelled to be. I can't quite explain it, but if it was left to Orlean's dictates, things would not be as they are. Yet, you might not appreciate this, either. But to make it plainer: Orlean has her mother's disposition, and that is not to assert her rights. Too bad.

"Well, there was a little incident that touched me the other day, and which I will tell you of. A certain lady was over and seeing her with the new shoes, she asked who had bought them. Poor Orlean! It is certainly to be regretted that a girl of her temperament, and kind disposition must be placed forever in a false light. Frankly it worries me. I trust you will understand that the true state of affairs has not been given to the public, and here I will draw a long line instead of saying what will be best left unsaid ———— But Orlean replied to the lady in these words: 'My husband bought them for me.'

"I wish you could understand that it is all one great mistake. I wish you knew the truth and the suffering this poor girl has been put to; for if you did you would know that she is a good girl, and loves the man she has married with all her soul — but Orlean is not like other women. She's weak and — oh, well, I must close here because it hurts me to tell more.

"I will, however, in conclusion say: Do not despair, or grow bitter toward her. This is a strange world, and strange things happen in it. Of but one thing I can assure you, and that is: The right must come and rule in the end. Yes, nothing but right can stand, all else passes. Therefore, hoping that you will be patient, and trust to that I speak of, believe me to be,

"Always your friend,
"E. M. Glavis."

Now it so happened that when Glavis had completed this letter, he was called to the phone, and later into the street. He was gone a half hour or more, and in the meantime, Ethel came upon it, and read it. Her evil little eyes narrowd to mere slits when she had finished. She had noted what had been going on — Orlean and her husband always finding each other's company so congenial.

"Well," she muttered after a time. "The time to strike iron is while it's hot. I'll have to get that man of mine straightened out." Whereupon she went to her room, and here is the letter she wrote:

CHICAGO, ILL., June 30th, 191—
"*The Reverend N. J. McCarthy, Cairo, Ill.*

"DEAR FATHER: We received your letter and were glad to hear you say that you expected to come to Chicago soon. I was just thinking awhile ago, that if you could come soon, real soon, it might be best. Certain matters need your attention. I will not state which, but I, you know, am aware of how you have been slandered and vilified by a certain person that you know. Well, that person is again finding a way to influence those who are near to us. So knowing how equal you are to the most arduous task, I take this means of communicating that which is most expedient.

"Hoping that your health is the best, and that we may see you real soon, believe me to be, as ever,

"Your loving daughter,
"ETHEL."

So it happened that out in the West where the most terrific and protracted drought the country had ever experienced was burning crops and hopes of the people included, Jean Baptiste was made joyful.

He understood Glavis' letter; he understood what he had said and what he had not said. He had suffered. He saw disaster creeping upon him from the drought rent fields.

Is it, therefore, but natural that in his moments of agony and unhappiness, shattered hopes and mortal anguish, that he should turn to the woman who had been his mate. To have her to talk to; her to tell the truth to and share what little happiness there was to be had in life, he became overly anxious? Thereupon he wrote her, sending another check for five dollars.

July 5th, 191—

" *My dear wife:*

" I am writing and sending you a little more money, and since you must be well by now, and realize how much I need you, I am enclosing a signed but not filled-in-amount check, with the request that you come home right away. You will start, say the 10th, that will place you in Winner on the night of the eleventh, on Saturday, where I will meet you.

" I will expect you, dear; and please don't disappoint me. I have not seen you for three months now, and that has not been my preference. The amount will be sufficient for your fare, and expenses please, and I will write no more; but should anything happen that you can not start on that date, then write or wire me that I may know.

" With love to you, I am,

" As ever, you husband,

" JEAN."

CHAPTER VIII

THE text of Reverend N. J. McCarthy's sermon to be delivered on Mothers' Day, was one of the most inexhaustible. Most of his sermons he did not prepare. But because this was one of the greatest days in the annual of the church, he spent a half a day in the preparation thereof. The title he selected for it suited him fully, and he called it: "The Claim of the Wicked."

Into it he put all the emotion that was in him. He drew a picture in illustrious words, of the wicked, the vicious man, and the weak, the undefended woman, and made many in his dark congregation burst into emotional discordance thereby. He ridiculed the vain; he denounced, scathingly, the hypocrite; he made scores in his audience turn with perspiration at the end of their noses with conscious guilt. Oh, never before in the years since he had mounted to the pulpit and begun what he chose to call, "an effort for the salvation of souls," had he preached such a soul stirring sermon.

"Live right, live right, I say!" he screamed at the top of his voice. "How many of you are there as you sit here before me, that have done evil unto thy neighbor; have made some one unhappy; have cast a soul into grief and eternal anguish? Think of it! Think of what it means before God to do evil, spite; vent your rotten deceit upon others! I stand before you in God's glory to beseech you to desist; to pray with you to live according to your consciences;

to dispense with that evil spirit that in the end you may face your God in peace! Go forth hereafter in this world of sin; go to those whom you have wronged and made thereby to suffer, and ask forgiveness; ask there and repent forthwith! Oh, I'll tell you it is a glorious feeling to know you have lived right," and he turned his eyes dramatically heavenward, and affected his audience by the aspect. " To feel that unto others you have been just; that you have been kind; that you have not caused them to suffer, but to feel happy! Think of the thrill, the sensation such must give you, and then let your conscience be henceforth your guide in all things!"

When the services were over, and he had shaken hands with all the sisters, and bowed to the brothers, a boy, the son of the lady where he stayed, approached and handed him a letter. He looked at it with his spectacles pinched upon his nose, and then read it. It was from Ethel, and we know the contents.

"So," he said easily as he read it. " The evil seeks to influence my household in subtle matters, eh! Oh, that man has the brain of a Cæsar, but the purpose of Satan! Drat him, and his infernal scheming! Ever since the day I first knew him in the country four miles from this town, he has been wont to annoy, to aggravate me — and after all my daughter, my poor daughter, and myself have done for him!"

He began preparation to go to Chicago at the earliest convenience. As his work was so urgent, he wrote Ethel in reply that same day:

" *My dear daughter:*

" I am in receipt of your letter and make haste to reply. To begin with, I am not surprised to hear what you wrote in your letter. I am not surprised to hear anything these days. Ever since your mother committed the unpardonable blunder of letting my poor child go straggling off into the West, that wild West, where only the rough and the uncivilized live, I have not been surprised with what each day might bring. It is certainly to be regretted that when one has sacrificed as much as I have to raise two of the nicest girls that ever saw the light of day, a fortune hunter should come along and bring misery into a peaceful home as that man has done. God be merciful! But it is to be hoped that we will see fit to adjust rightly the evil that we are threatened with.

" I cannot come to Chicago until a week from next Thursday or Friday. I am so behind with God's work, caused by the trip we made to that land of wilderness last spring, that I am almost compelled to be at Cairo next Sunday. But should anything transpire that will necessitate my presence before that time, wire or write me right quick and I will be there.

" From yours in Christ,
" N. JUSTINE McCARTHY."

In the West Jean Baptiste got ready for the homecoming of his wife. The small grain crop was gone. While the drought was now burning the corn to bits, his large crop of flax, which had been the most hopeful possible a few days before, was showing the effect of the drought now as well.

But with Jean Baptiste, he could almost forego anything and be happy with the prospects. In his mind this became so much so, until he looked forward to the day he had set for her coming as if all the world must become righted when she was once again near him.

Now during these months he had only his grandmother for company, and her he wanted to send home. But she would not leave him, always willing to wait until Orlean came back. During these long lonesome days he found a strange solace in talking to his horses. There, for instance, was John and Humpy, the mules that Orlean had driven her father out to their home with when he had come on his first visit. He told them that she was coming back now, and to him they appeared to answer. 'They had become round and plump since work had closed, and having fully shed their winter's hair, and not yet become sunburned their dapple gray coating made them very attractive.

He rearranged the house, bought a few pieces of much needed furniture, and made elaborate preparations for the homecoming. At last the day arrived.

It was Saturday morning. The wind had died down, and gave threats of rain for the first time in six long, hot dry weeks. He hitched John and Humpy to the spring wagon, and with a touch of his old enthusiasm, left his grandmother cheerfully — but for reasons of his own, did not tell her that he was going for Orlean. Perhaps he wished to surprise her, at least he did not tell her.

He drove to Winner more filled with hope than he had been for months.

The town was filled that day, and because there was an appearance of rain in the air, which could yet save much of the corn, there was an air of hope and cheer abroad. Jean thought to board a train and ride a few miles, and return on the evening train on which she would be. Then he decided he would wait for her and be ready to drive directly home. As the train was due shortly after nine P. M., he estimated that he could drive the distance in two hours, thereby getting to her claim before midnight and they could spend Sunday together celebrating their happy reunion.

He had longed to talk with her — and grieve with her

over their loss in the fine little boy who never knew his parents. He thought of all this and of the happy days they had spent together the summer before. He felt the love and the devotion she had given him then. He wondered sometimes whether he had ever loved her as he had dreamed he would love his wife; but this thought had ever been replaced by his sense of duty. Marriage was sacred; it was the institution of good; he always disliked to see people part. He felt then, as he had ever felt before, that nothing but infidelity could ever make him leave a woman that he had married. He was still an enemy of divorce. He recalled how they had gone to the Catholic church once in Gregory, and had heard a learned priest discourse on divorce and its attendant evils. Never before had anything so impressed him. How plain the priest had made his audience understand why the church did not tolerate divorce. How decidedly he had shown that divorce could and would be avoided if the people could be raised to feel that "until death do us part." And Baptiste and the woman he had married had discussed it afterward. They had found books and stories in the magazines to which they subscribed, and had read deeper into it, and had been united in their opinion on the subject. Divorce was bad; it was evil; it was avoidable in almost every case. Then why should it be?

They had agreed that duty toward each other was the first essential toward combating it; that selfishness was a thing that so often precipitated it. In all its phases he had discussed it with her, and in the end, she had agreed with him. And down in their hearts they had felt that such would never be necessitated in the union they had formed.

So he lived again through the life that had been his, he did not allow his mind to dwell on the evil that had come into and made his life unhappy; made his days and nights and very existence a misery. He did not, as he lingered on the platform of that little western station, think or dwell on the things that were best forgotten. For a time he became Jean Baptiste of old. Return to him then did all that old buoyancy, all that vigor and great hope, all that was his when he had longed for the love that should be every man's.

And she had been away on a visit, to recover from the illness that the delivery had given her. He was sorry for their loss, and he would talk with her this night as they drove along the trail. They would talk of that and all they had lost, and they would talk of that which was to come. Oh, it would be beautiful! Just to have a wife, the wife that gives all her love and thought to making her husband happy. And he would try to give her all that was in him. And his wife would soon be with him — in his arms, and they would be happy as they had once been!

There it was! From down the track the train whistled. It was coming, and his wait was to an end. Near he saw John and Humpy whom she had been delighted to drive. They were groomed for the occasion, and were anxious to go home. Tonight they would haul her and hear her voice. He rose suddenly to his feet when at last the light fell upon the rails and he could see the engine. The roar of the small locomotive was approaching. Around him were others whose wives had been away. They, too, were come to meet their loved ones. Some were alone while around the others were children — all waiting to meet those dear to their hearts.

The train came to a stop at last, and the people emerged from the coaches. There was the usual caressing as loved ones greeted loved ones. Little cries of "mama" and "papa" were heard, and for a moment there was quite a hubbub of exclamations. "Oh, John," and "Jim" with the attendant kiss. In the meantime he looked expectantly down the line to where the car doors opened, and not seeing the one for whom he was looking, he presently jumped aboard the first car, and passed through it. It was empty and he estimated that she would be in the rear car. It was the chair car, and the one in which he naturally would expect her to ride. He passed into it bravely, with his lips ready to greet her. The last of the passengers were filing out. The car was empty, and his wife had not come.

Slowly he passed out of the car as the brakeman rushed in to change his apparel for the street. Across the street was the team waiting. They seemed to know him before he came in sight and they greeted him as though they thought that she had come, too.

He got slowly into the wagon, and soon they were hurrying homeward.

CHAPTER IX

WHAT THE PEOPLE WERE SAYING

N. J. McCARTHY arrived in the city late on Friday afternoon and was met by both his daughters. Ethel had, of course, read the letters Jean Baptiste had written his wife requesting her to return home, and so she took Orlean with her to meet her father, instead of permitting her to go to the station to return to the husband who had asked for her. The Elder was due in about the same time the train that would have taken Orlean West was due out.

"Ah-ha," he cried as he stepped from the car. "And both my babies have come to meet their father! That is the way my children act. Always obedient to their father. Yes, yes. Never have contraried or disobeyed him," a compliment he meant for Orlean, but Ethel could share it this once, although the times she had contraried or sauced him would have been hard to recount.

Upon arriving home, they met Glavis just returning from work, and he was also greeted in the same effusive manner by the Reverend.

"And how is everything about the home, my son?" asked the Elder in a big voice. At the same time he eyed Glavis critically. He had come to the city with and for a purpose, and that purpose was to put down early the intimacy that had been reported as growing up between Glavis and Baptiste. So he had planned to attend to it diplomatically.

"Why everything is alright, father," glabbed Glavis,

grinning broadly and showing his teeth. He was ever affected by the other's lordlyism, and he had never tried matching his wits with those of the other's in an extraordinary manner. The Elder was aware of this, and it made him rather grateful. However, he regarded the other closely as Glavis stepped about in quick attention to his possible needs or desires. That was as he had hoped to have both his sons-in-law, wherefore his team would have been complete. It made him sigh now regretfully when he recalled how he had failed in the one case. He gave up momentarily to a siege of self pity. How different it would have been had Jean Baptiste chosen to admire him as Glavis apparently did. But — and he straightened up perceptibly when it occurred to him, instead of being as Glavis was, the other had chosen to be independent, to call him " Judge," " Colonel," " Reverend," and " Elder " and any other vulgar title he happened to think of on the moment. Moreover, he had also chosen to ask him a thousand questions about things he did not understand — that was the trouble, though the Elder had not seen it that way— asking him questions about things he did not understand. The Elder saw it as " impudent." He saw and regarded that persistency which had been the making of the man in Jean Baptiste as " hardheadedness." He regarded that tenacity to stick to anything in the other, sufficient to characterize " a bulldog."

" M-m, my boy," he said now to Glavis. " You are certainly a fine young man, just fine, fine, fine! " He paused briefly while Glavis could swallow the flattery, and then went on: " Never in the thirty years I have been a minister of the gospel and been compelled to be away from home in God's work, has it ever been like it has since you married Ethel. I simply do not have to worry at all now;

whereas, I used to have to worry all the time." Whereupon he paused again, affected a lordly sigh, and permitted Glavis to become inflated with vanity before going on.

"Now, before you married Ethel, I was a little dubious." He always said this for a purpose. "I am so well informed and understand men so well, and the ways of men, until I was hesitant to risk trusting you with my daughter's love. You will understand how it is when you have raised children with the care I have exercised in the training of my precious darlings. A man cannot be too careful, and for that reason, I was dubious regarding her marrying you. Besides, we, I think you understand, are among the best colored people of the city of Chicago, and the State of Illinois, so it behooved me to exercise discretion."

"Yes, father," Glavis swallowed. He felt then the dignity of his position as a member of such a distinguished family.

"Well," went on the other, "you know how much grief I must be enduring when I see this poor baby," pointing to Orlean, "as she is. The finest girl that ever trod the earth, and my heart always, and then to see her dragged down to this, and all this attendant gossip, grieves my old heart," whereupon big tears rolled down his dark face. All those about sighed in sympathy and were silent.

"Oh, it's a shame, a shame, my father, it is a shame!" he cried between sobs. "Oh, his immortal soul! Come in here like a thief in the night, and with his dirty tongue just deliberately stole her from her good home — her an innocent child to go out into that wilderness and sacrifice her poor soul to make him rich!" He ended with the eloquence that his years of preaching had given him. He shed more tears of mortification, and resumed:

"And my wife, her own mother, was a party to it!" He

was killing two birds with one stone now. Nothing was more gratifying to him than to seize every possible opportunity to place all his failures, all his shortcomings, all his blunders, and last, but not least, all the results of his evil nature, on the shoulders of his little helpless wife. For years — aye, since he had taken her as wife, had it been so. Never had she shared even in reflected light the honors that had come to him. She did as he requested, and endeavored to please him in every way. The love he had given her was an affected love. It was not from his heart. He had given her little that was due her as his wife.

"I went out there," he went on, "to find this child lying there in the bed with only his sister and grandmother to look after her. The doctor was coming twice a day, but that man asked him, when she could but open her eyes, whether such was necessary; and that when it wasn't, then to come but once. I sat there by her bed, I, her poor old father, and nursed her back to life from the brink of death, the death that surely would have come had it not been for me. And when she was well enough, I went to all the expense of bringing her out of that wilderness back to her home and health.

"And for that, for all that I have sacrificed, what am I given? Credit? Well, I guess not! I am being slandered; I'm being vilified by evil people — and right in my own church! Think of it! For thirty years I have preached the law of the gospel and saved so many souls from hell, and now, now when my poor old head its white and my soul is grieved with the evil that has come into my home, I am vilified!

"No longer than last week, I was approached by a woman, a woman purporting to be a child of God, but who ups to me and said: 'Reverend Mac., what is the matter with your daughter and the man she married? I hear they are parted?' I was so put out that I did not attempt to answer, but just regarded her coldly. But did that stop her mouth? Well, I guess not! She went right on as flip as she could be: 'Well, you know, Reverend, there is all kinds of reports about to various effects. One is that you didn't like him because of his independent ways, and because he was successful, and he didn't take much stock in you because he didn't like the way you had lived. And then there's other reports that he made an enemy of you because he didn't praise and flatter you, and that you did it to "get even." They say that you had your daughter to sign her husband's name to a check for a large sum of money and used it to slip away from him and so on. But the one thing that everybody seems to be agreed upon is, that there was nothing whatever wrong between the couple, and that they had never quarreled and never had thought of parting. That all the trouble is between you and your son-in-law.'

"I had stood her gab about as long as I could, I was so angry. So all I could say was: 'Woman, in the name of heaven, get you away from me before I forget I am a minister of the gospel and you a woman!' But before she had even observed how angry I was, she ups and says: 'Why, now, Elder, as much as you love the ladies, and then you'd abuse a poor woman like me,' and right there, after such a tonguing as she had let out, fell to crying!

"Those are some of the things I must endure, my son, in this work. I must endure slander, vilification, misunderstanding, and all that. It's terrible."

"People are certainly ungrateful," cried Ethel at this point. "And they don't try to learn the truth about anything before they start their rotten gossip. More, they have nerve with it! A certain woman stopped me on the street downtown the other day, a woman who claims to have been my friend and a friend of our family for years. And what do you think she had the nerve to say to me? Well, here's what it was, and I *hope* she said it: 'Why, Ethel, how is Orlean?' I replied that she was getting better. She says: 'Is she sick physically, or mentally?' I said: 'I don't understand you?' She looked at me kind of funny as she replied, 'Why, don't *you* know, Ethel Glavis, that it's the talk around Chicago — everybody is saying it, that you and your father went out West there, and made her forge his name to a check for a large sum of money and for spite and spite only, took poor Orlean away from her husband and came back here and spread all this gossip about her being sick and neglected when the doctor had come to see her every day? I know Jean Baptiste and I have not lived in this world for thirty-five years and not able yet to understand people. And Jesus Christ couldn't make me believe that Jean Baptiste would mistreat Orlean. Besides, all this talk comes from you and your father. Orlean has said nothing about it. She is just simple and easy like her mother and will take anything off you and your father. Now, it's none of my business; but I am a friend of humanity, and I want to say this, that anybody that is doing what you and your father are doing will suffer and burn in hell some day for it!' And she flies away from me and about her business."

"It's outrageous," the Reverend cried. "We hardly dare show our heads on the street; to greet old friends for fear we are going to be ridiculed and abused for what we have done."

"It's certainly an ungrateful world, that's all," agreed Ethel.

CHAPTER X

IT DID NOT rain the night Jean Baptiste went to Winner to meet the wife who failed to come, but the protracted drought continued on into July. For three weeks into this month it burned everything in its path. From Canada to Kansas, the crops were almost burned to a crisp, while in the country of our story proper, only the winter wheat, and rye, and some of the oats matured. And this was confined principally to the county where Jean Baptiste had homesteaded. Here a part of a crop of small grain was raised, but everything else was a failure.

His flaxseed crop in Tripp County which had given some promise if rain should come in time, had now fallen along with all else, and when he saw it next, after his trip to Winner, it was a scattered mass of sickly stems, with army worms everywhere cutting the stems off at the ground. The whole country as a result, was facing a financial panic. Interest would be hard to raise — and this, in view of the fact that the year before had seen less than half a crop produced, was not a cheerful prospect. With Baptiste, and others who had gone in heavily, disaster became a possibility; and, unless a radical change intervened, disaster appeared as an immediate probability.

During these days there was little to do. He had harvested what little crop he had raised, and having no hauling or anything, to engage him he found going fishing his only diversion. And it was at about this time that he received a letter. It bore the postmark of the town where he had met his wife in the beginning, and read:

"*My dear Jean:*

"I thought I would be bold this once and write you, since it is a fact that you are on my mind a great deal. You will, of course, remember me when I mention that it was in my home that you met your wife. Rather, the woman you married, whom, I suppose, from what I hear, has not proven very faithful. I daresay that your trip to my home that day was the beginning of this episode. But it is of him, the Reverend, her father, of whom I wish to speak.

"He used to speak of you. You see this town is in his itinerary, and I therefore, see him quite often. In fact, he is quite well known to me, and visits my home, and has been here recently. He was here just a week ago yesterday before going into Chicago, and I asked about you. He ups with his head when I did so, and I estimated that the trouble that is supposed to be between you and Orlean, is possibly between him and yourself.

"Well, you see, it is like this. After you married Orlean, we could hear nothing from him but you. You were the most wonderful, the most vigorous, the wealthiest — in fact you were everything according to his point of view. He preached of you in the pulpit; he set you up as the standard and model for other young men to follow. Therefore, you must imagine our surprise when almost over night you had changed so perceptibly. From everything a man should be — or try to be, as a young man, you became the embodiment of all a man should not be. Now it is rather singular. Apparently the Elder must have been possessed with very poor judgment to begin with, or you must have become in a few weeks an awfully bad man.

"Well, I don't know what to say; but in as much as I have known you some little time — before you met Orlean in the house where I write this, I cannot conceive or realize how you could change so quickly. But what is more to the point — I have known the august Elder even longer than I have you — know him since I have been large enough to

know anybody, and I have known him always to be as he
is yet. One wonders how such men can have the conscience to preach and tell people to live right, to do right,
so they may be prepared to die right. But somehow we
take the Elder's subtle conduct down this way as a matter
of course. We think no more — I daresay not as much —
of what he does in that way than we would the most common man in town. But it is too bad that his daughter must
suffer for his evil. Orlean is a good girl, but she has been
raised to regard that old father as a criterion of righteous-
ness, regardless of the life he does, and always has lived.
But withal, honestly, I do feel so sorry for you. I am
aware that this letter and the nature of its contents is un-
solicited, but it is and has been in my heart to say it. I
really feel that it is no more than honest to protest against
in some manner, the wrong that man is practicing. But to
the point.

" The last time he was here, and mama asked him about
you, and he was made angry because of it, he remarked
among the discredits he endeavored to pay the country
and you, that there was no church for her to attend. I remarked that you had said you attended the white churches.
Thereupon he became very demonstrative. He said you
did attend the white churches, and had taken her, but that
you went to the Catholic church where there was, of course,
no religion in the sense to which she had been raised. I
hardly knew how to reply to or counter this, but I thought
that if you had, and she had belonged to the Catholic
church, how easy it would be now for you to lay your
cause before the priest and have it considered. But if you
did such before the ministers of his church — oh, well, I
am saying too much.

" And only now have I arrived at the event I choose to
relate. It is always so when one chooses to gossip, to forget the things that may be of real interest. Well, word has
come that the Elder was taken violently ill in Chicago the
other day, and grave fears are held of his recovery. I
hear that he is very low, and perhaps the Lord might see
fit to remove a stumbling block. . . .

" I must close. I am sure I have bored you with such a long letter and so much gossip; but I have at least satisfied my own conscience. So hoping that all comes out well with you in the end, believe me to be,

" Your dear friend,
" JESSIE MANSFIELD."

It so happened that the exhausted Jean Baptiste turned to the hope that illness might claim his enemy, and he exchanged letters with Jessie Mansfield, regularly, and after a time, found her correspondence a great diversion.

And so the summer passed. Near the last days of July the severe drought was broken, but too late to benefit the crops which had been so badly burned by the drought. He managed to get considerable land into winter wheat, and the fall came on with only a crop of debts and overdue bills that made him regard the mail box dubiously.

Winter followed, one of the coldest ever known, and spring was approaching when Jean Baptiste decided to make his last attempt for a reunion with his wife.

In all the months that had followed his previous trip he had planned that if he could only see her, could only see her and be alone with her for a day, they would abridge the chasm that had been forced because of the Reverend. That one had not obliged him by dying by any means, but had regained his health in a measure, so Baptiste read in the letters he received from Jessie. However, she wrote, it seemed that something had come over him, for he was not the same. He had lost much of his great flesh, wore a haggard expression, and seemed to be weighted down with some strange burden.

It was April again when at last he took the train for Chicago, for the last time, he decided, on the same mission that had taken him there twice before. He planned now, to exercise more discretion. Inasmuch as the Reverend was as a rule, always out of the city, he trusted to fate that he would be out this time. The bitterness that had grown up in his heart toward the Elder, he feared, might make him forget to observe the law of the land if he chanced to encounter that adversary. So when he arrived in the great city, he went about the task of seeing his wife under cover.

He first visited a barber shop. He happened into one near Van Buren on State Street, where lady barbers did the trimming. He did not find them efficient, and was glad when he left the chair. He decided that he would act through Mrs. Pruitt, who he had heard from the fall before, and who was being charged along with Mrs. McCarthy, as being the cause of all the trouble.

He had not written her that he was coming, calculating that it would be best for her not to have too long to think it over. Upon leaving the barber shop, he ventured up State Street, through the notorious section of the " old tenderloin " to Taylor Street, and presently turned and discovered himself in the Polk and Dearborn Street station. He found that slipping about the street under cover like a sneak thief was much against his grain, and he was nervous. In all the months he had contemplated the trip, he had taken great care not to let Ethel or any of the family know in advance of his coming. He wanted his wife. The agony of living alone, the dreaded suspense, the long journey and the gradual breaking down of what he had built up, played havoc with his nerves, and he was trembling perceptibly when he took a seat in the station. He encountered a man upon arrival there, whom he had known years before, and because he had been so intent on keeping out of sight, the recognition by the other frightened him. He managed to control himself with an effort, and greeted the other casually. However, he was relieved when he recalled that the other knew nothing of his relations — not even that he had ever married.

After he felt his nerves sufficiently calm, he ventured to the telephone booth, and secured Mrs. Pruitt's number. He paused briefly before calling her to steady his nerves, and then got her in due time.

"Hello, Mrs. Pruitt," he called.

"'Hello," came back, and he caught the surprise in her voice. "Is it *you?*" she asked, and he noted that her voice was trembling.

"Yes," he called back nervously. "Do you recognize my voice?"

"Yes," he heard, and the uneasiness with which she answered discouraged him. He had great faith in Mrs. Pruitt. Notwithstanding the gossip that connected her name with the Elder's she was regarded as a woman of unusual ability and mental force. She was speaking again in a very low tone of voice. Almost in a whisper.

"Listen," said she. *"Call this same number in about ten minutes, understand?* Yes. Do that. I'll explain later."

He sat before the clock now, in the station, and watched the minutes pass. They seemed like hours. He was now aware that the strain of these months of grief and eternal mortification, had completely unnerved him. His composure was like that of an escaped convict with the guards near. His heart beat so loud until he looked around in cold fear wondering whether those near heard it. And all the while he sat in this nervous quandary, he kept repeating over, and over again: *"Mrs. Pruitt, Mrs. Pruitt — surely even you have not gone back on me, too. Oh, Mrs. Pruitt, you can't understand what it means to me, what I have suffered,— the agony, the disgrace — the hell!"* He regarded the telephone booth before him and his eyes were like glass. All the busy station was a hubbub. After what seemed to him an eternal waiting, he was slightly relieved to see that fifteen minutes had passed, and he got up and slipped back into the booth and called Mrs. Pruitt.

"Yes, I'm here, Jean," she called, "and the reason I told you to call later was that *your* people — *your father-in-law is right here in the house at this moment*. He was sitting right here by the 'phone when you called awhile ago, so now you understand."

"Oh," he cried, his head swimming, and everything grew dark around him. After one long year of agony, of eternal damnation, one long year of waiting and suspense, he had banked his chances, and encountered his enemy the first thing. Right under the telephone he had been! Jean Bap tiste who had once been a strong, brave and fearless man, was now trembling from head to foot.

"Now, Jean," he heard Mrs. Pruitt. "I understand *everything*. You are here to see and get Orlean if you can; but you want to do so without them knowing anything about it, and I agree with you. You wish me to help you, and I will. I'll do anything to right this terrible wrong, but give me time to plan, to think! In the meantime, he is so near that it is not safe for me to talk with you any longer. So you go somewhere, and come back, say: in about an hour. If he is still here, I will say: 'this is the wrong number.' Get it?"

"Yes, Mrs. Pruitt," he replied, controlling the storm of weakness that was passing over him. "I *get* you."

"Very well, until then."

"Until then," he called, and hung up the receiver.

CHAPTER XI

"IT'S THE WRONG NUMBER"

JEAN BAPTISTE had come eight hundred miles after one terrible year, to the feet of his father-in-law, and when he realized that such was the case upon hanging up the receiver, his composure was gone. Bitter agony beyond description overwhelmed him when he came from the booth at the end of his brief conversation with Mrs. Pruitt. Never in his life had he been as miserable as he now was. It seemed to him that in the next hour he must surely die of agony. He found a place in the station where he was very much alone, and for a time gave up to the grief and misery that had come over him.

"Unless I find some diversion, I will be unfit for anything but suicide!" he declared, trying to see before him. Out in the West all was wrong. He was now loaded down with debt. His interest was unpaid, also his taxes. His creditors for smaller amounts he had not even called upon to say that he was unable to meet his financial obligations. He had tried being blind to everything but the instance of his wife. He had just deliberately cast everything aside until he could have her. That was it. He had made himself believe that only was it necessary to see her alone, and together they would fly back to the West. He had not reckoned that his arch enemy would be lying like a great dog right at the door he was to enter.

And now, before he was hardly in the city, he was all but confronted with his hypocritical bulk.

"Oh, I can stand it no longer, no, no, no!" he cried in

agonizing tones. The world to him was lost. The strong shall be the weakest when it becomes so, it is said; and surely Jean Baptiste had come to it in this hour. He had no courage, he had no hope, he had no plans.

After minutes in which he reached nowhere; minutes when all the manhood in him crept out, and went away to hide, he staggered to his feet. He straightened his body, and also his face; he became an automaton. He had decided to seek artificial stimulation. Thereupon he made his way into the main waiting room. He looked about him as one in a daze, and finally turned his face toward the entrance of the station. When there he had arrived, he hesitated, and looked from right to left. As he did so, his mind went back to some years before when he first saw the city, and had gone about its streets in search of work. A block or two away he recalled Clark Street, that part of it which had been notorious. He recalled where one could go and see almost *anything* he wished.

Now, he was a man, was Jean Baptiste, a man who had loved a wife as men should; a man who had found a wife and a wife's comfort all he had longed for in life. But that one he had taken as wife had fled. She had left him to the world, and all that was worldly. He was breaking down under the strain, and his manhood was for the time gone. He became as men are, as men have been, and he was at a place where he did not care. He was alone in the world, the prairies had not been good to him, and he felt he must have rest, oh, rest.

He stepped from the station, and held himself erect with an effort. He turned to his left, and walked or rather ambled along. He did not know in particular where he was going, but going somewhere he was. He kept his face turned to the west, and after many steps, he came to a side street. It was a narrow street, and he recalled it vaguely. It was called Custom House Place, and its reputation for the worst, was equalled by none. Even from where he stood the sound of ragtime music came to his ears from a gorgeous saloon across its narrow way.

He listened to it without feeling, no thrill or inspiration did it give him. He turned into this street after some minutes, and ambled along its narrow walkway. As he went along, from force of habit, he studied the various forms of vice about. In and out of its many ways, he saw the familiar women, the painted faces and the gorgeous eyes. He came presently to where Negroes stood before a saloon. They, too, were of the type he understood. Characters with soft hands, and soft skin, and he knew they never worked. He turned into it. A bar was before him, and although for liquor he had never cared especially, he could drink. He went forward to the bar and ordered a cocktail. He drank it slowly, as he observed himself, all haggard and worn in the bar mirror, and as he did so, he could see what was passing behind him. A man sat in a small ante room near a door, and he observed that men would pass by this man to a door opening obviously to a stairway beyond. He wondered what *was* beyond. He ordered another cocktail, and drank it slowly, studying those who passed back and forth through the door that the man opened with a spring. He decided to venture thereforth.

When he had drank his cocktail, he wandered toward the door also, as if he had been accustomed to entering it. The door opened before him and he entered. He found himself in a hallway, with a flight of stairs before him, and a closed and locked door on the stairway. He stood regarding it, and espied a bell presently. This he approached and touched.

The door was opened straightway and the flight of stairs continued to the landing above. He looked up and beheld a woman standing at the top of the stairs, who had seemingly opened the door by pressing a button. He entered and approached her. As he did so, she turned and led him into a small room, then into a larger room, where sat many other women. He was directed to a chair, and became seated. He regarded all the women about wonderingly; for to him, none had said a word. He might as well have been in a house of tombstones, for they said naught to him, and did not even look at him.

He sat where he was for perhaps two minutes. Then he arose and walked to the door which he had entered, and turned to look back into the room. It was empty, every woman had disappeared without a sound in a twinkling, all except the woman who had admitted him. She stood behind, regarding him noncommittally.

" What is this place? " he inquired of her. She looked up at him, and he thought he caught something queer in her eyes. But she replied in a pleasant tone:

" Why, it is *anything.*"

" Oh," he echoed. She continued to stand, not urging him to go, nor to stay. He looked at her closely, and saw that she was a white woman, perhaps under thirty.

" A sort of cabaret? " he suggested.

" Yes," she replied, in the same pleasant tone of voice. " A *sort* of cabaret."

" So you serve drinks here, then? "

" Yes, we *serve* drinks here."

" Where? "

" Well," and she turned and he followed her to another room apparently the abode of some one. Included in the furniture there was a table and two chairs, and while he became seated in one, she took the other and her eyes asked what he wished.

"A cocktail," he said.

She went to a tube and called the order.

"And something for yourself," he said.

She did as he directed, and duplicated his order. She came back to where he sat by the table and sat before him, without words, but a pleasant demeanor.

"Here's luck," he said, when the drinks had been brought up.

"Same to you," she responded, and both drank.

He told her then to bring some beer, and when the order had been given, he bethought himself of his errand. Instantly he became oblivious of all about him, and the old agony again returned. He stretched across the table, and was not aware that he groaned. He did not hear the woman who stood over him when she returned with the beer. He was living the life of a few minutes before,— misery.

"Here is your beer," she said, but he made no move. Presently she touched him lightly upon the shoulder, whereupon he sat erect, and looked around him bewilderingly.

"Your beer," she said, and he regarded her oddly.

"What is the matter?" she said now, and regarded him inquiringly.

"I was thinking," he replied.

"Of something unusual," she ventured.

"Yes," he answered, wearily. "Of something *unusual.*"

She observed him more closely. She saw his haggard face; his tired, worn expression, and beneath it all she caught that sad distraction that had robbed him of his composure. In some way she really wished to help him. Here was an unusual case. She,— this woman who was for sale, became seated again, and regarding him kindly she said:

" You are in trouble."

He sighed but said no word.

" In great trouble."

He sighed again, and handed her the money for the beer.

" I wish I could help you," she said thoughtfully and her eyes fell upon the table. His hat lay there, and she saw therein the name of the town where it had been purchased.

" You don't live here? " she suggested then.

" No," he mumbled, trying to dispel the heaviness that was over him. If he could just forget. That was it. If he *could* forget and be normal; be as he had been until that evil genius had come back again into his life. " No," he repeated, " I don't live here."

" And — you — you — have just come? " she said. Her voice was kind. " Is it — it — a *woman?* "

He nodded slowly.

" Oh," she echoed. " Your wife, perhaps? "

He nodded again.

" Oh! "

They were both silent then for some moments; he struggling to forget, she wondering at the strange circumstances.

" Has some one come between you? " she inquired after a time.

" Yes," he whispered.

" Oh, that's bad," she uttered sympathetically. " It is bad to come between a man and his wife. And you —" she paused briefly then bit her lip in slight vexation, then observed him with head bent before her. It was rather unusual, and that was what had vexed her. Could it mean anything what a woman like her thought of or sympathized. Yet, she was moved by the condition of the stranger before her. She felt she had to say something. " And you —

you don't look like a bad fellow at all." He looked up at her with expressionless eyes. She returned the look and then went on:

"You have such honest, frank and truthful eyes. Honestly, I feel sorry for you."

"Oh, thank you," he said gratefully then. To have some one — even *such a woman* look at him so kindly, to say words of condolence was like water to the thirsty. He thought then again of that other, and the father that was hers, who at that moment sat in the company of another man's wife. He recalled that Mrs. Pruitt said that he had been in town for several days and every day since he had been there. Naturally. This man courted another man's wife openly, yet was ready with all the force in him, the moment Jean Baptiste sought his God-given mate, to rise up in pious dignity to oppose him. Wrath became his now, and his eyes narrowed. In the moment he wanted to go forth and slay the beast who was making this. He rose slightly. She saw it, and her eyes widened. She reached out and touched his hand where it gripped the table.

"Please don't do *that*," she said, and in her voice there was a slight appeal.

He regarded her oddly, and then understood. He sank back listlessly in the seat, and sighed.

"Poor boy," she said. "Some one has done you a terrible wrong. It is strange how the world is formed, and the ill fortune it brings to some. I can just see that some one has done you a terrible wrong, and that when you rose now you would have gone forth and killed him."

He regarded her with gratitude in his eyes, and the expression upon his face told her that she had spoken truly.

"But try to refrain from that desire. Oh, it's justifiable it seems. But then when we stop to think that we will never feel the same afterward about it, it's best to try to forget our grief. You are young, and there are worlds of nice girls who would love and make for you happiness. Some day that will be yours in spite of all. So please, just think and — don't kill the one who has done this."

"You are awfully kind," he whispered. He felt rather odd. Of all places, this was not where men came to be *consoled,* indeed. But herein he had gotten what he could not get on Vernon Avenue where church members were supposed to dwell. He arose now. . . . He reached out his hand and she took it. "I don't quite understand what has happened, but you have helped me." He reached into his pocket and withdrew some coins, and this he handed her. She drew back her hand, but he insisted.

"Yes, take it. *I* understand your life here. But you have helped me more than you can think. I was awfully discouraged when I came. Almost was I to something rash. Take it and try to remember that you have helped some one." He squeezed her hand, and she cast her eyes down, and as she did so, he saw a tear fall to the floor. He turned quickly then and left.

He retraced his steps toward the Polk Street station, and to the booth he had been inside of an hour before. He called Mrs. Pruitt, and after a time came back over the wire, in a low, meaning voice:

"*It's the wrong number.*"

CHAPTER XII

H E had some friends who lived on Federal Street and to their home he decided to go. He thought of the day when he had married. The man ran on the road. His wife he had known long, her name being Mildred, Mildred Merrill. She had been invited to his wedding but had not attended. When he had seen her a year later, and had asked her why she had not attended, she replied that she had been unable to purchase a suitable wedding gift.

Her parents had been lifelong friends of his parents, and he had been provoked because she stayed away. She and her husband had been quietly married in the court house and had since lived happily together.

" Oh, Jean," Mildred cried, when the door opened and she saw his face. " We have just been talking of you," as she swung the door wide for him to enter.

" Mama," she called, " here is Jean Baptiste!" Her mother came hurriedly forward, grasped his hand, and exchanged a meaning look with Mildred.

" And you are back *again*," she said as all three became seated.

" Yes," he said, and sighed.

" It's awful," commented her mother.

" Isn't it the truth, oh, my God, how can those people be so mean?" cried Mildred.

"He's in Chicago," said her mother.

"Yes," said Mildred, "and I'll bet right over at Mrs. Pruitt's every day."

"He wouldn't be *likely* to be home," commented her mother.

"He returns as a rule along about midnight." The two laughed then, and regarded the man.

"You ought to give her up, Jean," said Mildred. "A woman that has no more will power than she has, isn't fit — isn't worth the grief you are spending."

"Yes, Mildred, it does seem so, but she is my wife, and somehow I feel that I should give her every chance."

"The case *is* unusual," commented her mother again. "The man has a reputation for such actions — rather, he has been known to persecute, and does persecute the preachers that are under his dictation in the church. But that such would extend to the possible happiness of his own children! Indeed, it hardly seems credible."

"Vanity, mama. Reverend McCarthy is regarded as the most vain man in the church. Jean here has never flattered him — tickled his vanity, and this is the price he's paying."

"Well," said her mother. "Such as this *can't* keep up. Some day he's going to be called on to pay — and the debt will be large."

"Understand that he aspires for the bishopric in the convention next month," said Mildred.

"Shucks!" exclaimed her mother. "That's all bluff. He seeks to grab off a little cheap notoriety around Chicago before he goes to conference. There is as much chance of his being even entered as a candidate for the office as there is of me."

"That's what I think," from Mildred.

"What are your plans, Jean?" her mother now inquired of Baptiste who sat in a sort of stupor listening to their talk.

"I am trying to get to see her without the old man's knowledge." And he told them of his conversation with Mrs. Pruitt.

"Isn't that a wife, now!" exclaimed Mildred. "Afraid to meet the man she has married."

"Orlean and old lady McCarthy have no voice in that house," said her mother. "First it's the Reverend, and then follows Ethel."

"And it hardly seems credible when one knows how he has always flirted with other women," said Mildred.

"I asked Orlean the last time I saw her," said Mildred again, "what was the matter; was Jean mean to her, or had he neglected her. She said: No, that he was just as good to her as he could be, but that she could not stay out in that wild country; that it would impair her health, and she just couldn't stay out there, and that was all."

"Reverend McCarthy," said her mother.

"Of course. But that is one thing I have observed. They have never got her to lie as they have done, and say that he mistreated her." From Mildred.

"It's to be regretted that she has not more will to stand up for what she knows to be right," said her mother.

"You have taken it up with the right person, Jean," said Mildred. "If any one can help you in such a delicate undertaking, it is Mrs. Pruitt. She has more influence with that old rascal than his wife. In fact, his wife, from what I hear, has no influence at all."

"Well, Jean," said Mildred's mother, "you are to be ad-. mired for the patience you have exercised with Orlean. The average man would have knocked that old white headed rascal stiff and let Orlean go, and I don't wonder that if I was a man that I wouldn't have done so myself."

"If I were that weak, and could see things as I do now, I would want my husband to shoot me. I'm getting out of patience with Orlean's weakness," Mildred added.

"Well," said Baptiste at this point, "it is now eleven, and I will call up Mrs. Pruitt to go ahead with certain plans that I have in view. Have you a 'phone?"

"Just outside," said Mildred, and opened the door.

He got Mrs. Pruitt directly, and again came back over the wire:

"It's the wrong number!" But during the recent conversation he had forgotten for the moment the "counter sign," and continued calling back. Frantically he heard again and again, *"Tho wrong number! You have the wrong number!"* Suddenly he caught on, and as suddenly hung up the receiver with a jerk.

He didn't go to the Keystone that night. He felt as though he wanted to be near some friends. Accordingly he went to Miss Rankin's. She was glad to see him, and, like all his friends, knew his troubles, and welcomed him.

"You will awaken me early tomorrow — say, six o'clock?" he asked, and upon being assured she would, he went to bed.

All the night through his sleep was fitful. He saw gorgeous processions that frightened him, and then again he was thrilled; but never did he seem to feel just right. Then he saw his enemy. He dreamed that he came to him and kissed him; he heard him saying kind words, and saw his wife by his side. They were back in the West and his wife was returning from a visit. He was aroused, and jumped to his feet. He looked at the clock, and the time was half past five. All the agony of the day before came back with a rush, and he was overwhelmed. Thereupon he got him up, and, dressing quickly, hurried out of the house and caught a car to where Mrs. Pruitt lived on the west side, in the basement of an apartment building, of which her husband was janitor.

He estimated that the other would go home during the night, and early morning would be the time to form some plan of action. It seemed a long way to the west side, and it was after seven when he arrived there.

He was greeted by Mrs. Pruitt, and the expression upon her face did not disappoint him.

" Now, Jean," she said, " I have prepared you some break-fast, and you must eat first, for I'll wager that not a bite have you eaten since you talked with me yesterday."

" It is so, Mrs. Pruitt," said he, recalling then that eating had not occurred to him for the last eighteen hours or more.

" Well," said she, becoming seated, " *he* left here at al-most midnight, and I have been planning just what to do, that you may see Orlean. I certainly should have little patience with a girl that has no more gumption than Orlean; but since I know that she gets it from her mother, who has not as much as a chicken, I have accepted the in-evitable.

" Now, to begin with. If I called up and had her come over here, he would come with her, of course, and also maybe Ethel. And you know what that would mean. It is so unusual that such a thing could be, but that is Reverend McCarthy. He has always been this way, and I could not change him. You erred when you didn't flatter him. But that you did not have to do, and I don't blame you. He has done you dirty, and some day he's going to pay for it. I wouldn't be surprised if he did not soon, either. He is a disturbed man, he is. Never has he been happy as he was before he brought that girl home. The crime he has committed is weighing on him, and I wouldn't wonder if he wouldn't be glad to have Orlean go back with you. The only thing is, that he has been associated with a hard headed lot of Negro preachers so long, until his disposition is ingrained. He actually *couldn't* be as he should. He would let Orlean go back to you, but he would determine on a lot of ceremony, and something else that you are ill fitted to forego. So the best way, as I can see, is for you to meet Orlean somewhere, and there reason it out with her." She paused briefly then, and was thoughtful.

"She loves you as her mother loves, in a simple, weak way; but what is a love like that worth! In truth, while I admire your courage, and desire to uphold the sacredness of the marriage vow, you ought to get a divorce and marry a girl with some will and force."

"I realize so, Mrs. Pruitt, but I am determined to live with Orlean and protect her if it is within my power."

"I understand your convictions and sentiments, Jean, and admire you for it. If the world contained more men like you, the evil of divorce would lessen; but on the other hand, as long as it contains men like the Reverend, and women like Orlean, there will always be ground for divorce."

"But every man should exhaust all that is in him for what he feels is right, shouldn't he, Mrs. Pruitt?" spoke Baptiste.

"Of course," she said somewhat absently. She looked quickly at him then, and her eyes brightened with an inspiration.

"By the way, Jean," she said. "You remember Mrs. Merley?"

"Who? Blanche's mother?"

" The same."

" Most sure. Why "

" Well," said Mrs. Pruitt. " I have been thinking. She's a friend of yours, a good friend, although you might not have known it."

" It is news to me — that is, directly."

" Well, she is, and has been very much wrought up over the Reverend's treatment of you."

" Indeed ! "

" Yes, it is so. You see, moreover, she is a distant relation of Mrs. McCarthy's, and is fairly well-to-do."

" So I have understood."

" Yes, they are, and McCarthys sort of look up to them."

" Yes ? "

" Mrs. Merley is independent, and hasn't much patience with the Elder."

" So."

" No, and for that reason he admires her."

" Indeed."

" Yes, and she was over there and sort a ' bawled ' them out over what they were doing. Understand that she just spat it in the Elder's face and he had to take it."

" Well ? "

" Yes. You see Blanche got married this last summer, and didn't quite please her mother."

" Oh, is that so ? "

" Yes, Mary Merley is a friend of mine, and frankly she almost told me that she wished Blanche had married some one on your order.

" Oh ! . . ."

" Yes, she did. And meant it ! She admired your type, and I know she would have been more fully pleased in such an event."

He was silent.

"Anyhow, I have planned that it will be through her that you and Orlean may be brought together."

He was attentive.

"But before you go into it, my request is that my name shall be left out."

His eyes asked a question that she answered.

"It is so. While Mary is a friend of mine, she has certain habits that I don't like."

He regarded her more questioningly.

"I will say no more."

His face blanched, and then his mind went back two years. Orlean had made just such a remark. He was sorry.

"So I don't want you to mention me, since it would do no good."

"I understand."

"I want her to have the credit for whatever success might come of this."

"Yes."

"And my plans are that you go over there, and see her?"

"Yes."

"Jolly her a little, and don't let on that you are aware that she admires you."

"Very well."

"Get her to call Orlean up, and suggest a show."

"I get you."

"And there you are."

"Your plan is simple, but practical," and he smiled upon her thankfully.

He was standing now. He held out his hand. She grasped it, and bending forward, kissed him.

"Be careful, Jean," she said. "And don't do anything rash."

When he went his way, he understood.

CHAPTER XIII

MRS. MERLEY

THE APRIL morn shone beautifully over Chicago, when Jean Baptiste came from the basement of the apartment where Mrs. Pruitt lived, and had bade Godspeed to him. It was election day over all the state, a preferential primary for the purpose of choosing delegates to the G. O. P. convention to be held two months later. And when Jean Baptiste thought of it, he understood what had brought the Reverend to the city.

Baptiste arrived at Mrs. Merley's an hour after he left Mrs. Pruitt, went directly to the number and pulled the bell. It was responded to by a young woman he did not know, but she assured him that the one he sought was in, and after seating him in the parlor, hurried to tell Mrs. Merley.

She came at once all joy and gladness, and greeted him with a shake of both hands, and kissed him into the bargain.

"Sit right down, sit right down," she said profusely. "And, oh, my, how glad I am to see you!" she smiled upon him happily, proving how glad she really was, and he was moved.

"And you came to see me," she continued. "You could have called on no one who would have been more delighted to see you!"

"You do me too much honor, Mrs. Merley," said he gratefully.

"Indeed," she returned. "I could not do you enough."

"I hadn't hoped for so much kindness, I am sure."

"But, Jean, you don't know how much I have thought about you in the last two years, and I have longed to talk with you!"

"Oh, really! But I thought I was forgotten by everybody in Chicago."

"You have never been forgotten by us. And especially have we talked of you in this last year. . . ."

He was silent, though he felt he understood her reference.

"Some dirty sinner ought to be in torment!"

And still he did not speak.

"Oh, I know all that has been done to you, Jean," she went on tenderly.

"Your words give me much relief, Mrs. Merley."

"I wish they could give you more. It is my wish that an opportunity could be given me to help you."

He straightened. Now was the time to state his mission. But she was speaking again:

"I spoke my sentiments to his face, the rascal! All his dirty life has been given to making people miserable, wherever he could."

Jean said nothing, but was listening nevertheless.

"He has been a rascal for thirty-five years, and has made that simple cousin of mine he married, the goat." She paused to get her breath. "I saw Orlean not long ago, and asked her where her will was, or if she had any."

He was attentive. Always he liked to hear her.

"She, of course, tried to stand up for that arch hypocrite. But I waived that aside. Said I to her: 'Orlean, I could never believe you if you said Jean Baptiste abused, mistreated or neglected you.' She looked down when I had spoken and then said evenly. 'No, Jean did not do any of those things.' 'Then,' said I. 'Why do you live apart from him, the man you married? Where is your sense of duty?' 'But, Mrs. Merley,' she tried to protest. 'I just couldn't live out there in that wilderness, it was too lonesome.' 'Oh, Orlean,' I said disgustingly, 'do you expect me to believe that? And if even I believed you, how could I respect you?'

"But that is it, Jean. Here is this family posing as among the best Negro families in Chicago, but with no more regard for what is morally right than the worst thief. Indeed, no thief would do what that man is doing."

He mumbled something inaudible. She was out to talk, so he heard her on:

"I understand the whole line up, and their vain shielding of that old rascal, just because you didn't lie to him and become a hypocrite like he himself is. Everybody near him must bow to him and tell him he is great, else he will use what influence is his to 'get even.' So that's the whole output. He took her away from you because he raised her as he has willed my cousin, his wife, to subserve to him. And now he goes around here with all that dirty affected piety and wants people to sympathize with him in his evil." She paused again for breath, and then he spoke:

"I am glad to know you have taken the view of this you have, Mrs. Merley," he said slowly, "And I am wondering therefore, whether you would be willing to help me in a certain Christian cause."

"Why, Jean! Why ask me? You must know that I would help you in any way I could."

He then told her just what he had planned. She interrupted him at times with little bursts of enthusiasm, and there was no hesitancy on her part.

"Anything, Jean, anything! You don't know how anxious I am, and how glad I am to have the opportunity! The only thing I regret is that you ever married such a weakling. You might have heard that Blanche is married?"

"I have," he replied. "I trust she is happy."

"Well," said the other slowly, "she appears to be, withal. And for that reason I suppose I should be thankful. But she did not quite please me in her selection."

"Oh," he echoed.

"No," she said slowly, and as if she felt the disappointment keenly. "She did not. Her husband, it is true, is good to her, but he did not come up to my hope. Yet, and it is singular," she said thoughtfully, "to think that a man with all you possess financially, and mentally, should get '*in*' as you have." She paused again a little embarrassed, and then pursued:

"I wish Blanche had a husband of your disposition and attainments."

"Blanche, I thought, was a sweet girl," he said reflectively.

"And a good girl," said Mrs. Merley. "I would have given anything to have had her marry a promising young farmer of your order, and be now living in the West."

"I love the West, and had hoped others would be loving it too," he said ruefully.

"He came back here after his first visit, and sitting right where you are now, said that you was one of the race's most progressive young men. He added to this everywhere he had half a chance and eulogized you to the highest. It happened that the minister who married you, was here, and he, too, very much admired you, and voiced the same to the Reverend. That old devil just swelled up like a big frog with vanity. Three months later he comes back here, and, to seek to justify his action, he spreads the town with lies that nobody believes."

The other shifted his position.

"Well, Jean," she said now more soberly, "just what shall I do?"

"If you would not mind —"

"Oh, don't say that!"

"Very well, Mrs. Merley. I would like you to call her up and suggest a matinée."

"Why not just go to one?"

"That would please me if you would condescend?"

"I'd be glad to go, and in view of the circumstances, I think it would be a suggestive idea. Let her get used to your presence again, without coming directly to the point at once."

"A capital idea, I agree!"

"Call her up and ask her to come over and go with you to the matinée."

"That is the plan, and I understand."

"I will appreciate your kindness," said he heartily. She arose then and advancing toward him, embraced him impulsively.

Thereupon she went to the telephone, and succeeded in getting his wife on the wire. He heard her answer the call, and laugh over something humorous Mrs. Merley said. His heart beat faster, and he was conscious that he was more hopeful than he had been for a long time.

"Yes. . . ." Mrs. Merley was saying. "I want you to go with me to a matinée. . . . Be here at one forty-five. . . . Yes, I have the tickets. . . . And you'll not be late."

She was standing before him again, and her face was lighted up with the joy of what she had accomplished. He was grateful, and rose to thank her, whereupon she embraced him again. The next moment she went quickly up the stairs to prepare for the occasion.

"You may come upstairs, too, Jean," she invited, "and from the front room there, you can watch for yours."

"Oh, Mrs. Merley, you make me happier than I have been for a long time," he said, and almost was he emotional.

"And I have a nice spare bedroom for you and *her*, tonight. And tomorrow, she is *yours.*"

Jean Baptiste waited and watched, and then suddenly he heard a voice. It was that of the girl who had admitted him, who was also watching.

"Here she comes," she cried, excitedly. Jean Baptiste looked quickly out of the window and up the street, and saw his wife coming leisurely toward the house wherein he was sitting.

CHAPTER XIV

OH, MERCIFUL GOD, CLOSE THOU MINE EYES!

REVEREND NEWTON JUSTINE McCARTHY had once lived in Peoria, Illinois, and was well acquainted with the late Robert Ingersoll. Moreover, he had admired the noted orator, and although he had not the courage, in truth, he believed as Ingersoll believed. And because he did, and was forced to keep his true convictions a secret, while he preached the gospel he did not believe, he had grown to hate almost all people. But N. J. McCarthy was not aware of this fact himself.

Ever since he brought his daughter home, and had thereby parted her from the man she married, he had never been the same. Always he was troubled with something he could not understand. His dreams were bad. The awful sensations he very often experienced while in slumber, grew so annoying that at times he found that he was almost afraid to sleep. Then, a persistent illness continually knocked at his door. The truth of it was, that he was battling with a conscience he had for years crucified. But it would persist. So deep had he sowed the habits he followed, and so intrenched were the roots of these habits, until it was no easy task to uproot them.

He had left Mrs. Pruitt near midnight of the day when Jean Baptiste had arrived on his trip in a last effort to secure his wife. The family had retired before he arrived home, and having some business in the rear of the house, he passed through the room which contained the bed wherein his daughter, Orlean, lay in peaceful slumber. When he was returning he paused briefly to observe the face of the sleeping girl in the moonlight. Peacefully she slept, and for the first time in his life he saw therein something he had never seen before. He felt his flesh and wondered at the feeling that was come over him. It seemed that he was asleep, but positively he was awake. He *was* awake, and looking into the sleeping face of his daughter. But if he *was awake, what was it he saw?*

Surely not. But as he stood over her, he thought he could see her eyes open, and look at him strangely, regard him in a way she had never done before. And as she looked at him, he thought she raised her hand that lay under the cover, and with her forefinger leveled, she pointed at him. In the trance he imagined he could hear her voice. She called him:

" Father? " And betimes he answered.

" Yes, daughter."

" Where is my husband? " He gave a start. He thought he caught at something, and then he heard her again:

" You have sent him away, out of my life, and the day is coming when you will be called upon to answer for your sins ! "

He thought he was trembling. All about him was turmoil. He saw the people, the friends of the family, and all the people he had preached to in thirty years, and all were pointing an accusing finger at him. And out of the chaos he heard them crying: *" Shame, oh shame! That you should be so evil, so vile, such a hypocrite, and let your evil fall upon your own daughter!"* He saw then the wife he had taken from Speed. He saw that one in his misery, he saw him sink, and renounce from weakness the sentiments he had started in the world to teach. He saw him struggle vainly, and then saw him fall, low, lower, until at last the flames of hell had swallowed him up. "Merciful God," he cried, and he was sure he staggered. "Was it *I* who brought all this?" But before he could recover, the procession kept passing.

Behind Speed came the wife he had robbed him of. She carried in her arms a baby that he had given her. By the hand she led the other illegitimate offspring. There they were, the innocents that had no name. He saw the bent head of the woman, and saw the grief and anguish in her face. He saw her suddenly stop and fall, and while she lay upon the earth, her children were taken, and grew up surrounded with all that was bad and evil. He saw one suddenly dead, while still a boy, murdered by the companions he kept. He saw his young body in the morgue. And before all this had passed, he saw this one's mother again, the woman he had fooled, in the depth of the "tenderloin." He saw her a solicitor, and he could hear himself groan in agony.

The years passed, and while he grew older, other things came and went; a train of evil deeds he had committed, and at last came his own daughter. He saw her passing and when he saw her face, the agony therein frightened him. Was it so! Had *he,* done that, too? Was *he* the cause of what he saw in this girl's face? Suddeny he saw her change, and in the distance he saw Jean Baptiste, and all he had suffered. "*Oh, merciful God, close thou mine eyes,*" he thought he could hear himself call. But his eyes would not close, and the one to whom he appealed appeared to be deaf, and the procession continued.

He saw Orlean stretch her hands out to Baptiste, and he came toward her with arms outstretched, and he thought he heard a voice, the voice of the man Jean Baptiste. And

the words he cried rang in his ears: " My wife, oh, Orlean, my wife! Come unto me!"— But lo! When the
two had came close, and the man would have held her to
him, a shadow suddenly rose between them, and shut them
out from each other's sight. He thought he raised his
voice to call out to the one of the shadow. And when he
called to him, and the one of the shadow turned, and behold! It was himself! He suddenly came out of the
trance, to see Orlean sitting up in bed. He caught his
breath and held his hand over his heart, as he heard her
voice:

" Papa, is that you? My, how you frightened me! I —"
and then she quickly stopped. She had started to say, " I
thought it was Jean," for in truth she had dreamed of him,
and that he had come for her, and she was glad, and when
she arose to go she had awakened to find her father standing
over her.

" Yes, yes, my dear," he said rather awkwardly. " It is
I. I stopped to look at you and seemed to forget myself."
He hurried away then, and up the stairs to his room and
went to bed, but it was near morning when he fell asleep.

It so happened when Jean Baptiste had gone upstairs to
call on Mildred and her mother, he had knocked at the door
below. A man lived there whom he had known in the years
gone by and who had educated himself to be a lawyer. His
name was Towles, Joseph Towles. Always before when he
was in the city, he had called on Towles and his family,
and when their door rose before him, on the impulse he
had forgotten all else but to greet them. He pushed the
bell, and no sooner had he done so than he recalled his
mission, and that he was avoiding his acquaintances. He

quickly passed upstairs but not before Mrs. Towles had opened the door and caught a glimpse of him passing.

She was aware of his difficulty, and had pretended to sympathize with him. But Mrs. Towles was a gossipy, penurious woman, and did not get along with her neighbors overhead. So when she saw Jean Baptiste passing up the stairs, and hurrying from her without speaking, she at once became angry, and with it apprehensive. She went back to where she had been working over some sewing. She was thoughtful, and then regarded the clock.

" I wonder what he is doing here? " she mused to herself. And then she suddenly brightened with an inspiration. " *His wife,* of course," she cried, and fell to thinking further.

She happened to be a close friend of a certain lady who lived next door to the McCarthys on Vernon Avenue, and it was to her that she decided to pay a visit on the morrow. And, of course she would discuss the fact that she had gotten a glimpse of Jean Baptiste, and would try to find out what she could.

It was the following afternoon that she found the time to visit her friend in Vernon Avenue. She passed by the house wherein lived the McCarthys, and made up her mind to call there later in company with her friend to hear the news.

" Why, Mrs. Towles! " cried her friend when she saw her face upon opening the door. " How nice it was of you to call, when I was not expecting you! Such a pleasant surprise," whereupon they kissed in womanly fashion. She took a seat by the window, for she wished to look into the street. The other took a chair just facing her, and together they fell to talking. As they sat there, Orlean suddenly came out of the house next door, down the steps, and passed before Mrs. Towles' gaze as she went up the street to Wabash Avenue to·fill the engagement with Mrs. Merley.

" Oh, look," cried Mrs. Towles, pointing to the figure of the other. " There goes Orlean! "

The other strained her neck, and said:

" M-m."

" And I saw her husband last night."

" You did! " exclaimed the other in great surprise. She had a grown daughter who was very much accomplished, but unmarried. So she took a delight in such cases as Jean Baptiste's. . . .

" I did," replied the other, making herself comfortable and getting ready to relate his strange actions.

" Well, well, now! " echoed the other, all attention.

" Yes," said Mrs. Towles, and then related all that had passed which was not anything but catching a glimpse of Baptiste as he had disappeared up the steps.

" I don't think they know next door, that he is in town," suggested the other.

" Don't they? "

" Why, not likely. You know the last time he was here they wouldn't admit him! " They eyed each other jubilantly, and then went on.

" Then we ought to go right over and inform them at once! " said Mrs. Towles.

" Just what we should do," agreed the other.

And so it happened that the Reverend learned that Jean Baptiste was in the city; but for once he was not excited. Somehow, he hoped that Jean would meet Orlean, and he knew then that she had gone out for that purpose. He knew that she was supposed to go to a matinee, and he realized

from previous statements, that Mrs. Merley was the " go between."

So he took no part in the gossip that followed, nor did he for once sigh in self pity.

Perhaps after all he had decided not to interfere.

CHAPTER XV

"LOVE YOU — GOD, I HATE YOU!"

THE PLAY they witnessed that afternoon was an emotional play, and in a degree it sufficed to arouse the emotion in all three. The meeting between Orlean and her husband had been without excitement. As if she had been expecting him, she welcomed him, and they had proceeded directly to a play at the Studebaker Theater downtown.

When they were again in the street, they went to another theater where they purchased tickets to witness Robert Mantell in Richelieu. And, later, taking a surface car on State Street, proceeded to a restaurant near Thirty-first Street where they had supper, after which they retired to the home of Mrs. Merley.

Of course that one left them to themselves in due time, and in a few minutes they were engaged in congenial conversation. After a time Jean caught her hand, and despite the slight protest she made, he succeeded in drawing her up on his knee.

"I ought not to sit here," she said.

"Why not, Orlean?" he said kindly, placing his arm about her waist fondly.

"Because."

"Because what, dear?"

She looked at him quickly. He met her eyes appealingly. She looked away, and then down at her toes.

"How you have fleshened," he commented.

"Do you think so?" she returned, inclined to be sociable.

"It is quite noticeable. And you are better looking when you are so."

"Oh, you flatter me," she chimed.

"I would like to flatter my wife."

She did not reply to this. She appeared to be comfortable, and he went on.

"Don't you know that I have longed to see you, and that it has not been just right that I could not?"

And still she made no answer.

"I never want to live so again. I want you always, Orlean."

"When did you leave home?" she asked now.

"A couple of days ago."

"And how long have you been here?"

"I came yesterday afternoon."

"And when to Mrs. Merley's?"

"This morning."

She was thoughtful then. Indeed they were getting along better than he had hoped. There remained but one thing more. If he could persuade her to stay the night at Mrs. Merley's and not insist on going home. If he could keep her out of her father's sight until morning, he would have no more worry. That, indeed, was his one point of uneasiness. Keeping her out of her father's sight. He recalled how he had refrained from buying a revolver when he left home. It would not have been safe after all that had passed between himself and her father for him to have anything of the kind about, and he was glad now that he had been sensible.

He drew his wife's head down, turned her face to his, and kissed her lips. He caught the sigh that passed her lips. He saw her eyebrows begin to contract. What was passing in her mind? Duty? Then, to whom?

He kissed her again, and caressed her fondly. This meant much to him. He told her so then, too.

"It has been very hard on me, wife, for you to have stayed away a whole year. Awfully hard. It was never my plans or intention for such to be." He was full up now. He wanted to talk a long time with her. If they could just retire and talk far into the night as they had done in the eleven months that had been theirs.

His confidence was growing. All that was expedient now, he felt sure, was to keep the Reverend out of it until morning. By that time no further effort on his part would be necessary.

"Do you love me, Orlean?" he said now, drawing her face close to his again.

She made no reply audibly, but she seemed to be struggling with something within herself. In truth she did not want to say that she did, and she *would not* tell him she did not. She let her arm unconsciously encircle his neck. Her hand found his head and stroked his hair, while she was mentally meditative.

In the meantime, his head rested against her breast, and he could hear the beating of her heart.

"Oh, my wife," he cried, intended for himself but she heard it. It aroused her, her emotion began to assert itself. How long would it take for her to be his mate again at this rate?

"How is everything back home?" she asked, as if seeking a change. He hesitated. She looked down into his face to see why he did not answer directly. He caught her eyes, and she could see that he was not wishing to tell her something.

"What is the matter, Jean?" she asked now, slightly excited and anxious.

"Oh, nothing," he replied. He wanted to tell her the truth, all the truth, but it was not yet time he feared. Until she had given up to him, he decided to withhold anything serious.

"There is *something,* Jean, of that I am sure," she insisted, shifting where she could see his face more clearly.

"If there *is* anything, wife, I would discuss it later. Now,— I can think of but one thing, and that is you," whereupon he caressed her again fondly. She sighed then and her emotion was becoming more perceptible.

"You are going back home with me tomorrow, dear?" he dared to say presently.

For answer she shifted uneasily, and then her eyes espied the clock on the wall. It was five-thirty.

"I think I should call up home," she said thoughtfully. He caught his breath, and trembled perceptibly. She regarded him inquiringly.

And here again we must remark about Jean Baptiste. In the year of misery, of agony and suffering in general he had endured, he had settled upon one theory. And that was that if he and his wife were to ever live together again and be happy, the family were to be kept out of it. Perhaps if this could have been forgotten by him in this moment, we would not have had this story to tell; but when she mentioned her folks, all that he had wished to avoid — all that he felt he *must* avoid, came before him. As he saw it now, if she called her father, they would *never* live together again. He was nervous when he anticipated the fact. He started, and took on unconsciously a fearsome expression.

"Please don't, Orlean," he said, beseechingly.

"Don't what?" she asked, apprehensive of something she did not like.

"Call your father," he said. He wanted to tell her that if she called her father, it would mean the end of everything for them, but he withheld this.

"Now, I wish him to know where I am," she said, protestingly, and arose from his knee. She stood away from where he sat hesitatingly. In that moment, she was not aware that she stood between duty and subservience. As she saw it, she forgot from her training that there *was* a duty, she only remembered that she was obedient. Obedient to the father who had reared her so to be.

It was the psychological moment in their union. Near her the husband that she had taken, regarded her uneasily. He had come to her to do the duty that was his to do. They were estranged because of one thing, and one thing only, and that was her father, the man her husband would never yield to. And as she hesitated betwen obedience to one and duty toward the other, her life, her love and future was in the balance.

Which?

"Orlean," she heard now, from the lips of her husband. "Listen, *before you go to the 'phone.*" He became suddenly calm as he said this. "I married you two years gone now, for better or for worse, and ' until death do us part.' That was the vow that I took and also you. I've done my best by you under the circumstances. I gave you a home and bed that you left. I gave you my love, and am willing to give you my life if that be necessary. But, Orlean, I didn't contract to observe the ideas and be subservient to the opinion of others. To force me to regard this is to do me a grave injustice. You cannot imagine, appreciate, maybe, how humiliating it is to be placed in such a position. I can-

not explain it with you standing impatiently before me as
you are. I have come here to try and have you discuss
this matter with me from a practical point of view. Surely,
having taken me as your God-given mate, you owe me that.
You force me to honor and respect certain persons —"

"Don't you," she cried. "Don't you insinuate my
father!" She advanced toward him threateningly in her
excitement, and all sense of duty was gone. Only obedience
to the one who had made it so remained. That she should
rally to the support of his adversary, displaced his composure. He had hoped to have her reason it out with him,
and he had prayed that he be given a little time, and then
all would be well. He was aware that she was unequal to a
woman's task. Not one woman in a thousand he knew
would place a father before a husband; but his wife was
different. She had been trained to be devoutly subservient
to her father. For that reason he was willing to be
patient — he had been patient. But at the same time he had
suffered much, and her love and obedience to his worst
enemy — even if it was her father, unfitted him for that
with which he was now confronted. He was fast losing his
composure, likewise his patience. Nothing in the world
should stand between him and his wife. He became excited now, but calmed long enough to say:

"Go ahead, or come to me. There are two things a
woman cannot be at the same time," and he waved his hand
toward her resolutely. "A wife to the man she has
married, and a daughter to her father." With this statement he sank back into the chair from which he. had partly
risen. He had said the last statement with such forceful
logic, that it made her stop, pause uneasily, and then suddenly she straightened and turning, went to the telephone.

But when she called over the wire to her father, all the

composure that Jean Baptiste ever had left him. All the suffering and agony that he had experienced from the hand of the other asserted itself. He arose from the chair and came toward her. His eyes were bloodshot, his attitude was threatening. She called to her father, and the words she said were:

"Yes, papa. . . . Is this you. . . . Yes. . . . I am at Mrs. Merley's. . . . And — ah — papa," she hesitated and her voice broke from fear. "Ah — papa — a — Jean is here, papa. . . . Yes, Jean. He is here." She was trembling now, and the man standing behind her saw it. He saw her passing out of his life forever, and desperation overtook him. In that moment something within him seemed to snap.

He reached over her shoulder and grasped the receiver and pushed her roughly aside. The next instant she was protesting wildly, while Mrs. Merley was br ught to the front by his loud voice screaming over the 'phone.

"*Hell, hello, you!*" he cried savagely. "*Hello, I say! . . . How am I! My God, how could I be after what you have done to me, my life. . . . Why didn't I come to the house? . . . Why should I come to your house, when the last time I was there I was kicked out, virtually kicked out, do you hear?*"

"You get away from here!" he heard in his ear, and turned to see his wife gone wild with excitement. Her eyes were distraught, her attitude was menacing, as she struggled at his arm to try and wrest the receiver from his hand. He heard the other saying something in his ear. He did not understand it, he was too excited. Everything was in a whirl around him. He became conscious that he had dropped the receiver after a time. He felt himself in contact with some one, and saw the face of his wife. In her excitement she was striking him; she was trying to do him injury.

He became alive to what was going on, then. The receiver hung suspended; he was in a grapple with his excited wife.

"You — you!" she creamed. "You abuse my father, my poor father! You have abused him ever since I knew you. You will not respect him, and then come to ask me to live with you. You abuser! you devil! Do I love you? God, *I hate you!*"

He made no effort to protect himself. He allowed her to strike him at will and with a strength, born of excitement, she struck him in his face, in his eyes, she scratched him, she abused him so furiously until gradually he began to sink. He reached out and caught her around the waist as he lost his footing and fell to his knees. As he lingered in this position his face was upturned. She struck him then with all the force in her body. He groaned, as he gradually loosened his hold upon her, and slowly sank to the floor. And all the while she fought him, she punctuated her blows with words, some abusing him, others in defense of her father.

At last he lay upon the floor, while around her, Mrs. Merley and the other girl begged and beseeched. But she was as if gone insane. As he lay with eyes closed and a slight groan escaping from his lips at her feet, she suddenly raised her foot and kicked him viciously full in the face. This seemed, then, to make her more vicious, and thereupon she started to jump upon him with her feet, but Mrs. Merley suddenly caught her about the waist and drew her away.

How long he lay there he did not know, but he opened his eyes when from the outside he heard hurried footsteps. He continued to lay as he was, and then somebody pulled the bell vigorously. Mrs. Merley went to it, opened it, and let some one in. He looked up through half closed eyes to see the Reverend standing over him. In that instant he saw his wife dash past him and fall into the other's arms. He heard her saying words of love, while he was aware that the other pacified her with soft words. They took no notice of the man at their feet.

And then he saw them open the door, while the others stood about in awe. While the door was open he caught a glimpse of the street outside — and of Glavis on the sidewalk below.

The next instant the door closed softly behind them, and she went out of his life as a wife forever.

CHAPTER XVI

A STRANGE DREAM

WHEN the others had gone, Jean Baptiste rolled over again upon the floor, and was conscious that one eye was closed and swollen, filled with blood from a wound inflicted by his wife just below it. He rose to a sitting posture presently, and looked around him. He was in the hall, and when he looked through the open door into the parlor, he saw Mrs. Merley stretched on the settee before him weeping. He staggered to his feet, and went toward her.

She looked up when he approached, and dried her eyes. "You spoiled things, Jean," she accused, and he noted the disappointment in her voice, and also detected a note of impatience.

"Yes, I admit I did, Mrs. Merley, and I'm sorry — for you."

"For me?" she repeated, not understanding his import.

"Yes," he replied wearily. "For *you.*"

"But — but — why — *for me?*"

"Well," he said, with a sigh, "It *had* to be as it was. I wanted her. But it would have been disaster in the end on his account, because I could never have brought myself to honor him, and to have lived with her I should have been forced to — at least pretended to do so, and that would have been worse still.

She was thoughtfully silent then for some time, then she regarded him closely, and said as if to herself:

"Well, I fear you are right. Yes, I *know* you are when I recall how she abused you a while ago. Gracious! I did not know that it was in Orlean."

"Nor did I," he said, his face covered with his hands.

"*He* made her that way through the influence he has exerted over her. Evil influence. I have a feeling that there will come a day when that influence will work the other way," she said musingly, "*he* will be the victim, and the punishment will be severe."

Both were silent for a time, and nothing but the ticking of the clock on the mantel disturbed the quiet. He presently raised his head, and in so doing uncovered his face. It was dark and distorted, swollen a great deal, and one of his eyes was closed. She saw it then for the first time.

"My God, Jean!" she exclaimed, arising and hurrying to him. "Your face is swollen almost beyond recognition. Why, my dear, you are in a dreadful fix!" She stood over him scarcely knowing just what to do. Then she regained her composure. She caught at his arm, as she cried:

"Come with me, quick!" He arose and followed her upstairs and into the bedroom she had prepared for him and Orlean. In a corner there was a little basin, and to this she led him. She then had him hold his face over the basin while she carefully bathed it. This done, she asked him to go to bed while she went downstairs, returning presently with liniments and towels, and bathed his wounds again and bandaged his face carefully.

"Now, Jean," she said kindly, "I will leave you. But you will do this favor which I ask of you?"

He turned his face toward her.

"Don't advise Mr. Merley about what has occurred here tonight," she said.

"I understand," he replied quietly. Thereupon she left him to himself.

At the Vernon Avenue home of the McCarthys, the house was in an orgy of excitement. When the Reverend had been advised regarding his son-in-law's presence in the city, he recalled the séance he had experienced the night before. When the women came, he was preparing to go to the west side for his daily visit with Mrs. Pruitt. But upon this advice, he desisted, and decided to remain home.

When the mongers had taken their gossip from his presence, he fell into deep thought. For the first time since he had precipitated the trouble, he saw the situation clearly. He was aware that his act by this time, had helped nobody, had made no one happy or satisfied— not even himself. Almost he agreed with himself then, that he had miscalculated; Jean Baptiste was willing apparently, to forego his wife's loss and the loss of her homestead, before he would do as the Elder had planned and estimated he would. His conscience was disturbed. He recalled the unpleasant nights he had endured in the last few months. He recalled that while Orlean always pretended to him that she was satisfied, for the first time in his life, he saw that it was due to the training, the subservience to his will, and not to her own convictions.

He arose from his seat and walked the floor in meditation. Habit, however, had become such a force with him, that he could hardly resist the impulse to commit some action; to rush to Mrs. Merley's and make himself conspicuous. He struggled between impulse and conscience, and neither won fully. After an hour, however, he reached this decision: He would not go to or call up Mrs. Merley. He would just leave it to them to solve, and if they should finally reach some agreement between themselves, he would not stand in the way. When he had reached this conclusion, he went into the street, and was surprised at the relief he felt. Not for months had he enjoyed a walk as much as he did that one.

But while Newton Justine McCarthy had struggled with his conscience, and at last found solace in admitting at this late hour to what he should have done two years before, he had failed to reckon with other features that asserted themselves later. He had not estimated that if Jean Baptiste sought his wife secretly, it must have been because he wished to avoid him. He failed to see that this man had suffered bitterly through his evil machinations. He failed, moreover, to appreciate that his training of Orlean to the subservient attitude, would prevent her from returning to her husband or reaching any agreement with him until she had first ascertained that such would be agreeable to her father. Had he so reckoned the scene just related might not have occurred.

It was while they were sitting at supper that the telephone rang. When the conversation ensued, the Reverend sought not only to promulgate good will by leaving it to Jean Baptiste, but he thought also to encourage him by inviting him to the house, and in this he meant well. But behind him stood Ethel. She caught the gist of excitement and instantly began to scream.

" Get Orlean, go get my sister! Don't let that man have her, owee!" at the top of her voice, she yelled, and Glavis and her mother had to hold her. Some friends were having dinner with them, and they now stood toward the rear uncertain whether to leave or remain, and heard all that passed. The Reverend was laboring frantically to get an answer over the 'phone, and it was at this moment that Orlean had gone frantic and was abusing her husband.

In the excitement, Ethel kept up her tirade at the top of her voice, and in the end, the Reverend, followed by Glavis, had gone to Mrs. Merley's.

They had now returned, and Ethel was pacified. The visitors had departed to spread the gossip, and all but Ethel was downcast. Orlean, in unspoken remorse, had retired; while the Reverend, fully conscious at last of what his interposition had brought, was regretful, but not openly. And the others, not knowing that he had that day repented, sat at their distance and tried to form no conclusion.

"It is over — all over," cried Orlean now in the bed. "And as I have done all my life, I have failed at the most crucial moment. Oh, merciful God, what can you do with a weak woman like I! It has been I all along who has made misery for myself, for *him,* and for all those near me! I! I! *I!* That I could have cultivated the strength of my conviction; that I could have been the woman he wanted me to be. Out there he *tried* to make me one; he sought in every way he knew how. But a weakling I would remain! And because I have sought to please others and abuse him in doing so, I have brought everybody to the ditch of misery and despair." She cried for a long time, but her mind was afire. All that her weakness and subservience had caused, continued, and at last the event of the night.

"And what did I do to him?" she said now, rising in the bed. "I recall that he came to the telephone. He stood listening to what I was saying, and I recall that when I turned slightly and saw his face, it was terrible! Then I saw him suddenly snatch the receiver from my hand, and I heard him talking to papa. He was terribly excited, and I shall never forget the expression on his face. I cannot clearly remember what followed. I recall, however, that I struggled with him; that I struck him everywhere I could; that I scratched his face. . . . And, oh, my God, I recall what passed then!" She suddenly sank back upon the pil-

low and gave up to bitter anguish, when she recalled what
had followed. But the excitement was too great for her
to lay inert. She rose again upon her elbow, and looked
before her into the darkness of the room as she slowly repeated half aloud what had followed.

"Yes, I *recall*. *He made no resistance. He did not defend himself, but allowed me to strike him at will. And
under the fusillade of blows, I recall that he sank slowly to
his knees — sank there with his arms about me, and I striking him with all the strength in my body. Upon his knees
then, he lingered, while I rained blow after blow upon his
upturned face. And now I can recall that his eyes closed,
and from his lips I caught a sigh, and then he rolled to the
floor. And, here, oh, Lord, I added what will follow me
throughout my life and never again give me peace.*

"*While he lay there upon the floor, with his eyes closed
before me, I kicked him viciously full in the face! But
even then he did not resist, but only groaned wearily. Merciful Jesus! Nor did I stop there! I jumped on his face
with my feet, and then I recall that some one caught me and
saved me from further madness!*" She was exhausted
then, and lay without words for a long time. Almost in a
state of coma, she bordered, and while so, she fell into a
strange sleep. The night wore on, and the clock downstairs was striking the hour of two when she suddenly awakened. She sat straight up in bed, and jerked her hands to
her head, and screamed long and terribly. The household
was awakened, and came hurrying to where she lay. But
in the meantime she continued to scream loudly, at the top
of her voice. And all the while, perspiration flowed from
her body. It was nigh onto four o'clock before they succeeded in quieting her, and when they had done so she lay
back again upon the pillow with a groan, and the family

went back to their beds to wonder what had come over her. All felt strangely as if something evil had crept into their lives, and their excitement was great. All but Ethel, who, in her evil way, was delighted, and laughed gleefully when she had returned to bed.

"Laugh on, Ethel, you evil woman!" said Glavis at her side. "Evil has this night come into our lives. It *wasn't* right in the beginning; it *isn't* right now, nor was last night. Oh, I have never wanted to see this go along as it has. Because your father has trained Orlean to obey and subserve to his will, he has done something to her, and she has become a demon instead of a weakling. Last night I saw Jean Baptiste lying prone upon the floor, and knew that she had beaten him down to it, and he had not resisted. She told me as we came home what she had done, but was not aware that she was telling me. Nothing good can come of evil, and it is evil that we have practiced toward that man. He is through now, and never again will he make effort to get her to live with him. But just so sure as she has abused him, just so sure will *she* do injury to those who have brought this about." And with this he turned on his side and feigned sleep.

Alone Orlean lay trying vainly to forget something — something that stood like a spectre before her eyes. But she could not forget it, nor did she *ever* forget it. It had come, and it was inevitable. She had seen *it* in her sleep. *It* had all been so clear, and when she had awakened and screamed so long, she knew, then that it must in time be so. She would never forget it; but realizing its gravity, she decided thereupon never to tell it — the dream — to anybody.

The sun shone and the birds sang, and the day was beautiful without when she at last fell asleep again.

EPOCH THE FOURTH

EPOCH THE FOURTH

CHAPTER I

THE DROUGHT

JEAN BAPTISTE jumped from the bed and went quickly to where his trousers hung on a chair, and went through the pockets hurriedly. He laid them down when through, and got his breath slowly when he had done so, and the perspiration stood out on his forehead as he concluded that he had been robbed.

After a time he raised his hand to his forehead, and appeared puzzled. He was positive he had seen some one enter the room, go to the chair, and take the money from his pockets. It was rather singular, however, he now thought; for if such had happened, and he had seen it, then why had he not stopped the robber? He was deeply puzzled. He had seen the act committed, he felt sure but had made no effort whatever to stop the thief. He scratched his head in vexation, sat down, and as he did so, saw that his coat hung also upon the chair. Absently his hands wandered through the pockets, and found his purse and the money in an outside pocket.

He was awake then, and went to the basin, removed the bandages, and bathed his face. The swelling had gone down considerably, but the injured eye was dark. He realized then, that nobody had entered the room, for the door was locked with the key inside; but he couldn't recall having his money in his coat pocket. He was awake at last to the fact that it had been a dream.

When he had bathed and dressed, he slipped quietly down the stairs, and into the street, and found his way to the Thirty-fifth Street " L." station. He had no plans. He considered that his relations with his wife were at an end, and from his mind he dismissed this in so far as it was possible — and as far as future plans were concerned. But since he had made no plans, whatever in the event of failure, and since failure had come, he was undecided where he was going or what he would do at once.

He decided not to return home directly; he wanted to go somewhere, but did not care to stay in Chicago. He took the train that was going down-town, and when he reached the Twelfth Street station, suddenly decided to go to Southern Illinois, and visit the girl Jessie, with whom he had been corresponding.

While walking toward the Illinois Central Station, he purchased a paper, and was cheered to see that his candidate had carried the state in the preferential primary by an overwhelming majority. The train he was to take left at nine-forty, and he was able to forget his grief in the hour and a half he waited, by reading all the details of the election.

The journey three hundred miles south was uneventful, but when he arrived at Carbondale, the train that would have taken him to where he was going had left, and he was compelled to spend the night there. The next morning he caught an early train and reached the town in which she lived, his first visit there since he met the one he had married.

He found Jessie, and her kind sympathy, served to revive in a measure his usual composure, and when he left a few days later, he was much stronger emotionally than he had been for a year, and on his return West, determined to try to regain his fortunes that had been gradually slipping from him in the past two years.

When he had digested the state of his affairs at home he had a new problem to face. Decidedly he was almost " in bad." For a time his interest had been paid by his bankers; but they had left him to the mercy of the insurance companies who held the first mortgages. And these had been protesting and had lately threatened foreclosure. Even so, and if the crops be good, he was confident he could make it. But before he could even sow that year's crop, he would have to see a certain banker who lived in Nebraska. This man was represented by a son who conducted the bank he controlled at Gregory, and the son had issued an ultimatum, and if Baptiste would keep his stock that was mortgaged to the bank as security, he realized that it was best to see the boy's father, since the son had made plain his stand.

The banker was out of town when he arrived, and to save time, Baptiste judged that it would be best to go to Sioux City, where he could meet the banker on his way home, and on the way from Sioux City to the little town where the banker made his home, he could consult with him, and get an extension. In this he was successful, and returned home with an assurance that he would be given until fall to make good — but in truth, until fall to get ready.

To work he went with a sort of fleeting hope. The spring had been good. But he was apprehensive that the summer would be dry as the last, and it was with misgivings that he lived through the days and weeks that followed. Seed wheat and oats had been furnished to the settlers in Tripp County that spring by the county commissioners, and he had sowed a portion of his land with it.

Conditions in the new country had gone from bad to worse, and if the season should experience another drought, the worst was come. Already there were a few foreclosures in process, and excitement ran high. The country was financially embarrassed. To secure money now was almost impossible. Any number of farms were for sale, but buyers there were none.

A local shower fell over part of the country in the last days of May, wetting the ground perhaps an inch deep, and then hot winds began with the first day of June. For thirty days following, not a drop of rain fell on the earth. The heat became so intense that breathing was made difficult, and when the fourth of July arrived, not a kernel of corn that had been planted that spring, had sprouted. The small grain crops had been burned to a crisp, and disaster hung over the land. Everywhere there was a panic. From the West, people who had gone there three and four years before were returning panic stricken; the stock they were driving — when they drove — were hollow and gaunt and thin. Going hither the years before they had presented the type of aggressive pioneers. But now they were returning a tired, gaunt, defeated army. All hopes, all courage, all manhood gone, they presented a discouraging aspect.

From Canada on the north, to Texas on the south, the hot winds had laid the land seemingly bare. Everywhere cattle were being sold for a trifle, as there was no grass upon which they could feed.

To the north and the south, the east and the west in the country of our story, ruin was in the wake. Foreclosures became the order, and suits were minute affairs. From early morn to early morn again, the hot winds continued, and the air was surcharged with the smell of burning plants.

And with the hero of our story, he saw his hopes sink with the disaster that was around him; he saw his holdings gradually slipping from him, and after some time became resigned to the inevitable.

So it came to pass that another change came into his life, hence another epoch in the unusual life was his.

CHAPTER II

EARLY in July when the drought had burned the crops to a crisp, and plant life was beyond redemption, the Banks, Trust and Insurance Companies holding notes secured by mortgages against the land and stock of Jean Baptiste began proceedings for a foreclosure. He read with the cold perspiration upon his forehead the notices that appeared in the papers. Attachments were filed against all he personally possessed in Gregory County, as well as in Tripp County. The fact that he had not had his sister's homestead transferred to him, and that she had just made proof that summer, was a relief to him now, and with a sigh he laid down the newspapers containing the notices.

It was no surprise since he had been threatened with such for many months, he regarded it therefore as unavoidable. But when the grim reality of the situation dawned upon him, it weakened him. Never had he dreamed that it would come to this. He took mental inventory of his possessions and what he could lay claim to, and he happened to think about his wife's homestead. On this he had made his home since her departure, and no trouble had been given him. While the local land office had rendered a decision in her favor; the contestee had taken an appeal to the general land office and the commissioner and upon being represented by an attorney, the local land office's decision had been reversed. It had been up to him then to go further, which he had done, by appealing the case to the highest office in the land department, the Secretary of the Interior, and here it rested. To do this, he had agreed to pay the attorney $300 to win, and one hundred dollars in the event he should not, the latter amount he had paid, and so the case stood. He had formulated no plans regarding it beyond this as to how he would continue to hold it, since now it was a settled fact in his mind that he and the woman he had married were parted forever.

But poverty accompanied by crop failures for three years was a general and accepted thing now. And the fact that he was being foreclosed, occasioned no comment, and at least he could continue on without intensely feeling, the attendant disgrace.

It was at this juncture in life that a new thought came to Jean Baptiste. In all his life he had been a thinker, a practical thinker — a prolific thinker. Moreover, a great reader into the bargain. So the thought that struck him now, was writing. Perhaps he could write. If so then what would he write? So in the days that followed, gradually a plot formed in his mind, and when he had decided, he chose that he could write his own story — his life of hell, the work of an evil power!

Of writing he knew little and the art of composition appeared very difficult. But of thought, this he had a plenty. Well, after all that was the most essential. If one has thoughts to express, it is possible to learn very soon some method of construction. So after some weeks of speculation, he bought himself a tablet, some pencils and took up the art of writing.

He found no difficulty in saying something. The first day he wrote ten thousand words. The next day he reversed the tablet and wrote ten thousand more. In the next two days he re-wrote the twenty thousand, and on the fifth day he tore it into shreds and threw it to the winds.

He had raised a little wheat and when the foreclosures had been completed and the wheat had been threshed he sowed a large portion of the seed back into the ground on three hundred acres of ground upon which the crop that year had failed. According to the law of the state, when a foreclosure is completed, the party of the first part may redeem the land within one year from the date of the foreclosure. Or, better still, he may pay the interest, and taxes at the end of one year from the date of the foreclosure, and have still another year in which to redeem the land. So it is to be seen that if Jean Baptiste could pay his interest and taxes one year from this time, he would have two years in all to redeem his lost fortunes. Hence, in seeding a large acreage of wheat, he hoped for the best. The years, however, had been too adverse to now expect any returns when a crop was sown and it had been merely good fortune that he happened to secure the means with which to sow another, for credit there was for few any more.

When this was done, there was nothing to do but listen to the wind that blew dry still, although the protracted drought had been broken by light autumn rains. So took he up his pencil and fell to the task of writing again. Through the beautiful, windy autumn days, he labored at his difficult task, the task of telling a story. The greatest difficulty he encountered was that he thought faster than he could write. Therefore he often broke off right in the middle of a sentence to relate an incident that would occur to him to tell of something else. But at last he had written something that could be termed a story. He took what appeared to him to be quite sufficient for a book to a friend who had voiced an interest in his undertaking. In fact, although he had said nothing about it, the news had spread that he was writing a story of the country and everybody became curious.

Of course they were not aware of his limited knowledge of the art of composition. To them, a patriotic, boosting people — despite the ravages of drought which had swept the country, this was a new kind of boost,— a subtle method of advertising the country. So everybody began looking for the appearance of his story in all the leading magazines. The fact helped the newsdealers considerably. But to return to Jean Baptiste and the story he was writing.

The friend was baffled when he saw so many tablets and such writing. He pretended to be too busy, at the time to consider it, and sent him to another. But it was a long time before he found any one who was willing to attempt to rearrange his scribbled thoughts. But a lawyer who needed the wherewithal finally condescended to risk the task, and into it he plunged. He staggered along with much difficulty and managed to complete half of it by Christmas. The remainder was corrected by a woman who proved even more efficient than the lawyer, notwithstanding the fact that she was not as well trained. Besides, Jean Baptiste was of quick wit, and he soon saw where he was most largely in error, so he was very helpful in reconstructing the plot, and early in the next year, he had some sort of story to send the rounds of the publishers.

And here was the next great problem. He had, while writing, and before, read of the difficulties in getting a manuscript accepted for publication. But, like most writers in putting forth their first literary efforts, he was of the opinion that what he had written was so different from the usual line of literature offered the publishers, that it must therefore receive preference over all.

So with its completion, he wrapped it carefully, and sent it to a Chicago publisher, while he sighed with relief.

It seemed a long time before he heard from it, but in a few days he received a letter, stating that his manuscript had been received, and would be carefully examined, and also thanking him for sending it to them.

Well, that sounded very encouraging, he thought, so he took hope anew that it would be accepted.

In the meantime he was questioned daily as to when and where it would appear. He was mentioned in the local newspapers, and much speculation was the issue. Many inquired if he had featured them in the story, and were cheered if he said that he had, while others showed their disappointment when advised that they had not been mentioned. But with one and all, there was shown him deep appreciation of his literary effort.

So anxious did he become to receive their " decision " that as the days passed and he waited patiently, he finally went to town to board until he could receive a reply. And as time passed, he became more and more nervous. At last his anxiety reached a point where he was positive that if he received an adverse decision, it would surely kill him. Therefore he would entertain no possibility of a rejection. It *must* be accepted, and that was final. Added to this, he took note of all the publicity he had been accorded with regard to the same. How would he be able to face these friends if they failed to accept the book? Tell them that it had been rejected as unavailable? This fact worried him considerably, and made him persist in his own mind that the company would accept it.

Some of his less practical creditors extended his obligation anticipating that his work would net him the necessary funds for settlement — the question of acceptance they did not know enough about to consider. So it went, the time passed, and he could scarcely wait until the stage reached the little town where he now received his mail. He was never later than the second at the postoffice window. He had read in Jack London's *Martin Eden* that an acceptance meant a long thin envelope. Well, that was the kind he watched for — but of course, he estimated, it was possible for it to come in another form of envelope, so he wouldn't take that too seriously. Still, if such an envelope should be handed him, he would breathe easier until it was opened.

And then one day the letter came. The Postmaster, who knew everybody's business, regarded the publishers' name in the upper left hand corner, and said:

"There she is! Now read it aloud!"

Baptiste muttered something about that not being the one, and got out of the office. His heart was pounding like a trip hammer; for, while he had concluded that a long thin envelope would not necessarily mean an acceptance, his was a short one, and he was greatly excited.

He went blindly down the street, turned at the corner and sought a quiet place, a livery barn. Herein he found an empty stall that was dark enough not to be seen, and still afforded sufficient light to read in. He nervously held the letter for some minutes afraid to open and read the contents, and tried to stop the violent beating of his heart. At last, with forced courage, he broke the seal, drew the letter forth and read:

"Mr. Jean Baptiste,
"Dear Sir:
"As per our statement of some time ago, regarding the manuscript you were so kind as to send us, beg to advise that the same has been carefully examined, and we regret to state has been found unavailable for our needs. We are

therefore returning the same to you today by express.

" Regretting that we cannot write you more favorably, but thanking you for bringing this to our attention, believe us to be,

" Cordially and sincerely yours,

" A. C. McGraw & Co."

He gazed before him at nothing for some minutes. He was trying to believe he had read awrong. So he read it again. No, it read just the same as it had before. It was done; his last opportunity for redemption seemed to be gone. He turned and staggered from the barn and went blindly up the street. At the corner he met the deputy sheriff, who approached him jovially, and then gave him another shock when he said:

" I've got a writ here, Baptiste, and will be glad to have you tell me where this stuff of yours is so I can go and get it."

He raised his hand to his forehead then, and began thinking. He *had* to do something, for although all his land had been foreclosed on, he had two years to redeem the same. But this writ — well, the man was there to take the stock, then!

CHAPTER III

MEN of the type of Jean Baptiste don't waver and despair regardless as to how discouraged they may at times, under adverse circumstances, become. When he was confronted with the law with the papers to take from him the stock with which to seed his crop, his mental faculties became busy, and in the course of two hours he had been granted an extension on the note and the deputy sheriff had returned to Winner as he had come, empty handed.

But *what was he to do!* He had no money and no credit. He had the land in Tripp County that was broken into winter wheat, while that in the next county east was rented. He could, of course, rent some more land and put it to crop; but he was for the present through with any more large crops until the seasons became more normal. So he was at a loss how to engage himself for the months that were coming. He still lived on his wife's homestead, and had no plans and nowhere else to live. In these days he found reading a great diversion. He simply devoured books, studying every detail of construction, and learning a great deal as to style and effect.

Then he tried writing short stories, but like the book manuscript, they always came back. He concluded after a time that it was a waste of postage to send them around; that in truth they were not read — and again, that there was no fortune in writers' royalties always, anyhow.

He was possessed with a business turn of mind, and one

day he met a man who told him that it was possible for him to have his book printed and be his own publisher. That sounded very good — anything sounded good in these dark days in the life of Jean Baptiste. This was a splendid idea. But it was some time before he was able to find the proper persons with whom to take this up. But, he finally secured the address of a company who would manufacture a book to exceed 300 pages for fifty cents per book. Although this was the most encouraging thing he had encountered in his literary effort, the price seemed very high in view of what he had been told. He had planned that it could be made for much less. However he decided to consider it.

Now Jean Baptiste had less means at hand than he had ever had in his life. Not a dollar did he possess — not even did he have a suit of clothes any more, and wore every day his corduroys. He owed the promoters of the old townsite of Dallas more than he was likely to pay very soon, but they still were his friends. But to get to Dallas, fifty miles away, was still another problem. He went to a bank in the little town where he had other friends from whom he had never asked credit. They loaned him what he asked for, $5.00. With this he went to Dallas. The senior member of the firm was in town — that is, senior in age but not in position. Jean Baptiste possessed great personality, and to be near one was to effect that one with it.

" I believe you could do alright with that book, Baptiste," this one said when Baptiste had told him regarding the company who would put it out for him.

" Yes, I am confident I can, too, Graydon," replied Baptiste. " But I am clean, dead broke. I can't go down there."

The other was silent for a moment as he stood wrapped in thought. Presently he said:

" How much do you have to have to go down there? "

" Oh, thirty-five or forty dollars."

" I'll let you have fifty."

" I'm ready at any minute," so saying, he went to a store across the street where he had friends, and there was dressed from head to foot, charging the clothes to his account. Two days later he walked into the office of the printing firm with which he had been in correspondence. They were rather surprised when they saw that he was an Ethiopian, but he soon put them at ease.

After several days' of negotiating they finally reached an agreement whereby they would manufacture one thousand copies at seventy-five cents per copy. He was to pay one third of the amount before the book went to press, the balance he was to pay within a reasonable time. An outrageous price, he knew — at least felt. But he was to have all subsequent editions for one half the amount of the original edition, which was some consolation to look forward to.

Another fence: who would furnish that two hundred and fifty dollars and secure him for the remainder? Besides, what would he do with the books when he had them? Publishing meant distribution. But what did he know of such? He thought these things over carefully and finally decided that he would sell them himself. He communicated this fact to the firm. It was rather unusual for an author, perhaps, to sell his own works. Jean Baptiste had never sold anything by solicitation since he had grown up, but when he was young he had been a great peddler of garden vegetables. He would sell his book, and he seemed to convince them that he could.

They prepared some prospectuses for him, and back home he returned. He told, in answer to the volumes of inquiries that everything was all right, and that the book would appear soon. He said nothing, however, to the friends he had in view to put up the money and that necessary security. He believed in proving a thing, and all else would necessarily follow. He would go out and secure orders there at home among his friends and acquaintances. But the day he planned to start was very cold — the mercury stood twenty-seven below zero.

Starting in Dallas he received orders for one hundred forty-two copies the first day. Very good for a starter. He went to Winner the next day. Despite the fact that the drought had done no good to the people of that community and town, they all were acquainted with and admired Jean Baptiste. Besides, they would not see Dallas beat them. And one hundred fifty-three copies were ordered by them.

Jean Baptiste could prove anything in a fair fight if given a chance. He secured orders for fifteen hundred copies of his book in two weeks. The promoters went his security and put up the cash into the bargain, and he went back to the publishing house victorious.

The printers had evidenced their confidence in him, for they had been so impressed with his personality that they had begun work upon the copy when he returned. In thirty days it was ready, and in sixty days from the time he was penniless, he had deposited twenty-five hundred dollars to the credit of the book in the banks.

As he was winding up his business preparatory to interviewing his printers, establishing an office and going into the book business for a livelihood, he was the recipient of a telegram from Washington advising that the Honorable Secretary of the Interior had reversed the commissioner's decision, which had been adverse to his wife, with regard to the claim. He had won, but as to how he would ever prove up he didn't know, nor did he let it worry him. He was too flushed with success in his new field. He could still hold the claim, but it would be his wife who must offer proof on the same, and his wife he had not heard from for over a year.

He did not find his new field of endeavor so profitable when he began to work among strangers. Indeed, while he did business the money didn't seem to come in as it should. He conceived an idea of securing agents among the colored people, and in that way effect a good sale. To begin with, this was difficult, for the reason the black man's environment has not been conducive to the art of selling anything except those things that require little or no wide knowledge. They deal largely in hair goods to make their curls grow or hang straighter,— or in complexion creams to clarify and whiten the skin. Yet he succeeded in getting many to take the agency and these received orders and sent for the books. He had learned that it was a custom with subscription book companies to allow agents to have the books and give them thirty days in which to remit the money. This proved agreeable to his agents. However, the greater number of them took not only thirty days — but life, and did not send in the money when they died.

He was confronted then with the task of learning how he could get the books to them and be assured of his money. To learn this, he went on the road himself appointing agents and selling to bookstores. And it was upon this journey that he met one who had played a little part in his life some years before, at a time when conditions had been entirely different with him.

In Kansas City she occurred to him. He recalled that it was only twelve miles from the city where her father owned and lived upon one of the greatest farms in the country.

He thought of the last letter he had received from her, the letter that had come too late. And then he thought of what had passed since. Girls in her circumstances would not be likely to waste their sympathies with grasswidowers; but he wished that he might see her and look just once into the eyes that might have been his. But his courage failed him. He still had spirit and pride, so he gave it up for the time.

Late in the afternoon of that day, he was engaged with some acquaintances in the bar-room of a club. They became quite jolly as cocktails and red liquor flowed and tingled their veins. He thought again of Irene Grey, and the memory was exhilarating. And the cocktails gave him the necessary courage. He was bold at last and to the telephone he went and called her over long distance.

" Is this the Greys home? " he called.

" Yes," came back the answer, and he was thrilled at the mellowness of the voice at the other end.

" Is Miss Irene at home? " he called now.

" Yes," it said. " This is she."

He was sobered. All the effect of the cocktails went out of him on the instant. He choked blindly, groped for words, and finally said:

" Why — er — ah — this is a friend of yours. An old friend. Mayhap you have forgotten me."

" I don't know," she called back. " Who are you? "

He still didn't have the courage to tell her, but sought to make himself known by explaining. He then mentioned the state from whence he came, but no further did he get. It so happened that she had heard all about his troubles following his marriage, and, womanlike, feeling that she had been in a way displaced by the other, she had always been anxious to meet and know him.

" Oh," she cried, and the echo of her voice rang in his

ears over the wire for some moments. " Is this you? " she cried now, her voice evidencing the excitement she was laboring under.

" Yes," he admitted somewhat awkwardly, not knowing whether the fact had thrilled and joyed her, or, whether he was in for a rebuke for calling her up. But he was speedily reassured.

" Then why don't you come on out here? " she cried.

" I — I didn't know whether I would be welcome," he replied, happy in a new way.

" Oh, pshaw! Why *wouldn't* you be welcome? But now," her tone changed. " Where are you? "

" In Kansas Ctiy."

" Let me see," she said, and he knew she was thinking. " It is now four thirty, and a train leaves there that passes through here in forty minutes. It doesn't stop here; but you catch it and go to the station above here, do you understand? "

" Yes, yes," he replied eagerly.

" Well, now, listen! The station I refer to is only four miles above this, and when you get off there, catch another train that comes in a few minutes back this way, see? "

" Yes, yes."

" Well, that train stops at this station, and there I will meet you."

" Oh, fine," he cried. " I'll be there."

" Now you will be sure to catch it," she cautioned.

" Most assuredly! "

" I will depend on it."

" Count me there! "

" I want to talk to you, I'm going to talk all night."

" Good-by."

CHAPTER IV

WHAT MIGHT HAVE BEEN

JEAN BAPTISTE was so elated over being invited to call early to see Miss Irene Grey, that he went back to the bar where his acquaintances lingered, ordered drinks for all, and imbibed so freely that when he reached the depot, he found the train had left him. His disappointment was keen, and he was provoked with himself. However, since it was so, he went to a booth, called her up, and advised her of the fact.

"Now wasn't that careless of you," she complained. "I am sure you are *very* careless."

"I wouldn't have missed it for anything in the *world*," he told her. "Indeed, I was so delighted over the prospects of seeing you, after these many years, and I indulged so freely that I lost the sense of time."

"How is that — did you say that you *drank*?"

"Well, yes, I do," he admitted frankly; "but not in a dangerous sense. I do not recall having been drunk but once in my life, and trust that I will never have occasion to recall a second occurrence."

"Oh," she echoed. "I am relieved. I don't trust a drinker, and the fact that you were left made me suspect you."

"At least I can reassure you on that score. I am proud to say that I have the strength of my convictions."

"I am pleased to hear that. A man has a poor chance to succeed in the world otherwise."

" I agree with you."

" Well, now, let me see when you can get out here," she said meditatively. After a time he heard her voice again. He had never seen her, not even a photograph of her. He could only estimate her appearance from recalling her brother, and from what he had been told. But however she may appear, her voice, to say the least, was the most beautiful he thought that he had ever heard. He listened to every word she said, and thought the tone like sweet music.

" You will have to stay in K. C. all night now," she said regretfully. "And I must repeat that I am so disappointed. It had been my dream that I would talk with you all the night through," whereupon she laughed and this was even more beautiful than her voice when speaking. " But, now," she began again, admonishingly, " you will arise at eight — no, seven, do you understand, and catch a train that leaves the city at eight. I will be at the station to meet you again."

" I cross my heart that I will catch it."

" And if you do not — so help you God ! "

" I hope to die if I miss it."

" Well, if you do, don't die — but catch the train, that's all. Now good-by, and you are forgiven this once."

" Good-by."

Whatever happened it is irrelevant to relate, but Jean Baptiste missed the morning train, and so disgusted was he with himself that he boarded a train for Topeka where he went and appointed some agents, intending to get the train back that afternoon. But his " Jonah " still clung to him, and when he had it estimated that the train went at five-thirty, it had gone at four fifty-two and he was left again.

" I'll catch the morning train if I must sit here all the night through," he swore, so put out with himself that he could say no more.

He ascertained the exact minute the morning train left, and this train found him on time. It was Sunday in early June, and the day was beautiful. The air was rich, and the growing crops gave forth a sweet aroma. He reached the little town near where she lived, and even from the depot the splendid home in which they lived could be seen reposing vaingloriously upon a hillside. In the community her father was the wealthiest man, having made his fortune in the growing of potatoes and fruit.

She was not at the depot to meet him, and he had not expected her. It was perhaps two miles to the big residence on the hill, and to this he set out to walk. When he arrived, the house seemed to be deserted, and, as it was Sunday, he surmised that the family were at services. He went up to the front door and knocked loudly. He was conscious at once of whisperings from the inside. Presently the door was opened slowly an inch, and he saw an eye peeping out at him.

" Who are you? " a voice whispered.

He told the eye.

" Oh, yes," cried the voice and it happened to be a boy, and the cause of the whispering and quietness from the inside was due to certain pranks going on inside. " And you're that fellow from up in the Northwest," said the youngster, opening the door wide and stepping away to look at him curiously.

" Yes, I guess that's whom you refer to."

" We are certainly glad to see you around here," said the other. " Irene's been down to the train to meet you three times and she's sure fighting mad by this time."

" Oh, say, I really don't blame her a bit — to be put to so much trouble and be disappointed in the end. But, on the square, I had not anticipated being so highly honored."

" Aw, we've been anxious to know you for years. We boys had sort of planned when you was writing to Irene two or three years ago to come up there and get in on some of that land."

" That would have been a capital move."

" Yes, but you quit writing and got married, so we heard, and had bad luck in the end," whereupon he laughed. Baptiste looked embarrassed.

" Where is the family and how many are there of you? "

" Aw, say! We are so many around here that you'll have to get paper and pencil and mark us down to keep track of how many. My father is in Colorado on business, while Irene, mama and another sister are at the next town up the line attending a funeral."

" And the boys —"

" Just gettin' ready to go swimmin'. Wanta go long? "

" Say, there hasn't enough water fallen where I've lived for the last three years at the right time to fill a pond deep enough to go swimming in, so I'll just take you up," he cried, full of the idea.

It was in the early afternoon when they got back, to find that the folks had returned from the funeral. Following the boys, Baptiste entered by the kitchen door to encounter the mother and three daughters preparing the meal. Hereupon he was caused much embarrassment and discomfiture, for of the three girls, he knew not which one was Irene. Quickly seeing his confusion, they laughed long and heartily among themselves. Finally, his predicament became so awkward that an expression of distress crept into his face. At this point the most attractive one of the three girls walked forward, extended her hand, and he saw by the expression she now wore, that she was sorry for him, as she said:

"I'm Irene, and you are Mr. Jean Baptiste." She paused then, and looked away to hide the color that had rushed to her face, while he clutched the outstretched hand just a bit dubiously. She looked up then again, and seeing that he was still confused and perhaps in doubt, she reassured him:

"The joke is over now, thanks. I'm the one you called up and once wrote to. I'm Irene," and with this she led him to the front and showed him her picture, whereupon he was at last satisfied.

"And you came at last," she said later, when the two were seated in the parlor.

"At last," he laughed and observed her keenly. She noted it, and conjectured that it was from a curiosity that was some years old. It was true, and he was seeing her and perhaps thinking of what might have been.

She was beautiful, he could see. A mixed type of the present day Negro, she was slightly tall, and somewhat slender, with a figure straight and graceful. Her hair was of the silken wavy sort not uncommon among the Negro of this type. Such hair seems to have had its beginning with the cross between the Negro and the Indian — a result that has always been striking when it comes to the hair. Her face, like her figure was straight and slender; while her eyes were black, quick and small. Her nose was high bridged, and straight to a point while the mouth below was small and tempting. But what he observed most of all now, and admired forthwith was the chin. A wonderful chin, long and straight. A strong, firm chin, and as he regarded it he could seem to read the owner. Whatever she was or may be, he was confident then that she was possessed of a strong will and in that moment Orlean recurred to him. Orlean was regarded as a fairly attractive woman; but her chin, unlike that of the one before him, was inclined to retreat. And, of course, he knew only too well, that her will had been the weakest.

"You are very successful in missing trains," she ventured.

He laughed, and she joined him. He looked up then and caught her regarding him keenly out of her half closed eyes, and as she did so, she reminded him of an Indian princess such as he had seen in pictures and read about. There was more about her than he had at first observed, and which was made plain in the look she gave him. For in it there was passion — love to her meant much!

"Oh, I was so disappointed," she said.

"It was not you?"

"But how could you have missed the train so often?"

"I cannot account for it. I am not in the habit of doing so. Indeed, I think it was because I was overly anxious."

She laughed then, to herself, elfin like.

"I have been curious to see you for a long time."

He was silent, and his eyes did not return the look she had given him.

"Ever since I received *that* letter. . . ."

And still he did not reply. The subject was too suggestive, not to say embarrassing; but she was bold. He couldn't know now whether she was serious or merely joking; but notwithstanding it sounded pleasant to his ears. He could hear her voice for a long time, he was sure, and not grow weary. . . . We should pause at this point to make known — perhaps explain, that the persons of our story are the unconventional. And with the unconventional what was in their minds was most likely to be discussed. The woman, therefore, was the most curious.   She was a woman, and in truth she would have married the man beside her had he have come hither when he had gone to Chicago.

" What did you do with your little wife? "

He raised his eyes then, not to look at her, but because of something he did not himself understand.   Perhaps it just happened so?   She regarded him again; looked him full in the eyes, and his eyes spoke more than words. Strangely she understood all, almost in a flash, and was sorry.   She regretted that she had spoken so directly.   She admired him now.   When he had looked up, and like that, she had seemed to see and understand at last the man he was.

" Pardon me, please," she said, and rising quickly, took a chair nearer his.   She reached and touched him on the arm.   " I didn't — I — well, I didn't intend to be bold." She paused in confusion, and then went on:

" I hope you will pardon me.   I am sure I didn't intend to embarrass you."

" It is all right," he said.   " And since you have asked me, may I explain? "

It was she who was now embarrassed.   She looked away in great confusion.   She was bolder than the conventional girl as a rule; but the subject was delicate.   Yet she wanted to hear the story that she knew he would never tell.   If he did, he was not the type of man she had estimated.

" Of course you would think me a cad, a — well, I have my opinion of a man that would tell *his* side of such a story to a *woman*."

She looked at him then without any embarrassment in her eyes.   She was able to read the man and all that was him clearly.   She smiled a smile after this that was one of satisfaction, and at that moment her sisters called that the meal was ready.

CHAPTER V

"NOW I wish you would tell me all about yourself, that is, all you *care* to tell," said Irene Grey to the man who sat beside her on the veranda of their beautiful home, some time after luncheon had been served. "I have always been peculiarly interested in you and your life alone off there in the Northwest," whereupon she made herself comfortable and prepared to listen.

"Oh," he said hesitatingly, thinking of the series of dry years and their attendant disaster, and hoping that he could find some way of avoiding a conversation in which that was involved. "I really don't consider there is much to relate. My life has been rather — well, in a measure uneventful."

"Oh, but it hasn't, I know," she protested. "All alone you were for so many years, and you have been, so I have been told, an untiring worker." She was anxious, he could see, but withal sincere, and in the course of the afternoon, she told him of how her father had came to Kansas a poor man, bought the land now a part of what they owned on payments, found that raising potatoes was profitable — especially when they were ready for the early market, and later after his marriage to her mother, and with her mother's assistance, had succeeded. From where they sat, their property stretched before them in the valley of the Kaw, and comprised several hundred acres of the richest soil in the state. Indeed, his success was widely known, and Jean

Baptiste had been rather curious to know the family intimately.

After some time he walked with her through three hundred acres of potatoes that lay in the valley before the house, and he had for the first time in his life, the opportunity to study potato raising on a large scale.

" From your conversation it seems that you raise potatoes on the same ground every year.   I am curious to know how this is done, for even on the blackest soil in the country I live, this is regarded as quite impossible with any success."

" Well, it is generally so; but we have found that to plow the land after the potatoes have been dug, and then seed the same in turnips is practical.   When the turnips, with their wealth of green leaves are at their best, then, we plow them under and the freezing does the rest."

" A wonderful mulch!"

" It is very simple when one looks into it."   They were walking through the fields, and without her knowing it, he studied her.   The kind of girl and the kind of family his race needed, he could see.   In his observation of the clan to which he had been born, practicability was the greatest need.   Indeed he was sometimes surprised that his race could be so impracticable.   Further west in this State, his uncles, who, like all Negroes previous to the emancipation, had been born slaves, had gone West in the latter seventies and early eighties, and settled on land.   With time this land had mounted to great values and the holders had been made well-to-do thereby.   A case of evolution, on all sides.   Over all the Central West, this had been so.   At the price land now brought it would have been impossible for any to own land.   There happened, then as had recently, a series of dry years — seemingly about every twenty years.   To pull through such a siege, the old settlers usually did much bet-

ter than the new. To begin with, they were financially better able; but on the other hand, they did not, as a rule, take
the chances new settlers were inclined to take. Because
two or three years were seasonable, and crops were good,
they did not become overly enthusiastic and plunge deeply
into debt as he had done. He could see his error now, and
the chances new settlers were inclined to take. Because
moreover, he had been so much alone — his wedded life had
been so brief, and even during it, he was confused so much
with disadvantages, that he had never attempted to subsi-
dize his farming with stock raising. Perhaps this had been
his most serious mistake; to have had a hundred head of
cattle during such a period as had just passed, would have
been to have gone through it without disaster.

He felt rather guilty as he strolled beside this girl whose
father had succeeded. But one thing he would not do, and
that was make excuses. He had ever been opposed to ex-
cusing away his failures. If he had failed, he had failed,
no excuses should be resorted to. But as they strolled
through the fields of potatoes he could not help observe the
contrast between the woman he had married, and the one
now beside him that he might have had for wife. Here
was one, and he did not know her so well as to conclude
what kind of girl in all things she was, but it was a self
evident fact that she was practical. Whereas, he had only
to recall that not only had his wife been impractical, but
that her father before her had been so. He recalled that
awful night before he had taken her away, at Colome, when
that worthy when he chanced to use the word practical, had
exclaimed: "I'm so tired of hearing that word I do not
know what to do!" and it was seconded by his cohort in
evil, Ethel.

His race was filled with such as N. J. McCarthy, he

knew; but not only were they hypocrites, and in a measure enemies to success but enemies to society as well. How many were there in his race who purported to be sacrificing their very soul for the cause of Ethiopia but when so little as medical aid was required in their families, called in a white physician to administer the same. This had been the case of his august father-in-law all his evil life.

"Would you like to walk down by the river?" she said now, and looked up into his face. She had been silent while he was so deeply engrossed in thought, and upon hearing her voice he started abruptly.

"What — why — what's the matter?" she inquired anxiously.

"Nothing," he said quickly, coloring guiltily. "I was just thinking."

"Of what?" she asked artfully.

"Of you," he said evasively.

"No, you weren't," she said easily. "On the contrary, I venture to suggest that you were thinking of yourself, your life and what it has been."

"You are psychological."

"But I have guessed correctly, haven't I?"

"I'm compelled to agree that you have."

They had reached the river now, and took a seat where they could look out over its swiftly moving waters.

"Frankly I wish you would tell me of your life," she said seriously. "My brother who, as you know is now dead, told me so much of you. Indeed, he was so very much impressed with you and your ways. He used to tell me of what an extraordinary character you were, and I was so anxious to meet you."

He was silent, but she was an unconventionally bold person. She was curious, and the more he was silent on such topics, the more anxious she became to know the secret that he held.

"I appreciate your silence," she said, and gave him the spell of her wonderful eyes. Stretched there under a walnut she was the picture of enchantment. Almost he wanted to forget the years and what had passed with them since she wrote him that letter that he had received too late.

"I want to ask you one question — have wanted to ask it for years," she pursued. "I want to ask it because, somehow, I am not able to regard you as a flirt." She paused then, and regarded him with her quick eyes, expectantly. But he made no answer, so she went on. "From what *I* have heard, I think I may be free to discuss this," and she paused again, with her eyes asking that she may.

He nodded.

"Well, of course," she resumed, as if glad that she might tell what was in her mind. "It is not — should not be the woman to ask it, either; but won't you tell me why you didn't answer the last letter I wrote you — tell me why you *didn't* come on the visit you suggested?"

He caught his breath sharply, whereat, she looked up and into his eyes. His lips had parted, but merely to exclaim, but upon quick thought he had hesitated.

"Yes?"

"I heard you."

"Well?"

"I hardly know how to answer you."

"Please."

"Don't insist on a reply."

"I don't want to, but —"

"I'd rather not tell."

" Well, I don't know as I ought to have asked you. It was perhaps unladylike in me so to do; but honestly I *would* like to know the truth."

He permitted his eyes to rest on the other bank, and as a pastime he picked up small pebbles and cast them into the river, and watched the ripples they made subside. He thought long and deeply. He had almost forgotten the circumstances that led up to the unfortunate climax. She, by his side, he estimated, was merely curious. Should he confess? Would it be worth while? Of course it would not; but at this moment he felt her hand on his arm.

" We'll go now."

They arose then, and went between the rows of potatoes back to the house. When they arrived there was some excitement, and she was greeted anxiously.

" Papa has returned," said one of the boys, coming to meet them.

" Oh, he has," whereupon she caught his hand and led him hurriedly into the presence of the man who was widely known as Junius N. Grey, the Negro Potato King.

CHAPTER VI

THE STORY

JUNIUS GREY inquired at length concerning the land whence he had come, of the prospects, of the climate, and at last relieved Baptiste by inquiring as to whether the drought had swept over that section as well as other westerly parts.

"I have had the same result with twenty-two hundred acres I own in the western part of the State. But such will come — have come every once in a while since I have been here," he assured him. "If you have been caught with considerable debt to annoy you, and succeed in pulling through, it will be a lesson to you as it has been to others."

"It *has* been a lesson, I admit," said Baptiste a little awkwardly. Irene, who seemed to be her father's favorite, sat near, and regarded him kindly while he related how the drought had swept over the land, and the disaster that followed. He did not tell them *all*; that he had been foreclosed, but that, he felt, was not necessary.

Withal, he had met those in his race whom he had longed to meet. Of business they could discourse with intelligence, and that was not common. Grey's holdings were much, and Baptiste was cheered to see that he was possessed with the sagacity and understanding to manage the same with profit to himself. Besides, the family about him, while not as conventional as he had found among the more intelligent classes of his race, had grown into the business ways and assisted him.

"Would you like to attend services at the church this

evening," said Irene after a time, and when they were again alone.

" Why, I suppose I might as well."

" Then I'll get ready." She disappeared then, to return shortly, dressed in a striking black dress covered with fine lace; while on her head she wore a wide, drooping hat that set off her appearance with much artistic effect.

" What is your denomination," she asked when they went down the walkway to the road. The church was not far distant, and, in fact was at the corner of his property, and was largely kept up by her father he had been told.

" The *big* church, I guess," he said amusedly.

" Indeed!" she exclaimed, feigning surprise.

" And yours?"

" Oh, Baptist, of course," she replied easily.

When she held his arm like she now did, it made him feel peculiar. Never, three years before, would he have thought that he would be company again for another woman — at least, under such circumstances.

" What do you think of protestantism?"

" Well," he replied thoughtfully, " it has not been until lately that I have considered it seriously."

" So?"

" And sometimes I am not inclined to think it has been for the best."

" How so?"

" Well, it appears to me that organization is lacking in so many of the protestant churches."

" But is that the fault of protestantism?"

" I hardly know how to reply to you. It seems, however, that inasmuch as catholicism requires more effort, more concentration of will force on the part of their members to come up and live up to their standard of religion; and

that since it is obviously easier to be some kind of a protestant, then protestantism has afforded a less organized appreciation of the Christ."

" You make it very plain. And especially is it so in the
church to which I belong. But I am sure, however, if the
standard of requirement was raised within the Negro Bap-
tists, it would be better for all."

" You mean —"

" If it was compulsory for the ministers to possess a
college education and attendance for at least three years at
a theological seminary, the standard would be raised in the
churches conducted by Negroes."

" I agree with you; and do you know, that since I have
been in the book business only these few short months, it
has been my experience that ours is a race of notoriously
poor readers."

" Isn't it so! Oh, it is dreadful when we come to consider how much needy knowledge we lose thereby."

" It is staggering."

" Why is it so?"

" Well, to begin with. There is little encouragement to
become a reader among Negroes themselves. Take, for instance, the preacher. By all circumstances a minister — at
least should be a reader. Is it not so?"

" Certainly."

" Well, are they as a whole?"

" Lord, no!"

" Then, how can you expect their followers to be?"

" We cannot."

" Another disadvantage, is separate schools."

" I don't quite understand?"

" Well, mix the Negro children daily with the whites, and
they are sure to become enamored of their ways."

" I gather your trend."

" The most helpful thing on earth. Negro children thereby are able, in a measure, to eradicate the little evils that come from poor homes; homes wherein the parents, ignorant often, are compelled to be away at work."

" Evil environment, bad influence! "

" That is it. There is no encouragement to read, therefore no opportunity to develop thought, and the habit of observation."

" How plain you make everything."

" And now we have come unto the church, and must end our conversation."

" I'm sorry."

He was, too, but they filed into the little church.

In and around where they now sat, there was quite a settlement of Negroes, mostly small farmers. Perhaps it was due to the inspiration of the successful Grey. She had, earlier in the evening, pointed out here and there where a Negro family owned five acres; where somewhere else they lived on and farmed ten acres and fifteen acres and so on. After slavery there had been a tendency on the part of the Negro to continue in the industrious ways he had been left in by his former master. The cultivation was strong; but strangely there had come a desire to go into town to see, and to loaf. Perhaps it was because he had not been given such a privilege during the days of bondage. But here in this little valley of the Kaw, he was cheered to see his race on a practical and sensible basis. Only in the pursuit of agriculture can the black man not complain that he is discriminated against on account of his color.

When the service was over, they walked leisurely homeward, and their conversation became more intimate. The feeling of a woman by his side thrilled Jean Baptiste. In his life on the prairies, this had never been afforded, so to him it was something new, and something gloriously sweet. Or was it her presence? At least he was moved. He decided that he would go his way soon, because it was dangerous for him to linger in her radiating presence without regretting what fate had willed.

" Isn't it warm tonight? " she said, when they reached the porch.

" Dreadfully so down here in your valley."

" Perhaps you will not care to retire, and would rather sit out where the air is best," she suggested.

" I would be glad to."

" Very well, then," and she found a seat where they were hidden by vines and the shade of the big house. " I'll return presently, when I have put my hat away."

When she returned, her curiosity to know why he had not visited her was, he could see again, her chief anxiety. She tried to have him divulge why in subtle ways. Late into the night they lingered on the veranda, and he found himself on the verge of confessing all to her.

He succeeded in keeping it from her that night, but she was resourceful. Moreover, her curiosity had reached a point bordering on desperation. Accordingly, she had the boys to hitch a team to a buggy and took him driving over the great estate. For hours during the cool of the morning, she drove him through orchards, and over wheat-fields where the wheat now reposed in shocks. She chatted freely, discoursed on almost every topic, and during it all he saw what a wonderfully courageous woman she was.

He loved the study of human nature, and wit. Here, he could see, was a rare woman, but withal there was about her something that disturbed him. What was it? He kept trying to understand. He never quite succeeded until that night.

A heavy rain had fallen in the afternoon, and he lingered in her company at her invitation and encouragement. That night the sky was overcast, the air was sultry, and the night was very dark. She took him to their favorite seat within the vines, and where nothing but the darkness was their company. And there she resumed her artful efforts to have him tell her all.

Never in his life had Jean Baptiste the opportunity to be perfectly free. He had once loved dearly, and he had sought to forget the one he had so loved because of the *Custom of the Country* and its law. Out of his life she had apparently gone, and we know the fate of the other. There is nothing in the world so sweet as to love a woman. But, on the other hand, mayhap all that is considered love is not so; it may be merely passion, and it was passion he discovered that was guiding Irene Grey. He saw when this occurred to him, that in such a respect she was unusual. Well, his life had been an unhappy life; love free and openly he had never tasted but once, but a law higher than the law of the land had willed against that love, and he had subserved to custom. So he decided to tell her all, and leave on the morrow.

" Please, Jean," she begged, calling him by his first name. " Won't you tell it to *me*? "

He regarded her in the darkness beside him. She was very close, and he could feel the warmth of her body against his. He reached him out then, and boldly placed his arm about her. She yielded to the embrace without objection. He could feel the soft down of her hair against his face, and it served to intoxicate him; aroused the passion and desire in his hungry soul.

" *Yes*, Irene," he said then. " I will tell *you* the story, and tomorrow I will go away."

" No," she said, and drew closer to him. On the impulse he embraced her, and in the darkness found her lips, and the kiss was like a soul touch. He sighed when he turned away, but she caught his face and drew his lips where she could hear him closely.

" Tell me," she repeated. " For so long I have wanted to hear."

" Well, it was like this. You know — rather, perhaps you recall the circumstances under which we met."

" I remember *everything*, Jean."

" I was in love with no one, I can say, but I *had* loved outside of our race."

" Our race ? "

" Yes."

" You mean," she said, straightening curiously, " that you loved an Indian up there? That, I recall is the home of the Sioux ? "

" No, I have *never* loved an Indian."

" Then *what* ? "

" A white girl."

" *Oh, Jean,*" she said, and drew slightly away. He drew her back to him, and she yielded and settled closely in the curve of his arm, and he told her the story.

" Honestly, that was too bad. You sacrificed much. And to think that you *loved* a white girl ! "

" It was so."

" So it came that you sacrificed the real love to be loyal to the race we belong to? "

" I guess you may call it that."

" It was manly, though. I admire your strength."

" It was then I wrote you."

" Yes.   And —"

" Others."

" I understand.   You loved none of us, perhaps, and it was because you had not had the opportunity, maybe? "

" Perhaps it was so."

" And now I will hear how it happened."

" I must first confess something that pains me."

" Oh, that confession!   But maybe I am entitled to hear it? "

" Well, yes, I think so.   There were three."

" Oh . . ."

" And you were the first choice."

" *Me?* "

" But I waited for your letter.   There was a *time* limit."

" And I was away."

" Therefore never received it in time."

" And you? "

" At Omaha I hesitated, and then decided that you did not favor it."

" O-oh! "

" So I went to Chicago, to meet the second choice."

" Such an unusual proceeding, but interesting, oh, *so* much so.   Please go on."

" *She* lived in New York."

" In New York? "

" Was a maid on the Twentieth Century Limited."

" O-oh! "

" But sickness overtook her.   She didn't get into Chicago when she was due."

" Such fate."

" I wonder at it."

" And then you got the *last* choice."

" That is it."

Not knowing what else to do, she was so carried away with the story, she stared before her into the darkness.

"And when *did* you receive my letter? I understand about the claim business."

"When I returned with her to Gregory."

She was silent. He was too. Both were in deep thought and what was in the mind of both was:

What might have been.

CHAPTER VII

HER BIRTHRIGHT "FOR A MESS OF POTTAGE"

THE people of Winner and vicinity had no opportunity to rush to the Farmers' State Bank, of which Eugene Crook, mentioned earlier in our story was president, and draw any portion of their money before the bank examiner's notice greeted them one morning.

The bank was closed by order of the public examiner, so that was settled. The causes became apparent the day before, although those directly interested did not understand. It was in the shape of drafts they had bought and sent away, which came back to them indirectly, marked by the bank upon which they were drawn: "No funds."

Not much excitement followed the closing, although in some manner Crook had worked into the confidence of the people since moving the bank to Winner, and was leading the four banks in the town in point of deposits. Of course it hit many needy ones quite hard, but the people of the country had become so accustomed to adversities, that even bank failures included did not excite them.

But there happened a few days after the failure an incident that has some connection with our story. Crook went upon a journey. He was gone several days and when he returned, the unexpected happened. It caused about as much excitement as had the failure of the bank because of its cunningness.

When Jean Baptiste had ended his visit with Irene Grey, he returned to his office at the publishing house to find considerable mail awaiting him. One letter was from his attorney in Washington, and since he had won the claim for Baptiste's wife in the contest, Baptiste naturally took it for granted that it was a request for the balance of his fee. So he laid the letter aside until he had attended to all other business, and later opened and read it.

> "WASHINGTON, D. C., July, 191 —
> "*Mr. Jean Baptiste,*
> "MY DEAR SIR: I am informed through your attorney at Gregory, that your wife has sold her relinquishment on the homestead I was successful in getting the Secretary of the Interior to reverse the land commissioners decision on. I am not informed further; but inasmuch as you are living on the place, my advice is that you stick right there, and hold it. You may write and advance me the details concerning the matter, and I will assist you in a legal way in pressing your right to hold the same.
> "In the meantime, kindly send me a remittance on the fee that is past due at your earliest convenience, and oblige,
> "Very truly,
> "PATRICK H. LOUGHRAN."

He reread the letter to be positive that he had understood it correctly. He was thoughtful as he allowed the substance to become clear. His wife had sold her relinquishment on the claim that he had spent thirty-five hundred dollars cash for. And in so doing she had sacrificed his confidence; *had sold her birthright for a mess of pottage.* And she had not received, he was sure, perhaps one tenth part of the amount he had expended for it. He thought a little longer, and as he did so, a vision of his arch enemy rose before him. His mind went back to a day when N. J. McCarthy in all his lordliness had with much vituperation, denounced and condemned Eugene Crook for having contested his poor daughter's place, and all the white race with him.

"And Newton Justine McCarthy," muttered Baptiste, "this is *more* of your work."

He was very calm over it, was Jean Baptiste; but the *turning point* in his life had come. At last his manhood had returned, *and he was ready to fight*.

He wrote his attorney at once at Gregory, and the reply that came back in due time was:

"GREGORY, S. D., July — 191 —

"*Mr. Jean Baptiste,*

"FRIEND JEAN: Replying to yours regarding the claim, it was Eugene Crook who got it. He went to Chicago and bought it from your wife, through her father. I understand that your wife refused to sell, whereupon, Crook sent for the Reverend who was at Cairo, sending him the railroad fare to Chicago at the same time. I do not, of course, know just what followed, but it is the report here, that the Reverend had his daughter to execute the relinquishment, and Crook returned and filed on the claim.

"I understand, further, that Crook got the idea from reading your book, wherein you told of the preacher and what he had done, although anonymously. It is also reported that Crook paid the Elder $300 for the claim.

"Very truly yours,

"WM. MCCONNELL."

Jean Baptiste laughed when he had completed the letter, picked up one of his books and looking through it, found the place. "Well, old boy, I guess you lost me more than I'll make out of you; but you've given me what I ought to have had three years ago!" He was silent then, but his face took on a cold, hard expression, whereupon he laughed again.

"N. J. McCarthy, we vied twenty-five years ago, and we encountered three years since. On both occasions you had me at a disadvantage. . . . We are *going* to *vie* again, now; *but it will be upon an equal basis*." So saying, he looked before him at nothing; his eyes narrowed to mere slits.

An hour later his grip was packed. He went that afternoon back to Tripp County. His three hundred acres of wheat had failed, so he was unencumbered. He returned to Winner, and the next morning he boarded a train for Chicago.

And of the battle that he fought with his august contemporary, will be the continuance of our story.

CHAPTER VIII

ACTION

JEAN BAPTISTE went directly to an attorney, a Negro attorney with offices in the loop district, upon his arrival in Chicago, and did not lurk around the depots to keep from being seen this time. He was well acquainted with the one upon whom he called and they greeted each other cordially when he walked into the office.

"Well, White," he said. "I think I have a little work for you."

"That's what I'm here to look after," said the other aimiably.

"A suit — want to obtain a judgment?"

"We obtain judgments in this old town every day. The question is —"

"Are they worth anything?" laughed his prospective client.

After indulging in a bit of humor the which he was at times given to, his face cleared, his eye-brows contracted and he related the business upon which he was bent, and questioned the attorney concerning the law covering such cases or instances.

"Yes," said the other, after looking it up in the Illinois Statutes, "it can be done."

"Then we will begin at once," said Baptiste decidedly.

"I'll have the papers drawn up, and have the same ready for service tomorrow afternoon."

"Very well," said the other, handing him a check for

twenty-five dollars as a retainer, and straightway left the office.

He caught the State Street car and went to visit his friends on Federal Street. They were delighted and surprised to see him looking so well, and so carefree.

" Why — what has happened to you," said Mildred's mother, looking him over carefully from head to foot.

" You infer that I have forgotten my troubles? "

" Of course," and she laughed.

" You'll know in a few days," he returned. Soon he bade them good-by and went over to the Keystone where he encountered Speed.

" Well, I have everything ready now," said the attorney when Jean called at his office the following afternoon.

" So the next is to get service on my friend," said Baptiste.

" That's it. Where shall we find him? " inquired the lawyer.

" I don't know. I suppose you might call up his wife on Vernon Avenue and find out. Of course, she need not know what our business is with her old man. . . ."

" Of course not."

In a few minutes he was talking to her over the telephone. " The Elder is in the southern part of the State," Baptiste could hear.

" Yes, madam; but what place. . . . I see. . . . He will be there over Sunday you say? . . . I understand. . . . What do I want with him? Why, I have a little *personal* matter with him. . . . Yes . . . that is all."

The attorney turned and advised him where the Elder was, and would be there until after Sunday, and as that day was Wednesday, Baptiste breathed a sigh of relief.

" That's the town near where I first knew him. I was born within four miles of it."

" Indeed! Something of a coincidence."

" Indeed so."

" I'll get these papers off to the sheriff down there on the evening train. We'll get them tomorrow morning, and should get service on him tomorrow afternoon."

" Then I'll see you about Saturday."

" All right," and Jean was gone.

The little town near where Jean Baptiste was born, and where he had met the man who was now his acknowledged enemy, had not changed much. Perched on the banks of the Ohio, it still lingered in a state of dull lethargy; loafers held to the corners, and arguments were the usual daily routine. When he had left the town, the Odd Fellows' hall, an old frame building, three stories high, had stood conspicuously on a corner, and had been the rendezvous for loafers for years untold. This had been torn down and replaced since by a more commanding brick structure, at the front of which a shed spread over the walk and made welcome shade in the afternoon. And under it on benches the usual crowd gathered reposing comfortably thereunder from day to day. Under it the preachers sometimes paused on their return from the postoffice where they received their mail every afternoon. And it was the afternoon train that brought the papers for N. Justine McCarthy. The sheriff who happened at the postoffice at the same time the Elder did, received them, and upon his return to his office in the court house, laid the mail on his desk and went at once to serve the papers.

He knew that Odd Fellows' hall was where Negroes might be easily found; at least the information as to the whereabouts of any particular one might be obtained.   So to that spot he went directly.

It so happened that a large crowd of Negroes were gathered there this particular afternoon, and that the Reverend had paused there on his way from the postoffice to listen to the heated argument that was a daily diversion.   At that moment the sheriff came up, listened a moment to the usual harangue, and then inquired aloud for Rev. N. J. McCarthy.   When the crowd saw who he was the argument desisted forthwith, the crowd became quiet and respectful, moreover expectant.

" You refer to me? " said the Elder, and wondered what the sheriff could possibly want with him.

" N. J. McCarthy? " the other repeated.

" That's me," replied the Elder.   The crowd looked on with curious interest.

" Some papers," and handed him the same, turned on his heel and went his way.

The Reverend went down the street later reading the papers.   He had never had any experience in legal proceedings, and knew little of such, but he understood the papers and was thoroughly angry.

" Well," greeted the attorney, " got service right off on your friend."

" Good! "

" Yes, got my return, and now we may as well draw up the complaint."

This they did, but in the meantime, while passing downtown, Glavis had espied Baptiste.   Thinking that he was on another mission of trying to persuade his wife to return, and having been loyal to the Reverend in his fight on Baptiste, he went at once to advise her of the fact.

Orlean had secured a position in a ladies' tailoring establishment at five dollars and fifty cents a week, and there he went. She was out so he did not get to tell her that her husband was in town. Since the selling of her homestead the entire family had been apprehensive of him. They appreciated by now that he was not the kind to give up without a fight, therefore they were on the lookout.

In some way the Negro papers got hold of enough of it to give the Elder a great deal of free advertising; but since McCarthys did not get the papers, they knew nothing of it until the next morning which was Sunday. That morning they espied a copy of the paper in their mail box. They never knew how it got there, but thinking it was by mistake, Glavis took it into the house and spread it out.

Pandemonium reigned when they had read the account, and in the same hour they received a special from the Elder announcing that he was leaving for Chicago that night. That would place him in the city the following morning, and they were anxious all that day.

It was the talk of Dark Chicago that day, and for days and weeks following. Moreover, it circulated over all the state where the Elder was well known, and gave the gossips great food for delight.

The Elder arrived the next morning, and after being greeted by the family, with Glavis, went at once to a white attorney. They laid the case before him.

" And so you are sued for ten thousand dollars," said the attorney, " and by your son-in-law? "

" It seems that way," replied the Elder. " And to me it looks like a joke."

" How so? "

" Did you ever know a Negro preacher that was worth such an amount? "

The attorney shared the obvious joke with his prospective client and Glavis, and then took on a rather serious expression.

" And you are not worth ten thousand? "

" Lord, no! "

The other bit the cigar he held between his teeth, got up and brought a statute from among his many volumes, glanced through it, and stopped at a page and read it.

He returned the book to its place and came back and sat down.

" What do you think of it? " inquired the Elder, still seeming to take it as a joke.

" Have you ever considered the outcome in case he should get a judgment against you? He accuses you of having alienated the affections of his wife, your daughter."

" Granting that he secured a judgment? "

" And you could not pay it? "

" Certainly, I could not."

" Then he could remand you to jail for six months by paying your keep."

When the Elder, accompanied by Glavis, returned home, both understood Jean Baptiste a little better than they had ever before. . . .

CHAPTER IX

GOSSIP

"I'VE BEEN over to the McCarthys today," cried Mildred Merrill, greeting her mother, as she returned home the Sunday following the filing of the suit. "And, oh, mama, they are certainly excited over there!"

"Mm! Guess they'll understand that Jean Baptiste better now. Because he had wished to settle their difficulties — if there were any — like a man, they thought he was afraid of the Reverend."

"That was it — positively!"

"What was the conversation?"

"Of course it was Ethel who was making the most of the noise."

"Naturally."

"And she *made some* noise!"

"I'd wager."

"To begin with, they didn't know Jean had sued the Reverend until they read it in the paper."

"Is that so!"

"Yes! You see, it was like this. Orlean sold her farm."

"Gave it away."

"Quite likely."

"It was so. Why I understand that Baptiste had paid over thirty-five hundred dollars into it, and that the place was supposed to be worth about forty dollars an acre, with one hundred sixty acres bringing the sum of sixty-four hundred dollars. That insurance companies would lend two thousand five hundred dollars on the place if she had proved up on the same as other people were doing and had done, and secured a patent."

" Isn't that a shame ! "

" Nigga's ! "

" Negroes proper ! "

" Well, what did they say ? "

" Oh, yes ! Orlean sold her farm some time ago."

" For three hundred dollars."

" Is that all she received ? "

" Every cent."

" Well, what do you think of that ! "

" It was the Reverend's work, of course."

" That dirty old rascal."

" Ignorant into the bargain."

" If I were Baptiste I'd kill him."

" That would do no good."

" No, I guess not."

" Would make him appear a martyr, also."

" Well, ever since Orlean sold her place, you see, they have been uneasy."

" I guess so."

" So they had been sort of looking to hear from him."

" And they have."

Mildred laughed.

" And they'll hear from him some more ! "

Both laughed.

" Now, Orlean heard that Jean was in town before the rest of the family did, and told me so."

" She's waited a long time to tell other people things she hasn't told the folks first. . . ."

" Yes," thoughtfully. " Anyhow, Glavis met Baptiste on

the streets downtown, and, of course, Glavis, not knowing Baptiste's mission, thought he was here after Orlean again."

" Just like him."

" The truth."

" He was by here awhile ago."

" He was?"

" Yes; but I'll tell you about that later. Go on."

" When he met Jean on the street — rather, after, he goes around to where Orlean worked to warn her."

" Sneak!"

" But Orlean was out."

" Yes?"

" So when she returned, and was told that a colored man had called and inquired for her, she —"

" Thought it had been Baptiste."

" Yes."

" I'll try to quit interrupting you."

" Well, Orlean told me that she was provoked. She wished that Jean would not be calling at where she worked to bother her."

" She got fooled — excuse me!"

" But she didn't say anything to the folks about it, and they knew nothing of his presence in town — Glavis didn't tell it seems, either — until Sunday morning."

" Indeed!"

" No, none of them had gone out Saturday night, so they hadn't heard any of the talk that was going the rounds."

" Well, Glavis went outside Sunday morning and found the *Defender* in the mail box."

" So?"

" You see, they do not subscribe for it, but the people next door get it —"

" And knowing they were not subscribers, they take the paper and place it where they could get it."

Mildred laughed.

" So," resumed Mildred, " when they saw the paper, all was excitement."

" Goody ! "

" So Glavis (he is the Reverend's faithful lieutenant, you know), went out to look up Baptiste and have a talk with him."

" Ump ! "

" He didn't find him."

" That was how he happened by here."

" But the funny part about it is, that they don't know what Baptiste is up to. They don't know that if he secures a judgment, he can remand the Elder to jail for six months."

" Now won't there be some excitement when they learn ! "

Mildred laughed again, her mother joined her.

" But getting back to Ethel."

" Tell me about her."

" Oh, she was on the war path. ' You see,' she cried, standing over Orlean. ' You see what you've done by your hard-headedness. I told you all the time not to marry that man ! ' "

" Wouldn't that disgust you ! "

" ' But you *would* go ahead and marry him ! You *would* go ahead and marry him, after all papa and *I* tried to persuade you not to ! And now ! You are going to *kill* your father; going to *kill your poor old father.*' Orlean just hung her head like a silly and took it. ' Yes,' went on Ethel, turning her little slender body around and twisting her jaws as if to grind it out. ' You got him all mixed up with that nigga', and here he comes in here and sues him. Think of it! *Sues him!* And now all the nigga's in Chicago have the laugh on us — we daren't show our faces in the street!

"'And what has he done it for?' 'But, Ethel,' Orlean protested, 'Papa isn't worth anything. He *can't* do anything with papa if he gets a judgment.' 'What do you know about judgments,' Ethel flew up. Well,' said Orlean, 'I recall hearing Jean say that if a man was worth nothing, then a judgment was of little or no good.' 'You heard *Jean* say it!' screamed Ethel, looking at Orlean severely. And then she turned to me. 'Do you know, Mildred,' she rang out, '*This* fool woman loves that man yet. Yes. Y-e-s! *Loves* him yet and would go back to him tomorrow if it wasn't for us!'"

"Doesn't it beat anything you ever saw!"

Mildred laughed again as she paused for breath.

"Well, Ethel went on: 'And don't you think that nigga' is a fool. No, no! *Never!* That's a scheming nigga'. He's the schemingest nigga' in the world! *He* knows what he's about. Believe me! He knows papa isn't worth anything. And, besides, he isn't *after* money, he's after papa. He don't *want* no money. A scheming nigga' like him can make all the money he wants. Oh, yes! He's up to *something* else.'"

"Seems they are willing to admit very readily now that which they were not as long as he tried to deal with them like a man."

"I should think so," returned Mildred. "Well, Ethel was so excited that she walked up and down the floor in a rage. Every little while she would stop before me, and glare into my face: 'But what can he do, what can he do!' 'I have nothing to do with it, Ethel,' I replied. 'Yes, you have, yes, *you* have! You know! I know you and I know Jean Baptiste! He never comes to Chicago without coming to see you all. He's told you what he's *up* to, and I know it! *Oh, that nigga'!*'

"I looked at Orlean, and she sat by looking like the man who has murdered his wife and regrets it. When she met my eyes she sighed, and then said: 'Do you think he can hurt papa, Mildred? I'm worried. You see, I know Jean some. He's shrewd, Jean is very shrewd.' I confess that I was rather uncomfortable, knowing what I did. So hoping to find some way to get out of it, I suggested that they walk out. 'No,' exclaimed Ethel. 'I'm afraid I'll run into that nigga'.'"

"When do they look for the Reverend in?"

"In the morning. They are afraid to go out until he comes."

"I'd like to be around there when they found out what Jean is up to."

Mildred laughed again, and then cried: "And oh, yes, I forgot to tell you that Orlean asked me whether Jean came direct from the farm here."

"What did you tell her?"

"Why, I said I thought he was visiting down in Kansas before coming here."

"Hump."

"She said: 'I guess he was calling on Miss Irene Grey.'"

Her mother giggled.

"I said I thought he remarked something about having visited there, whereupon Orlean said: 'He ought to have married her.'"

"Jealousy."

"Yes, that was it."

"Look! There is Glavis," cried Mildred's mother, pointing to his figure crossing the street.

"Now for some fun," said Mildred, whereupon, both feigned sleepiness, and prepared for some good interesting gossip.

"Oh, Mr. Glavis," exclaimed Mildred, answering the rap on the door and admitting him.

"And how is everybody?" asked Glavis, coming in with his head bared, and smiling in his usual way.

"Fine, Mr. Glavis," replied Mildred's mother, arising to greet him for the second time that day.

"And where is my friend, Baptiste?" said Glavis. "I've just come from the Keystone, and while he stops there, I can never catch him in."

"He has not been here today, Glavis," replied Mildred.

"That's funny. I'd certainly like to see him."

"Why would *you* want to see him?" inquired Mildred's mother.

"Oh, I want to see him, of course, about all this scandal that's in the air."

"Hump! This appears to be the first time that you have wanted to see him since your father-in-law brought Orlean home."

"Well, of course," said Glavis, a little embarrassed. "It has always been a bad affair. A bad affair, and I certainly have wished Orlean would have kept us out of all the mess."

"Why not say you *wished the Reverend* had kept you out of all the mess," ventured Mildred's mother, who was out of patience with their conduct.

"Well, it's rather awkward. Baptiste is a little in fault himself."

"How's that?"

" Oh, he sorter had it in for father before he even married Orlean. He didn't come into the family like *I* did."

Mildred and her mother regarded each other as Glavis went on thoughtfully.

" Yes, Baptiste is a good fellow, and I have always rather liked him. But he has always had it in for father; has never treated him as I have. . . . If he would have, I'm sure we would not be the bone of this scandal."

" It seems that this enmity between your ' father ' and Baptiste, begun way back in the southern part of this state, when Baptiste was a small boy. . . ."

" I've heard something concerning that, but of course he oughtn't hold such things against a man when he has grown up."

" You seem to hold Baptiste in fault for everything, when it's common knowledge, from ·what I can hear, Glavis," argued Mildred's mother, " that the Elder went up there and just broke Orlean and Baptiste up; made her sign his name to a check for a big sum of money — and a whole lot of other things. How dò you account for or explain that? "

" Well, Baptiste could have settled this without all that. If he'd come and seen me before starting this suit," Glavis was evasive, " I would have had him and Orlean meet and reason their differences out together."

" Why have *you* waited so long to take such action, Glavis? You had years almosĭ to have gotten them to-gether — to have been at least fair to Baptiste. As it is, you have treated — all of you — Baptiste like a dog, like a dog. And because he tried to settle an affair like it ought to have been settled, you just ground him — pride and all right into the ditch."

Glavis winced under the fusillade with which the elder lady of the house bombarded him.

" And now after you do him all the injury you can, you cry about him making a scandal! Just because he didn't come around again a whining like the dog you have tried to make him, you profess to be shocked at his conduct. Moreover, you had Orlean to give away the farm he gave her, and from what I can hear, to the man that tried every way known to law to beat her out of it and failed. And at Baptiste's expense! "

Glavis was very uncomfortable. He shifted uneasily, while his handkerchief was kept busy mopping the perspiration from his brow.

" I heard that the Reverend just scored the man about trying to beat poor Orlean out of her place: Preached a great sermon on the evil and intriguing of the white race, and just gave that man, a banker, the devil. Then upon top of that he comes down here to Chicago and sends your ' father ' the money to come here from Cairo to sell him the place that Baptiste was man enough to trust her with for nothing. I can't figure out where any of you have any cry coming."

" Well," said Glavis, rising, " I want to see Baptiste anyhow. If you see him, tell him to come over to the house."

" No, Glavis, I have nothing to do with it, and I oughtn't to be gossiping as I have been; but I have known Baptiste since he was a little boy, and I just can't help protesting — as I have always heretofore protested, about the way you people have treated him."

" Well, I guess Baptiste hates all of us enough to make up."

" Baptiste has nothing against any one in that house over there but your ' father.' But there would be no use in my telling him to call over there. No use at all, for let me tell you," she said, following him to the door; " The day of

Baptiste beholding unto you for his wife is past. I don't think he wants Orlean any more, and don't blame him after what she has allowed to happen to him through her lack of womanhood. Nawsiree, Baptiste didn't come into Chicago this time crying, he came here like *a man,* and it's the *man* in him with which you'll have to fight now."

"Oh, well, I don't know," said Glavis, taking a little courage, "I don't think he is so wise after all. Any man that will sue a man like father for ten thousand dollars, wouldn't seem so wise."

"Well," returned the elder lady, "Perhaps you had *better* wait until you see a lawyer."

CHAPTER X

A DISCOVERY — AND A SURPRISE

JEAN BAPTISTE called by to see the Merrills before leaving the city, and took Mildred and her mother one afternoon to a matinée at the Colonial theatre. It was a musical repertoire, and a delightful entertainment. Before one of the numbers was to appear, the director of the orchestra came upon the stage and announced:

"Ladies and gentlemen: If I may have your kind attention, I wish to announce that the next number is an extraordinary specialty. Miss Inez Maryland, the young prima donna who has made considerable of a reputation by her beautiful singing in the last year, will this afternoon sing in an introduction, a song that is destined by the critics to be one of the most popular of recent production." Whereat, he stepped to one side, and led upon the stage, a charming blonde who was greeted profusely.

"I am glad to have you meet Miss Maryland, who will now sing the discovery of the season, *O, My Homesteader*, by Miss Agnes Stewart."

In the moment Jean Baptiste did not quite recall the name, or rather, he did not connect it with an instance in his life; but as the sweet mezzo soprano voice, combined with the strains of the orchestra, floated out over the audience, the years gone by, to him were recalled. He listened to it with a peculiar and growing enchantment, and the night he had lain upon the ground and would have frozen, but for the now composer, came fresh again into his mind.

" Beautiful."

" Wonderful."

" Grand!" came to his ears from over all the theatre and then followed the storm of applause. Again and again did the singer have to return to satisfy the audience before her, and when the crowds poured into the street at the close of the performance, every one seemed to be humming the tune that had that afternoon began its initial success.

As it would take nine months or a year for the suit to come to trial, Jean resumed his efforts in the book business, and was able by borrowing a little, to meet the interest and taxes on the foreclosed property, and was given the customary year's extension.

He traveled now from town to town, from city to city, and found agents for his book, and was able in a small way to recuperate his finances. He hired an engine to plow all his land that was not prepared, besides renting a little more, and also took a flier in wheat. The war abroad had been going on a year, and he conceived that if it " happened " to rain at the right time he *might* get a crop and redeem his land. At least, he could lose only what he put into it by risking the same, so he took the chance. So with all he could get hold of until the last days of October of that year, he put it into winter wheat on his land, and succeeded in getting over 700 acres seeded.

And everywhere he went, the people were playing and singing *O, My Homesteader*. Never, whether it was fifty times a day, or one, could he seem to tire of hearing it. At the stores he saw hundreds of copies of it, and in every home it was. And always it took him back to his youthful days in the land where he had gone with the great hope.

And then one day he saw a picture of her. It was in a musical review. It spoke at length of her, and of the simple life she had lived. That she was a product of the prairies and a wonderful future was in store for her because of the fact that her work was original.

So the winter passed and springtime came again with all its beauty, and he continued in his book business. He made a trip to Gregory and Winner to see what the prospects were again in the Northwest. The winter for the wheat, he was cheered to learn, had been ideal; but the spring was dry, and that was not to the wheat's advantage. However, he had the best prospects he had had for years, and he returned to the book business with renewed hope.

And now we are compelled by the course of events to return to certain characters who were conspicuous in the early part of our story.

When Jack Stewart left the farm he had rented near the property of Jean Baptiste and went West and took a homestead and had George and Bill and Agnes to do likewise, he was obsessed with a dream that riches had come to him at last. Agnes was delighted with the prospects, also, and so they looked forward to a great future in the new land.

But there was something that troubled Jack Stewart, and for days when alone he would shake his head and cry: "Dang it. Dang it! I oughtn't to have let it go that far, dang it!" But he had kept what was now the cause of his worry to himself so long that he would not bring himself to confess it even to Agnes after what had occurred. But never did he forget Jean Baptiste, and to Agnes he would mention him quite often.

"By the way, my girl," he said one day when they were settled on their claims, staying mostly on his, of course, for the prospects were hopeful. "Do you know that. I never did learn who saved me from that foreclosure. No, sir, I never did! I paid the note and was so glad that it was paid, that I tore it up and forgot the whole matter.

"Now *who* do you reckon it was that interceded for me?"

She paused and looked up from her sewing, and then bent over it again, as she said:

"Jean Baptiste."

"Jean Baptiste!" he exclaimed incredibly.

"It was him."

"Why the stinkin' rascal, he never told me!"

She was silent.

"And it was him that came to my assistance," the other mused reflectively. "Well, now since I come to recall him, it was just like him to do something like that and keep it to himself. Well, well, I do say!" He paused then, and looked down at the toe of his boot. Suddenly he looked up, and concentrated his gaze on Agnes.

"And *you knew* it all the time. He told you."

"He didn't tell me."

"Didn't tell you!"

"I knew it when you returned home that morning."

"Well, well. . . ."

"I was positive the administrator hadn't granted you an extension, nor wouldn't have, so it must have been some one near. So who else could it have been but Jean Baptiste."

"Of course not, now that I recall it; but did you tell him about it?"

Her eyes had business in her lap at the moment, *very* much business. She saw the sewing and she didn't see it. What she was seeing again was *what had happened one day when she had gone to carry his and her brother's luncheon.*

. . . It passed before her, as it had done many times since. *Never,* she knew, would she be able to forget *that day, that day* when the harvest was on, and he had said sweet words to her. . . . It was all past now, forever, but it was as fresh as the day it was done.

She understood why he had gone away, and when he returned and she had seen his face she understood then his sacrifice. She knew that the man's honor, his respect for his race and their struggle had brought him to commit the sacrifice. And strangely, she loved him the more for it. It had been an evidence of his great courage, the great strength with which he was possessed. It was strange that the only man she, a white girl, had ever loved was a Negro, and now when that was history, it seemed to relieve her when she could recall that he had been a *man.*

" Did you hear me, Aggie? " her father called now again. She started.

" Why — yes, father — I heard you," she said, straightening up. " And — of course — I told him about it. . . ."

" Now I'm glad to hear that you did. It seems that you ought to have told me at the time — at least before we left there, so that I could have thanked him." He was silent for a time then and reflective.

" I wonder what sort of woman he married," he mused after a time.

" I don't know."

" I am sometimes a little afraid that he didn't get the right kind of woman.

" He was such a prince of a good fellow, that it would most likely have been his luck to have gotten a woman who would betray him in some way. It is all rather strange, for I don't think he loved any woman but *you,* Aggie."

He darted his eyes quickly in her direction, recalling a

time before when he had intimated something of the kind. This time, however, she did not cry out, but continued at her sewing as though he had not spoken.

As he slowly walked out, what was in his mind was the thing that had worried him before.

She looked after him and sighed. It was her effort then to forget the past, and in so doing, the inspiration with regard to music came again, and developed in her mind. But her efforts had brought so little encouragement from those to whom she had submitted her compositions that she for a long time despaired of making another effort.

So it was not until the great drought swept over the land and drove almost all the settlers from their claims in a search for food, that made her again resort to the effort.

The drought was even worse in the part of the country they now called home than it had been in Tripp County and other parts farther East. Corn that was planted under the sod one spring had actually not sprouted for two years, for the moisture that fell had never wet the earth that deep. So, after two years in which they came nearer to starvation than they had ever before, she secured a position in a hotel in a town farther West, and the money earned thereby, she gave to her father and brothers to live on.

It was then she had returned to compositions in a desperate effort and hope to save them from disaster. For a long time she met with the usual rejections, and it was a year or more before anything she composed received any notice.

But *O, My Homesteader* was an instantaneous success. While she still worked in the kitchen of the little hotel in the western village, the royalties came pouring in upon her so fast until she could hardly believe it. And coincident with the same, she became the recipient of numerous offers from almost everywhere. Most were for compositions; while many were offers to go on the stage, at which she was compelled to laugh. The very thought of her, a dishwasher in a country hotel, going on the stage! But she resigned her position and went back to her father and brothers on the farm. She used her money to pay off their debts and started them to farming, and made herself contented with staying on as she had done before, and keeping house for her father and the boys. She refused to submit any more manuscripts until the success of her first song was growing old, and then she released others which followed with a measure of success.

The offers from the East persisted; and with them, drought in the West continued and they saw that trying to farm so far west was, for the present time, at least, impractical. So they returned to Gregory where she purchased the place they had lived on. Owing to the fact that the drought had been severe there, also, she secured the place at a fair bargain, and they returned to farming the summer following the publication of Baptiste's book.

When she read it, she hardly knew what to think; but it was rather unusual she thought, because he had told a true story in every detail; but had chosen to leave his experiences with her out of it. She heard of him, and the disaster that had overcome him, and was sorry. She felt that if she could only help him in some way, it would give her relief. And so the time passed, and he came again into her life in a strange and mysterious manner.

She was surprised one day to receive a visit in person from the publisher of her works. She was, to say the least, also flattered. He had come direct from Chicago to persuade her to come to the city, and while she was flattered and was really anxious to see the city, she refrained from going, but promised to write more music.

In the months that followed, he wrote to her, and the experience was new. Then his letters grew serious, and later she received the surprise. He came again to see her and proposed. She hardly knew how to accept it, but he was so persistent. To be offered the love of a man of such a type, carried her off her feet, and she made him promise to wait.

He was very patient about it, and at last she concluded that while she did not feel that she really loved him yet, she was a woman, and growing no younger, and, besides, he was a successful publisher and the match seemed logical. So after some months in which she tried to make herself appear like the woman she knew he wished her to be, she accepted, but left the date for their wedding indefinite.

CHAPTER XI

THE REVEREND McCARTHY was commonly regarded as a good politician in church affairs, meaning, that he was successful with the Bishop in being
able to hold the office of Presiding Elder over such a long
period. At every conference other aspirants attempted to
oust him. But he had always held with the Bishop and had
succeeded himself annually until the five-year limit had expired. At the end of this time he had usually succeeded in
manipulating matters in such a manner that he had invariably been successful in securing the same appointment
over another district in the state. Over this he presided another five years, and was then automatically transferred
back to the district over which he had formerly presided.
For twenty years he had been successful in keeping this up,
but in the conference that was to convene after he had been
sued by his son-in-law, it became known and talked about
that he would not be re-appointed to the Presiding Eldership, and would necessarily be sent to a charge for a year or
more.

Accordingly, he began early to seek a charge which he
was in position to know would be lucrative, since there were
few outside the large churches in Chicago that would pay
as well as the Presiding Eldership.

The fact was, however, he regretted going back to a
charge, for his former experience in such work, in gaining

and retaining the confidence of the members of his church had not been ideal, to say the least. And again, it was expedient that he should have his family, especially his wife, living in the town with him where he held the charge. Perhaps that made it awkward for him, as he was not accustomed to having his wife in such close proximity with him daily. His regard for her was such that he could not bear the thought of that close association. For his experience had been that it was impossible for him to be in the house with her a matter of two days without losing his patience and speaking harshly to her. To avoid this unpleasant domestic state of affairs it had been agreed that Orlean should be his housekeeper, and this was settled on before conference — and before he had been sued.

This pending suit, however, brought added complications. Ever since he had brought Orlean home, he had been embarrassed by gossips. Nowhere had he been able to turn unless some busy-body must stop him and inquire with regard to his daughter; what was the matter, etc., and so on. It kept him explaining and re-explaining, a subject that was to say the least, delicate. He had, however, succeeded in explaining and conveying the impression that the man she married had mistreated and neglected her, and that he had been compelled to go and get her in order to save her life. This was not satisfactory to him in view of the fact that he decided once to let her return, but Jean Baptiste not knowing that he had reached such a decision, had felt that his only chance to secure her again was to keep away from her father — well, we know the result of that effort.

But inasmuch as that Jean Baptiste had refused to argue with him over her, he had used this as an excuse to become his old self again, which, after all, was so much easier. So when 'Gene Crook had approached him with an offer, and convinced him that Baptiste was what the Elder knew he was not (because the Elder was easily to be convinced of anything toward the detriment of his adversary) he easily secured the place and the Elder had felt himself ahead. Three hundred dollars was a great deal of money to him, and went a long way in taking up the payments in which they were in arrears on the home they were buying in Chicago. True, it twitched his conscience, but N. J. McCarthy had a practice — long in effect — of crucifying conscience. So when he had closed the deal — and had been reimbursed for his traveling expenses — he went directly back to his work, and had not been in the city since until called in on the suit.

When he left the lawyer's office and returned home, he discussed the matter with Glavis, who in turn discussed the matter with white friends who advised him how to answer to the charge. Returning to the lawyer's office they engaged counsel. It was very annoying — more than ever — to the Elder when he was required to put up twenty-five dollars in cash as a retainer. He had become so accustomed to posing his way through in so many matters — letting some one else put up the money, that when he was forced to part with that amount of money he straightway appreciated the seriousness of the situation. It was no pleasant anticipation in looking forward to the trial, for there he would be compelled to counter the other on equal terms.

He was very disagreeable about the house when he returned home, and his wife adroitly kept out of his sight. He sought the street to walk off his anger and perturbation, only to run into a Mrs. Jones, teacher in the Sunday school of one of the large Negro churches, and with whom he had been long acquainted. It was, in a measure, because his acquaintances were of long standing that gave them, they felt, the right to question him regarding such delicate affairs. So when he met Mrs. Jones, he doffed his hat in his usual lordly manner, and paused when she came to a stop.

" Good evening, Reverend Mac.," she exclaimed, and extended her long, lean hand. He grasped it, and bowing with accustomed dignity, replied:

" Good evening, Sister Jones. I trust that your health is the best."

" My health is good, Reverend Mac. But, say, Reverend Mac., you don't look so well."

" Indeed so, my dear madame, I have not been in the best of health for some months."

" Well, well, that is too bad, indeed I hear that you have not been, Reverend Mac. And say, Brother McCarthy, what is this I read in the paper about your son-in-law coming in here and suing you for breaking up Orlean and he? "

His Majesty's head went up, while he colored unseen, and would have passed on, but Mrs. Jones was standing in such a manner that he was unable to do so without some difficulty.

" The man is crazy," he retorted shortly, and stiffened. But it took more than stiffness to satisfy this gossip.

" Well, I thought something was the matter, Reverend. For you see, I've heard that you went out there and brought her home to save him from killing her, so you see it is rather strange. That fellow, as a boy — and even yet, when he is in Chicago — attends Sunday school and sits in my class, and I was rather surprised that he should treat Orlean as it is said you said he did."

Reverend McCarthy would liked very well to have moved on. But Mrs. Jones was very much interested.

"There's all kind of talk around town about it. They say that if he gets a judgment against you, Elder, he will put you in jail, and all that; but of course that couldn't be. You stand too well in the church. But you know, Reverend, the only thing that looks kind a bad for you is, they say that he wouldn't dare start such a suit unless he had good ground for action. They say —"

The Elder had extricated himself at last, and now sailed down the street with high head. "May the God crush that hard-headed bulldog into the earth," he muttered between compressed lips, so angry that he could not see clearly. "How long am I to be aggravated with this rotten gossip!"

He changed his mind about walking far, and at a convenient corner, he turned back toward home. But when he arrived there, he was confronted with another, and more serious problem. It had been his intention before arriving there, to arraign his wife again for having let Orlean go West in the beginning. But now he was confronted with his august honorary, the Bishop.

"And, now, Reverend," said the Bishop, after they had gone through the usual formalities, "I am forced to come around to something that embarrasses me very much, in view of our long and intimate relations," and he paused to look grave. The Reverend tried to still his thumping heart. All his life he had been a coward, he had bluffed himself into believing, and having his family believe, that he was a brave man, but Orlean had told Baptiste on several occasions that her father might have risen higher in the church, but for his lack of confidence.

"It pertains to all this gossip and notoriety that is going the rounds. I suppose you are aware of what I refer to." The other swallowed, and nodded.

"You can appreciate that it is very embarrassing to me,

and to the church, more, because I have struggled to raise the standard in this church.   We have in the years gone by been subjected to unfair gossip, and some fair because of the subtle practices of some of our ministers.   And now, with conference convening in two weeks, it is very awkward that we should be confronted with such a predicament with regard to you, one of our oldest ministers.   The subject is made more embarrassing because of its — er, rather personal nature.   I would regard it as very enlightening if you would give me an explanation — but, of course, in the name of the church."

The Reverend swallowed again, struggled to keep his eyes dry, for the rush of self pity almost overcame him.   It was, however, no time or place for self pity.   The Bishop was *not* an emotional man; he was *not* given to patience with those who pitied themselves — in short, the Bishop was *very much* of a cold hearted business man, notwithstanding his position.   He was waiting in calm austerity for the other's reply.

" Ah-m ahem ! " began the Reverend with a great effort at self composure.   " It is, to say the least, my dear Bishop, with much regret that I am compelled to explain a matter that has caused me no end of grief.   To begin with :   It was not with my consent that my daughter was allowed to go off into the West and file on a homestead."

The other's face was like a tomb upon hearing this. Indeed, the Elder would have to put forth a more logical excuse.   It has been said that the Bishop was a practical man which in truth he was, and the fact is, he regarded it as far more timely if a larger number of the members of his race in the city would have taken up homesteads in the West, than for them to have been frequenting State Street and aping the rich.   Also, the Bishop had read Baptiste's book — although the Reverend was not aware of it,— and was constrained to feel that a man could not conscientiously write that which was absolutely false.

"But I came into the city here after a conference to find that my daughter had been herded off out West in a wild country to take a homestead."

"Now, just a minute, Reverend," interposed the Bishop astutely. "Regarding this claim your daughter filed on. What was the nature of the land? You have been over it, I dare say."

"Of course, of course, my dear Bishop! It was a piece of wild, undeveloped land. At the time she took it, it was fifty miles or such a matter from the railroad. She gave birth to a child —"

"But," interposed the Bishop again, "you say the land was a considerable distance from the railroad at the time your daughter filed on the place? Very well. Now, Reverend, isn't it a fact that in the history of this country, all new countries when opened to the settler may have been some distance from the railroad in the beginning? For instance, somebody started Chicago, which was certainly not the convenient place then that it is now in which to live."

"Of course, my dear Bishop, of course."

"So the fact that the railroad was, as you say, fifty miles away, could not be held as an argument against it. Besides, is it not a fact that there were other people, men and women, who were as far from the railroad and therefore placed at an equal disadvantage?"

"Of course, of course."

"Then, my dear Reverend, it does not appear to me that that should be a fact to be condemned."

"I have not condemned it, my dear Bishop. No."

"Very well, then, my dear Reverend, please proceed."

Now the interposition of the Bishop, had rather disconcerted the Elder. Had he been allowed to proceed in the
manner he had planned and started to, he might have made
the case from his standpoint, and under the circumstances
very clear to the Bishop. But the latter's questions threw
him off his line, and he started again with some embarrassment, and with the perspiration beginning to appear around
the point of his nose. Appreciating, however that he was
expected to explain, he went resolutely back to the task.

"Well, my wife allowed my daughter to be taken out
there and file on this land that this man had secured on his
representation that he wished to marry her, and when I came
into the city it was all settled."

"Pardon me for interrupting you again, my dear Elder.
But is it not a fact that Mrs. Pruitt, with whom you
are well acquainted, accompanied your daughter on this
trip?"

"It is so, Bishop."

"And is it not a fact that Mrs. Pruitt as well as your
daughter, explained it all at the time with satisfaction to
you?"

"Well, ah — yes, she did."

"You admit to this, then, my dear Reverend?"

"Under the circumstances at the time, I was rather compelled to, my dear Bishop."

"Meaning that since she had gone and taken the land,
you were morally bound to look into and consider the matter favorably?"

"Yes, I think that explains it."

"Now, Reverend. Is it not a fact that a considerable
write-up appeared in the Chicago *Defender* shortly after this
visit, detailing considerable, and with much illustration regarding the trip; that, in short, your daughter had come into

considerable land and was regarded as having been very fortunate?"

" I think so, my dear Bishop."

" Very well, Reverend. Now — a — who solicited that write-up? Did the editor not have a conversation with you before the article appeared?"

" I believe he did, yes, sir. I think he did."

" Well, now, Reverend, if I remember correctly, this young man visited the city the Christmas following, and I was introduced to him by you in this same room?"

" I think so. Yes, Bishop, I remember having introduced him to you myself."

" And do I quote correctly when I say that you called me up the following spring to perform the ceremony that made your daughter and this Jean Baptiste man and wife?"

" I think you quote correctly, my dear Bishop."

" M-m. Yes, I recall that I was indisposed at the time and was very sorry I could not perform the ceremony," said the Bishop thoughtfully, but more to himself than to the other.

" Well, now. After they had been married some months, my wife visited your wife, and the latter seemed to be greatly impressed with the union. I think if I am correctly informed that you went on a visit to them yourself that fall."

" I did, my dear Bishop. Yes, I did."

" And at the conference on your return, you, if I am not mistaken, called on me at my home and discussed the young man at considerable length."

" Yes, my dear Bishop. I did that."

" Yes," mused the Bishop again thoughtfully and as if to himself. " And you appeared greatly delighted with their union. You seemed to regard him as an extraordinary young man, and, from what I have heard, I have been inclined to feel so myself. Now it seems that a few months after you were speaking in high praise of him, you made a trip West and on your return brought your girl home with you, and she has not since returned to her husband. Of course," he added slowly, "that is your personal affair, but since it has reached the public, the church is concerned, so I am ready to listen to further explanation."

"I went out there and found my girl in dire circumstances," defended the Elder. "I found her in neglect; I found her without proper medical attention — no nurse was there to administer her needs. In short, I was prevailed upon by my love and regard for my daughter's health, to expedite the step I took."

"Nobly said, Reverend, nobly said," said the Bishop, and for the first time during his explanation, the Elder felt encouraged.

"The man did not marry her for love," the Elder went on now somewhat more confident. "He did not marry her to make her happy and comfortable. He married her to secure more land. It is true that I was impressed with him in a way, because the man was rather — er, inspiring, and I entertained hopes. Our race does not possess successful men in such a number that we can be oblivious to apparent success as on a young man's part. This man seemed to be such a man — in fact, I grant him that. The man was popular with those who knew him; he was a pusher; but he *was so ambitious to get rich* that he was in the act of killing my child to accomplish his ends." The Reverend finished this with a touch of emotion that made the other nod thoughtfully. And while he paused to gather force and words for further justification of his interposition, the Bishop said:

"I note by the reports in the newspaper that you are

accused of having coerced the girl; that you had her write her husband's name on a check with which you secured the money to bring her from the West."

" He gave my daughter the privilege of securing money by such a method for her needs, and it was not I that had her do any such a thing."

" But it was — er, rather — a little irregular, was it not? It does not seem reasonable to suppose that he granted her the privilege to sign his name to checks to secure money with which to leave him?" The question was put rather testily and caused the other to shift uncomfortably before making answer.

" Well, under the circumstances, methods *had* to be resorted to — er, rather to fit the occasion." The Elder's defence was artful.

The Bishop, not pretending to take his question seriously, pursued:

" I note, further, that he accuses you of disposing of some property. . . ."

" My daughter sold her place. It was hers, in her name, and the transaction did not require his consent."

" M-m — I see. It seems that the property, so he claims, represented an outlay of some thirty-five hundred dollars in cash, and he purports the same as being worth something like sixty-four hundred dollars. What is your opinion, having been on the property, of its actual worth?"

" Well, I have some sense of values, since I am buying this home, and I do not regard the property as being worth such a sum."

" I see," said the other, stroking his beard which was thick and flowing.

" A piece of wild, raw land such as that I could not estimate it as being so valuable."

" M-m. Have you any knowledge of what land has brought in that neighborhood, Reverend. You see, value is a very delicate thing to estimate. We cannot always be the judge in such matters. The usual estimate of what anything is worth is what some one is willing to pay. Do you recall of having ever heard your daughter or any one say what deeded land in that section sold for? "

" Well, I have heard my daughter say that a place near there had brought five thousand dollars."

" Which would not compare with the value you put on the place your daughter held."

" It would not seem to."

" M-m. You say this was your daughter's place entirely? "

" It was," returned the Reverend promptly.

" And she paid for it out of her own money? "

" Well, no. She did not."

" I see. M-m. Then who purchased it for her, Reverend? "

" I think he did that. Yes, I think he did."

" I see. Do you recall the consideration. I understand that he purchased what is called a relinquishment. I understand such transactions slightly. I have read of such deals in Oklahoma. Seems to be a sort of recognized custom in securing land in new countries, notwithstanding the subtlety of the transaction."

" I think he claimed to have paid two thousand dollars for the relinquishment, which I would consider too much, considerably too much."

" But, inasmuch as your knowledge of new countries has been brief, perhaps, you would not set your judgment up as a standard for values there," suggested the Bishop, pointedly. " You will grant that the individual in the controversy would likely be able to judge more correctly with regard to values?"

"It is obvious."

"Yes, yes. Quite likely." The Reverend was very uncomfortable. If the Bishop would only stop where he was it wouldn't be so bad, but if he kept on with such questions. That was what he had disliked about Jean Baptiste. . . . He had a habit of asking questions — too many questions, he had thought; but this man before him was the Bishop, a law unto himself. And he must answer. The Bishop knew a great deal more about the West than he had thought he did, however.

"Who bought your daughter's place, my dear Elder? A white man or a Negro? Which of course, doesn't matter, but if I understand all the details, it would be more clear, you understand."

"Of course, my dear Bishop. Naturally. A white man bought the place."

"I understand now. A *white* man," he repeated thoughtfully. During all the questioning, the Bishop had looked into the Reverend's eyes only occasionally. Most of the time he had kept his eyes upon the carpet before him, as if he were studying a spot thereon.

"It seems by the paper that the man, according to the accusations set forth in the complaint, had once contested the claim."

"Yes, he had done so, Doctor, he had."

"I see. Why did he contest the place, my dear Reverend?"

"Why, I do not understand clearly, but such methods appear to be a recognized custom in those parts," countered the Elder evasively.

"But isn't it a fact that he tried to contest her out of

the place, and if he had been successful, he would have had the place for nothing in so far as she was concerned?"

"It is quite likely." The Elder had nothing but evasive answers now. He tried counters no more.

"But he failed, it seems, to get the place through contest, regardless of the fact that your daughter was here in Chicago instead of being on her claim."

"It seems that way."

"And then, forsooth, it must have been your daughter's husband who was instrumental in saving the place for her?"

"Yes."

"And after this, your daughter sold the place to the man who had struggled to beat her out of it and failed through the instrumentalities of her husband, and without consulting her husband with regard to the bargain."

"I counciled her, my dear Bishop."

"Ah, *you* counciled her," and for the first time he turned his sharp, searching eyes on the Elder and seemingly looked directly through him. The next moment they were back on the carpet before him, and he resumed his questions. He was thinking then, thinking of what he had read in the book by Jean Baptiste, and what had recently appeared in all the papers. It seemed to him that the Elder's defence was not quite clear; but he would see it through.

"It was reported that this man, a banker, whose bank had failed . . . sent you the money for your railroad fare from Cairo to this city, and also reimbursed for the return. Is that quite true?"

"That was — the railroad fare — a part of the transaction."

"Ah-ha. A *part* of the transaction. You never, I suppose, informed her husband regarding the *transaction* after the deal was closed?"

" No."

" What was the consideration, Reverend, for this piece of land that your daughter's husband bought, for which he paid $2000, placing a house and barn thereon, digging a well, and making other improvements, fighting off a three years' contest — placed there by the man who tried to beat her out of it? What did he pay for the place?"

" Three hundred dollars." Such an awful moment! The Elder's head dropped as he said this. But the Bishop's eyes were still upon the spot in the carpet.

" And so this young man comes hither and accuses and sues you, accusing you of breaking up he and his wife. He published all that you have told me and if he should secure a judgment it is known that he can remand you to jail for six months."

He paused again, regarded the spot in the carpet before him very keenly and then arose. The Elder arose also, but he was unable to find his voice. In the meantime the Bishop was moving toward the door, his hand was upon the knob, and when the door was open, he turned, and looking at the one behind him, said:

" Well, see you at the conference, Newt," and was gone.

The other stood regarding the closed door. His brain was in a whirl and he could not quite understand what had happened. But *something* in that hour had transpired, and while he could not seem to realize what it was just then, he knew he would learn it in due time.

CHAPTER XII

THE conference that followed was one of grave apprehensions for the Reverend McCarthy. Before, he had always looked forward to this occasion with considerable anxiety. He had usually prepared himself for the battle that was a rule on such occasions. For thirty-five years he had not missed a conference; he had never come away in defeat. True, he had not risen very high, but he had, at least, always been able to hold his own.

But, for the first time in his long experience, he went to meet this conference with a feeling in his heart that he would come away defeated. That he was not to be re-appointed Presiding Elder, was a foregone conclusion, but he entertained doubts about getting the appointment he had hoped to secure. Ever since the Bishop had paid him the visit, he had been uncomfortable. When the prelate bade him good-by that day, he had never been able to get out of his mind the idea that the other had convicted him in his own heart, and had purposely avoided his company. It worried him, and he had been losing flesh for two years, therefore he did not present now the same robust, striking figure as when he had met the conference heretofore year after year.

And then, moreover, he had been hounded almost to insanity by gossips. From over all his circuit it was the talk, they brought it to conference and discussed it freely and did not take the trouble to get out of his hearing to do so. Nowhere was there, as he well knew, a body that would have delighted more in his downfall than those brother preachers who met the conference that year. Always had they been ready to oppose him, but always before the Bishop had been with him. He had been able by subtle methods to place himself in the Bishop's favor, but this time that august individual artfully kept from meeting him directly. Besides, he had not the conscience to seek him, and he had not been able to meet the Bishop in the free atmosphere as before.

The charge that he had picked out was very good, and it was convenient for his needs for many reasons. Of course there were scores of others after the same charge, but with his old influence he need not have worried. However, he had not and could not see the Bishop privately long enough to secure from him a promise. And so he met the conference for the first time, unsettled as to where he was to preach the ensuing year.

Never had a conference seemed so long as that session. The week wore slowly away, and he was forced to be aware of the fact that on all sides they were discussing him, and the fact that he had been sued, and was likely to be remanded to jail as a result, since no one credited him with so large a sum as ten thousand dollars. He could see the uncon-cealed delight, and the malice that had always been, but which before he had been able to ignore. Affairs reached such a point until it was almost a conclusion that it mat-tered little as to where he was sent, for he would be unable to fill the pulpit because of the fact that he would have to go to jail shortly. It nettled him; it broke down his habitual composure, and it was a relief to him when the conference came to a close.

And not until the secretary arose to call the various

charges and who had been sent thither, did he know where he was to go. So it was with a sinking of the heart when his name was reached:

" Reverend McCarthy to Mitchfield! "

" *Reverend McCarthy to Mitchfield!* " was the echo all through the audience. Impossible! *Reverend McCarthy,* one of the oldest, and regarded as one of the strongest, one of the ablest ministers to such a forsaken charge. Indeed they could hardly have sent him to a poorer charge, to a less dignified place. It seemed incredible, and the rest of the calls were almost drowned out in the consternation that followed.

Well, it was done. He had been all but silenced, and lowered as much as the Bishop dared to lower him. That was settled, and he returned to Chicago without telegraphing the fact to his family.

With resignation he made the necessary preparations for the trip, and taking Orlean with him, went to the small town. They rented a house, for the place didn't afford a parsonage, and began the long dreary year that was to follow. It was his good fortune, however, when the school board met and decided to separate the Negro children from the whites in the public schools, that they employed his daughter to teach the colored pupils for the year. In this way they were able to get along in very good comfort in the months that followed. So the autumn passed, and also the winter. Spring came and went, and summer had set in when his attorney wrote him that the case had been called, to come into Chicago, and prepare to stand trial in the case of Jean Baptiste, plaintiff, versus Newton Justine McCarthy, defendant.

CHAPTER XIII

WHERE THE WEAK MUST BE STRONG

THE TRIAL was called for early June, and Baptiste reached the city a week or ten days before the time set. He had become very friendly with the Negro lawyer who was conducting his case. He also secured a Gregory lawyer, the one who had conducted the contest case. When he arrived in the city, the lawyer advised that, inasmuch as they had a spare bedroom at his home, and that it would be imperative for them to be close to discuss various phases of the prosecution, he could have the room if he liked. So he accepted it.

It so happened that the lawyer's home was located in the same block on Vernon Avenue as was the McCarthys, and on the same side of the street. Moreover, it had been built at the same time as had that of the McCarthys, and was very much like in appearance the one in which they were living.

One afternoon a few days before the trial, while lingering at the bar of the Keystone Hotel, Baptiste was approached by Glavis, who invited him to a table nearby, where they were very much alone. He ordered the drinks, and when they were served he began:

"Now, Baptiste, it seems we ought to be able to get together on this case without going into court."

"Yes?" replied Baptiste, regarding the other noncommittally.

"Yes, I think we could, and should. I think you and

Orlean ought to be able to console your differences without such an extreme."

" You *think* so? "

" Why, I do. Orlean has always — ah — rather loved you, Baptiste, and I think you two could make up."

" But this is not between Orlean and me, Glavis. You seem to misunderstand. It is between N. Justine McCarthy and me."

" Of course, but it is over Orlean. You have sued father for this sum, a sum you know he cannot pay in the event you should secure judgment. So there would be nothing left for you but to remand him to jail, which seems to be your desire."

" Possibly so." The other was still noncommittal.

" Then why not you and I get together on this proposition before the trial is called? "

" I don't see as I can oblige you, Glavis. There comes a time when compromise is impossible, only vindication can suffice. And it's vindication that I want now and, regret to advise, am determined to have."

" That seems rather severe, Baptiste."

" Why so? "

" Well, you see, I understand that the old man kinda — er, gave you the worst of it, but you ought to forget some things. Look at it from a broad viewpoint. See how expensive it is going to be, and all that."

" I considered all that before I went into it, Glavis," replied Baptiste calmly.

" Well, now, Baptiste, I want to stop this thing before it goes to court. If you had of kinda flattered the old man a little in the beginning as I did, all would have been well."

" Why should I have done so when I didn't feel to? "

" Oh, Baptiste, you are *so* severe! "

" When a man has suffered as I have, it is time to be severe, my friend. For your own benefit, I will say that I do not trust your father-in-law. I do not love him and never have. If it wasn't because I wish to observe and subserve to the law of the land, I would have killed him long ago. *Even when I think of it now,* my bitterness is so great at times that I must repel the inclination to strike him down for the coward he is. So if that's all, we will call the meeting to an end," so saying he arose, strode toward the bar and ordered drinks for both. He drank his with a gulp when served, and turned and left the saloon.

Glavis proceeded to his lawyer, and advised him of his inability to dissuade the plaintiff.

" Couldn't dissuade him, eh? "

" Couldn't do a thing! "

" That's too bad. It might be to your advantage if you could settle this case out of court. When will your father-in-law be in? "

" I'm looking for him here in a day or so, now."

" M-m." The attorney was thoughtful. " This is rather an unusual case," he resumed, " and I have been studying the complaint of the plaintiff. The old man, it seems to me, committed some very grave blunders."

" You think so? "

" Quite obvious. And while it will be difficult for the plaintiff to secure a judgment in such a case; it is, however, apparent that the sympathy of the court will be against your father-in-law in the proceedings."

Glavis was uncomfortable.

" Now I take notice here that the plaintiff states that his wife drew a check for two hundred dollars unknown to her husband, and that the Reverend had it cashed. That may be regular, but it will not help her father's case. Again, he complains that her father influenced the girl to sell a quarter section of land for less than one-tenth what it cost the plaintiff. Of course these are technicalities that while they cannot justify a judgment will win the sympathy of the jury. What the plaintiff must show, however, is that his father-in-law actually was the direct cause of and did alienate the affections of his wife. Such a case is not without parallel, but it is uncommon. A father alienating the affections of his daughter.

" Now where is your sister-in-law? "

" At home."

" Wish you'd bring her down. This is a complicated case, and we've got to conduct it with directness. She can be of great assistance in extricating her father from this predicament."

" All right, sir. When shall I bring her? "

" Oh, any time that is convenient. Tomorrow morning at nine will perhaps be the best. And, now, say! Have you any idea who the plaintiff is going to use as witnesses? "

" Why, I think he plans to bring his grandmother from what I can hear, for one."

" His grandmother? What does she know about it? "

" Well, she was in the house when my father-in-law went on the visit and the girl came away with him."

" I see. I'd like to know just what passed and what she heard and will testify to. I wonder whether she will testify that she overheard your father-in-law abusing this Baptiste to his wife? "

" I really don't know."

" Who else? "

" I heard something about him going to bring a doctor down, and also a lawyer."

" The doctor, eh? " He shook his head then a little

dubiously. " This physician attended the girl while she was confined ? "

" I think so."

" M-m. I see here where we have recorded that your father-in-law claims that the girl was neglected; didn't have proper medical attention. What about this? Have you any knowledge as to how many visits this doctor made to the bedside of this girl when she was sick? Any knowledge of what kind of bill was rendered by him ? "

" I hear that his bill amounted to something like two hundred dollars."

" Two hundred! Great Scott! And for a dead baby! Gee! We'll have to keep away from neglect as an excuse. That's a fact. No jury will believe such a statement if that fellow shows where he's paid such a bill as that! "

Glavis shifted uneasily. He was seeing another side of the controversy. Before he had only seen one side of it, and that side was as the Reverend had had him see it.

" You send or bring the girl down here tomorrow. It will be up to *her* to keep her father out of jail, that's all. It will be up to *her* to convince the court that she never loved this man, that all he did for her was by persuasion, and that her father only followed her instructions. In short, it's almost directly up to her; for the plaintiff has certainly got the goods on her dad if he can prove that she ever loved him."

Glavis was much disturbed when he went home. For the first time he was able to appreciate the full circumstances. It would be up to Orlean to save her father, and that he could see. He would take her to the lawyer, and have her carefully drilled. The success for them depended on her; on her falsifying to the court, for it could not be otherwise. For her to testify that she did not love — and had never

loved Jean Baptiste, he knew would be a deliberate falsehood. It worried him, but he had to go through with it.

He accompanied her to the lawyer's office as agreed, and
there she was made to understand the gravity of the situation, that everything depended on her statements, *and her
statements only.*

Her father arrived the following day, and at the attorney's office in company with Orlean and Glavis, he was
impressed with the nature of the defense. All were finally
drilled in their course of action.

That night Orlean faced the most serious period in her
life. She was a weak woman and her weakness had been
the cause of it all. The trial was approaching — and the
result was *up to her.* Her father's freedom, his continuance in the pulpit, his vindication of the action he had taken
depended upon *her,* and *her strength.*

And that strength — for on that day she would *have* to be
strong,— *depended upon a lie.*

CHAPTER XIV

THE TRIAL — THE LIE —" AS GUILTY AS HELL!"

"*N*OT *guilty, your honor!*"

The court room was silent for a time before any one stirred. It had been apparent that the decision would be so; because there were several reasons why the jury was constrained to render such a verdict.

Among the reasons, chiefly, was the fact that the plaintiff had failed to produce sufficient evidence to justify a verdict in his favor. His grandmother, his corroborating witness, had answered her last call just before she was to start for Chicago to give hers, the most incriminating testimony. The doctor who had attended his wife during her confinement was indisposed, and was represented only by an affidavit. But what had gone harder than anything against the plaintiff was his wife's testimony. Under the most severe examination, and cross examinations, she had stood on her statements. She had never loved her husband, and had not been, therefore, actuated by her father's influence into leaving him. She had instructed her father in all he had done, and that he was in no wise guilty as accused.

No jury could have rendered a verdict to the contrary under such circumstances, and no one — not even the plaintiff, had expected or even hoped that they would.

But in the minds of every man and woman in the crowded court room, N. J. McCarthy stood a guilty man. Not even the faintest semblance of doubt as to this lingered in their minds. It was merely a case of insufficient evidence to convict. And while the people filed out into the air at the conclusion, every one had a vision of that arch hypocrite in his evil perpetuation. In their ears would always ring the story Jean Baptiste had told. Told without a tremor, he had recited the evils from the day he had married her up until the day she had sold her birthright for a mess of pottage. So vivid did he make it all that the court was held in a thraldom. For an hour and a half he detailed the evil of his enemy, his sinister purpose and action, his lordly deceit, and his artful cunningness, and brought women to tears by the sorrow in his face, his apparent grief and external mortification.

Never had the black population of the city listened to or witnessed a more eloquent appeal. But justice had been unable to interfere. The trial was over, and Newton Justine McCarthy left the court room a free man, with head held high, and walking with sure step.

Jean Baptiste left it calmly in company with his lawyers. They had anticipated losing the case before going into court, for it had been apparent to them that the outcome rested entirely with Baptiste's wife. If they failed to shake her testimony; that she had never loved him, then they knew it was hopeless. It had all depended on her — *and she had stood by her father.*

" Well, I'm satisfied," said Baptiste as they went through the street.

" I suppose so, in a way."

" I wanted vindication. I wanted the people to know the truth."

" And they know it now. He goes free, but the people know he is a guilty man, and that your wife *lied* to save him."

" Yes," said Baptiste a little wearily.

Somehow he felt relieved. It seemed that a great burden had been lifted from his mind, and he closed his eyes as if shutting out the past now forever. He was free. Never would the instance that had brought turmoil and strife into his life trouble him again. Always before there had seemed to be a peculiar bond between him and the woman he had taken as wife. Always he seemed to have a claim upon her in spite of all and she upon him. But, by the decision of the court, all this had been swept away, and he sighed as if in peace.

They found their way to the " L " station that was nearest, and there took a train for the south side. At Thirty-first Street Baptiste left his lawyer and slowly betook himself toward the familiar scenes on State Street.

While he lost himself in the traffic of State Street, the Reverend, in company with Glavis, Ethel, and Orlean, boarded an Indiana Avenue surface car. The Reverend was cheery for a great fear had passed. A coward by nature, he had been on the verge of a nervous breakdown before the trial, thinking of what might happen. But now that was over. He was free. That meant everything. The fact that he was guilty in the minds of everybody who heard the trial, did not worry him now. He was free and could claim by the verdict that he was vindicated in the action he had taken. That was the great question. Always before he had been sensitive of the fingers of accusation that were upon him, and the worry had greatly impaired his usual appearance.

And while he was relieved, Glavis, sitting proudly by him, was also. He talked cheerfully of the trial, of the decision, and of the future that was before them. He smiled at all times, and the Reverend's large face was also lighted up with a peculiar delight. But there was another who, in spite of the fact that the testimony from her lips had saved the day for the Reverend, was not happy, not cheerful, not in a mood to discuss the case.

This one was Orlean. Few knew — in fact maybe only one other, and that was her husband — or appreciated how much that false testimony had cost her. She had lied; lied freely; lied stoutly; lied at every point of the case — *and this for the man who had brought her to it*. And *now* when it was over she felt not at ease. While Jean Baptiste was conscious that a burden had been lifted from his mind, and Glavis and her father chatted freely, she sat silently by without even a clear thought. She was only conscious that she had lied, that after a life of weakness, a life that had made no one happy or cheerful or gay, she had for the first time in her life, deliberately lied. And as she became more conscious of what had passed, she felt a burden upon her. Never since the day she had abused her husband; never since the suffering her actions had brought him; never since as a climax to all this, when he lay upon the floor and she had kicked him viciously in the face, had she experienced a happy or a cheerful day.

But today — after that terrible ordeal, she felt as if life held little for her, that she was now unfit to perform any womanly duty. She found no consolation in the fact that she had been encouraged to do as she had done by those who claimed to love her. That seemed to annoy her if anything. She could now, for the first time in her life, realize clearly what duty meant. Duty could not be side-tracked, regardless of what might have passed. Her husband had been good to her. He had given her the love that was his. Never had he abused her in any way, never had he used a cross word in her presence. But she had done everything to him. And as a climax to it all, she had *lied*. Oh, that lie would haunt her forever!

They arrived at the street where they must leave the car for home. She arose along with the rest. When they stood upon the walkway and had started toward home, her father paused.

"By the way, children," he said cheerfully. "I think I should call at the lawyer's office and thank him." He turned his eyes to Glavis, his worthy counsellor at all times, and read agreement in his face before the other opened his lips to give sanction.

"I think that you should, too, father," he said, where-upon he turned to accompany him.

"Well, I'll drop by his office. You may go on home with the girls, Glavis," he said. So saying he turned toward the attorney's office to settle his account and talk over the case.

As he walked along his way, he became reflective. He allowed his mind to wander back into the past — back many years to the time when he had gone into the country to take a meal. He recalled that day at the dinner table where he had sat near a certain school teacher. She had been an attractive teacher, a rare woman in those days. And he admired her. It was a privilege to sit so close to her at the table, to wait on her, and be the recipient of her charming smiles. He saw himself now more clearly in retrospection. He saw a little boy standing hungrily at a distance. He saw again now, that same small boy approach the teacher; saw the teacher's motherly face and her arms reached out and caught that youth and then smother his face with kisses. He felt again the anger that little boy's action had aroused in him. He heard again the cries from the summer kitchen as the mother administered punishment for the same. He recalled briefly the years that followed. He recounted the testimony at the trial. For many, many months he had endeavored to make Baptiste suffer, and this day he had succeeded. But still he was not satisfied. The joy that had come of being freed of the accusation after his unhappy and nervous state of fear, had shut all else out of his mind for a time. After all freedom is so much. But was freedom all? He could not account for the feeling that was suddenly come over him. He recalled then again the severe chastisement he had caused Jean Baptiste to receive when he was a mere child. He recalled also how he had been instrumental in separating him from his daughter. He recalled now the lies, oh, the lies she had resorted to that had kept him out of jail, the tears he had shed from self pity, while Baptiste stood stoically by.

And thinking thusly, he reached his destination.

He found the attorney alone, busy over some papers. He approached him courteously, bowed, and thrusting his hand in his pocket, said:

"Yes, sir. I thought I would drop in and pay you the balance of the fee that is now due, and thank you for your services." He smiled pleasantly as he spoke, and never appeared more impressive. The other regarded him a moment, held out his hand, accepted his fee, and said:

"Well, it's over, and you are free."

"Yes," said the Elder, but now found it rather hard to smile. "I am glad it is over for it was a very awkward affair, I must confess." He paused then, perforce. The lawyer was regarding him, and the Elder wondered at his expression. He had never seen that look in his face before. What did it mean? He was not kept long in suspense, for soon the other spoke.

"Yes, you are free and fortunate."

"Fortunate," the Reverend repeated, thoughtfully, and

looking up found the lawyer's eyes upon him. They were looking straight into his with the same expression of a moment before.

"Yes," said the lawyer then coldly, "you are *free* and *fortunate*, because *you were as guilty as hell!*"

CHAPTER XV

AGNES decided to visit Chicago and planned to be married there. Besides, since she was now engaged, the legacy in the bank at Rensselaer must be secured, and, according to her mother's will, consulted before she was married. She was curious to know what it was all about. Indeed, she was almost as anxious, if not more so to learn the contents of the legacy than she was to become the wife of the man she had consented to marry.

Accordingly, before the train reached Chicago, she became very anxious. It gave her a peculiar and new thrill to recline in the luxurious Pullman, to have her needs answered and attended to by servants, and to be pointed out by curious people as the writer and composer of a song that had delighted the whole country. She was experiencing how very convenient life is when one has sufficient means to satisfy one's needs. This had been her privilege only a short time. A newsboy boarded the train and passed hurriedly through the cars with the morning papers. She purchased one, and glanced through the headlines. In the index she saw an account of the suit of Jean Baptiste, versus his father-in-law. Curiously and anxiously she turned to the account and read the proceedings of the trial. She laid the paper aside when through and reviewed her acquaintance with him in retrospection. How strange it all seemed at this late date. Beside her, a long, narrow mirror fit between the double windows. In this she studied her face a moment. Some years had passed since that day — and the other day, too, at the sod house. She thought of the man that was to be her mate and of what he would think should he ever know that the only man who had ever touched her lips before him, was a Negro. She found herself comparing the two men, and she was rather surprised at the difference she could distinguish. She tried to estimate what true love was. The life she had so recently entered was the life she had aspired to. She had hopes for it. The life that could now be hers was the goal of her ambition — and she had attained it! She should be satisfied. But was she?

As the train with its luxurious appointments sped along, she felt after all that she was going out of the life that she really loved. Was it because she had always been so poor and unable to have the things she could now partake of at will, that such had become a habit, and indispensable to her happiness? For indeed she had a longing for the old life, the dash and open it afforded. She had a vision of Jean Baptiste and his honor. He had sacrificed her to be loyal to the race in which he belonged. Had it not been for this, she knew she would not be journeying to the great city to become the wife of another. But amid all these thoughts and introspectives and otherwise, there constantly recurred to her mind the man she was to marry and what he would think if he knew that she had once loved and would have married — *and even kissed a Negro.*

She was glad when at last the train drew into the outskirts of the city, and the excitement about drove such reminiscences out of her mind. She had wired him, and of course, she expected him to meet her.

"Oh, here you are," he cried as she stood upon the platform a half hour later. On hearing him her eyes wandered toward where he stood, and regarded him keenly for a moment. A really handsome man, immaculately attired in the finest tailored clothes and in the fashion of the day. He caught her in his arms and she did not resist the hot kisses he planted upon her cheeks. Still, she was greatly confused, and feared that she would create a scene before she had become accustomed to the ways and dash of the city.

He had her arm — held it close, as they passed through the station and crossed the walkway to where an inclosed auto stood. Into this he ushered her, attended to her luggage, and a moment later followed her inside. Through the city with all its bustle and excitement they sped.

" I'm going to take you to my aunt's," he said, when they had gotten started.

" Oh," she chimed. At that moment she could think of nothing to say. It was all so confusing to her. She was so unaccustomed to any kind of a city that she was actually in a fear. She did not realize because of the distinction to which she had attained, that any awkwardness on her part would be looked upon as the eccentricity of a genius. She decided, however, to say as little as possible, to speak only when spoken to. In that way she would try not to cause him any embarrassment or mortification.

" You have certainly been a hard one to pull off the farm, dear," she heard now.

" Oh, do you think so? " she said coyly.

" Do I think so? " he laughed. " Well, say, now, there isn't one person in a thousand who, after writing the hit you have composed, wouldn't have been over all this old land by this time, letting people see them."

" Oh, I could never wish that," she said quickly.

" Oh, come, now! Get into the limelight." He eyed her artfully, winked playfully, and continued: " You'll like it when you get the modesty out of yourself."

" I don't think so."

He regarded her quickly out of the corner of his eye, and then looked ahead.

" Ever heard of State Street?" he inquired.

" Oh, yes. Is this it?"

" This is State Street," he said, and she looked out and started. She didn't know just what she had expected to see, but what met her gaze and made her start was the sight of so many Negroes.

" What's the matter, dear?" he said, glancing at her quickly.

" Why — ah — oh, nothing."

" I wondered why you started," and he again looked ahead. They were across it now, and approaching Wabash Avenue. He turned into this, to where his aunt lived some distance out in the most exclusive part of its residence section.

Agnes, sitting by his side, despite the excitement, the great buildings and fine streets, was thinking of the past, and of what she had just seen. Negroes, Negroes, and *that* would have been her life had she married Jean Baptiste. All such was foreign to her, but she could estimate what it would have meant. She was sure she could never have become accustomed to such an association, it wouldn't have seemed natural. And then she thought of Jean Baptiste, the man. Oh, of him, it was always so different. In her mind he was like no other person in the world. How strange, and singularly sweet had been her acquaintance with him. Never had she understood any one as she understood him. She tried to shut him out of her life, for the time had come, and she must. But *could* she? When she dared close her eyes she seemed to see him more clearly.

The car had stopped now, and he was lifting her out before a large house that stood back from the street some distance in sumptuous splendor. As they went up the walkway, the large front doors parted, and a handsome elderly woman came forth. Upon her face was written refinement and culture.

"Oh, aunt, here we are."

"I saw you coming because I was watching," said his aunt, coming forward, the personification of dignity. She held out her arms, and Agnes felt herself being embraced and kissed. Her head was in a whirl. How could *she* readily become accustomed to such without displaying awkwardness.

Arm in arm they mounted the steps, were met by the butler, who took her bags, and a moment later she found herself in a large, richly furnished room.

"Come now, dear," he said, and led her to a couch. She heard his aunt going upstairs to prepare her room, and the next moment she felt him draw her to him, and whatever difference there was in this convenient life, all men loved alike.

Jean Baptiste lingered late at the Keystone bar. He was alone in the world, he felt, so company of the kind about seemed the best, and was, at least, diverting. It was twelve o'clock and after when he left. He still retained his room at the attorney's residence, and to this he strolled slowly. He attempted to formulate some plans in his mind, and after a time it occurred to him that he should go back West to Gregory. He had hired more than seven hundred fifty acres put into wheat. He hadn't heard how it was, or whether there was any wheat there or not. But he had seen in the papers that a drought had affected much of the crop in Kansas and Nebraska. He half heartedly assumed that it would naturally hit his country also. If so, there was nothing left for him to do but leave that section. But he would depart from the city on the morrow and see what there was up there, and with this settled in his mind, he quickened his step, and hurried to his room.

He turned into the right number, as he thought, but upon trying to insert the key in the lock he found that he had made a mistake. He glanced up in confusion and almost uttered a cry. It was not the attorney's home, but that of the Reverend McCarthy.

"Chump!" he said to himself as he turned and started back down the steps. "I'll never sleep inside that house again," and laughed.

Upon the walk he heard steps, and when he had reached the street, looked up to meet Glavis and a strange Negro just turning in. Glavis glared at him as if to say, "Well, what business have you here, now?" But Baptiste mumbled some word of apology about having turned in at the wrong number, went directly to his room, retired and forgot the incident.

He had no idea how long he had been asleep or what time it was when he was awakened suddenly by a drumming on his door, and the attorney's voice, saying:

"Heh! Heh! Baptiste, wake up, wake up, you're wanted!"

He turned on his side and drew his hand to his forehead to assure himself that he was awake. Then, realizing that he was, he jumped from the bed and going forward, opened the door.

Two officers, the attorney in a bath robe, and Glavis

stood at the door. He regarded them curiously. " What is this? " he managed to say, as they came into the room.

" Seems that they want you," said the attorney.

" Me? " he chimed.

" Yep," said one of the officers. " Will you go along peacefully or shall we have to put the bracelets on. You're arrested for murder."

" For murder! *Me,* for murder? "

" Just go with the officers, Baptiste. If you'd been a little earlier you might have gotten away; but it so happened that I met you coming out just as I was going in."

" But I don't understand what you're talking about — all of you," persisted Baptiste. " Who has been murdered, and why am I accused? "

The lawyer had been observing him keenly, and now he interposed.

" Why, your wife and her father have just been found murdered, and Glavis here and another assert they met you coming out of the house at midnight or a little after."

The incident of the night came back to him then, " Well," he muttered, and began to get into his clothes. When he was fully dressed he turned to the attorney and said:

" Glavis is right in part, White." He was very calm. " I'll call you up when I need you." And then he turned to the officers and said. " I'm ready. The cuffs will not be necessary."

CHAPTER XVI

A FRIEND

BECAUSE she feared that rising as early as she had been accustomed to might serve to embarrass her fiancé and his aunt, Agnes took a magazine from her bag, returned to bed and tried to interest herself in a story the morning following her arrival in the city. About seven, some one knocked lightly at her door, and, upon opening it, she found the maid with the morning paper.

"Would you care for it?" she asked courteously.

"I would be glad to have it," she said as she took it, returned to the bed, and once again therein, turned to read the news. It was but a moment before she started up quickly as she read:

STRANGE MURDER CASE ON VERNON AVENUE

Negro Minister and His Daughter Found Murdered about Midnight

JEAN BAPTISTE, WHO HAD LOST SUIT AGAINST PREACHER, ARRESTED AND HELD WITHOUT BAIL AS SUSPECT. WAS MET LEAVING THE HOUSE JUST BEFORE DISCOVERY OF THE MURDER.

Jean Baptiste, Negro author and rancher is under arrest at the county jail this morning, accused of the murder of his wife and father-in-law, the Reverend N. J. McCarthy, at 3—— Vernon Avenue. The dead bodies of the preacher and his daughter were discovered shortly after midnight last night by his daughter Ethel and her husband, upon his return from State Street where he had seen Baptiste leave the Keystone saloon a few minutes after twelve.

The murder appears to be the sequence of a long enmity between the preacher and his son-in-law, Baptiste. Some years ago Baptiste had the preacher's daughter take a homestead in the West, on which he had purchased a relinquishment for her. Some months later they were married and went to live on the claim he had secured. It seems that bad blood existed between the preacher and Baptiste, and some time after the marriage the preacher went on a trip West and when he returned brought his daughter back with him. It is said that the rancher visited Chicago several times following in an effort to persuade her to return. About a year ago, the daughter sold a relinquishment on the homestead and Baptiste accused the preacher of having influenced her to do so. He also accused him of other things that contributed to the separation, and finally sued the minister in the circuit court of Cook County for ten thousand dollars for alienating his wife's affections. The case was brought up, tried, and, yesterday, the minister was adjudged not guilty by the jury. The rancher and author made a strong case against the minister, and it was the consensus of opinion in the court room that the minister was guilty. But it was his daughter's alibi that saved him: she testified that she did not and never had loved her husband, and because the plaintiff was unable to prove conclusively that she had, the jury's verdict was " not guilty."

E. M. Glavis, also a son-in-law of the dead man, testified and was corroborated by another, a minister, that just as he turned into his yard last night, he met Jean Baptiste coming out. He moreover claims, that a few days before the trial, he tried to dissuade Baptiste from going through with the case, and to settle it out of court. But that Baptiste refused to consider it; that he showed his bitterness toward the now dead man, by declaring that if he hadn't wished to observe and subserve to the law, he would have killed the preacher long ago.

It is therefore the consensus of opinion that Baptiste, disappointed by losing the suit, entered the house and murdered his wife and father-in-law while they slept. The circumstantial evidence is strong, and it looks rather bad for the author. Only one phase of the case seems to puzzle the police, however, and that is that the preacher and his daughter were found dead in the same room, the room which the minister occupied. Both had been stabbed with a knife that had long been in that same room. The minister's body lay in bed as if he had been murdered while he was sleeping, while that of the daughter lay near the door. It is the opinion also of those who feel Baptiste guilty, that he entered the house and went to the preacher's room, and there killed him while he lay sleeping; and that the daughter, who was sleeping downstairs near her mother, was possibly aroused by the noise, went up to the room, and was murdered as the intruder was about to leave.

Baptiste refused to make any comment further than that he was innocent.

"Accused of murder!" Agnes echoed, staring before her in much excitement. "*Jean Baptiste accused of murder!*" She read the account again. She arose and stood on the floor. "He *is* innocent, *he is innocent!*" she cried to herself. "*Jean Baptiste would not commit murder, no, no, no! No, not even if he was justified in doing so.*" Suddenly she seized her clothes, and in the next instant was getting hurriedly into them.

She completed her toilet quickly, opened the door and slipped down the stairs. The maid was at work in the hall, and she approached her, and said:

" Will you kindly advise the lady of the house that I have gone downtown on some very urgent business. That I shall return later in the day? "

She stepped outside, crossed to State Street, inquired of an officer the way to the county jail, and a few minutes later boarded a car for the north side.

She had no plans as to what she would or could do, but she was going to him. All that he had been to her in the past had arisen the instant she saw that he was in trouble. Especially did she recall his having saved them from fore-closure and disgrace years before. She was determined. She was *going* to him, he was innocent, she was positive, and she would do all in her power to save him.

It was rather awkward, going to a place she had never dreamed of going to, the county jail, but she shook this resolutely from her mind, and a few minutes following her arrival, there she stood before the bailiff.

" I am a friend of a man who was arrested in connection with a murder last night," she explained to the officer. " And — ah, would it be possible for me to see and consult with him? "

" You refer to that case on Vernon Avenue, madam? "

" Yes, sir."

" And you would like to see this Jean Baptiste? "

" That is the one."

They regarded her closely, and was finally asked to follow the bailiff.

They stopped presently before a cell, and when the light had been turned on, she saw Baptiste sitting on a cot. He looked up, and upon recognizing her, came forward.

"Why, Agnes — Miss Stewart, *you!*" he cried in great surprise. He regarded her as if afraid to try to understand her presence there.

"Yes, Jean," she answered quickly. "It is *I*." She hesitated in her excitement, and as she did so, he caught that same mystery in her eyes. They were blue, and again he could swear that they were brown. Despite his precarious position and predicament, he could not help regarding her, and marking the changes that had come in the years since he had seen her. She seemed to have grown a trifle stouter, while her hair appeared there in the light more beautiful. Her face was stronger, while her lips were as red as ever. Withal, she had grown more serious looking. She reminded him as she stood there then, of a serious young literary woman, and he was made hopeful by her visit.

"Now, Jean, I've read all about it in the papers. I happened to be in the city, and so came right over. I know nothing about anything like this, and don't suppose you do either. But, Jean," she spoke excitedly, anxiously, and hurriedly, "I am willing to do anything you ask me to, just anything, Jean." And she regarded him tenderly. He was affected by it, he choked confusedly. It was all so sudden. She noted his confusion, and cried in a strained little voice,

"You must just tell *me*, Jean."

"Why, Agnes — I. Well, I don't know what to say. I don't feel that I ought to involve you in such a mess as this. I —"

"Oh, you must not speak that way, Jean. No, no, no! I'm here to help you. You *didn't* kill him, you *didn't* kill *her — you didn't kill anybody, did you, Jean?*"

"Of course I didn't kill anybody, Agnes."

"Of course you didn't, Jean!" she cried with relief. "I

knew you were innocent. I said so, and I got out of bed and came at once, I did."

"How brave, how noble, how kind," he murmured as if to himself, but she reached and placed her hand over his where it rested upon the bar.

"Shall I hire a lawyer, Jean? A great lawyer — the best in the city. That would be the first thing to do, wouldn't it, Jean?"

He looked at her, and could not believe it was so, but finally he murmured:

"I have a lawyer — a friend of mine. You may call on him, Agnes. His number is 3——Vernon Avenue. He will tell me what to do."

"And *me,*" she said quickly.

"Yes — *you,*" he repeated, and lowered his eyes.

"Well, I'm going now, Jean," and she reached for his hand.

He was almost overcome, and could not look at her directly.

"Be strong, Jean. It will come out all right — it must come out all right —"

"Oh, Agnes, this is too much. Forget it. You should not —"

"Please hush, Jean," she said imploringly, and he glanced up to see tears in her eyes. She looked away to hide them. As she did so, she cried: "Oh, Jean, I know what *they* have been doing to you — how you have been made to suffer. And — and — I — could *never* stand to see it after all —" she broke away then, and rushed from him and out of the building. He watched her and when she was gone, he went back to the cot and sat him down, and murmured.

"Agnes, oh, Agnes,— *and after all that has passed!*"

CHAPTER XVII

THE MYSTERY

AFTER AGNES had consulted with the lawyer, who was glad to go into the case, and agreed to engage a worthy assistant, she returned to Baptiste and said: " Now, Jean. Don't you think that if I secured a good detective to look into it — this case, it would be the proper thing? "

" Why — yes, Agnes," he said. He could hardly accustom himself to her in such a situation.

" I think that would be best," she resumed. " As I was coming downtown on the car I observed the Pinkerton Office on 5th Avenue and now, Jean, if you think that would be a practical.move, I will go there at once and have them send a man to you. I'll bring him."

" That would be practical, Agnes. Yes," he said thoughtfully, " since you insist —"

" No more, please," and she affected a little smile. " Just let me work until we arrive somewhere," and she was gone, returning in due time with a man.

" I represent the Pinkerton agency, Mr. Baptiste," he said, after greeting the prisoner, " and now if you will state just where you were; what time, as near as you can recall, that you reached home; also what time you turned into this place where the murder was committed, I shall be glad to get down to work on the case."

Since Baptiste had observed the time by the clock in the Keystone before leaving there, he was quite accurate in fixing the time he reached his room. Since we have followed him to his room, we know this phase of the case.

"Well, I'll hike over there and squint around a little. Hope I'll get there before the inquest is held." And so saying, he was gone.

"I will go back to where I am staying, now, Jean," said Agnes, after the detective had departed, "and you may expect me at any time. I want to see you out of here as soon as possible, and I will do all in my power to get you out," and she dashed away.

The detective went to the McCarthy home forthwith. The bodies had been removed and were then at the morgue. He looked into the room where the tragedy had been committed, and then sought Glavis.

"Who discovered the murder, Mr. Glavis?" he inquired when they stood in the death room.

"Why myself and another fellow returned home just after it had been committed."

"How did *you* know it had just been committed?"

"Well — why, my wife was in the hall-way, and when we entered she had just discovered the bodies."

"But that doesn't prove that they had just been murdered."

"But my wife says she was awakened by her sister's scream."

"I see. So it was your wife who first discovered the bodies, or that they had just been murdered."

"Yes."

"Where had you been, and what time did you return home?"

"I had been around town, to the Keystone where Baptiste was until shortly after midnight."

"You saw this Baptiste leave the hotel?"

" I did."

" How long after Baptiste left was it, before you followed? "

" Perhaps fifteen minutes."

" *Perhaps* fifteen minutes; but you are not positive? "

" No, but I am quite certain."

" When you left the hotel, where did you go? "

" I came here."

" You came directly here. Didn't stop on the way anywhere? "

" I did not."

" And when you arrived, what happened? Did you meet anybody on the way? "

" I passed people of whom I took no notice on the way here, of course. The only person I took notice of was Jean Baptiste."

" Where did you meet him? "

" Coming out of the house upon my arrival."

" You met him coming out of the house upon your arrival? "

" Well, out of the yard. I saw him come down the steps that leads up to the house."

" But you *didn't* see him come out of the house? "

" Well, no, I didn't see that."

" Did you exchange any words with him when you met him? Did you stop and talk? "

" No. But I heard him mutter something."

" Did you understand the words or any words he muttered? "

" I thought he said something about having turned in at the wrong place."

" How do you account for him having done so — if so? "

" Well, the house where he stops is just a few doors — about a half dozen — up the street —"

" On the same side or the opposite? "

" The same side. And he was stopping there."

" Did you have any conversation with Baptiste after the trial in which he sued your father-in-law? "

" No; but I tried to have him settle the case before going to court."

" What did he say to it? "

" Refused to consider it."

" Did he give reasons? "

" Yes. He said he wanted vindication."

" Anything else? "

" That he would have killed the Elder if it had not been that he was an observer of the law."

" Where were they murdered? "

" She lay near the door, while he lay in bed."

" Any evidence of a struggle? "

" No, not as I could see."

" With what were they murdered? "

" With a knife that has been in the room here for two or three years."

" Was Baptiste aware that such a knife was in the room? "

" Not that I know of."

" When, to your knowledge, was Baptiste last in the house? "

" He has not been in the house for more than three years."

" Then he couldn't have known the knife was there."

" Well, unless he discovered it when he entered the room."

" Providing he *entered* the room. Was he aware also that the preacher occupied this particular room? Is it not reasonable to suppose that he would not know where the preacher slept if he had not been in the house for three years?"

"But he could have looked around."

"Possibly. But how do you account for the girl's body being here in the room also. Where did she sleep?"

"Downstairs near her mother. It is my theory that she was disturbed by the sound of some one walking, went upstairs, and was in time to see the tragedy of her father, and was in turn murdered by her husband."

"That is your *theory*. But why was there no evidence of a struggle? It hardly seems reasonable that she would have allowed herself to be stabbed without some effort to save herself."

"Well, that is beyond me. Jean Baptiste acted suspicious in my opinion, and it is certainly strange that he should have been in the position he was at such a crucial time."

"May I consult with your wife?"

Glavis looked around, uneasily. "She is very much torn up by the incident," he suggested.

"But this is a very grave matter."

"Well," and he turned and entered the room wherein Ethel had enclosed herself.

"Ethel, an officer has called and wishes to consult with you."

"No, no, no!" she yelled. "Send him away. Didn't I tell you I didn't want to see no police," and she fell to crying. The detective had entered the room in the meantime, and when she looked up, she saw him.

"What are you doing in here?" she fairly screamed. He did not flinch under the glare she turned upon him. Indeed, the day was at last come when she could frighten no one. The one she had been able to drive to any lengths with such a propaganda, lay stiff at the morgue. The detective regarded her searchingly, and upon realizing he was not going to jump and run, she ceased that unseemly noise making and began crying, woefully.

"You discovered this tragedy, madam?" he inquired calmly, but with a note of firmness in his tone.

"Yes, yes! — oh, my poor sister! My poor father — and that low down man!"

"When did you discover this, madam?"

"Just as soon as it was done, oh me!"

"How did you come to discover it, lady?"

"By my sister's scream. She screamed so loud it seemed everybody must have heard it. Screamed when he stuck that knife into her breast!"

"How long after you heard her scream was it before you came out of the room — your room?"

"I came at once," she said sulkily, and tried to cry louder. The detective was thoughtful.

"So you came at once! And what did *you see* when you came out?"

At this she seemed overcome, and it was some moments before he could get her answer, and that was after he had repeated.

"My sister and father lying murdered in the room there."

"Is *that all* you saw?"

She was sulky again. After a time she muttered. She wrinkled her face but the tears would not come. Presently she said, and the detective caught an effort on her part to say it.

"Yes. But I think I heard a door slam downstairs."

"You *think* you heard a door slam? What happened next?"

"My husband came."

" How long after the door slammed was it before your husband came? "

" Not long."

" Is it not possible that when you heard the door slam, that it was your husband coming in? "

" No. I heard the door slam behind him, too." Again he thought he detected something singular in her manner, as if she were not telling all she knew. . . .

The detective went downstairs and talked with Mrs. McCarthy a few minutes, and then took his leave. He called up Agnes, and made an appointment and met her some hours later.

" What have you discovered? " she inquired anxiously, her eyes searching his face.

" Well," said he, slowly, " a few things, I think."

" And Jean — Mr. Baptiste? " He looked up sharply and searched her face.

" He is innocent."

" Thank God! " And she clasped her hands and looked down in great relief. Quickly, she looked up, however, and cried: " But the proof. Will you — can you *prove* it? "

He toyed idly with a pencil he held in his hands, and after a time, drawled: " I think so. *When the proper time comes.*"

" The *proper* time? And — when will that be? " Her voice was controlled, but the anxiety was apparent.

" Well, we'll say at the preliminary hearing tomorrow morning."

" And — and — you have no more to report? "

" Not today. I shall attend the inquest, of course. And where may I see you — say, tomorrow? "

" At the hearing."

" Very well, then. Good day."

" Good day."

CHAPTER XVIII

VENGEANCE IS MINE. I WILL REPAY

"JEAN," she cried joyfully. "The detective says that you are innocent; and that he feels he will be able to place the crime where it belongs!"

"I'm glad," he said solemnly. She bestowed upon him a kind smile as she said:

"So I thought I would just come over and cheer you up. There is something mysterious about it all, and the newspapers are devoting much space to it. Oh, I'm so glad to hope that it will be all over tomorrow, and you will be let out of this place, so you can go back home and cut your wheat."

"My wheat?"

"Yes, of course, Jean. You have a fine crop of wheat on all your land."

"I have?"

"Yes, it is so," she reassured him. And then she paused, as something seemed to occur to her. "Because of the fact that you have had several failures you cannot realize that you have actually raised a crop, a big crop, better than any crop since — since." She stopped short, and he understood and suppressed a sigh. When he looked up, she was moving down the hallway, her mind filled with something she had almost forgotten during the past two days.

He knew of it. She had been given quite a write-up in the social columns of a Chicago paper and many lovers of her musical hit, were, unknown to her, curious with regard to her coming marriage.

The detective Agnes had retained, called on Baptiste's lawyers and held a lengthy consultation. When he left them, an understanding had been reached with regard to the hearing, and silence was agreed upon.

At the magistrate's office the following morning, the court room was crowded. Scores were turned away, and all the family had been subpœnaed.

Glavis was first called, and related what he knew, which has already been related. Next came Mrs. McCarthy who knew even less. She was followed by Ethel, and the detective and two lawyers questioned her closely.

"Now, you say you heard your sister scream," said the lawyer after the usual formalities had passed. "Will you kindly state to the court just what you overheard and know regarding this affair?"

She glared at him, and then her eyes met those of Baptiste, and she glared again. She told a varied story of the case, and made it very brief.

"You say, madame, that after you heard your sister scream you rushed from your room and to where she was?"

"Yes," she answered, and those near noticed the sulkiness.

"And when you arrived you found her dead near the door, while your father lay murdered in the bed?"

"Yes."

"Do you recall, Mrs. Glavis, whether she screamed long, or whether it was brief?"

She hesitated, somewhat confused. Presently, she stiffened and said: "It was long."

"Did it last until after you had left your bed?"

"It did."

"Until you had left the room you were in?"

"Yes."

"In fact she was screaming still when you arrived at the

door of the room, no doubt?" the lawyer's tone was very careless, just as though he were not in the least serious. Her reply was prompt.

"Yes."

"Now Mrs. Glavis, do you recall having ever heard your sister scream before in a like manner?"

She started perceptibly. Her eyes widened, as if she were recalling an incident. Suddenly she became oblivious of her present surroundings, and conscious of a night two years before. . . . When she resumed her testimony, she was seen to be weaker.

"No," she said bravely.

Now it so happened that the attorneys for the defense had consulted with a chemist, who was in the court room by request. At this juncture he was called to the stand. He was asked a number of questions, and then Ethel was again placed on the stand.

"Now, madame, the court has decided to investigate this matter thoroughly. You are positive Jean Baptiste, here, killed your sister, also your father? You remember, of course, in giving your testimony, *that we are going to investigate the case and prosecute for perjury!*" She had been seen to raise her handkerchief to her eyes with the first announcement regarding the investigation. Now she uttered a loud cry as the tears flowed unchecked. Suddenly she dropped her handkerchief, and with her arms stretched forward, she screamed:

"*No, no! Orlean, Orlean! Oh, my God, Orlean!*" And in the next instant she would have fallen in a dead faint had those near not caught her. For this is how it happened.

When the family returned from the court house, Orlean

had retired at once, complaining of a headache. Since she had very often since her father brought her home complained of such, no particular attention had been paid it. She stayed in bed until late in the afternoon. In the meantime her father went over to the west side, presumably to call on Mrs. Pruitt. It was late when he returned, about eleven o'clock, that night.

Orlean retired again about ten, and had fallen into a troubled sleep. She felt the same as she did the night she had returned from Mrs. Merley's, and she could not account for the strange nausea that lingered over her.

When N. J. McCarthy returned, he went to the kitchen for a drink of water, after which, he must return through the room in which his daughter, Orlean, lay sleeping. As he had done on that occasion two years before, he had paused at the foot of the bed to observe his sleeping daughter. How long he stood thus, he never knew, but after a time he became conscious of that strange sensation that had come over him on the memorable night before. He tried to throw off the uncanny feeling, but it seemed to hang on like grim death. And as he stood enmeshed in its sinister thraldom, he thought he again saw her rise and point an accusing finger at him. Out of it all he was sure he heard again her voice in all its agony as it had spoken that other night. But tonight the accusation was more severe.

"*There you are again, my betrayer,*" she said coldly. "*Today you completed your nefarious task; you completed the evil that began more than thirty years ago, oh, debaser of women! Where is Speed, and the wife of his you ruined? Where? In hell and its tortures did you say? Yes, and where are my brothers? Oh, don't tremble, for you should know! No, you made me pretend to feel that you had not committed that sin, and other sins, also. But I knew —*"

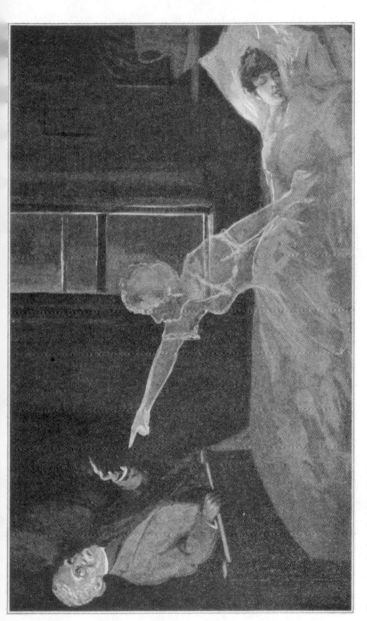

From a painting by W. M. Farrow.

HE TRIED TO THROW OFF THE UNCANNY FEELING, BUT IT SEEMED TO HANG ON LIKE GRIM DEATH. AND AS HE STOOD ENMESHED IN ITS SINISTER THRALDOM, HE THOUGHT HE SAW HER RISE AND POINT AN ACCUSING FINGER AT HIM.

*yes, I knew! You never told me I had brothers. You said
foolish things to deceive me and the mother of mine. You
called me by a boy's name, Jim, and pretended, because you
did not recognize your illegitimate off-spring, that there were
none. And then came Jean. Oh, you had him at a disadvantage always! When he was a little boy, you started
your evil, and twenty years later you renewed it. Why,
oh, you vain sinner, you know! He married me — perhaps
he didn't love me then as he might have — as he would have
had I tried to be the woman he wished me to be. But you
took advantage of the weakness that was in me by the heritage of my mother, and you made me subservient unto your
evil will!*

*" Well, it's all over now, and from this day henceforth
you will never see peace. The evil and misery you have
brought unto others, shall now be cast upon you. You are
my father, and the creator of my weakness, but you have
taken my husband and soul mate, and made a new genera-
tion impossible for me to lead. And now I say unto you, go
forth and repent. Begone from me. For from this day
evermore though in weak flesh I may pretend to love you,
know that I must hate you!"*

He shook himself, and succeeded in casting off the depression. When he looked again, Orlean was sitting up in bed,
regarding him sleepily. He started, and wondered whether
what had passed was real, but in the next moment he was
relieved.

"Papa," she said in her usual, but sleepy-like voice, " Is
that you?"

"Yes, daughter," he replied quickly, and as if to still the
excitement in his heart, he passed quickly around to where
she reposed, and planted a kiss upon her lips, and turning,
hurried upstairs.

She sat upright for some minutes after he had gone, and became conscious of that singular feeling that she had felt all the day, still lingering over her. As she sat there, she heard the little clock on the table beside her mother strike 11 :30. She lay down again, and a few minutes later she was asleep.

The Reverend retired quickly and wished he could sleep and forget what he thought he had seen and heard. He was successful, and soon he was snoring. He could not understand upon being awakened slowly how long he had slept, but he became conscious that the light was burning brightly. He turned on his back, and when he could see clearly, his eyes fell upon Orlean.

She stood between him and the door, and he regarded her with a puzzled expression. Presently his eyes met hers, and he started up. *What was the matter with her?* Her eyes were like coals of burning fire ; her stiff, bushy hair, was unbraided and stood *away from her head giving her the appearance of a savage. But it was the expression of her eyes that disturbed him.* He was held in a thraldom of fear as she slowly advanced toward the bed.

" Orlean," he at last managed to say. " What is the —"

" *I have come at last to right a wrong,*" she began in an uncanny voice. Never had he seen her appear like that before, nor heard her speak in such a voice. She paused when she was beside the bed, and stood looking down upon him in that demented fashion. The cold perspiration broke out all over him, and he trembled.

" *Oh, you told me my husband did not love me. While he worked to make us comfortable and happy out there on the claim you sat beside my sick bed and told me lies. While he grieved over the loss of our little one, you conceived a vile plot to ' get even.' Oh, you — liar! You sunk his soul into hell for spite. And then today — yesterday you reached your climax by having me go on the stand and testify to a greater lie! To save your wretched soul from disgrace, I swore to the most miserable lie a woman could tell! And now that you have made him suffer unjustly, and spoiled all life held for me, the judgment of God is upon you. The God that you have lied to and made a laughing idol of seeks restitution! So you sinner of all the sins, vengeance is mine, I will repay!"*

So saying, she reached quickly and grasped the knife he had found years before, a desperate looking instrument with a six-inch blade and bone handle. She raised it high, and for the first time he was fully awakened. He attempted to struggle upward, but with a strength borne of excitement, she pushed him and he felled backward upon the bed.

"*Orlean, my child, Orlean! My God — oh, my heaven, what do you —*" he got no further. Quickly her poised arm descended, and the knife she held sank deeply into his heart.

"*Oh, God — my beloved God — ah — oh — Christ! Christo. . . .*" he struggled upward while she stood over him with that same white expression upon her face. As the blood clogged in the cut the knife had made, and all the pulsations concentrated, struggled before ceasing their functions for all time, he turned his dying eyes toward her. Regarded her blindly for a moment, and then, dropped limply back from where he had risen, dead. In that moment she regained her sanity.

She regarded him a moment wildly, and then she closed her eyes to try to shut out the awful thing she had done and screamed long and wildly — just as she had done that night when she returned from Mrs. Merley's. Then, as the echo died away, the door was pushed open, and before her stood Ethel. One terrible look and the mad girl went quickly forward, halted, swayed, and then with a moan, raised the knife and sank it into her own breast. Drawing it forth she regarded Ethel wildly, and then, throwing the knife against the wall of the room, dropped dead at Ethel's feet, just as Glavis' steps were heard in the hall below.

When he heard his wife scream, and had rushed upstairs, saw the dead father-in-law and her sister, he cried:

"Jean Baptiste did this! I just met him coming out of the house as I entered," and catching his wife he quickly took her back to the room, and proceeded to spread the alarm.

Even with the grief she was cast into, Ethel had quickly seen a chance to spite the man she hated, and instead of telling the truth, she had chosen to keep silent and let Jean Baptiste be convicted if possible for the crime he knew nothing of.

The people were filing out of the court room. Ethel's confession, born out of the excitement when the lawyer had mentioned investigating the crime deeply, had cleared everything, and Jean Baptiste was free.

In the court room during the hearing he had observed Agnes, but when the trial was over, she was nowhere to be seen. He looked around, but failed to find any trace of her. At last, with a sigh, he went with the lawyers and a few days later was home, to harvest the wheat she had told him was the best, and so he found it.

He was saved thereby, and went into the harvest with Bill and George again shocking as they had done years before. But there was no Agnes to bring the luncheon now, and Jean Baptiste lived in the memory of what had once been.

CHAPTER XIX

WHEN THE TRUTH BECAME KNOWN

"I HAVE hardly seen you for two days, my dear," he complained when Agnes had returned from the hearing.

"I have been consumed with some very delicate business," she said, and notwithstanding the excitement she was laboring under, allowed him to caress her. At the same time he was regarding her strangely. For the first time he seemed to be aware of the fact that she was a rather strange person. He was trying to understand her eyes as everybody else had done, even herself.

"Will Agnes tell me what has kept her so busy and away, I know not where?" he asked tenderly. "Or would she rather not — now."

"She'd *rather* not — now," and she tried to be jolly, although she knew she must have failed miserably.

"Very well, my dear. But, sweet one, when are you going to become my own?"

She started. In the excitement she had so recently been through, the fact that she was engaged and expected to marry soon, had gone entirely out of her mind.

"Why, really — when?" She paused in her confusion, and he said quickly:

"Let's just get married — today!"

"Oh, no, please don't ask me to so soon."

He frowned. Then he was pleasant again. "Then, when, Agnes?"

She was still confused, and in that moment thought of the legacy. She was more confused. He caught her hand then, and touched her cheek with his lips.

After an hour she had told him of the legacy.

"That place is less than a hundred miles from Chicago and we can just run down there today and back this evening!" he exclaimed, shifting in anxious excitement. "We can go there and back today, and be married tomorrow."

"No," she said slowly. "I'll suggest that we have the legacy brought here, and attended to according to the will and all that has for a lifetime to me been a mystery, be cleared here in your and your aunt's presence. And the day after — I will marry you." She dropped her eyes then in peculiar solemnity. He didn't understand her but the thrill of what was to come overwhelmed him, and in the next instant he held her in his arms.

They explained their plans to his aunt, who, because she disliked notoriety, readily agreed, and by special messenger the papers were brought to the city the following day and opened according to her mother's will.

The night before, as they were returning from the theatre, he said to her:

"Agnes, do you know — and I trust you will pardon me if it seems singular, but there is something about you I can never — somehow feel I never *will,* understand." He paused then and she could see he was embarrassed.

"It is in your eyes. I see them in this hour and they are blue, but in the next they are brown. Has any one ever observed the fact before?" he ended.

She nodded, affirmatively.

"Why is it, dear?"

"I don't know."

"And you — you have noticed it yourself?"

" Yes."

" And — can't you understand it, either? "

She acknowledged the fact with her eyes.

" It is strange. I'll be glad when we understand this legacy."

" I will, too."

" It makes me feel that something's going to happen. Perhaps we — you are going to prove to be an heiress."

She laughed cheerfully.

" And then you will not want to marry me, maybe."

She laughed again.

" But nothing would keep me from loving you always, Agnes," he said with deep feeling.

" Even if the papers would show me to be descended from some horrible pirate or worse."

" Nothing in the world could make a difference.   Indeed, should the papers connect you with something out of the ordinary, I think I would like you better — that is, it would add even more mystery to your already mysterious self."

" Wonderful! "

He kissed her impulsively, and in the next hour she went off to bed.

" What is this? " said her fiancé's aunt, as the lawyer lifted a small package from the box of documents, and as he did so, an old photograph slipped and fell to the floor. It was yellow with age; but the reflection of the person was clearly discernible. All three looked at it in wonderment. Then her fiancé and his aunt regarded her with apprehension. The package was untied, and all the papers gone through and much history was therein contained. But one fact stood above all others.

" Is *this* a fact? " said the aunt coldly.   Never had she

appeared more dignified. Her nephew stood away, regarding Agnes out of eyes in which she could see a growing fear.

"Well, I hope everything is clear," said the lawyer astutely. "It seems that you have come into something, madam, and I trust it will prove of value." She mumbled something in reply, and stood gazing at the two pictures she now held. All that had been so strange to her in life was at last clear. She understood the changing color of her eyes, and her father's statements that he had never quite explained. *At last she knew who she was.*

She turned to find herself alone. She opened her lips and started to call the others, and then hesitated. *Why had they left her?* She looked at the photographs she held — *and understood.*

She gathered the documents and placed them in the box, went upstairs, slowly packed her belongings, and called a cab.

Jean Baptiste came into the granary on the old claim, and looked out over the place. And as he did so, he regarded the spot where the sod house had once stood and wherein he had spent many happy days. As he thought of it, the past rose before him, and he lived through the sweetness again that a harvest had once brought him. That was years before, and in that moment he wished he could bring it back again. *The Custom of the Country and its law* had forbid, and he had *paid the penalty.* He wondered whether he would do the same again and sacrifice all that had been dear and risk the misery that had followed.

He shifted, and in so doing his back was toward the road. "Withal, it would have been awkward to have married a white woman," he muttered, and reached for the cold lunch he had brought for his meal. Bill and George were eating in the field where they worked.

"Batching is hell," he muttered aloud, and picked up a sandwich.

"How very bad you are, Jean," he heard, and almost strained his neck in turning so quickly.

"*Agnes!*"

"Well, *why* not?"

"But — but — oh, tell me," and then he became silent and looked away, raising the sandwich to his mouth mechanically.

"Don't eat the cold lunch, Jean. I have brought some that is warm," so saying she uncovered the basket she carried, and he regarded it eagerly.

"But, Agnes, how came you here? I — I — thought you — were *getting married*. Are you here on — on your *wedding trip?*"

"Oh, Lord, no! No, Jean, I am not going to marry."

"*Not going to marry!*"

She shook her head and affected to be sad, but a little smile played around her lips that he saw but didn't understand.

"But — Agnes, *why?*"

"Because the one to whom I was engaged — well, he wouldn't marry me," and she laughed.

"I wish you would make it all clear. At least tell me what it means — that it is so."

"It *is* so!" she said stoutly, and he believed her when he saw her eyes.

"Well, I guess I'll understand by and by."

"You *will* understand, soon, Jean," she said kindly. "Papa will explain — *everything*." She turned her eyes away then, and in the moment he reached and grasped her hand. In the next instant he had dropped it, as a far away expression came into his eyes as if he had suddenly recalled something he would forget.

"Jean," she cried, and came close to him. She looked up into his eyes and saw what was troubling him. She got beside him closely then. She placed an arm around him, and with her free hand she lifted his left hand over her shoulder and held his fingers as she looked away across the harvest fields, and sighed lightly as she said:

"Something happened and I was strangely glad and came here because — because I — just *had* to see you, Jean."

"Please, Jean. You — will — forget that *now*." She paused and was not aware that her arm was around him, and that his hand rested over her shoulder. Her eyes were as they had been that day near this selfsame spot years before, kind and endearing. She did not resist as she saw his manly love and felt his body quiver.

And almost were his lips touching hers when suddenly, she saw him hesitate, and despite the darkness of his face, she could see that in that moment the blood seemed to leave it. He dropped the arms that had embraced her, and almost groaned aloud. As she stood regarding him he turned and walked away with his eyes upon the earth.

She turned then and retraced her steps, but as she went along the roadway she was thinking of him and herself and *who she was at last*. She sighed, strangely contented, and was positive — knew that in due time *he too* must come to understand.

CHAPTER XX

I T WAS in the autumn time, after the wheat and the oats, the rye, the barley and the flaxseed had all been gathered, and threshed, and also after the corn had been husked. Wheat, he had raised, thousands and thousands of bushels. And because there was war over all the old world, and the great powers of the land were in the grim struggle of trying to crush each other from the face of the earth, the power under which he lived was struggling with the task of feeding a portion of those engaged in the struggle. And because Black Rust had impaired the spring wheat yield those thousands of bushels he raised, he had sold at a price so high that he had sufficient to redeem at last the land he was about to lose and money left for future development into the bargain.

He sat alone at this moment in a stateroom aboard a great continental limited, just out of Omaha and speeding westward to the Pacific coast. As was his customary wont, his thoughts were prolific. But for once — and maybe for the first time, on the whole, he was satisfied,— he was contented — and last, but not least, he was happy.

Being happy, however, is not quite possible alone. No, and Jean Baptiste was *not* alone. And here is what had happened.

Jack Stewart had told him the story. And in the story told, one great mystery was solved. He now understood why Agnes' eyes had been so baffling. Simple, too, in a measure. To begin with, her mother had possessed rare brown eyes, he had seen by her picture, because Agnes' mother had not been a white woman at all, but in truth was of Ethiopian extraction. This was a part of the story Jack Stewart had told him. He had met and married her mother on a trip from the West Indies where she had lived, to Glasgow; the marriage being decided upon quickly, for in truth the woman was fleeing. In London some years before, she had been the pupil of a learned minister, who had become an infidel, and also unscrupulous. But we know the story — at least a part of it — of Augustus M. Barr, alias, Isaac M. Barr; alias — but it does not matter. We are concerned with Agnes' mother. Her mother had inherited a small fortune from Agnes' grandma and this Barr had sought to secure. To do so, he had followed Jack Stewart and his wife, Agnes' mother to Jerusalem. There he had met Isaac Syfe, the Jew, whom he later brought to America. He did not find the woman he had followed there, but on his return to England he *did* find Peter Kaden who was married to Christine. Kaden was involved in a murder case, was accused, and had been sentenced to Australia for the rest of his natural life. It was Barr who saved him, and the fee Kaden paid was Christine. Barr accommodated him by bringing him to America where he placed all three, including himself, on homesteads. Syfe settled with him in cash by taking a large loan on his homestead and giving Barr the proceeds.

But Kaden was in the way. He had never been comfortable in the new country with Christine the wife of another and living so near, so Barr sent Christine away and drove Kaden to suicide. Later at Lincoln, Nebraska she left him and went out of his life forever. Barr had secured Kaden's homestead, and all this Jack Stewart knew, but had never disclosed.   Barr lost track of Agnes' mother, but knew that somewhere in the world there was a treasure but not as great as he had thought it was — about ten thousand dollars in all.

While Jean Baptiste was absorbed in these thoughts, the door was opened quietly, and closed.   Some one had entered the stateroom and his ears caught the light rustle of a skirt. His eyes were upon the landscape, but suddenly they saw nothing, for his eyes had been covered by a pair of soft hands.

"I knew it was you," he said, happily, as he drew her into the seat beside him, between himself and the window.

"What are you thinking of, my Jean," she said then.

"Of what I have been thinking ever since the day when we understood that you and I after all are of the same blood."

"Oh, you have," she chimed, and drawing his face close with her hands, she kissed him ardently.

"Isn't it beautiful, Agnes?   Just grand!"

"Oh, Jean, you make me so happy."

"You are *honestly* happy, dear?" he inquired for the hundredth time.

"I *couldn't* be happier," and she reposed in his arms.

"Have truly forgotten that you are *an Ethiopian,* and *must share* what is Ethiopia's?"

"Will share what is *yours,* my Jean."

"Always so beautifully have you said that."

"Have I, now, really?"

"Do you recall the day when I forgot, dear, *The Custom of the Country — and its law!*"

"How could I forget it?"

"And what followed?"

"I cannot forget that, either.   But Jean, do you want me to?"

" Agnes, we must both forget what followed.   Still, when we think how kind fate has been to us, after all, we must feel grateful."

" Oh, how much I do.   But, Jean — it was *such* a sacrifice. . . ."

He was thoughtful for a time, and from the expression on his face, the present was far away.

" Please, dear," she said, taking his hand and fondling it. " When you happen to think of it; will you try never to allow yourself to resume that expression — *that* expression again ? "

He looked down at her.

" Expression ? "

" Like you wore just then."

" Oh."

" You see, it seems to bring back events in your life that we want to forget."

" You mean, I —"

" Yes," she said slowly, " you — we understand each other and everything that has concerned each other, don't we, Jean? "

" Of course we do, Agnes.   We have always — but there, now ! " and he smothered the rest of it in a fond caress.

" Wasn't it strange," she mused after a time.   " I could never understand it.   I saw it in my eyes before we left Indiana.   And then I had that strange dream and saw you." She paused and played with his fingers.   " But I never felt the same afterwards.   Somehow I felt that something strange, something unusual was going to happen in my life, and now when I look back upon it and am so happy," whereupon she grasped tightly the fingers she held —" I feel it just had to be."

"Do you reckon your father understood the love that was between us?"

"I think he did. And he started more than once about that time to tell me something. He went so far once as to say that if you liked me, and I cut him off. Afterwards I could see that it worried you and my heart went out to you more than ever. And then you reached your decision. I saw it, and it seems that I liked you more for the man you were."

"Did you love the man you were engaged to?"

"Jean!"

He laughed sheepishly, and patted her shoulder. He was sorry, that he had asked her such a question, and he resolved thereupon never to do so again. Something dark passed before him — terrible years when he had suffered much. She was speaking again.

"You know I never loved any one in the world but you."

THE END